Alex Ince

THE CHRONICLES OF ERIC MASON

BOOK ONE

THE BEASTS AND THE DARKNESS

Alex Ince

THE CHRONICLES OF
ERIC MASON

BOOK ONE

THE BEASTS AND THE DARKNESS

MEREO
Cirencester

Mereo Books

1A The Wool Market Dyer Street Cirencester Gloucestershire GL7 2PR
An imprint of Memoirs Publishing www.mereobooks.com

The chronicles of ERIC MASON: 978-1-86151-750-0

First published in Great Britain in 2017
by Mereo Books, an imprint of Memoirs Publishing

The address for Memoirs Publishing Group Limited can be found at
www.memoirspublishing.com

The Memoirs Publishing Group Ltd Reg. No. 7834348

The Memoirs Publishing Group supports both The Forest Stewardship Council®
(FSC®) and the PEFC® leading international forest-certification organisations. Our
books carrying both the FSC label and the PEFC® and are printed on FSC®-certified
paper. FSC® is the only forest-certification scheme supported by the leading
environmental organisations including Greenpeace. Our paper procurement policy
can be found at www.memoirspublishing.com/environment

Typeset in 9/14pt Century Schoolbook
by Wiltshire Associates Publisher Services Ltd. Printed and bound in Great Britain
by Printondemand-Worldwide, Peterborough PE2 6XD

Dedicated to Oliver Ince (1981 – 2015)

THE CHRONICLES OF ERIC MASON

BOOK 1
The Beasts and the Darkness

Created by
THE BROTHERS INCE

Written By
ALEX INCE

A BIG THANK YOU TO...

Family
Irina and Michael, David and Sheila, Jemma and Dean,
Liz and Jim, Tina and James, Dylan, Mollie, Marcus, Grace,
Alex, Simon, Joseph, Megan, Ellie.

Friends
Francesca Dale, Anthony Woodley, Helen Kingston,
Tolley Brown, James Ayres, Donna Ayres, John Mansfield,
Jacqui Harvey, David Monypenny, Robert Frith, Tom McGuire,
Martin Lewis, Kate Lewis, James Littlewoods, Jason Hill,
Tommy Leedham, Darren Stoneham, Edward Llewelyn,
Rob Jones, Matthew Jackson, Phillip Padgett, Julie Duff,
Samantha Smith.

#TheBrothersInce
@AbsoluteInce
@TheoImighty

CONTENTS

ERIC MASON WOKE UP. HE HURT. EVERY PART
OF HIS BODY WAS SCREAMING AT HIM IN PAIN.
HE OPENED HIS EYES, SLOWLY GOT TO HIS FEET,
AND SAVED THE WORLD.
AGAIN.

CHAPTER 1

ERIC MASON

Eric Mason woke up. He hurt; every part of his body was screaming at him in pain. He opened his eyes, but nothing happened. He closed them, then opened them again. He couldn't see a thing. It was either very dark, or he had gone blind, and annoyingly he couldn't quite decide which it was.

He was lying on his front, that much was certain, so he tried turning his head to one side, but his neck sent a warning shot up and down his spine which buried itself deep into his brain, ordering him not to try again. He tried blinking, but even his eyelids hurt as they tried to open and shut over his dry and tired eyes.

'Great, now where am I?' he muttered to himself through the haze of pain, hoping for a voice in his head to give him an answer, but none came.

This was bad. He had never felt this level of pain before; it was as if he had pins and needles all over his entire body. His muscles felt like there was molten metal pumping through them, and his skin felt as if it was covered in a thin layer of ice. His hands and fingers were numb, and he was starting to shiver. Although he was freezing cold, at the same time a small mist of sweat was forming and dripping down his head, face, and back.

He racked his brains, trying to kick some life into them. He needed to know where the hell he was, find out how to get away from here, and most importantly get some clothes on. He could feel that he was naked, because each time he tried to move he felt grit underneath him pressing and rubbing against his bare skin.

It felt as though he was lying on a rocky beach. He did not know where he was, but judging by the absolute darkness around him, it had to be the middle of the night.

CHAPTER 2

IN THE BEGINNING

In the beginning, when the universe was young and fresh, there was nothing. A deep and penetrating darkness stretched across the nothingness of space. This wasn't the kind of darkness you got from the absence of light, but rather the rich full darkness of there never, ever, having been any light in the first place.

Yet there were creatures. They were without form, like oil floating on water, and they slithered and flowed throughout the darkness. For hundreds of thousands of years, nothing had disturbed their peaceful existence. Until the noise came, and it changed everything.

It started off faintly, barely audible despite the sheer silence, but as it got louder it became a rumbling and growling vibration which reverberated across the universe, striking fear and dread into every creature that heard it. Not that they had ears to hear it of course, or had ever felt fear before, but the vibrations could be felt far and wide.

Their movements slowed almost to a stop, and they looked at one another, questioning this new turn of event. Not that they had eyes, or faces for that matter. The rumbling vibration got louder still, until it climaxed into one enormous tsunami of sound that ripped its way through everything.

After the mighty wave of sound had travelled as far as it could, the universe settled down slightly, like a pond after a rock has been thrown into it. Nothing moved, and nothing made a sound. Collectively the oily creatures waited to see what would happen next, but they all instinctively knew that things were soon going to change, and nothing would be the same again.

CHAPTER 3

The Darkness

Eric Mason had been lying in the same position for what felt like hours, his face pressed up against the freezing cold, gritty surface he had woken up on. But it could easily have been only twenty or thirty minutes; there was no time here, in this total darkness. He was trying to mentally order his body to stop being in pain, or at least to stop shivering. Every time the cold made him shiver, the movement would take the pain to a new and excruciating level which would cause him to spasm, and the cycle would start again. He couldn't get to sleep and his eyes and body were tired beyond measure, but the pain was forcing him to stay awake.

Mercifully, the pain in his body now started to die down, until after a while it was merely excruciating. Eric decided to take advantage of this moment of relative calmness, and tried to move as fast as he could manage. He summoned all the energy he could, forced his arms to tuck his still numb hands underneath his body, and waited a moment. Once the red and blue spots of pain had stopped bouncing around the inside of his eyeballs, he pushed down hard and rolled over like a slug, groaning all the way. It took some time and a lot of effort, but after forcing all his limbs to work together as a team, he was finally lying on his back.

The pain he now felt could not be described in mere mortal terms. If he thought it had been bad before, it was nothing compared to how he felt now. But at least he was facing the right way up, which had to be an improvement.

He opened his eyes and squinted at the sky above him. There was nothing there. He was still totally surrounded by blackness, and it seemed to stretch out forever, making him feel very small indeed. This wasn't a feeling Eric was used to, and it was making him very uncomfortable.

When the coloured dots of pain dancing around his eyeballs finally disappeared and his night vision started to kick in, he saw hundreds of thousands of tiny dots spread out all around him. The effect was really quite beautiful. That was a lot of stars. No wonder he was so cold. It was clearly the middle of the night.

He tried to make out the star signs in the sky above him, but alarmingly he could not recognise any of them. Eric did not know all the constellations of course, as he had never had the interest or the patience to learn them, but all those he could make out were either seriously warped or in completely the wrong place. One patch of stars to his right, if you screwed up your eyes just right, looked like Leo, although the lion's head seemed curiously distorted. But he couldn't have travelled that far, could he? He must have got very drunk to wake up in another part of the galaxy.

After a few minutes of mentally willing the stars to move back into their correct places he gave up, and decided to turn his attention to his aching body and brain. The feeling was very slowly coming back to his hands and arms, but this simply meant he was getting pain from more places. As his hands explored his body, he quickly discovered that he wasn't wearing very much, which probably explained the freezing cold he was feeling. He could feel what might have once been a pair of combat trousers, and what used to be a T-shirt and shirt, but they all had a large number of alarming gaps in them. Careful inspection of the edges showed that the holes in the material had a strange melted feel to them, which was confirmed by the burnt, exposed skin. He could feel the rough and smooth texture where the skin had been badly burnt and blistered and was trying to heal itself.

One hand explored his face, head, and neck; thankfully they seemed to have all the right parts in the right places. He was relieved not to find his face burnt and disfigured. It had happened once before, and he hadn't cared for it one bit.

What the hell had happened to him? He gently touched the burnt skin on his torso. Had he had a plane crash or something? But he couldn't see or smell any burning. It was so dark that he could be lying next to the burnt-out carcass of a jumbo jet and never see it, although presumably he would have been able to smell or hear it - you couldn't have a plane crash without oil or smoke in the air. But no other options sprung to mind about how he could have become this badly damaged.

"Hello?" he said in a dry and croaky voice, and heard the word get swallowed up by the darkness. He waited a few moments in case his question was answered, but no reply seemed to be coming, so he decided he was either alone, or anyone else there was either dead or still unconscious. Just him then. Great.

He turned his attention to more important stuff. At the top of his list of current priorities was figuring out where he was, how he had got there, and who he was going to kill for putting him there. He searched his memory banks. It was like looking through an old empty house that hadn't been used in a while. He ran from room to dust-covered room, opening every door he could find, but all the rooms in his mind were filled with ornaments of memories of days gone past. Nothing was new; not one single room had any memories that hadn't been there a long, long time.

This was hopeless. He couldn't for the life of him remember the events leading up to him lying on some rocky beach, in the middle of the night, and wearing clothes that were burnt and shredded. Either he had been at one hell of a party or he was in big trouble, and if history had taught him anything, it probably wasn't the first.

The problem with the beach theory was that he couldn't hear any water. Surely if he was on a beach he would be able to hear waves crashing, or birds. But the silence from all around him was almost as claustrophobic as the darkness. He couldn't even hear or feel a breeze. He needed to get up and get moving. He didn't like this place; it was time to try to find some form of civilisation. But by the feel of things this was not going to be anytime soon.

He shut his eyes, as if that would make any difference, and decided sleep should be higher up on his priorities. Everything would look better in the morning, and hopefully the pain would not be as bad. He switched off his mind and ignored it, and fell quickly into a deep sleep.

CHAPTER 4

END OF THE BEGINNING

The universe had been quiet for a while. Not the quiet from before, which had taken millennia to achieve; this had only lasted since the vibration of sound had died down and the dark oily creatures had relaxed a little. The sound had put them all on edge, as far as it could anyhow, and soon they were about to get a much bigger shock.

From the centre of where the tsunami of sound had originated from, lights pierced into the world. They were small at first, no more than pinpricks in the darkness. The black, shapeless creatures slithered over and around each other trying to get a closer look. The lights were round, like balls, but different from anything they had ever seen before. The tiny balls of light began spitting and biting at the darkness that surrounded them, and at the black creatures, who were getting more and more captivated.

Curiosity got the better of some of them, and they were forced to get even closer to the small balls of fire, their light illuminating the oily shapelessness of their bodies. They had no eyes to see, or mouths to speak, and yet even without form they seemed to have an inquisitive look to them.

Eventually curiosity became too much for one of the bigger creatures, and it reached out a long area of its body and touched the small ball of light. But the ball of fire instantly grappled and bit at the creature, then swallowed it whole. The ball of light grew a little bigger, fatter and fuller after its new meal.

The shapeless creatures had never felt fear before now. In the timelessness before the noise or light, they had all lived in harmony. Nothing ate them, and they ate nothing. They had never had to deal with either predator or prey, but right now, a very real chill ran down the back of every creature which was close enough to see what had happened. The creatures panicked, and if they could have screamed they would have. They slipped and slithered over each other in a bid to get away from the balls of fire, forcing each other out of the way in their desperate attempt to escape. But the smaller creatures were pushed too far back, and couldn't get past the bigger ones, and one by one they were consumed by the fire, feeding the light, causing the balls to grow bigger and stronger. Soon the balls of fire were strong enough to stretch out in all directions, sending out hundreds of tentacle-like arms to catch more food and pull more creatures towards them. As the balls of light got bigger they began to heat up, and their tentacles of light stretched further out into the darkness like elastic spears. Little fingers of light tested the darkness of space, investigating their new home, and any creature not fast enough to get away was caught and dragged back. The black oily creatures instinctively huddled together as far out of reach as they could, and eventually the balls of fire stopped their growth and the universe was illuminated for the first time in its long, long existence.

New light was stretching out in all directions, illuminating all the dust and reflecting off newly-born stars, creating wide prisms of colour. The creatures looked around at their world for the first time. They had never experienced colour before, and if it hadn't been for the terrifying fear they all felt at this incursion of light, they might have described what they saw as beautiful.

As the balls of light got hotter and stronger, and realised they couldn't reach any of the creatures, a strong gravity force began to form around them, starting to pull everything towards them. One sun in particular, which seemed to be bigger and stronger than the others, started to illuminate nine very large round objects. The gravity of the newly-formed sun was strong, but not quite strong enough to pull these orbs directly to it. Instead they start to revolve around it in big long arcs. As they did so, they slowly started to rotate on their axes, causing them to spin. With nothing to slow them down but dust and the occasional meteorite, they quickly built up speed.

The creatures, if they had had mouths, would have stared at all this new movement in jaw-dropping surprise and confusion.

One of these objects seemed different from the others. If you lined them all up it would be the third one out from this newly-born sun. Where most of the other objects were made from solid rock or mostly gas, this one had a mixture of rock, liquid water and gas of its very own. Even the rock and water were different from any found on the other orbs. The water that covered this particular orb glistened and shone in the light of this new sun. As it built up speed, rotating with the others, a smaller round rock got caught in its rotation, and began travelling alongside it as they both passed around the sun, becoming a moon. The moon's magnetism started to move the waters on its new parent body, pushing the liquid around its surface, causing it to rise and fall and create waves that splashed and soaked any areas of rock that were not already covered. The faster the new moon revolved around the planet, the faster the water would move around, and soon rock began to dislodge far under the water and bubble up to the surface. Soon entire areas of land could be seen.

If the light had scared the black creatures, it was nothing compared to the fear they felt for these new moving planets. They were angry too, angry that this light had turned their entire world upside down, angry that their home had started moving, and angry that that they were powerless to stop it.

Some of the creatures decided to hide from the light on some of the darker planets, those that were too far from the sun's warm embrace, while others retreated to the far corners of space which none of the light had managed to explore. They vowed that one day they would return and bring order back to their world.

CHAPTER 5

THE ARMY TRUCK

Eric Mason woke up. He hurt, again. He dreaded what he was going to see, but he opened his eyes anyway. His eyesight was blurred, and he knew the hangover would kick in any minute, so he had to quickly work out where he was and assess the situation. It was very difficult to concentrate; there was a deafening sound of roaring wind all around him, like a cruel mixture of radio static and the applause of thousands of pairs of hands.

His body hurt all over. Eric could not count the number of times he had woken up like this, but as ever, he knew there was probably some horribly amusing reason – amusing to someone else, of course. He had been on binge drinking weekends, and drowned his sorrows until the barman ran out of whisky, but even those hangovers combined wouldn't be this bad. His body felt weak and his stomach was churning, but he doubted he was hydrated enough to be sick.

Whatever he was lying on was hard, metallic and moving. He could tell because occasionally his bed would go over a bump or in and out of a dip, and everything would jump a few inches off the ground and come crashing down all around him. He rubbed his dry eyes and tried to force them to focus on his surroundings. It didn't work. He tried sitting up, but was immediately hit by a burst of wind that forced him onto his back again, hitting his head hard on the metal floor. He shook the ringing out of his ears and groaned in pain as he felt his brain slosh around inside his skull. He rubbed the back of his head where it had hit the floor, and tried sitting up again.

He had been lying in the back of what looked like a basic pickup truck, the sort you might find on farms, or on an army barracks. An Army truck? He inspected the paintwork. It wasn't the usual colour for the Army, but then again, these days Army vehicles were in short supply, and most trucks or vans they came across were 'liberated' for the war effort.

His bed for the night had been the cold, very hard metal floor of the truck's baggage compartment, in amongst what looked like bags and rolled-up tents which would probably have made a much nicer bed than the floor he had woken up on. The bags and rolled up tents mocked him by bouncing up and down a few times, pulling on their moorings like happy dogs on their leads as the truck went over yet another bump in the road. But he didn't have time to think about this now. He needed to find out why he was there, and where the hell he was going. This was definitely not where he had wanted to wake up. A bed would have been nice but not essential, and he didn't even need a blanket or duvet. But anything was better than a truck.

He looked around. Above him was deep blue sky as far as the eye could see. The only part of the sky that wasn't blue was the sun, which appeared to be trying to fry him alive. The sun was fairly high in the sky, so between this and his stomach rumbling, he figured it must be about lunchtime. Underneath the sky, stretching for miles in all directions, was sand and rocks. A single dirt road crossed the landscape, littered with potholes and rocks, which would explain all the jumping about the truck was doing. Each time a wheel went into a pothole or over a rock, it was like taking a punch to both his kidneys at the same time, and it nearly forced his stomach up and out of his mouth.

"Desert? What the fuck am I doing in the desert?" he exclaimed out loud.

In front of him Eric could make out two figures in the truck's cab. He couldn't make out who they were, but they looked like they were dressed exactly the same, which meant uniform, which meant bad news. He weighed up all the available data and considered jumping overboard, but judging by the speed they were travelling it wouldn't be a pleasant landing. Besides, he had no intention of being stranded in the middle of a desert with no water or food and a raging hangover.

He very slowly and carefully edged his way to the cab window, inch by inch, begging his fuzzy mind to focus on the task at hand, and banged on the glass with his fist. Neither of the shapes on the other side of the glass moved. He tried banging again, louder this time and nearly breaking the glass. The shape that wasn't driving the truck half turned and raised a hand over its shoulder. It slid open the window a fraction, posted a canteen and a pair of sunglasses through the narrow gap, and slammed the window shut before Eric could get a word in.

Eric looked confused at the items that had been dropped into his lap. They looked completely alien to him right now, so he banged on the window again, but again the shapes inside the cab ignored him. Eventually gave up in a huff and slumped back down, trying to move out of the wind. That meant sitting with his back up against the cab, but now he was travelling backwards, and this did nothing for a hangover.

Turning his attention downwards, he decided to put on the sunglasses. They were pretty badly scratched, and one side was slightly bent, but at least they dulled the blinding brightness of the midday sun. He inspected the canteen next. It wasn't very big, but he could hear liquid sloshing around inside. He unscrewed the cap, poured the liquid down his dehydrated throat, and immediately regretted it. The liquid burnt a trail of fire all the way down to his stomach; it was rough whisky. Acting on instinct, he launched himself onto his side, and was just about able to get all the sick over the edge of the truck. As it came up, the whisky and stomach acid burnt his throat and mouth even further, but after it had finished he was actually quite glad to get the demons out of him.

Eric had always visualised a hangover as being attacked from the inside by tiny demons with pitchforks and sledgehammers, and anyone who had ever had to endure a really bad one would probably agree. Not the sort of hangover that gave you an annoying headache and a delicate stomach, a dry throat and a hunger for something greasy, but the sort that only comes from really pushing the boundaries of what your body can handle, the sort of hangover you get from several bottles of whisky, or a keg of beer.

When he was sure he had completely finished throwing up and the dry heaving had finally stopped, he wiped his mouth with the back of his hand. Over the roar of the wind he could hear muffled laughter from inside the cab. He groaned and swore under his breath and sat back down with his back to the cab, striking his head.

"Arseholes!" he shouted to the air in general, and rubbed the back of his head.

The laughter continued, but after a few minutes the cab window slid open again and a hand extended through the gap waving a plastic bottle. This time Eric could see there was water inside. Eric wasn't taking any chances this time. He unscrewed the lid and sniffed at the contents. It smelt all right, and after a small taste, he decided it was indeed water, so he drained the lot in one quick, smooth motion.

With the minor problems of sight and thirst solved, he turned his attention to the bigger problem at hand. Where was he, and where were the silly brothers taking him? He carefully moved into a crouched position. A few bumps and dips in the road made the truck buck up and down, and for a moment Eric looked like he was riding a runaway bull. Anger and frustration began to bubble up inside him, and he growled a little under his breath. He was just about to put his boot through the cab window, fully prepared to smash the glass and kill anything moving inside with his bare hands, when something caught his eye. Off in the very far distance, just coming over the horizon, was what appeared to be a city made of tents and sandbag walls. Any hope in Eric's heart that this was just some kind of misunderstanding fizzled away. This truck belonged to the New Global Army.

"Oh shitty bollocks!" sighed Eric. His words were whipped out of his mouth by the wind and thrown into the nothingness of the desert.

Eric hated the Army. Nothing good was going to come of this. He seriously contemplated for the second time jumping overboard and taking his chances in the desert, and quickly scanned the luggage for some kind of weapon. Maybe he could make a club or a spear out of one of the tent poles. They had been clever enough not to leave any guns or knives he could see.

He looked back at the city of tents. It was enormous; bigger than any barracks or camp he had ever seen, and unfortunately for Eric, he had seen far more than his fair share.

CHAPTER 6

The War-Torn City

It was a very wet night. The rain came down so hard that it was as if the clouds had some deep and meaningful grudge against the earth and all its inhabitants. Each raindrop seemed the size of a tennis ball and came down with the force of a meteorite, but on the upside, the rainwater was washing away the dirt and stench of the dark, remote city down the drains.

The city was fairly new, just a few hundred years old, and before the War it had had a very vibrant population, and had been growing every day as men, women, and families flocked to it in their hundreds. Now however, the streets were dark and ominous; most of the street lamps had been smashed or covered with thick blankets, and even the windows had big thick block-out sheets across them to catch any escaping light.

The streets were completely empty. A person could explore for hours and never see anyone else, yet feel that there were eyes on them at all times. The roads were littered with the debris of crumbling buildings and abandoned vehicles left to rust and rot. Everything about this city seemed to scream just how much it didn't want to be seen. The streets were silent, except for the occasional sound of an invisible footstep splashing through the rushing rivers in the gutters. No one wanted to be outside, not on a night like this, and certainly not when the front line of the War was creeping ever closer. It could be on their doorstep any day now.

After the War had broken out, most of the city's population had scoffed at how far away all the fighting was, and doubted in a very arrogant way that it would ever reach this far out. And annoyingly they were right, in a way. The front line was an ever-shifting and changing snake, and just as unpredictable. But after many attacks from enemy forces, and the New Global Army's desperate need for constant recruits to join their ranks, the population was now a fraction of its former size. Mothers and fathers had lost sons and daughters, husbands had lost wives, brothers had lost sisters.

The Zarda forces of the enemy, cruel lizard-man hybrids, were everywhere. Almost every week they heard of another city or town being overrun, and they were getting closer and closer. So the city's population collectively made the decision to lock down the city; they rarely went outside if they could help it, and any time they needed to get to somewhere they used the paths they had built through buildings by knocking down walls, or underground in the city's sewer system. The main aim of the game was to keep the streets clear.

Since there weren't too many people around any more, the sewers were relatively clean and dry, but you'd still needed to cover your mouth and nose with a fragrant cloth because of the smell. No amount of bleach could take away the scent of hundreds of years of decaying muck. A lot of walkways had been built between buildings because of the smell, so people could dart from one to another quickly, without being seen. If Zarda troops did happen to pass by, they would just find empty streets and buildings and carry on moving. So far it had worked.

One of the buildings in the city was never empty though, and saw more than its fair share of foot traffic. It was a bar, of course, but not a very good one. On first entering the place it was clear to see it had once been brightly and colourfully light by neon lights and lamps running across its walls, but now it was just as dark and dingy as the rest of the city. The drinkers were no longer the fun-time junkies, loudmouth students spending pocket-money from their parents or first-time lovers on a date.

There were no students any more, not really, not like in the old days before the War. Nearly everyone was sent to one of the New Global Army's Military Academy schools, sometimes against their wishes, but they didn't have much choice. It was easier for the schools; they just changed names, or shipped all the kids off to the nearest Military Academy. But the older students, who thought they were old enough and clever enough to do what they wanted, often had to be rounded up and shipped there.

Now the bar's main trade consisted of Army soldiers and a few locals that remained. Neither group really got on with each other, but they both tended to have the same aim in mind – drink to forget what they had seen in the War, drink to numb the pains of wounds suffered from the War, or drink to lift what spirits they had left. Either way, if you saw someone on their own in this bar, drinking several people's worth of drinks to themselves, you left them well alone because they probably had good reason to be there.

Eric hated having to interact with the Army. He certainly didn't deal with them by choice, but they paid well for the little jobs he did for them, and sold him ammunition on the occasions he had a need for it. Shortly after the War had started, so many years ago now, individual countries' armies became redundant. The old

United Nations took charge over each country's armed forces, whether they liked it or not, and the New Global Army was now in control of everything.

There was a large barracks not too far outside the city limits. The locals didn't want it because it stood to reason that if the Zarda were to attack the barracks, they would soon move to the city too. The city was practically defenceless, so they would probably find the bunkers fairly quickly, and all the inhabitants would be slaughtered. But the Army based their barracks there anyway, and as a sign of goodwill, they sent patrolling units to guard the city. The soldiers had, of course, decided that this meant they were in charge, and took it upon themselves to shout at the locals and boss them around at every opportunity they got. Most of the soldiers resented having to babysit a bunch of locals who should, based on the propaganda they had been subjected to, have been sent to an Academy as they had to do their bit for the War. According to the Army's propaganda, it was everyone's duty to register themselves and join the New Global Army with a smile on their faces. On the whole the two groups got along through mutual hatred for each other, and simply tried their best to stay out of each other's way. Occasionally there were fights and punch-ups, which were probably unavoidable, but overall these weren't too serious. Other soldiers and locals usually turned up to pull the groups apart, after they had got a few good punches in themselves.

Eric Mason hated this city. The soldiers tried to boss him about, which didn't work because he didn't do as he was told, and that just made the soldiers angry, so they'd try to fight him, and lose. It was a vicious circle.

The locals were wary of Eric because he looked like an officer; he had a high level of intelligence, which was usually manifested through logical thinking or sarcasm, and he knew how to fight. To the locals, this meant he had to be a deserter or a spy, which they also hated for some reason. Eric had assumed, correctly, that maybe the locals just didn't like anyone who wasn't one of them, and made any excuse to take all of life's little frustrations out on someone they thought they could beat in a fight. They were wrong most of the time with Eric, who wasn't the sort of person to back down from a fight, especially if he was in a bad mood. Which seemed to be nearly every day.

But the main reason Eric hated the city was that it always seemed to be raining there. So many nights he had been staring out the window at the constant wetness and thinking how he could have wound up on some sunny island somewhere instead. He wouldn't have the sparkling conversation or company of all these city folk or soldiers, but at least he wouldn't smell damp every day, and he could even get a suntan.

He had found the bar fairly quickly, like most people, mainly because he could smell a mile away the telltale mixture of alcohol and depression which go hand in hand in such bars. He enjoyed them; everyone tended to avoid him, and he could get down to some serious uninterrupted drinking. This bar in particular was helpfully split into two groups, the locals and the Army, and there was a fairly wide no-man's-land between them to avoid 'accidental' conflict.

He was on his fifth drink when a group of young soldiers came in through the front door. It made him smile that even in a world scarred by war and death, a soldier could still get a good strong drink, and maybe have a laugh or two with your squad. There weren't too many laughs being had in here tonight, but Eric really wasn't in a laughing mood anyway, so getting violently drunk seemed like his only viable option for fun

Eric did enjoy getting into fights, mostly because he always won, but he only really enjoyed it when he had a good opponent. There's no fun in in getting into a fight with someone who doesn't know what they are doing, because it rarely lasts longer than a few seconds. Even the local looters and pickpockets had learnt to avoid Eric, especially when he was drunk. He looked like an easy target, but he wasn't. Occasionally he still got the odd one or two who hadn't learnt their lesson yet, and he was forced to show them the error of their ways.

He had been in the city for a little while, maybe four or five months, because he tended to move around a lot lately and lose track of time. Most days seemed to blur together, and whole weeks could pass in a blink of the eye. He never liked staying in the same place for too long, and he hated whatever town or city he found himself in. For now it was somewhere he could just lie low and not be bothered by anyone. He did the odd job here and there for the Army to earn some cash, but he kept his dealings with them to an absolute minimum. No sense in inviting attention.

No one would think to look for him here, no one he wanted to be found by anyway. He had chosen this city in the hope that it might be the last place anyone would look for him, as it was so close to a large army barracks. They'd surely think he would have to be stupid to lie low right under their noses. The city was big enough to have adequate hiding places, and currently he was using three which he rotated at random. He could probably hide out in this city forever and never get found. It wasn't that he was hiding from anyone in particular, more just hiding away from the world in general, and those he might owe money to in particular.

When the soldiers burst in, he could tell straight away that they were new to the uniform and had not seen much of the War, because they were still smiling and laughing, and their uniforms were clean and smart. If he had had to guess, Eric would have said they were straight out of the Military Academy. They'd probably seen a few camps and outposts, and had now been transferred to the big boys' barracks outside the city. They probably thought they were in the War here, and that made them grown up enough to hit the city and drink in bars with the big boys.

Once they were all inside and had wiped the rain off their

uniforms, the boldest of the soldiers, the alpha male of the group, addressed the room. "If there are any ladies here, please form an orderly queue," he announced, grinning like a tiger approaching its hunting ground.

The soldier took in the clientele and quickly deduced that there were only two types of women in the room. There were the ones who obviously worked at the bar, or rather in the rooms upstairs, and who could be very interested in the soldier for a negotiable, and surely affordable, price. And then there was the other type of woman, those who were sensibly dressed for the weather, and were not paying attention to anything other than the drinks in their hands or the husbands sitting next to them. Most of the local women ignored the soldiers from the barracks. A few took an interest, until their fathers or brothers found out, and another fight would break out. The female soldiers were almost as bad as the male ones, not caring for the local's situation, married or otherwise, so long as they got what they wanted out of the fleeting exchanges.

The young soldiers noisily marched to the bar. The alpha male banged heavily on the counter, demanding a round of the strongest but cheapest drink the bar had to offer. A wave of laughter and joking spread through the squad, and the group set about moving the furniture around so they could all sit on the same table. The noise made everyone in the bar stop their conversations and look up, while the barman busied himself pouring watered-down but brightly-coloured drinks.

The squad leader paid the barman in Army Credits, a form of currency introduced by the New Global Army in order to put the entire planet on the same standard. Then he picked up the tray of drinks and shouted at the others to get out of his way. Eric couldn't help thinking that if these soldiers had only just begun their night out, not all of them were going to make it home alive. Which was fine by him. He hadn't had a scrap in a few hours, and he had seen a few soldiers he wouldn't mind going a second round with. He could already see one or two of the hardened drinkers beginning to get violent thoughts, and hands were reaching down to unclip sidearm holsters. Out of the corner of his eye Eric noticed that one table of men had produced hunting knives the size of their forearms and laid them on the table ready.

Eric leaned back in his chair. He was sitting at the far end of the room beneath a big window that had been blocked out with a thick curtain. He had sat at this particular table every night, and for a very good reason. Not only was it mostly bathed in a shadow that hid his face and upper body, from this position he could see the entire bar and everyone in it. Anyone wanting to sneak up on him from behind would have to be extremely talented.

He watched the group of young soldiers for a little while. There were nine of them in total, three women and six men. The Army liked squads of nine or more, so in a pinch they could form three rotating tripods and cover their perimeter better. It was a move Eric was proud of, although he never got any credit for it.

Eric stood up quietly, draining the last of the drink, and whilst keeping an eye on the soldiers, he made his way to the bar to get another. He would have one more and then head back to the room. These probably weren't the only fresh units on leave tonight and it was starting to get a little crowded. The influx of fresh young soldiers could be a bad sign; the barracks must be getting ready for a big fight.

He signalled to the barman, who reached past the watered-down whisky reserved for the soldiers and other undesirables to the slightly less watered-down whisky at the back. Eric had won the right to the slightly better whisky after the barman had got caught in a gang fight between the locals and the Army. He hadn't wanted to step in, and wasn't going to, until one of the locals mistook him for a soldier and hit him. The fight hadn't last long after Eric had joined in.

The barman was a kind man. He knew his customers well, and he poured Eric a very large measure. After all, Eric had saved his life.

Eric paid for the drink in Army credits, flimsy pieces of paper similar to old currencies but with a very simple and basic design, and returned to his seat to the sound of laughter and shouting from the soldiers. He sat down and stared at his new drink. He wished it could have been longer and stronger, but the credits in his pocket were getting worryingly low.

"Time for another job" he sighed to himself. He sloshed the brown liquid around the glass and took a big swig.

CHAPTER 7

THE ARMY CONVOY

The convoy of army trucks continued on the dirt road at high speed towards the enormous barracks, and Eric stared in disbelief at the sea of tents in the distance. The wind was howling all around him, whipping at his clothes and hair, and in truth the breeze did help his hangover a little.

This was not where he wanted to be. He vaguely remembered the bar last night, and the group of soldiers that had come in making all the noise. He remembered telling himself he would have one more drink and then retire for the night. He had been staying in an abandoned building not too far from the bar. He remembered buying a drink and sitting down at his table... he paused, trying to remember through the haze of his hangover, but there was nothing. Surely that sixth drink wouldn't have got him so drunk that he had thought it was a good idea to sleep it off in the back of an army truck.

Especially one headed for the biggest barracks he had ever seen. It was as big as a city. As they got closer Eric could make out lots of ant-sized people walking from tent to tent. He could make out soldiers lined up in the various training areas, practising their punching and kicking in unison. As they got closer still he could make out shooting ranges, and soldiers in different stances firing weapons at easy-to-hit targets. There must have been thousands of squads stationed there. He would have more luck trying to count the stars in the night sky than the number of soldiers he could see. This place looked like trouble.

Eric shook his head in disbelief and sat back down, resting his head against the back of the cab again. He'd probably been in worse situations than this – he could think of a few – but he doubted that he'd be able to get out of this in the same way. He wished there was more water, and the heat was starting to make him sweat.

From his seat in the back he could hear muffled voices coming from inside the cab. People were taking it in turn to speak loudly and clearly, and it sounded suspiciously like lots of different people were checking in on a CB radio. He couldn't quite make out what the voices were saying, but it all sounded very official.

The shaking of the truck started to ease, and Eric realised they must be getting pretty close now, because they were slowing down. He racked his brain trying to think of a good excuse for falling asleep in the back of this truck, but not many sprang to mind. But then again, the drivers had known he was back here, because they had passed him water and sunglasses. How long had they known? Didn't one of them think it was odd, or thought to drop him off somewhere? Eric would have rather woken up in a ditch covered in boot marks and no wallet.

Annoyingly, Eric couldn't decide if he was a stowaway or a prisoner, which was probably something a person in this situation really ought to know. If he was a prisoner, shouldn't he be in chains or something? He'd never known the Army to be casual about prisoner transport. Surely he hadn't got into this situation voluntarily? Even drunk out of his skull he would have tried to resist arrest, and most likely got away. Drunk or not, Eric's speed and reaction times were far better than most people's at the best of times. The soldiers tended to put up as little fight as the city locals; one good punch somewhere they weren't expecting it and they dropped to the floor like anybody else.

The truck slowed down to enter the barracks and Eric shifted position so he could see as much as possible, but the surrounding area was a blur of tents and soldiers. When the truck finally skidded to a halt on the sands, Eric surmised that they had stopped practically central. Which meant if he ran now, it probably wouldn't make much difference which way he headed.

There were soldiers of all sorts and sizes milling around the roughly-parked trucks, and he could hear the shouting of several drill instructors off in the distance. He could feel eyes on him from every direction, so he tried to look like he belonged there, which was difficult as he was sitting in amongst all the baggage and wearing bad sunglasses. He ran an absent-minded hand through his sweat-soaked hair and tried his best to not look quite so hung over.

From the back of the truck came a loud bang as the tailgate was dropped down. Several unhappy-looking faces appeared and started clawing at the bags and tents. It was like watching a squid with hundreds of tentacles grabbing at the truck's contents. A soldier was lifted up and pushed into the back of the truck, and angrily shouted for Eric to get out of his way. Eric theatrically shuffled out of the way as best he could, with his friendliest smile plastered across his face. The man looked flustered, as if he had the job of unloading all the trucks that came here and didn't much enjoy it.

Suddenly Eric jumped. A large hand had wrapped itself around his ankle. He couldn't see past the soldier, who was now practically standing on him, so he tried to kick it off. "I'm not a tent!" he shouted. He kicked a little more, but the hand simply gripped his ankle harder. Then, with a sharp pull, Eric was dragged clean across the truck's baggage area. A second hand joined the first, and he was pulled the rest of the way. Eric hit the ground with a painful thump and rolled a little way across the gritty sand floor.

When he looked up there was a ring of faces staring down at him. He sighed a little, and brushed the sand and dirt off his clothes and hands. Then, without warning, he jumped to his feet, smiling slightly to himself when the ring of soldiers cautiously widened around him a little bit. He dusted himself off, and smiled a little more when a few of the younger soldiers flinched. So, prisoner it was then. Good. He was glad to get that sorted out.

He looked past the ring of faces and noticed a couple of officers strolling towards them. When they reached the ring of soldiers, they waved them all away like someone shooing away stray cats, and gave orders to hurry up and get the trucks unloaded. A few soldiers stayed nearby to guard the trucks, but the majority vanished. Eric was left standing in front of two very large, very well-fed men. He looked at their ranks. One was a Knight and looked like he had seen a lot of action. His face had a few scars running across it, and his nose had clearly been broken more than once. The Knight rank, named after the armoured knights from hundreds of years ago, was given to the big heavy juggernauts. These were broadly regarded as the brave, or as Eric suspected the stupidest, of all the ranks in the New Global Army. They were heavily armoured, usually carrying a big, heavy gun that could deal out death at an extremely high rate, and were one of the first waves sent into any battle to weed out the Zarda's front line forces. They couldn't move very fast under their weight, but they were difficult to stop once they had got up a good momentum, and fully loaded machine gun.

The other officer was a Captain. He was looking down his nose and sneering at Eric's dirty and crumpled clothes. This Captain had clearly not seen as much of the War as the Knight. His hands and skin looked smooth and tanned, and he stood with the casual air of an officer who has not had to earn his rank in the field. They were the sort of people who expected everything to be handed to them on a silver platter, because that's what happened. Expensive schools, expensive rank and big dinners too, it would seem, mused Eric.

"Is this him?" said the Knight in a deep voice, looking Eric up and down disapprovingly.

"That's who we were sent to find, this is who we found, so yes that's him" replied the Captain, in what Eric thought might be the sort of voice a rodent or a vulture might use if they could talk. He sounded frustrated, as if he had been on the road a long time and just wanted to file a report and get a drink and some much-deserved rest.

"Yes, yes, all right Jones" said the Knight, holding up a hand. He was clearly the more level-headed of the pair. "No one wanted that mission, not after all the other failures." He stared Eric in the eye. Then, with lightning speed, he reached over and snatched the sunglasses off Eric's face. The shock of light made Eric recoil and wince in pain, nearly hitting his head on the back of the truck, before standing up straight again and squinting.

"He doesn't look so dangerous to me," the Knight continued in a jovial tone. "OK then, get him to the General's tent as quick as you can."

The Captain nodded and ordered two nearby soldiers to escort their prisoner. The soldiers jumped to it and gripped Eric on either shoulder to lead him away from the trucks. Eric was still reeling from the blinding sun on his tired eyes, or he would never have let this weasel-faced man manhandle him like this. As he was pulled away, Eric saw the Knight turn his attention to the soldiers by the trucks and shout for them to get them put away. He was clearly one of those officers who loved to bellow orders at the lower ranks, just to hear his own voice.

"Where am I?" Eric asked, but all the Captain could muster was a snort of disdain. Clearly he felt far too important to waste his breath on answering a stupid question from the likes of Eric.

As they proceeded through the streams of soldiers, Eric pinballed around, bumping into everything and everyone they passed, sometimes just to annoy the soldiers on either side of him. They tutted each time he did it, and Eric found himself counting under his breath. He was aiming for a hundred, but it could easily be two hundred, depending on how far they were going.

"Any water?" he asked hopefully, but his question was ignored. "I suppose a kick in the testicles is out of the question?" he asked sarcastically, and thankfully this too was ignored.

The Captain led their little group straight to a big tent. It had to be the General's tent, because it was easily the biggest around. Eric doubted that even the food hall, which would be large enough to house several hungry squads, would be as big as this one. Maybe the General had seen his tent going up, seen the food hall and thought, 'that's what I need, a really big tent to do some really big thinking in. There were two soldiers standing guard at the tent entrance, and they quickly stood to attention when they saw the Captain and his prisoner approach. The Captain reached back without looking, gripped Eric's clothes and heaved him through the opening. Eric rolled a few times on the hard dirt floor and lay there for a moment, trying to stop his brain from dripping out of his ears

Eric had to hand it to the Captain – he had more strength than it seemed. He would have to remember that when it came to killing him.

The tent was full of noise. Men and women were shouting at each other, each voice trying to make its point by saying it louder than the others. Eric lay on his back for a moment. The dirt ground was more comfortable than the back of that truck, mainly because it wasn't shaking or jumping up and down.

"Is that Eric Mason?" came a surprised voice from across the tent.

Eric recognised that voice, and it was not one he wanted to hear right now. It was the voice of a man he had come into contact with far more frequently than he would have wanted. He was a friend of sorts, but someone who could quite easily get you killed.

Eric stretched his neck to see above him and saw an upside-down group of men and women, all staring at him wide-eyed. It wasn't every day that a prisoner came rolling through their door, or rather tent flap. Normally they were simply taken to the nearest Sergeant to throw in the brig. Only the really bad criminals were dragged in front of proper officers. Every one was an officer, from Captain all the way up to a two-star General it would seem, so there was enough brass and fake gold medals in this room to sink a ship.

Eric very slowly turned onto his front and sprang to his feet to address the group. They all flinched, which made Eric smile a little. They reminded him of a group of meerkats watching a predator. He was just about to ask who was in charge, but thought better of it when one of the officers stepped through the group with open arms. It was the owner of the familiar voice.

"Eric Mason, I don't believe it! Found you at long last! I thought someone like you could stay hidden forever."

Eric rarely forgot a face, but this one had changed. It had aged, and there were several scars across it that he didn't remember.

"Tolley" said Eric in a low, dry voice. "That can't be you, surely. Last time I saw you, you were doing something stupid, like trying to be a hero somewhere."

"That's Major Tolley now," the Major said, tapping his rank with a finger. "They promoted me when we got back from... er..."

His voice drifted off when he realised the eyes of the officers were staring at him intently.

"Did they really, you poor bastard?" said Eric with a laugh. "I guess it was because you were the only one to make it back alive." He could feel the eyes of the other officers change direction to burn a hole through his skull. "What's with the face? I'm sure you weren't this pretty when I last saw you." He followed the line of one of the scars with his finger. Several of them looked like claw marks.

"Well" said Major Tolley, feeling the heat from the other officers and trying to speed things up and change the subject. "You're not the only one that can fight his way out of a tight spot, you know." He laughed and absentmindedly rubbed one of the scars on his neck. Eric noticed Tolley's hand had its fair share of scars too.

A polite, yet authoritative, cough from one of the officers made Tolley jump and turn around. They were all still staring intently at him.

"Yes, well… sorry to have to bring you in like this, Commander Mason" said Tolley in his most official voice. He saw a tick in Eric's eye at the mention of his rank. "I hope you didn't hurt too many of our men on your way in?" he asked.

"One minute I was in a bar having a wonderful time, and the next thing I knew I woke up in one of those trucks" said Eric. The heat and dehydration were starting to get to him, and he was swaying slightly. "You could have just asked, you know."

Tolley stifled a laugh. "Would you have agreed to come in if I had asked politely?" he asked, raising a quizzical eyebrow at Eric.

"No, I would have told you to piss off."

"There you are then. Drastic times call for drastic measures and all that. Needs must when the devil vomits in your kettle and calls it soup – you told me that once."

"Who is this… gentleman, Major?" asked one of the officers

around the small central table.

"Looks like a bit of scruff to me."

The man who had spoken was another Major, and he had a very upper-class look to him. He could probably trace his great grandparents back to so the last world war this planet had.

Major Tolley turned and addressed the officers around the table as a whole, like an actor addressing a packed theatre. "Please, ladies and gentlemen, this is Commander Eric Mason. He's a good man, even though he'd probably never admit it himself, and he's been on more missions than all of us combined." He paused for effect. "He proved invaluable when I was a mere foot soldier, stationed deep inside one of the quarantine zones, and a fair few times after that too, as I recall. He wasn't much more agreeable then either, but when duty called and he found himself stuck with my unit, he had little choice but to help us. He even rescued a few soldiers from the grip of the Zarda, didn't you Eric?" The question had daggers in it. Eric instinctively nodded agreement, and smiled at the group of officers.

"Yep, woke up in the middle of beast country, not unlike this morning. Quite the holiday, if I do say so myself" said Eric through gritted teeth. "What is it this time Tolley? I thought I made my feelings quite clear the last time we spoke." His tone was close to a growl, but he continued smiling so as not to confuse the officers.

"Please Eric, you look very tired," said Tolley quickly. "I'm sure you could use a good rest, or at least something to eat? And maybe a wash? I did ask the Captain to try to bring you in peacefully, but if you woke up in the truck then he must have used the whole bottle on you." Tolley laughed nervously. "Didn't fancy his chances of taking you on himself, I guess." He was trying to laugh off the look Eric was giving him. He knew full well that if they had been alone Eric would probably have knocked him to the ground by now.

The eyes of some of the nearest officers gave away that there was movement behind Eric. He turned to see the Captain who had thrown him into the tent. A vague recollection started to creep across his mind. This was the soldier who had been making all the noise in the bar last night. They must have been wearing foot soldier's uniforms, no wonder they had all looked so clean and fresh. Faint memories flickered across his tired brain. He scolded himself for not thinking about this at the time, but that may have been because of the whisky he'd been drinking. The man must have paid the barman to put something in his drink. It wouldn't have been a difficult sale – wave enough money in front of a man's nose and he'd betray his own mother.

The Captain must have noticed Eric's recollection, because he had a knowing smile on his face. But Eric wasn't about to do anything about it here and now, not in front of all these officers and soldiers. He vowed to find a way to wipe that smile away the first chance he got. A broken bottle would be favourite, he thought nastily, but aloud he mumbled, "I suppose I could do with a drink, and maybe a clean set of clothes."

"Excellent," said the Major and signalled to the Captain to join them. "Please make Eric comfortable Captain, I believe there is already some accommodation for him? Good, and a clean set of clothes would be a good idea too."

The Captain put a hand on Eric's shoulder, which Eric shrugged off immediately. He had to fight the urge to punch a hole in the weasel-faced man's chest.

"Tell me where I am, Tolley!" said Eric angrily tone.

"You dare speak to an officer in that tone, Commander?" exclaimed the Captain next to Eric in shock. He had never seen anyone talk back to an officer, let alone in the presence of several high ranking colleagues.

"Piss off, Captain" said Eric, still keeping firm eye contact with Tolley. "Prick." He said it under his breath, and was sure only the Major and the Captain heard it. Even in his dazed and dehydrated state, Eric was fully prepared to fight and kill his way to the nearest truck and get as far away from there as possible. All he needed was a good enough reason. In fact, even a bad reason would probably do, with the sort of mood he was in. But first he wanted answers to all the questions racing across his mind, and any others he could think up after that.

"OK, OK," said Major Tolley dismissively, before the Captain could explode. "Eric, I am sure you are very tired, please rest and..."

"Where am I, you fucking bastard?" demanded Eric again. "This isn't a game. You can't just drug someone and drag them to another fucking country without at least telling them where they are!" He was really angry now, and his fists were clenching.

The Major flinched at Eric's outburst, before replying, "Don't you recognise it, Eric? This is Outpost 2151... well, Fort 2151 now, the biggest training and military intelligence facility the Army has to offer." There was a rumbling chorus and murmurs of agreement from the officers.

"Outpost 99!" exclaimed Eric. "I was there a few years ago, back then it was..." He paused when he realised he might have a higher clearance level than a lot of the people in the tent, Tolley included.

"Yes Eric, that's the one," nodded Tolley.

"But back then it was a... testing facility," Eric continued, taking care over which word to use to describe the horrors he had seen being done to man and beast. Outpost 99 was a silent facility, which meant you'd never find any paperwork or evidence of its existence. Eric hadn't liked it much, or their experiments trying to manufacture the perfect soldier to fight the Zarda and their beasts. "The man in charge then was called Captain Knock, a dog-faced fool of a man who would sooner wet himself than face any of the Zarda soldiers" he added, laughing.

"Yeah that's the man, I nearly forgot about him. Wasn't much back then was it? But look at us now!" said Major Tolley, pointing a finger at the tent opening.

"What about all of his… experiments? Surely those aren't still going on here?" exclaimed Eric, who had a good memory for people he hated, and Captain Knock was certainly one of them. Or at least he had been one of them, until that day when a few of his 'experiments' had got loose and ripped him to shreds. Eric hadn't enjoyed the screams, and the locks on the monster's cages had been a little tricky, but he felt the world was a little bit better now that Captain Knock wasn't in it.

"I can assure you, Eric, that that sort of thing is not still going on here. We are a training facility now, providing only the very best that the Army has to offer," Tolley concluded, and gestured to the door again.

Eric nodded whilst keeping eye contact with him. The look said, 'I will get answers, one way or another'. He reluctantly allowed himself to be led away.

With their exchange over, Tolley turned back to his patiently-waiting audience. He was about to apologise for the interruption when Eric called from the tent entrance.

"Remember, Tolley, if I don't like the reason I have been brought here, I will get very angry" he intoned, violence and blood dripping off every word.

The Major half turned and grinned at Eric. "No worries Commander, I will explain everything later. Eat something – you look hungry. And get a bit of rest, there's a good fellow, and I'll fill you in later. Thank you Captain, you may take him away this time." He could feel Eric's stare trying to burn holes through the back of him.

Eric shut his eyes and shook his head. He could tell he wasn't going to enjoy the explanation. He'd never had anything but bad luck when it came to the Army, and it was highly unlikely to change any time soon.

He was pulled out of the officer's tent into the brilliant midday heat and sunshine, and allowed the Captain to drag him through the maze of tents and walkways. The Captain showed Eric to a one of a long line of small tents. Eric ducked down to enter and immediately the Captain walked away. "What, no tour?" grunted Eric sarcastically.

The tent wasn't very big. Eric could just about stand up straight in the middle, and his head would brush against the canvas if he needed to reach anything outside the centre. There was nothing on the ground. He could see the footprints of the two men who had set the tent up, and it looked like they had done it in a hurry. The interior was as meagre as expected. There was a small chest of three drawers, and on top of this were a small battery-powered lamp and a foldable cot bed. Eric hated these beds with a passion. They consisted of an inch-thick piece of fabric stretched tightly across a thin metal frame, which kept you off the ground by about a foot and a half. At no point in history was this bed designed with comfort in mind; it was purely functional. They were simply designed for a tired soldier who was too tired to care about comfort to pass out on for a few hours before getting back to work.

At one end of the cot was a sad-looking pillow sitting on top of a neatly-folded, rough-looking, wool blanket. The Army really didn't care if their soldiers were having a good night's sleep or not. So long as they weren't passing out on duty, it didn't matter.

Eric checked the chest of drawers and found two sets of identical uniforms with the 'Priest' rank sewn into the collar and sleeve. They consisted of a black T-shirt, a black shirt and a pair of black combat trousers. They were nothing special. The Army had gone for cheap but durable cloth for their uniforms, and the only alternative was the jumpsuits that the engineers and roaming squads wore. You didn't need to be smartly dressed when you were up to your elbows in oil, or out in one of the many quarantined zones.

Down to one side of the small chest Eric found a pair of black boots. He had tried the boots once before, and they were terrible, so this pair got thrown out of the tent immediately, hitting a very surprised passer-by.

The black uniform was usually reserved for the Priest soldiers, holy men and woman who did their best to solve any issues the soldiers had that could not be resolved by the officers, which was most of them. Eric remembered the old days, when priests were a big force on the battlefield, bellowing at the soldiers to fight harder or else their god would send them straight to hell for an eternity in fiery damnation. That normally did the trick. These days the priests reminded Eric more of primary school teachers; they pretty much acted as counsellors to the whiners and those prone to complain, and read stories from the book for their particular brand of religion rather than rallying the troops.

Eric dressed slowly. The clean clothes were far better than the ones he had been wearing for the past week or so, and they smelt better too. He turned his attention to the sad excuse for a bed. There was a large bottle of water next to it which took barely a minute to pick up and drain. He lay down on the bed, stared up at the canvas ceiling and thought about how much he really didn't want to be there. He hated the Army. Many years before the War he'd tried to warn them that there was something strange in the air, but they had just laughed at him and called him paranoid. Then as soon as the attacks had come, they were quick to demand his help, which Eric translated as bailing them out of the biggest war the world had ever seen. Eric remembered how he had argued with all the different generals, majors, scientists, chiefs of staff, and all the different countries' leaders until he was nearly blue in the face. That had annoyed him greatly, as they hadn't believed that such a war could ever be possible. When the War finally broke out, instead of jumping into action, they decided to argue amongst themselves, and assigning blame was more important than actually doing something. But eventually the New Global Army was created, and all the soldiers got a brand new uniform to wear.

Eric lay there, the hangover demons swimming laps across his brain, but it was starting to simmer down as his brain cells started healing. Sounds from outside were filtering through the cheap canvas, and he could hear in the distance drill instructors and officers shouting at unseen soldiers. Behind that Eric could make out the banging and crashing white noise of the barracks hard at work. In the distance he could hear the thump-thump of helicopter blades. They got louder as they got closer, until the sound became a deafening roar as they flew over the camp. They were too loud to be simple goods and provision transporters; this was the heavy thump-thump of soldier transport choppers, big, fat and heavy brutes that were usually heavily weighted down with soldiers and supplies, and because of this they had to fly very low in the air. They must be skimming the radio towers. This city-sized barracks was growing fast, stretching outwards like a tumour on the landscape. Why had they been so desperate to get him here? Why did they seem to be rushing to build and stock these barracks? If Eric didn't know better, they were either expecting to launch a big attack, or preparing to defend one.

He decided to switch off his brain and turn uncomfortably onto his side. The water had helped, and so had the clean clothes, but what he really needed now was sleep. He would rest for a couple of hours and then beat all the answers out of Tolley, whether he liked it or not.

Eric shut his eyes and instantly fell into a deep and uncomfortable sleep, dreams of past adventures streaking across his slumbering mind.

CHAPTER 8

A WALK IN THE DARK

Eric Mason woke up from his deep slumber with a jolt. His body still ached, but at least parts of him weren't screaming at him in pain any more. He slowly opened his eyes, fully expecting them to be filled with light, but this didn't happen; it was still dark. Even though his body told him he had been asleep for several hours, the sun still hadn't crept over the horizon.

The stars were still shining bright far above, and he lay there trying to plot them against what he could remember through the haze of pain before his sleep. They seemed to be in the same places as before, the same wrong places, in the sky above him. Either he was dreaming, which he doubted because his whole body still ached from whatever mystery attack had befallen him, or he was on a planet that didn't turn, and in a different part of the universe from where he last remembered being. Given the choice, he'd prefer the second option, but only because it would be something a little different or fun. He couldn't help thinking that this option was a little far-fetched. A very real chill of doubt was running across his mind, cutting through him like a ship through icy waves.

He decided to try and move again, but not all at once this time; he wasn't crazy enough to attempt standing up just yet. Even the thought of getting all the way up sent a shiver of pain up and down his spine. He tried lifting his arms, which seemed like the easiest option to go for first. His elbows and shoulders clicked as his joints popped back into place, and he managed to stretch his tired arms out in front of him. He couldn't see his hands, which was very disconcerting. He knew they were there because he could feel the air against them as they waved, but he couldn't see even a faint outline of them. His biceps, forearms and chest screamed at him as he tried to stretch out further. It felt as though he was trying to lift an almighty weight, like a building or a truck, off his chest, and he felt the sweat starting to run down the sides of his face.

With the test over, he relaxed and dropped his hands back down by his sides, feeling the gritty sand underneath his fingertips. Overall it wasn't too bad, he could just about handle the pain without blacking out, which had to be a good sign, so he tried bending his knees too. This had the same result. His knees clicked as they bent, and lightning bolts of pain shot up and down his spine as he moved. Again the pain wasn't anything he couldn't ignore, for now.

But now it was time for the big push. Eric slowly, and very carefully, got to his feet. Parts of him creaked and groaned, and he had to stop a couple times to catch his breath, alarmed at some of the bovine noises he made in the process. If it hadn't been so dark he would probably have looked like an old man trying to get up from an overly-comfortable armchair. But eventually he was upright, and it was a good job there wasn't any kind of breeze here, because right here and now he could have been knocked down by a feather.

"Right" sighed Eric. His throat and his lungs were dry and rough, causing him to cough and dry-heave a little, which sent more spasms of pain ripping through him. Each cough and spasm brought a different swear word, until he was sure it was over, for now.

His words echoed off in all directions, which surprised even him. He wasn't sure what to expect any more, but he certainly wasn't expecting an echo. He normally had pretty good eyesight in the dark, but here he couldn't see a damn thing, except for the stars above him. He turned around in a little circle, hoping that he might catch a sound or smell he could follow, but still nothing.

He tried taking a small step. As he raised his foot his knee creaked and he wobbled and had to throw out his hands in front of him for balance. When his foot finally reached the ground, he looked like a trapeze artist on a high-wire without a safety net. He stood for a moment and let the almost orgasmic waves of pins and needles wash up and down his legs before taking another careful step and waiting for another wave. The next wave of pain was less severe than the first, so he tried again, and again. With each step the waves of pain got more and more manageable, until they were barely noticeable.

He walked a few metres with his hands stretched out in front of him, he looked like a toddler first learning to walk. Or a drunk trying to get home at three o'clock in the morning after a very heavy night out.

"Bugger!" he exclaimed loudly. He had walked into something hard and invisible. The collision knocked him off balance a little, and he swayed for a moment, grasping his head in his hands and trying to stay upright, but eventually he fell and landed like a fallen tree hard on the rocky ground beneath him. He felt like a fool lying there. He could do nothing but laugh at his current predicament.

He raised his pounding head. The point of impact was

radiating rings of hurt, and he could feel a thin trickle of blood running down his face. He got slowly to his feet and wiped it away from his eye with one hand, while with the other he felt for the object he had walked into. He took a small step forward, stumbled on a loose rock, and fell forward, slamming into his invisible attacker.

It was definitely rock. It was reasonably flat, like the side of a cliff, and just as solid. Eric stood motionless for a moment hugging the rock face. He rallied himself and pushed away, and used his hands to explore the rock face in front of him. Eric walked along it, feeling his way with both hands and occasionally banging his head on unexpected bulges of rock, which made the wound on his forehead a little bigger each time. Eventually he decided it had to be a wall of some sort, possibly made from rough stone bricks.

The theory that he might have fallen off a cliff drunk would possibly explain why every inch of his body had been screaming at him in pain, but it wouldn't explain the burnt skin or clothes. A wall would be useful. It meant that people came here often enough to have the need to build something here, so he might bump into one of them at some point, and they could take him to safety. Or they would try to kill him, if they turned out to be the Zarda. Considering he had no idea where he was, and the front line of the War was ever changing, this could be a very serious reality.

He turned around and leaned against the hard rock surface, trying again to squint into the darkness. He still couldn't see anything despite not being anywhere near where he had woken up. It was hopeless to keep trying. Where the hell was the light? He would have given all the possessions he had for just a flash of light, just enough to give him a split second to see where he was, and which way he should go.

'Possessions!' shouted a thought in the back of his mind. Why hadn't he checked his pockets yet? He didn't have an answer. He quickly patted his body down, trying to avoid the burnt skin. One pocket was no more; it hung down from his trousers like the tongue of a happy dog. He checked another, and another, but both came up with nothing more than dust and lint.

But the last one he came to felt full, the one just above his left knee. He fumbled inside and cut his hand on something sharp. He winced and sucked the blood on his hand, as it had cut quite deep. He carefully tried again and fished out what felt like a sliver of glass not much bigger than the palm of his hand. Where the hell did he get that from? And what had possessed him to put it in his pocket?

He hefted the shard in his hand. It was heavier than expected. He put it back in his pocket and made a mental note to try to fall on his other side. He readied himself and walked a few steps away from the wall with his hands stretched out and waving in all directions, he felt a little better knowing he at least had some sort of weapon on him now. He had done a lot more with a lot less in the past.

The occasional loose rock underfoot turned his journey into a small obstacle course, as some of the rocks he was stepping, or tripping, over were the size of footballs. He managed to walk a whole ten minutes before walking into something else big and solid, and once again he found himself lying on his back.

"Bugger!" he exclaimed in a loud voice, rubbing the second wound on his head. He could feel the blood trickling down his face and connecting with the other one to create a steady river of blood.

Eric lay there for a few minutes in disbelief. How the hell had he got himself into this situation? He descended into his memory house again, but deeper this time, and searched all the rooms he could find. Some of them had big metal chains across the doors, locked for very good reasons. But nothing he could find would give him any suggestion as to why he was now bumbling around in the dark like an idiot. Every room was covered in dust, nothing new or different anywhere. His mental personification ran from room to room, picking up newer-looking objects, which would cause a burst of memories pertaining to it, but nothing useful. Or at least, nothing that answered any of the questions he had.

It didn't look like the sun was ever going to rise, so Eric took a deep breath, got to his feet again and wiped away the blood from his face. He felt his way to what he had walked into. The blood was really gushing down his face now, and he was starting to feel a little light-headed. This wasn't normal, his body was usually pretty good at healing any cuts and bruises he got on his many travels.

His hands explored the rocky surface in front of him, and he walked alongside it, never lifting his fingertips. His rate of movement quickened, and again a shiver of extreme doubt ran through his body when he didn't seem to be able to find an edge or a corner. It couldn't be round, could it? It didn't feel like he'd just gone around in a circle. It had to be another wall. Two walls, maybe twenty or twenty-five metres apart, running parallel to each other maybe? Was he on some kind of road that someone had lined with a big rock wall? He reached up as he had done on the other rock, and again he couldn't seem to reach a ledge; the wall simply went up and up above him. He knew he wasn't a giant, he was only six foot and some inches tall, which meant his arm span was about three feet. Who would have built two walls facing each other, over nine feet tall? It didn't make any sense to him, unless he had found himself in a town or village somewhere, but that had to be very unlikely, didn't it? Because if it was a town or village, surely there'd be people, or fires, or something.

He bent down and fumbled around on the ground looking for something. The darkness was starting to piss him off. Even in the darkest room there was always a little bit of light to see by, but not here. He found a rock no bigger than a tennis ball, took a few uneasy steps away from the second wall and launched the rock into the air.

The sound he was expecting didn't come. He expected to hear

nothing until the rock hit the floor some distance away on the other side of the wall and rolled away. What he didn't expect to hear was a loud bang as the rock hit the wall a few feet above where he had reached up to. It echoed loudly all around him, and he felt the swish of air as the rock narrowly missed his head.

The echo of rock hitting rock travelled far and wide, and when the noise finally died down, all he could hear was the sound of his heart beating in his chest. Alarm bells that had been patiently and quietly ringing at the back of his mind started to turn up their volume, and now they were all fighting for his attention.

He had been here before. A vague memory flickered across his mind's eye. It was just a flash, but it was definitely déjà vu. Eric looked up to see the stars above him still shining bright in the cloudless sky. Now that his eyes were starting to focus a little more he could make out a slight green tint around each one. The déjà vu had shaken him a little, and something about the sky had been bugging him since he'd first stared up at it. He'd seen it before, but a very long time ago.

Suddenly Eric felt doors in his memory house open. His mind had the answers. It had all the information he needed, if he could only find the right door, he'd know exactly where he was.

He opened a room; it was dark, darker than any other room in his mind. But in the centre was a memory, a strong one. It sat alone, which was completely unusual.

Eric stepped into the room, and the door slammed behind him. He needed to make sure. Fragments of memory were spinning past his eyes. He couldn't catch them, or put them in any kind or sensible order, but they were there.

He scrabbled on the floor again and found another rock, and used his body to launch it as high as he could. It bounced off one of the star clusters. The stars shattered immediately, sending sparks and small glowing flakes into the air that gently drifted down to where Eric was standing. He watched the flakes slowly land on the ground around his feet. They definitely were not stars, and he had not been looking up at a sky.

He knew exactly where he was, and streams of vague memories came flooding back to him from all corners of his memory house. Doors opened and slammed as the torrent of memories rushed to escape their bondage. He didn't understand how he hadn't recognised this place immediately; it wasn't a place you would easily forget in a hurry.

Another chill ran down his spine as he stared at the glowing flakes on the ground, and one by one they started to fade away to nothingness. He had no idea how he had managed to wind up here, or who on the planet could have brought him here, but it was somewhere he had no intention of staying. It was in a place that couldn't be drawn on any map, a place only a few people knew about, and even fewer knew the secrets that were held here. He was in the cave network underneath the Mountain, a place he hadn't been in years, and had wished he'd never be in again.

"Fuck" he exclaimed under his breath, when he finally started breathing again.

CHAPTER 9

THE BATTLE BETWEEN LIGHT AND DARKNESS

The universe continued to turn, planets and rocks orbited their new suns, stars and gas giants were born and died, and everything was fine and peaceful. As there is no such thing as time, it's difficult to put into terms how long the world has been turning, years, centuries, millennia, it's all the same. The universe lives in the ever constant here and now.

On Earth, the third planet from the sun, the land had been forced to move by the waters covering it, and had crashed together to form mountains and valleys. Huge continents had grown and separated, and joined others elsewhere. The waters formed great oceans and lakes, rivers with rushing waters carving their way through the rough landscapes. The entire planet was a perfect picture of paradise.

It was now, however, the time for the dark creatures to return. The creatures were focused, all with the same driving purpose, and they swarmed forward in a big cloud of oily shapeless bodies to destroy the suns that had completely devastated their world. The suns had sucked in and chewed up many of their kind, and they wanted revenge. They wanted the light gone, and the cool darkness to envelop them again, as it always was, and as it always should be.

The sun in this galaxy in particular was the largest of its kind, and the creatures of darkness knew they had to destroy this one first. They mounted their attack, and sent wave upon wave of oily, formless, bodies to suffocate the sun. With each wave of darkness the sun got bigger again, but their determination blinded them from the hopeless fact that they could not win. The sun grew larger, and larger still, gorging and eating each creature as it charged to its death.

The sun started to rumble and vibrate. It shook and lashed out with its tentacles of warm light. Like a small child who has eaten too many sweets, it was irritated and uncomfortable. Its surface swelled and bulged in places, and when the pressure got too much, it let off violent explosions of fire. Colossal fireballs were fired in all directions, killing more of the dark creatures. Wrapped in fear, the Darkness backed away; the blobs had not expected this and did not know what it meant.

The balls of fire screamed as they flew through the ranks of Darkness, sucking the blobs in and gaining momentum with each mouthful. Some of the fireballs disappeared off into the darker recesses of space, hitting stars and moons and causing great blasts of colour to flash against all the other planets and stars. Many of the fireballs headed for Earth, its gravity pulling them in from far and wide, and they rained down like meteorites onto the planet's surface. The creatures watched, hoping that the balls of fire would destroy these new planets, but something strange happened to them when they reached their final destination. The balls of light that hit the water sank deep below the surface and out of sight, where they grew scales and fins, became fish and other water creatures, and expanded to happily fill each of the great oceans and lakes. Some were bigger than others, growing into sharks with fierce teeth and minds, or huge whale-sized monsters that could swim deeper than the others, and play on the sea bed.

Other balls of light developed wings and feathers before they hit the ground or the water, and became birds which could feel the winds beneath them lifting them up, and they spread out to fill the skies. Many of them flocked to the high mountain tops to live amongst the rocks and cliffs, losing their feathers and growing tough scales instead, and breathing the fire of dragons. The air soon became thick with bodies of all sizes, floating on the winds and letting the air currents spread them out throughout the higher places.

Balls of screaming light and fire slammed into the various landscapes too. They stretched and elongated, like a shape inside was trying to break free, until they had produced feet and tails. They grew big and strong, and fought amongst themselves to find the best land to breed on and grass to eat. These land-walking dinosaurs had teeth and tusks, and divided naturally into slow ones that ate the lush foliage of the land, and fast ones that ate the slow-moving grass eaters. Some were able to lift themselves onto their hind legs, allowing them extra height to see out across their new home and see predators stalking towards them. A lot of the dinosaurs grew big and hungry. Some of them were taller than the newly-grown trees, and could easily pick off smaller and weaker dinosaurs, or reach the leaves on the higher branches.

Earth was full of life and movement for the first time since the planet had first started to revolve around its mother sun. The dark creatures looked down upon the surface, watching all the movement of these newly-formed Earth creatures with great interest. They observed them like expectant scientists looking through a microscope. They saw each dinosaur moving and enjoying the sun's warmth, and they hated them for it. They watched as this new life spread across the lands, seas, and skies. They watched as the new life bred and multiplied uncontrollably. New families formed packs and herds, searching for the best food and the best place to enjoy the sunshine. The dark creatures decided there and then that if they couldn't kill the sun, they would have to kill the sun's offspring instead, and this filled the creatures with deadly and revengeful energy that could never be extinguished.

Without a further thought, the dark creatures in unison swarmed down to the planet like ink shooting from an octopus. It was a huge Brownian motion of pure darkness, contrasting against the thousands of colourful plants and animals below, with nothing but destruction on their singular mind. Riding, twisting, and flying on the wind, thick with their collective oily black bodies, they flew in and around the land masses, devouring the land creatures almost whole.

An unsuspecting three-horned dinosaur, walking across a grass plane with its two small offspring in tow, was unlucky enough to find itself in the path of this destruction. The mother screamed a warning, and the young ran for the nearby woods, but the mother was completely engulfed by the stream of darkness, which choked her lungs and broke her bones. When the young three young ones looked back, their mother was no more, and soon the Darkness caught up with them too.

Dinosaurs all across the lands and seas fled as fast as they could, but they had no hope of out running, or hiding, from this black, unforgiving purge. Parents screamed out for their young over the cries of pain and suffering from the rest of their herds, but their cries were unheard by their already dead children. The new world was full of suffering, and nothing was able to put up a fight. There seemed to be no end to the global decimation of life.

After killing all it found in the oceans and lands, the Darkness continued on its purge. The mass of oily creatures headed up high, to where the bigger birds and dragons lived, and found a hole in one of the larger mountains. It wasn't a big hole, more of a big cave with tunnels running down inside the mountains like veins. But this mountain didn't seem the same as the others the Darkness had found; it was alone, far from any other, which interested the creatures.

The cave was the entrance to a labyrinthine network of underground caves and tunnels. All the mountains on Earth were full of them, but this mountain in particular had the most direct route to the centre of the planet, and the Darkness guessed correctly that it could use this tunnel as a direct highway to the molten centre of the planet. Using their collective mind, they decided that if they were able to destroy the planet's heart, then the planet would wither and die.

The swarm picked up speed, fed off as many dinosaurs as it could find, and boosted its strength for their final assault. This would be the final blow. They would kill the sun's children and crumble their home. The swarm dived and swooped, banked and swayed, until it was ready to strike. The darkness reached speeds it had not found so far. Its mind was focused, its purpose was clear, and it charged the Mountain at full strength, but its entrance was blocked at the last minute. A shining ball of light, which had been searching the lands and seas for a home to call its own, was hovering in the way. It was much bigger than any of the other balls of light, and it too had seen the cave when it had first landed not too far away.

It had gone to investigate, and found the hot centre of the planet, which had been growing hotter and hotter with every turn the planet made of the sun. It heated the planet, melting all the surrounding rock, ever turning, ever churning, and had a power that could even rival the sun itself. The ball of light had decided to call it home. The heat and energy of the planet had infused the ball with extra power, and it was feeling very, very strong. It knew the Darkness should never reach the centre of the planet. It knew instinctively that it should protect its new home from this evil.

The light grew in size as best it could, pulsating its anger at the Darkness and warning it to leave, and barricaded the cave entrance. The darkness, unperturbed by this new-found guardian, speeded up, and charged at the ball of light with all its combined strength. But the light, fuelled by the planet's incredible heat, managed to hold back the tide of darkness, causing the black, greasy creatures to rebound and ricochet off in all directions.

The dark creatures rallied, anger filling up inside each one at this defiance. They forced their bloodlust into overdrive, and once more threw a wave of bodies against the ball of light. But again the ball of light managed to hold them back. Not a single black creature managed to claw itself past the light. It was too big, it was too strong, and now it was glowing brighter than the sun itself. The creatures of darkness were relentless, their bodies crashing again and again into the light, hoping to find some part of weakness, or a gap they could exploit to get past.

When the Darkness' collective mind realised that this was hopeless, they retreated to a safer distance, killing any animal or dinosaur in their path. What they needed was strength in numbers. The entire planet was covered in smaller swarms of black creatures, and from above you could see the trails of oily blackness seeping around the planet, wiping it clear of life and leaving nothing but bones in their wake.

The Darkness summoned all the creatures to one spot, not too far from the light at the top of the lonely mountain, and swarmed and dived and collected more and more bodies. With every extra swarm the mass got bigger and stronger, until it started to level whole forests and small mountain ranges with the sheer weight and energy of the mass of shapeless bodies. And as the mass got bigger, and stronger, it got closer and closer to the base of the Mountain.

The light, still floating in the cave at the top of the Mountain, bulged and expanded in readiness, and bounced around the inside of the cave leaving small splashes of light, which shone brightly but slowly dissolved. Just as the mother sun had done before, it grew bigger and stronger, and soon it was facing every dark creature that had descended to the planet. Their black shapeless bodies slipped and slid over each other like waves of oil, pulling each other higher and higher.

The glistening ball of light refused to back down, despite being heavily outnumbered. The tsunami of darkness crept ever closer as they got higher up the Mountain. The effect was like watching a dirty waterfall, only backwards. The bodies clambered from rock to rock, killing any plants and animals in their path.

The defiant ball of light bulged and stretched and out in all directions, and with one final burst of light, it split into ten smaller ones, each almost as bright as the one they came from, and bounced around the cave at a speed that was difficult to keep track of. Although they were now separate, they were still connected by tendrils of light so thin is was difficult to see, and they slowly expanded until they formed a line of defence in front of the cave entrance.

The two opposing forces lined up parallel and slowly crept closer to each other. The darkness was forming a cloud stronger than any storm the planet had ever seen. Thunder was rumbling in its centre, and lightning was spitting at the balls of light. The darkness was cautious not to get too close though. Its force had not performed well against the one big light, and now they were facing ten smaller, and much faster, spheres. But they were fuelled by hate and rage.

The ten smaller balls of bright light started to vibrate as the larger one had done only minutes before, causing the Darkness to back down a little, and watched helplessly as the lights started to bulge. But this was different from before, they stretched out in new and even stranger ways. The smaller balls of light seemed to charge up their energy, and with one final push they stretched out in different directions and grew arms and legs. At the end of each of these small fingers began to emerge. But they did not look like the other animals the Darkness had destroyed; these were very different. The thumb was in a slightly different place, like the monkeys that lived in the trees and jungles, but strong and nimble, as if they had been designed to do fine intricate work. Their feet were strange too, not like a monkey's that could work as hands but flat and spaced out, almost like the fins of fish.

Even in the brilliant glow of their charged-up energy, faces could soon be made out on their newly-formed heads, the brightest light coming from their eyes and the thin slit mouths. Collectively they looked from one to another, as if an extremely complicated and silent conversation was going around the small group. They stared at each other, and at their newly-formed hands, tensing them, feeling new strength in this form. The light inside each one pulsed in the rhythm of a heartbeat, and each one slowly sank until its feet touched the ground.

A surge of energy ripped through each one when they felt the solidity of earth and rock beneath them, and they glared at the storm-cloud of floating blackness and the hundreds of evil-looking creatures glared back. But something was happening to them too. They too were growing arms and legs, but unlike the golden beings of light, their hands had sharp claws, and long black tails hung down by their taloned feet. Their heads were contorted into horned faces, their heads and bodies covered in oily black scales that shone eerily in the light, and their mouths were full of razor-sharp black teeth.

As their bodies began to take shape, they dropped from the cloud. They were no longer creature of space and shadow, but whole and strong. They flexed the strong muscles under scales or fur, and shook their heads, creating waterfalls of black oily hair that cascaded down. Their eyes glowed red with anger, contrasting with their black bodies, and very soon the beings of light were facing thousands of pairs of red eyes.

The golden beings screamed a warning at the creatures, their brightly-lit mouths forming complex syllables that floated in the air between the two forces, demanding that they leave this planet and go back to the depths of space where they belonged. But the Darkness had no such thought in its collective mind, and without warning they charged, their glowing bodies full of anger and bile.

The dark creatures swarmed up the mountainside like ants, but the Beings of Light were ready, their new hands clenching into fists, their new muscles bulging under their glowing skin, their eyes narrowed. Every time the glowing Beings of Light connected a punch, or a kicking foot, a creature of the Darkness turned to ash, like fighting a statue made from wet sand. Each one crumbled instantly, and the black ash landed like dirty snow all around their glowing feet.

The creatures of Darkness were big, but slow, each one trying to crush or grapple with the Beings of Light, but the Beings were fast and nimble. They seemed to effortlessly twist and spin around each other, punching and kicking, ducking and diving, and all the while staying in a smart line defence in front of their mountain entrance. Each arm and leg motion was followed by a golden trail of light, which glowed brighter when the being needed a little more energy. But the sheer numbers of all the attacking monsters at once was overwhelming, and the Beings of Light were forced back inside the cave.

The cloud of darkness could see it was starting to win the battle, and quickly forced more and more of its kind to drop from the cloud, nearly covering the whole of the mountainside. The monsters rallied into a tight bunch, claws and fangs at the ready, and charged like a wrecking ball. The beings of light pushed as hard as they could against the wall of monstrous blackness, but their weight and combined strength was too much.

Some of the newly-formed dark creatures, which had grown tentacles instead of claws, wrapped themselves around the necks and chest of the weaker Beings of Light like snakes, choking the air out of their lungs and crushing them. More and more joined them until the Beings of Light were completely engulfed in their oily blackness. Black teeth and claws found gaps where they could rip and tear at the glowing skin. If the Beings of Light had had voices they would have screamed out in pain, but for now all they could do was open and shut their mouths in agonised surprise.

Very soon the Beings of Light were forced further into the cave, and into the Mountain itself. The darkness in here was deep, and only strengthened the forces of darkness further. By the time they had reached the heart of the Mountain, there were very few Beings of Light left to hold back the tide. Strange and eerie shadows flashed up against the walls of the underground caverns and tunnels each time a Being of Light managed to get a better footing, or had managed to take down a few of their enemies.

As the mass got closer and closer to the centre of the planet, the warmth and energy from the planet's core fuelled the Beings of Light, and enabled them to keep fighting. The darkness was all around them, suffocating them, choking them at every turn and trying to dim their light, but they refused to back down or surrender. This was their home now, and this was where they were going to stay.

The Beings of Light and the forces of darkness battled deep below the planet's surface, completely unknown to those dinosaurs who had escaped the purge, who never knew the struggle the Beings of Light had trying to keep their home, or which side would win in the end.

CHAPTER 10

FORT 21-51

Eric Mason was sleeping in a very thin and uncomfortable army cot, in a place he didn't want to be, in a war he didn't want to fight any more, and he had been brought there by someone he didn't want to talk to. All in all, things weren't going as well as he'd hoped.

It was still hot, but the heat of the day was starting to simmer down a little. Inside his tent, Eric was sweating hard. He was having a nightmare; his face was scrunched up as if he was in serious pain from invisible demons, and he had sweat dripping down his face and through his already-soaked hair.

He was breathing heavily too, gasping for air like a man choking in a burning building, and he suddenly awoke, sucking in a huge lungful of air, and sat bolt upright. His eyes were wide as he scanned the contents of the tent. Only after deciding that the forces of darkness weren't actually trying to suffocate him, as they had been in his dream, he relaxed a little. He let his lungs deflate with a long hissing sound, and tried to catch his breath as he swung his feet over the side of the army cot.

His head was pounding worse than when he had woken up with a hangover, and whatever that bastard Captain had put in his drink hadn't helped. The sounds filtering in from outside his tent seemed deafening; he could even hear his heart beating wildly in his chest. This had to be the result of whatever drugs they'd used. There was definitely a headache from dehydration, this he recognised from years of experience, so he fumbled around under his cot until he found the very nearly empty bottle of water he had dropped there before his sleep. The water was warm, but he didn't care right now because the liquid felt amazing on his dry throat. He'd hoped that the temperature would have simmered down a little after a few hours of sleep, but the sun had managed to bake so much heat into the surrounding land and air that it was impossible to escape the high temperatures. He wiped the sweat off his face and watched hypnotised as the droplets fell from his hand, hitting the dry dirt below him, each drop sending up a mini-explosion of dust.

He looked down at where he had been sleeping, and eyed the soaking wet pillow and the damp patch on the cot's thin fabric. He was having that nightmare more and more these days, though years had gone by without it. But now the War was getting worse, and the nightmares seemed to have taken up permanent residence in his sleeping mind. He hadn't been there at the time, of course, it was a story he had read when he was a child that had really stuck with him. He had often thought about how hard the Beings of Light must have fought, and how terrified they must have felt being forced back inside the Mountain, to be engulfed in darkness and be choked by monsters that were more shadow than flesh and blood.

The noise from outside his tent seemed to dull down a little as his hearing adjusted, until it was just about bearable. But now there were definite sounds of urgency, with shouted voices and running feet. A thump by the tent opening made him look over; one of the running feet had tripped and fallen into the side of his tent, spilling the pile of boxes it was carrying. The body swore loudly as only a soldier could, and jumped back up and fumbled around for the spilt packages before hurriedly running away. One of the small boxes the soldier had been carrying had fallen just inside his tent, so Eric got up slowly, not taking his eyes off the box, and when he was sure the unseen soldier wasn't looking for it, he walked over and picked it up.

It was a box of dried meat. The origin of the animal was indeterminable, and the language on the packet was not something he could read, but there was a crude drawing of some kind of animal with four legs on the cover smiling at him with a big cartoon grin. He scanned the box's contents. It didn't look very appetising, but his hungry stomach took control, and he ate a small amount. It was chewy and it tasted like meat. He wouldn't be able to tell what animal it came from by taste, but this was enough for now. His stomach growled its distrust of the new arrival, and told Eric that more recognisable food would be required soon.

He pocketed the small box of dried meat and gingerly opened the tent flap, stepped outside, and jumped backwards immediately to avoid getting trampled by a group of soldiers running at top speed down the path between tents. They were all carrying boxes and containers, all with similar labels to the one in his pocket. When he couldn't hear any running footsteps coming towards him, he tried leaving the tent again. He stepped outside and walked down the path.

All around him there seemed to be chaos. Officers were running around and stopping only to shout orders at any soldier stupid enough to be standing still. Eric casually dodged and weaved through the tents. He seemed to be the only one not rushing to be somewhere they weren't.

It quickly turned into a game. He dodged around the bustling throng of soldiers, picking bits of fruit and food out of the boxes they were carrying, using the sleight of hand he had picked up over the years. It helped that he had excellent hand-eye co-ordination and the reaction speeds of a cat on speed. He would tip a bread roll off one crate with one hand and catch it in the other, whilst at the same time spinning round to distract another person, causing them to drop some other food, which also went into one of the several pockets he had in his new uniform. He emerged from the rushing crowd a happy man, with enough breakfast secreted about his person to feed two or three hungry men, and he had every intention of eating the lot. That is, if he could find a quiet spot to sit down and enjoy the bounty.

He carried on, letting his feet do the orienteering to the spot from which he had been rudely dragged by that Captain. He reach into his pockets for food as he walked, appearing without a care in the world. The sun was starting to get low in the sky, and it was starting to feel like a nice evening. Eric wasn't in much of a rush. In fact, he couldn't help but smile about being the only one not in a hurry. The breeze was pleasantly fresh. It must have been coming off the seemingly endless deserts surrounding this city of tents, and it moved the stale heat around without giving a chill. Eric stood still for a moment, enjoying a mouthful of miscellaneous meat and listening to the ambient hubbub.

"Hey you!" came a voice behind Eric. He turned and saw a small fat man glaring at him. A quick look at the man's rank told Eric this was a Sergeant. "Who are you eyeballing?"

"Who, me?" asked Eric, mystified that someone was actually paying attention to him. Everyone else seemed to think he was invisible.

"Yeah, you soldier! And you will address me as yes Sergeant," continued the Sergeant, who had also seen Eric's rank as priest. "Do you notice anything strange around here?"

Eric looked around theatrically and took in their surroundings, then shook his head at the man "No, yes Sergeant, I don't" he said honestly, as if the sight of thousands of soldiers frantically packing everything up was a daily occurrence.

"Well I do" said the Sergeant and marched a few steps closer to Eric, which was probably meant to intimidate him, but in fact it didn't improve matters because Eric was a good foot taller. "I see something very strange indeed!" the Sergeant shouted, having to look up as he did so. "I notice everyone else is rushing around and working hard to get stuff done. Whereas you, priest, are standing there with a silly grin on your face!"

Eric liked Sergeants, they didn't need diplomacy unless they were speaking to an officer, and if they didn't like you, you knew about it.

"I had noticed that, yes Sergeant. Quite the commotion it would seem, is it a race of some sort?" asked Eric conversationally. "What's going on?" He absent-mindedly pulled a bread roll out of his pocket and took a big bite.

Eric saw the anger rise in the Sergeant's eyes, and his cheeks started going redder than any cheek should ever be forced to go.

"What's going on is that you are the laziest, poorest excuse for a soldier I have ever seen!" shouted the Sergeant. Eric opened his mouth to say something, but the Sergeant carried on "Get to bloody work you maggot!" Then he knocked the bread roll out of Eric's hand.

Eric watched the bread roll somersault away like tumbleweed and fall under the wheel of a fast-moving truck. He stood staring at the fallen meal like it was an injured soldier, even though there were two more in his pocket. The Sergeant continued to shout abuse at Eric, who wasn't really listening. Just then he saw out of the corner a very nearly empty pack of cigarettes on the floor. It must have been dropped by one of the rushing soldiers, and it had boot prints and tyre tracks across it, but the last remaining cigarette inside still looked good. Ignoring the still-shouting Sergeant, Eric bent down and picked it up. Then he removed the last cigarette from it and lit up.

The Sergeant glared at Eric dumbfounded. He had never seen a soldier ignore him before.

"I said... are you listening to me, boy?" shouted the Sergeant.

Eric had forgotten that the Sergeant was there for a moment. He turned around, breathing a big cloud of smoke. "Pardon?" asked Eric, and regretted it when he saw the Sergeant's face. His eyes were fixed on the cigarette in Eric's hand, and the man was shaking as if he was about to explode. Eric moved the cigarette a few times, and watched the Sergeant's eyes dance in time with his hand.

"Soldier!" shouted the Sergeant, snapping out of his trance, "never in all my career have I ever seen a soldier worse than you! Put that cigarette out! Pick up those boxes over there! And get them to where they need to be!" He barked the orders like an angry dog, and to Eric's surprise he found himself dropping the cigarette and picking up a box.

With his duty done the Sergeant smiled, spun on his heel and marched away in search of more soldiers to shout at. Eric watched him go, and then looked down at the boxes he was holding, mystified as to how they had got there. He casually dropped them back on the pile they had come from and picked up his cigarette. He breathed a bit of life back into it, and as if the exchange with the bitter sergeant hadn't happened, he nonchalantly continued down the path.

Eric knew his good mood wouldn't last because he was heading towards to the officer's tent, and Tolley was going to tell him exactly why he had been brought there, even if Eric had to beat the reason out of him. He doubted it was for a reason he was going to like, it never was with the Army, and he'd be damned if he was going to put his neck on the line by fighting their damned war, again.

It was at this point that Eric started to feel a little lost. He had never had the best sense of direction in a new environment. He should have been able to simply retrace the steps he and that weasel Captain had walked only a few hours before, but something about his surroundings was different. Tents had vanished, or at least moved. He kicked the dirt in a space where he remembered a water tower had stood; there was some drying mud underneath the top layer of dusty sand, but that could have easily have just been a spilt container; everyone was rushing around so much he was surprised there weren't more crashes and spillages all over the place. But the ground did look disturbed, as if the three tripod legs of the tower had skidded as it was dragged away down the path, so Eric decided to follow them.

He carried on down the path, certain that he was headed in the right direction. His feet were telling him that just around the corner he was approaching was the spot where he had met Major Tolley and the other officers. But instead of the big tent full of people, there was nothing – just a gap in the scenery.

Eric stood staring at the spot the tent had been in, willing it to appear and apologise for moving without asking. The space was the same size as the officers' tent, so he relaxed a little, reassured that he wasn't going mad. But nothing about this situation made any sense. Why had they moved it in the first place?

At that point the individual voices of the soldiers around him started filtering through his ears a little better, and he was beginning to pick up whole sentences rather than general white noise. They were shouts of packing up, bugging out, and confusion over how they were going to put away all the gear. He spun around and stared at all the soldiers working like ants, picking up all they could in their arms and all rushing off with it. It took a moment to realise the pattern, but every soldier was rushing off in the same direction with everything that wasn't nailed down. Which must be why none of the tents seemed to be packed, except for the big officers' tent.

"Hey you, why is everyone packing up?" he shouted at the nearest soldier, who looked up for a second before carrying on as if he hadn't seen or heard Eric. Eric didn't like being ignored, not when he didn't want to be that is, and he was about to lose his calm. He clenched his right fist tight, and was just about to punch the soldier for ignoring him when he heard a familiar voice call out behind him.

"Eric?" came the shouted voice above the rest of the humdrum noises. "I wouldn't do that if I were you."

Eric spun around and saw Major Tolley making his way through the mass of tents towards him. "Oh yeah? Give me three good reasons why not?" asked Eric.

"Because every soldier here has been handpicked from the very best training academies around the world" said Tolley casually as he crossed the pathway to where Eric was standing. "You touch one of them, and you'll be sorry." He smiled, probably hoping Eric wouldn't call his bluff.

Eric appeared to think about this for a moment. Then he turned and pushed the soldier into a tent. It wasn't a big push, but the soldier wasn't expecting it, so he went flying head first. The boxes and bags the soldier was carrying flew up in the air and hit the ground with the sound of several things breaking inside. All you could see of the soldier was two boots sticking out of the collapsed tent. The man was moving about a little, but in the slow motion manner of someone trying to understand what had happened, how it had happened, and how to get out of a collapsed tent without looking foolish.

"A very deadly force indeed" muttered Eric sarcastically, before turning his attention back to Tolley, who was trying to stifle a laugh. "Why am I here Tolley, and where the fuck are all your soldiers going with everything?"

Behind him soldiers rushed to help their fallen comrade, and quickly got the man back onto his feet and dusted him down a little. The soldier had emerged from the crumpled tent red-faced and furious, and vowing to find whoever had pushed him and rip them into tiny little bits. He spotted a few people subtly pointing at Eric, and was just about to grab him by the arm when he caught Major Tolley's eye. Major Tolley shook his head a little as way of a warning, and the soldier decided to think better of it. He wasn't happy about it, but the look he'd been given had warned more about a future of bruises and broken bones, rather than being court martialled for getting into a fight. Grumbling and swearing, the soldier scooped up what he had dropped and carried it off down the path with the other soldiers.

"You just make friends wherever you go don't you Eric?" remarked Tolley with a laugh.

"I take it it's you who's been training them up, is it?" said Eric.

"What are you trying to say?" asked Tolley sarcastically.

The wind started to pick up and dust and sand was filling the air over the tents, so Tolley put a hand on Eric's shoulder and gestured for them to go inside one of the slightly larger tents. Eric nodded in agreement, and the pair only just made it to an abandoned tent before the wind really picked up. They stood for a moment brushing the sand and dust off their clothes. Immediately they were done, Eric's hands shot out and grabbed Tolley by his jacket, and pulled him so their faces were barely a few inches apart.

"Why did you send soldiers after me?" Eric growled. "I've had nothing but trouble recently, bloody soldiers chasing me wherever I go! The Zarda sending their bastard assassins after me! Is that what this is all about? Why did you bring me here? What the fuck is going on?" Eric barked the questions one after the other through gritted teeth, not letting Tolley get a word in.

"Easy Eric, easy" said Tolley calmly. "I couldn't exactly send you a letter or call you on the phone could I? I had to send the brain trust out to get you and bring you here." He put a hand on Eric's and tried to pull it away, but Eric's grip was like a steel vice. "It took months to track you down, it wasn't as if I sent for you and here you are!" There was a twinge of panic in Tolley's voice now.

On Tolley's third attempt Eric loosened his grip a little, and Tolley pulled his hand off his jacket and took a few steps back. "We need your help Eric," Tolley explained, smoothing out the creases on his jacket.

"I'm not fighting your damn war any more Tolley, remember the last time we met? That wasn't the first time I've found myself mixed up in your fucking war!" Eric shouted.

"It won't be like last time," Tolley tried to explain. "We need more than one man to win this war, we need an army of men like you."

"I am not fighting in this war any more," Eric repeated, but slowly this time, so as to be sure Tolley heard him properly. "Every time the shit hits the fan, I seem to wind up right back in the middle of it, surrounded by idiots and bloody heroes." He was beginning to get tired of repeating himself to officers who didn't understand.

It flashed across Eric's mind how easy it would be to beat the living hell out of Tolley, right there with no eyes watching them, make his way to the nearest truck, drive as far as the petrol lasted, and then walk the rest of the way to civilisation. His biggest problem right now was that he hated the Zarda even more than he hated the Army. The Zarda had spies pretty much everywhere, and they always seemed to follow Eric around from place to place. He was always in the War, there was no getting away from it any more. It was everywhere across the globe in all the major cities, and even worse out in open spaces. But he preferred to do his part for the war effort in his own way. The Zarda had to be stopped, that much was obvious, but Eric preferred to do his bit alone, without having to look after anyone, or having to rescue some idiot who thought they were clever enough to do something stupid. Or having the Army's eyes watching every move he made, and then attempt to tell him off for it not doing it how they would want it, which he never really paid any attention to. After all, what could they really do to him?

"We don't want you to fight the War for us Eric," Tolley lied. "We need you to train the soldiers. I was there with you last time, and you're right. Our soldiers aren't trained or ready for what the Zarda can do. Believe me when I say that we brought you here with the best of intentions."

"You, Tolley" said Eric through gritted teeth, "are a complete bell-end. Those beasts are just pets, a test, to see how well we handled being attacked. I don't think even the Zarda expected them to work so well. Now I doubt even I would be able to visit some of the areas where the main nests are. Their numbers still continue to grow, and I told your generals then, and I'll tell you now, just nuke the fucking areas and be done with it." Eric's anger was written all over his body. He had done his best in the beginning, before the War had broken out across the planet, but now it was years later he was well past the stage of caring.

"We can't just go around nuking places Eric, the fallout alone would… anyway, we need to be prepared, and who better to train the soldiers than you?" explained Tolley patiently. "We'll pay you this time… and feed you?" It was worth a shot.

Eric pulled another bread roll out of a pocket as if he didn't have a care in the world, and took a large bite out of it, keeping his eyes on Tolley. "I can always find food and money" he said through a mouthful of bread, and spat crumbs in Tolley's direction.

"OK… how about a good bed to sleep in each night, and I'll give you a key to the alcohol storage?" bargained Tolley. He knew this would at least get a reaction, and his eyes lit up when Eric stopped chewing.

Eric thoughtfully swallowed his mouthful, whilst still keeping perfect eye contact. "And I just have to train your soldiers?" Eric said carefully, as if testing each word. "This isn't some trick to put me on the front line, or ask me to take a few newly-trained units into a quarantined zone to their certain deaths?"

Tolley held his hands up theatrically. "Would I do that to you? Trust me Eric." He was trying to keep his grin going.

"Tolley," Eric sighed, "You're an officer now, and if there's one thing I know not to do is trust any of you bastards. Are you authorised to make such an offer? Because you know who I'll be coming after if it all goes sour."

Tolley laughed and held out his hand. Eric stared at it for a moment before raising a quizzical eyebrow at Tolley, then, against his better judgement, he shook it.

Tolley put his other hand on Eric's shoulder and laughed again. "Let's face it Eric, how much danger could you be in, training soldiers this far from Zarda lines? Most soldiers are trained and experienced before we even think of transferring them here, so it's not like they don't already know how to fight. All you need to do is fine tune their skills a bit."

Eric still stared at Tolley. It wasn't that he didn't trust the man, Eric didn't trust anyone, but he had to give him points for effort. It must have taken some convincing to get authorisation from senior officers to send out squads looking for him time and again, especially when they returned with nothing more interesting than a few broken bones and a warning not to do it again. He could see the man was desperate. It couldn't hurt to find out what this was all about. Besides, with a massing army like this, maybe the Army was finally taking the war to the Zarda for once.

The thought of punching Tolley, stealing a truck and driving off was still at the top of Eric's to-do list, but he might as well see how this all played out. Besides, he was right, what was the worst that could happen? And the truck would be a better idea if he filled it from the storage areas. A few crates of food and booze could go a long way if he got lost in the desert.

Tolley stopped shaking Eric's hand and reached out to open the tent for them to leave, but they were both forced to take a step backwards when a howling gust of sandy wind came blowing in. They exchanged glances and Tolley, still grinning, pulled a pair of very expensive-looking aviator sunglasses out of his inside jacket pocket and slipped them on. Seeing this, Eric patted his own pockets and fumbled about his person until he found the sunglasses he had been given earlier, and put them on. The scratched and broken glass gave him a kaleidoscope view of Tolley in one eye, and the lens looked seconds from falling out in the other, but it had do for now. Tolley stared at the broken glasses on Eric's face, trying not to snigger, but he shrugged and they both turned to face the exit.

"We should probably get you another pair of sunglasses," said Tolley.

"Some more clean clothes would be nice too" murmured Eric.

"You don't like the priest look?" Tolley laughed. "I thought they would suit you down to the ground."

"Not quite my style" replied Eric, looking down at himself. He hated priests.

The pair stepped forward as one, and with Tolley holding opening the tent flap, they walked into the dusty storm.

CHAPTER 11

THE FOREST

Most landscapes these days were completely overgrown, and most farms were decommissioned if they were growing food that wasn't on the New Global Army's approved food list, or in a dangerous area. There were a lot of foods the Army had deemed unnecessary after they had the bright idea of monitoring everything people did, and anything fattening, or bad for you, was discontinued immediately. Salt mines were derelict, cocoa plantations grew wild without anyone to tend to them, and a lot of work was put into farming corn and sustainable foods from which their scientists could extract proteins.

This was good in the sense that people got food more for sustenance rather than enjoyment, leaving many chefs and food critics out of work. Their elegant meals soon became a thing of the past, and a tear would form in their eye as they attempted to chow down on their new army rations.

It also left the countryside wild and untamed, so any traveller could get lost four or five times before they had even reached the other end of what used to be a field they were in. Maps helped, but because of the changing landscape, and the war damage that turned landmarks and buildings into rubble, it was easy to lose your bearings, and usually by the time you found your way again, the Zarda had found you. Or worse, their Lykor pets.

Eric Mason was running at full speed. His clothes were ripped in places, showing bruises and cut marks, and he was dripping blood and sweat in a long trail behind him. But he was still managing to move at very high speed, from years of practice at running either towards or away from danger.

The path he was carving through the forest put several low-hanging branches and fallen trees in his way, and he was having to perform a very energetic mixture of high jumps and low skids to keep going in a reasonable straight line. Annoyingly, he wasn't able to duck under or jump over every obstacle in his path, and each mistimed or misjudged hit left a small patch of blood and sweat behind him.

In situations like this he'd have preferred to be in a wide open space where he could really put his head down and sprint, like a road or field. However this was the path he was on, and annoyingly, he couldn't seem to avoid leaving an extremely easily-tracked trail behind him. But right now he didn't have time to care; he was late.

Down the slope ahead was a big rotten tree trunk. As he leapt over it he caught his foot on a hidden root. The trip sent him straight to the ground, where he rolled head-over-heels and jumped back onto his feet, again without missing a beat. The landing had hurt a bit, but the momentum was still there and he was quickly running again. He was beginning to get out of breath and the bangs to the head and that little trip would have cost him a few seconds, maybe a minute or two, but if he could keep up this momentum, it might not matter.

Eric was fairly fit, but it had been a long time since he had had to run cross-country. In the old days he had been forced to walk, or run, for days to get anywhere, but right here he wouldn't mind finding a dirt-bike or something.

He was running along a narrow ridge at the top of a small dirt cliff when he came to a fallen tree. He launched himself high over it, but as soon as he was in the air, he saw what was waiting for him, and he swore loudly. There was a thirty-foot drop on the other side, and there was nothing he could do to avoid it. He managed to twist his body around in mid-air, and reached out to the cliff face. There were thin and wiry tree roots sticking out of the soil, but as he grappled for them they came away from the soft dirt without resistance.

Eric hit the ground hard, and felt his left ankle bend painfully under the weight of his body. He crumpled onto the floor like a pile of dirty laundry. The shock and pain rippled up through his body, making Eric let out a primal roar, and the sound echoed off in all directions. Birds flew from trees, squirrels stopped chasing each other and searched for the monster that had created such a sound. He rocked and rolled on his back a few times, cradling his twisted ankle with both hands and hissing through his teeth. He was trying desperately not to scream out in pain again and give away his position any more.

Don't just lie there, get up, keep moving, run, shouted a voice in his head. It was the voice of self-preservation, and it had got him through many a difficult situation. Its answer to most situations was to tell him to run away.

Eric looked around. He was lying in what must have once been a lake, or a very wide river mouth, which had long ago dried up, leaving a surface as hard as concrete. There was nothing nearby that he could use as a weapon if he had to fight, not that he'd be able to right now. At least if whatever was chasing him caught up, he'd give it one hell of a shock. Eric wasn't about to die easily. If only he could find a sturdy branch to use as a club. His eyes scanned every item in the vicinity, judging each one for weapon potential.

A distant sound sent a look of panic across Eric's face, and he went as still as a rock, ignoring the screaming pain in his ankle. He was listening for something. He could hear a few birds in the trees up above, and feel the light breeze through the leaves. He shut his eyes to aid his concentration and projected his mind's ear a little, searching for more sounds. His heart rate slowed slightly. It was almost as if time had decided to slow down a little for him.

CHAPTER 12

The Lykor

From deep inside the forest came the sound of pounding feet, like the hoofbeats of a wild horse. They were moving fast and getting faster as the animal picked up momentum. The scent of its prey was getting a little stronger the closer it got, and it should soon be tasting fresh blood.

Now Eric could hear heavy panting, snarling and growling. The low branches weren't a problem for this monstrous predator as it zipped between trees and undergrowth. The fallen tree trunks and thick bushes weren't putting up much resistance either; if this hunter couldn't go through them, it could leap over them with ease.

This was one of the dreaded wolf-beasts or Lykor, creatures with the speed and strength of lions, but much harder to kill. Many called them werewolves, although there was no such thing, at least in the traditional sense, as men turning into wolves in the light of a full moon. That was just a story born from the imagination of man hundreds of years ago, when it had probably been a metaphor for madness. Eric had searched for werewolves once. He had and come back empty-handed and feeling cheated, especially as he had spent all that money on silver.

Eric had a theory that the Lykor had been super-evolved by the Zarda some years before the War had broken out. the Zarda must have taken a wolf-creature considered to be the best killing machine available, with the best mind, and speeded up its evolution to make it bigger, stronger, faster, and much more intelligent and vicious. The result was a creation no man on earth had ever had to defend himself against. It immediately knocked mankind off the top of the food chain.

When the Lykor started turning up in hunting packs in the more rural areas, Eric knew that the Zarda were going to be very difficult to fight this time. He had never seen anything like them before, and even he had a job avoiding their keen senses. He had tried warning all the officers he knew, and some he didn't, but they refused to listen, believing he was crazy. He had argued until he was blue in the face, and had even gone out and captured a Lykor cub, risking life and limb in the process, to show the scientists. Still they did nothing to prepare for the war Eric was predicting. It wasn't until reports started coming through from remote towns and villages, screaming voice messages and blood-soaked letters describing attacks by packs of giant wolves, that they started taking him a little more seriously. The FBI, National Security, MI5 and even Scotland Yard sent agent after agent to find out the truth behind the attacks, and agent after agent died or disappeared without a trace.

But by then it was too late, and Eric had gone into hiding. Soon after the War broke out, whole countries were overrun by the fur-covered killing machines. The New Global Army tried to evacuate as many civilians as they could to safe zones and transportation far, far away, only to find that no matter how far they went, they faced more ways to die at the hands of the Zarda and their Lykor assassins. The New Global Army had only one choice left to it, and that was to build massive fortifications for the refugees to live in. But rather than simply building within a new space, they built up and around existing cities and towns. Men, women, and families crammed into every available space, often forced to sleep in dead people's beds, surrounded by happy smiling ghosts in picture frames.

Although these new complexes were big, they were cramped, and the Army tried to cram as many people in as quickly and cheaply as they could. Eric had seen inside some of these fortifications, where half the population had nothing but a blanket and a bag of clothes to their name, and some didn't even have that. Previously wealthy men and women were forced to beg, borrow, and steal from each other to survive. The result was chaos.

One officer had the bright idea of executing all the inmates of high-security prisons and housing some of the people in the newly-vacated cells. It amused Eric that this idea was not met with much opposition. A few families of the condemned protested, the few that were still alive that is, but they were silenced pretty quickly by those who were happy with the fortification. But these compounds fell to attacking packs of Lykor just like any other town or village. Their walls were high, thick and sturdy and the fences were electrified, but nothing seemed to be able to keep them out. They did hold out longer than Eric had expected, but because these prisons were thought to be impregnable, they were not heavily staffed and did not have enough firepower. From up in the guard towers, men and women opened fire on the fast-moving Lykor without a single kill. Nowhere was safe. They said the Lykor could smell blood from five miles away, and that their eyesight was equally perfect by day and by night. They could travel across land faster than a man on horseback, and had even caught up and slaughtered soldiers in fast-moving trucks and Jeeps. But what really scared Eric was that even the Lykor were not the worst weapon the Zarda had.

CHAPTER 13

THE DRIED-UP LAKE

Eric Mason lay on the hard bed of a dried-up lake. His ankle was screaming at him in pain, his brain was telling him to get up and run, and all the hairs on his neck and arms were sticking up. He was as still as a rock, straining to hear the oncoming pack of killing machines on four legs which was surely not far away now. He could imagine their snarling teeth dripping with drool, their feet pounding the dirt and their noses catching his scent. It wouldn't be long before they'd be right on top of him, and then... well, he wasn't sure what he'd do.

Yet there was silence. When he finally decided he couldn't hear anything close by, he very slowly got to his feet, limping slightly on his hurt ankle, which made him do a little hopping jig. Maybe they had gone the wrong way. But he scolded himself for being so stupid. They would easily be able to follow his trail, and he had probably now lost any time advantage he had had on them.

His ankle hurt when he tried to put weight on it, and he took a few hobbling steps forward. He tried shaking the pain out of his foot; it wasn't broken, and he'd walked off worse than this. His mind was racing. Memories flashed across his mind of the fall he'd survived up in the snowy mountains once, when he had lost his grip and slid down a mountainside hitting every block of ice and rock along the way.

Another memory was of when he'd been chased across the rooftops of a small city, and he had mistimed a gap between the buildings and fallen through someone's window. The glass had cut all the way up both arms and legs, and some had been pretty deep. They'd taken him ages to heal, not to mention he was still being chased at the time, and had to hobble up and down flights of stairs to get back on to the rooftop run. Now that had really hurt.

He shook the thoughts from his head, tried walking a few more steps and wiped the sweat from his face with a bloody hand. This was definitely not the time to be reminiscing on old memories. He needed to get his bearings, so he rummaged around in a pocket until he fished out a very old-looking brass compass. He tapped it a few times to make the needle point in the right direction, and looked around.

He had just made his decision about which direction to go when he heard a sound. It was quiet at first, but it was getting louder; a howl, it was coming from behind him, up the cliff he had just fallen down, and in the forest somewhere near. The Lykor were catching up, fast.

Eric quickly checked the compass again to make sure, rammed it back in his pocket and tried walking as quickly as his hurt ankle would allow. He could hear crashing noises far off in the distance, the sound of big, heavy objects were smashing their way through bushes and low branches. They sounded fast too, faster than he could run right now with this ankle, for certain. He shook his leg a few more times, letting the pain shoot up and down his nerves to try to get used to it, and headed off at high speed, grumbling and swearing as he did so and skipping every few steps to give the ankle a break.

He had to be very careful; there was absolutely no knowing how many were chasing him. He'd set a couple of traps before he had started running, so there might not be too many pursuers left. But this wasn't a gamble he was willing to take. Lykor rarely hunted in small groups; the smallest he'd ever seen was three or four – but you could never tell, the entire nest might be bearing down on him in a tsunami of fur and teeth. As with velociraptors back in the dinosaur age, if you were being hunted by a small pack, you might catch sight of one or two, if you were very lucky, but it was the third or fourth that would catch you unawares, and then you were in real trouble. Eric had seen unlucky soldiers in the past firing their weapons in every direction possible, desperately hoping to hit something, anything, before they got taken down. But Eric didn't have a weapon on him. He had lost his pistol a few miles back, when he had jumped off the bridge into the river to put the beasts off his scent. He hadn't, however, considered that the river would be full of sharp rocks, which had cut and bruised his body as he had been dragged along the riverbed in the strong current. He had left a pretty obvious trail when he had eventually climbed up the riverbank. But it had bought him a few minutes, ten, maybe fifteen at the most. All he had right now was speed and his wits, and right now he didn't have much speed with this ankle in this condition.

Eric was managing to get up to quite a high speed now, despite his foot threatening to drop off at any minute, but the adrenalin was pumping its magic brew around his body and he could just about ignore the pain. About a hundred metres in front of him he could see a line of trees. He put his head down and his arms and legs starting pumping like pistons. He burst through some low branches, sending leaves and twigs exploding into the air in all directions, and found himself at the top of a long slope of tall grass. Once this had probably been farmland, but over years of neglect the grass and plant life had got a little Jurassic.

He stood for a moment, confusion mixing with the urge to admire the view and his need to get away. The sun was shining in the big blue sky above, and a breeze was moving the sea of green grass this way and that. If he had been in any other situation, he'd probably have sat down to enjoy it all. But not now, not when he was so close to getting away. So he picked a direction at random, and set off again at a sprint.

Still moving at high speed, he fished a dirty and crumpled piece of paper from his pocket and scanned it carefully. The paper had lines and rough markings drawn on it in pencil; it was tough to make out what was drawn and what was just a crease in the paper. He tried comparing features of the landscape to the roughly-drawn markings of a man who had clearly never been here before. The markings looked as though someone had tried to compress into the piece of paper as much geographical information about this area as he could from a much more detailed map, but hadn't been bothered about distance or scale.

Off in the distance he could make out an ivy-covered building which could be the church drawing on the map, and to his right he could see what could be described as a farm house. So he changed direction and headed towards the farmhouse, swearing vengeance under his breath to the map maker if this went wrong. The fields seemed to surround the forest he'd been running through, and he resisted the thought that he could have been out much sooner if he'd gone in a different direction. And now in the distance, at the bottom of the slope, he could see safety.

CHAPTER 14

THE SCOUTING MISSION

The soldiers were beginning to get impatient. They had been hanging around an overgrown field for nearly four hours, and tempers and boredom were getting to an all-time high. The other scouting squads had left ages ago, and the soldiers were beginning to wonder if they shouldn't just leave too and go back to base with the others.

Sitting inside the truck were three soldiers, a Sergeant, a sniper, and a radio operative, and standing outside by the driver's door was their Captain. None of them looked particularly thrilled to be this close to a newly-discovered nest, and they would much prefer to be back at camp, drinking hot coffee or trying to swallow whatever crap they were serving in the mess hall. It wasn't good food, normally tasting like old boots, but it was hot, and it filled you up for a bit.

"We don't have to stay for him," the Captain was saying in the tone of voice of someone who had repeatedly had to say this to his squad, "but there's good men in there with him."

"But they're probably dead," moaned the Sergeant in the driver's seat. "And he's probably dead too. Let's just go, sir. If we go now we might still get some dinner." He was not a man to mince his words, which was probably why he'd never got past the rank of Sergeant.

The Captain looked around at the countryside. They were some distance from the forest, sitting at the bottom of a long grassy slope. There were several tyre tracks in the mud around them, left by the other scouting Jeeps and trucks as they had skidded away. He looked up at the two soldiers in the back of the Jeep, who were both nodding in agreement with the Sergeant. These men were low, even for foot soldiers. How had he managed to get to the scouting unit that would rather go back to camp and eat dinner, than wait to make sure their fellow soldiers were back safe? He shook his head in disbelief.

"We'll stay a little longer" announced the Captain firmly to the Sergeant, "unless one – or all of you – are volunteering to go into the forest to find them? Hmm?" He gestured theatrically towards the forest in the distance. "Well? Any volunteers? Because we are not leaving until those men are back here safe, or I see some bodies."

"But they're dead!" the sniper in the back pleaded. "I'm not going in there to get killed myself. It's going to get dark in a couple of hours, and they hunt better at night. How long are we going to wait here?"

"As long as it takes," said the Captain testily, but he paused a moment. He too had noticed that the sun would be going down soon. They had all heard the stories; the Lykor could smell your fear from a mile away, they could see in the dark as clearly as they could during the day, and they were as silent as the wind. He didn't want to be out there after dark any more than his squad did, but he had to appear fearless – it didn't do to show weakness in front of the lower ranks.

"If we have to wait here all night, we will and I want no complaints," he said at last, but without much conviction.

"What's that over there?" interrupted the radio soldier, standing up and pointing. The Sergeant stood bolt upright in his seat and passed the Captain his weapon, whilst picking up his own, and both men cocked their weapons immediately. The Captain squinted, trying to see what the radio soldier was pointing at.

"Right there," the radio soldier shouted again, and tried pointing harder, "near the top of the slope, to the right. Can't you see it?"

The sniper slowly stood up, raising his rifle with its high-powered telescopic sight, and squinted into the scope, trying to focus on the treeline. "I can't... yes I can, there's something over there about two clicks to the right. It's moving very quickly." His finger was hovering over the trigger.

The Sergeant and the radio soldier both scrambled out of the Jeep and took position on either side, aiming their weapons at the horizon. They could just make out something running along the slope parallel to the treeline, but it was like trying to watch an ant from the second floor of a building.

"Steady men," ordered the Captain, raising a hand. "Sniper, can you make out what it is?"

The sniper relaxed a little and lowered his weapon. "It's a man" he said, breathing a sigh of relief.

"Finally" breathed the Captain to himself. "I told you they would be back. Start the engine Sergeant, let's go pick them up and get home."

The Sergeant and the radio operator relaxed and lowered their weapons, and they all clambered back into their seats. The sniper looked through the scope again.

"Hold on… it's not all of them, sir, it's just him, he's alone and I don't see the others" the sniper reported, scanning the treeline. "Wait! He's not alone, there's something else behind him, coming up fast… shit!" He looked at the Sergeant with a worried expression.

"Lykor?" exclaimed the Sergeant. "How many?"

The sniper checked the scope again, and started counting under his breath.

CHAPTER 15

THE CHASE

Eric was managing to keep up a constant high speed now that he could see the finish line ahead. The ankle felt a little better than before, and the downward slope was helping to keep his momentum up. Down the slope waiting for him he could see the Jeep. He had to squint a little, but he managed to make out the soldiers jumping into it, and saw the Jeep shaking as the engine started. Were they leaving? He knew he was way behind time, and he was a little surprised they were still there waiting, but they didn't need to leave just when he was so close. Maybe they hadn't seen him. He threw both hands in the air, waving frantically. But the Jeep wasn't leaving; in fact it was heading straight for him. They must be coming to pick him up.

Instantly he felt a little silly for waving his hands like a child, and slowed down to a gentle jog, to the approval of this legs and feet. But even at this distance he could hear the changing gears; something didn't seem right. The Jeep was hurtling towards him too fast to be simply coming to meet him. There was a sense of urgency about the way it was headed directly for him. 'If they run me over I'm going to kill them,' he muttered.

The Jeep came to a skidding stop twenty metres in front of him and the soldiers jumped out and started sprinting towards him, raising their weapons. Had they turned on him? He hadn't wanted the others to die, in fact he had tried to keep them alive – it wasn't his fault. He would have had that blonde guy with him, but he had died when they hit the riverbed.

Eric slowed to an even gentler jog, and stared at the four soldiers aiming their weapons straight at him. He fought the urge to sprint a zig-zag and attack, mostly because he doubted he could dodge every bullet, and raised his hands into the air and slowed to a walk. Bloody army! He glared at the soldiers and slowly placed his hands on the back of his head.

Then something caught Eric's eye. The Sergeant's face was a picture of terror, and he had started frantically waving and pointing to the ground. Eric also noticed something about the Captain's eyes. They were not looking at him but off to one side. He was staring at something behind Eric.

As Eric spun around time felt slower, and the air felt thicker. "Get down!" came the Sergeant's shout over Eric's shoulder. It sounded slow and drawn out, as if time had slowed everything down. Eric slowly completed a full one hundred and eighty-degree spin. His eyes widened when he saw what was behind him. Three bear-sized Lykor were stalking towards him less than twenty metres away, each staring intently at him, their prey. These were the Lykor. They had to be nearly eleven feet long.

Their teeth looked as sharp as razors, some of them nearly four inches long, and largely dark brown from eating raw meat. They too were moving in slow motion; their big heavy feet were bringing them ever closer, their growls radiating out from their snarling, drooling jaws, and their eyes were sharp and fixed on him. They weren't happy that Eric had managed to get away from them, or that he had somehow managed to outrun them through the dense forest.

"Get down, now!" the Sergeant shouted again, and in a long-drawn-out motion, Eric dropped to the ground, bending at the knees. The Lykor, as if telepathically linked, in unison bent down low, their large muscles bulging and swelling under their fur. Their energy was unleashed all in one go, and the massive wolf-beasts took to the air and pounced on their prey.

Eric heard several pops and bangs coming from behind him, but nothing would make him lose eye contact with the lead Lykor, which was bearing down at him through the air. The banging sounds became louder and more frequent, and bullets started zipping past his head like tiny meteorites.

Time slowed even more when Eric finally hit the ground on his back. The shock made him blink, and broke the slow-motion spell. Time came rushing back, speeding everything back up to normal, and when Eric opened his eyes again, the biggest of the creatures was on top of him, teeth ready to bite his throat out, claws aching to slash the meat off his bones.

In a lightning reaction Eric instinctively raised both hands. He was just able to put one around the beast's throat and his other against its chest before it could sink its teeth into Eric. The beast roared and growled its anger inches away from his face. It bore down heavily, testing Eric's strength, and finding it much greater than it had anticipated.

The Lykor's teeth were barely an inch from Eric's cheek. He tried twisting and turning to give more room, but nothing seemed to work. Each time Eric tried to move, the beast snapped its strong jaws at him, and he felt the hot breath all around him. He grimaced, refusing to let the monster win. He pushed up hard, and managed to lift the Lykor away from himself a little, much to its surprise.

From somewhere behind the Lykor's head blood and fur started to fill the air. The soldiers were firing as fast as they could, and now concentrating on the big brute above Eric, but the bullets didn't do much damage through its thick armour-like hide.

The beast's hot breath stank of rotting flesh, and its warm saliva started to run down Eric's hands and arms as he moved his hand up its throat to get a better hold. The beast snapped its jaws, sending drool splashing all over Eric, and tried putting the full force of its weight down on him, trying to crush him. But Eric's strength held out. His arms were like iron bars right now, but they were beginning to shake a little under the pressure. Eric was vaguely aware of whines of pain coming from behind the monster, but he didn't care about that, he had enough to concentrate on.

He pushed back at the beast, actually managing to lift it off its front paws slightly. The beast's eyes narrowed on Eric and used its massive claws to scratch and dig at his shoulders, slicing his shirt and revealing his skin underneath. Eric grimaced in pain and nearly lost his grip on his adversary. The mighty jaws snapped shut a hair's breadth away.

Eric felt the whiskers tickling his face, and knew it was now or never. He swore, loudly and through gritted teeth. It wasn't a language any of the soldiers had heard before, but a swearword shouted out like that was universal, no matter where you were. He huffed, he puffed, he summoned every inch of energy and strength left, and forced it all into his muscles to push the creature away. The Lykor's eyes widened in surprise. This prey was stronger than anything else it had faced, and he'd managed to bite a hole through a tank. It found itself being lifted up a good foot or two above its prey, and left totally open to the soldier's guns.

"Shoot the bastard!" screamed Eric.

A hailstorm of bullets flew through the air between the pair on the ground, many of them penetrating the beast's thick underbelly, causing it to howl loudly. Eric felt the weight lessen as the beast arched its back, trying to get out of his grip, and watched as bullet after bullet hit their mark. He gripped as much fur and skin as he could, and held the Lykor in place. No way was this monster going to escape its fate. Eric felt the last few bullets cut through his already bloody and painful shoulders and arms, but he didn't care so long as some of them hit their mark.

Mercifully the bullets slowed to a stop, and the butt of a rifle came swinging into Eric's view. It hit the Lykor under the jaw, and several pairs of hands came in to catch the limp body as it fell. The dead weight of the Lykor landing on him drove all the air out of Eric's body, and he fought for breath in amongst all the foul-smelling fur. He felt the hands come in from all angles, tucking neatly under his arms, until his body was dragged out from under the animal and across the grass.

As Eric was pulled onto his feet he could hear shouts from the soldiers, asking if he was still breathing, swearing at the dead Lykor and calling for the sniper to finish the last one off. He looked around just in time to see the smallest of the three creatures fleeing back up the slope to the forest. The sniper holding Eric steady ran a few steps forward, loading this weapon with a fresh bullet, and took careful aim. A single shot rang out and the fleeing Lykor rolled across the ground dead. The bullet had caught it at the base of its skull.

The captain patted Eric on the shoulder, making him wince "I've never seen someone take on a pack leader before," he said. "Not bare-handed and survive for that matter."

"You're lucky we pulled you out from under it" said the sniper, turning around and looking Eric up and down suspiciously. "I've seen one of them crush a man." He absentmindedly walked over to the dead Lykor and kicked it. "Let alone a brute this size."

Eric looked the animal over and sighed with relief. A lot of adrenalin had been pumping through his body, fuelling his speed and determination to get as far away from that nest as possible. Now he felt a little weak at the knees, and the lack of blood and water in his system was making him feel a quite dizzy.

"Anyone got any water?" he asked. His voice was dry and his words were mumbled.

"Where are the others?" demanded the Sergeant, ignoring Eric's question. The Sergeant marched purposefully around the pair of dead Lykor to the rear, and grabbed Eric by the shoulder. "I said, where are the others?" he shouted into Eric's ear.

Eric's natural reactions took over. He didn't like people shouting at him, he didn't like people telling him what to do. Most of all he hated the Army, because the soldiers tried to do both to him at the same time. In one smooth movement he reached up and removed the Sergeant's hand from his painful shoulder, then twisted it so the man had to bend almost double to save his arm from breaking. With his other hand Eric made a fist and slammed it into the Sergeant's ear, making him drop to the ground whimpering. Eric quickly stepped over him and used one hand to pick the limp body up by its collar, whilst raising his fist to unleash a second blow.

"Eric Mason!" barked the Captain "leave it – please. I can only imagine the horrors you have gone through scouting that nest. Clearly you came across some difficulties, and I'm sure you will be able to give us a full report when we get back to base camp. But right now we would like to know where the other men are." He spoke in the voice you might ask a naughty child where it had hidden the pet goldfish. Eric Mason was not someone you demanded things from, not unless you wanted a punch to the head, which clearly the Sergeant hadn't heard about.

The ground shook a little under their feet, and a gust of wind carried the sound of an explosion from far away. In unison they all looked up the slope, and saw a large plume of smoke rising above the tree tops of the forest. Eric gestured at the smoke by way of explanation. Then he walked past the Captain in the direction of the Jeep, and found where they had stored the supplies. The soldiers all pivoted slowly to look at Eric, who had dug out a protein bar and a big canteen of water.

"What?" he asked when he noticed that they were all staring at him. "I couldn't just leave the nest there, that Lykor wasn't the biggest, in fact I'm surprised they sent three of the smaller ones after me." He gestured in the direction of the nest with the protein bar.

There was another explosion, closer this time, and a second column of black smoke rose up and joined the first, but instead of the silence that had followed the first, the wind was full of howls. First one pierced the air, then another joined it, then the harmony was made up of what sounded like hundreds of angry, blood curdling wails and howls.

"What happened to the others, Eric?" asked the Captain suspiciously.

"Do you really need me to draw you a picture?" said Eric, his words slightly muffled by the mouthful of food and water he was chewing.

"I think we would all like to know, especially if there are still men in there," said the Captain carefully.

Eric shrugged and swallowed his mouthful. "Two died pretty much straight away in the nest, one of the other scouts tried to warn them not to go too far in, and another two died when the nest were alerted to our presence, and..."

"Names!" interrupted the sniper angrily. "They have names, you know."

"Yes, true, but they all died, does it matter which one died when?" Eric asked. He took another big bite of protein bar. "One of them, the blond one, he was the least wounded. I tried to get him out but he died on the run from the nest to here."

"And what were those explosions?"

"When the ginger lad had most or his chest scratched out, I figured I might as well turn his grenades into a trip trap." He paused when he saw the shocked faces. "I used my own too, down the road, and ran back here as fast I could with the blond lad over my shoulders."

"You used Gary as bait?" exclaimed the Captain, shocked. "Was he still alive?"

Eric paused, his eyes fixed on the Captain, then shook his head. He doubted they would understand, or even believe the truth. How the young soldier had fallen while they were trying to get away, how his blood had sprayed into the air and all around them, instantly giving the beasts a target, and what it was like to see a man's still-beating heart exposed in his chest. He doubted they would believe how the soldier had held up the grenades in his trembling, bloody hands, and told Eric to rig a trip wire. Eric hadn't wanted to, but there was no arguing with a dead man. He had run the trip wire, and ran off to the sounds of the soldier firing his weapon in the air and shouting invitations for the beasts to come and get him.

To be honest, Eric was surprised it had taken that long to set off the trip wire. The soldier must have died before they had got to him. An inquisitive or hungry Lykor must have had an awful shock when it went sniffing around the body.

The soldiers were staring at Eric with open mouths. They couldn't believe what he had just told them. the Army Academy was very strict on instilling the moto 'Never leave a man behind'. Many of them had seen whole squads returning to dangerous situations, just to retrieve a fallen brother's blood-soaked body. The thought that Eric had simply left a dying a man to his fate, and not carried the other to safety, was completely alien to them all.

"I think we had better leave" said Eric simply. "We're losing the light, and we may have the entire nest coming down that hill any minute." He got into the back of the truck.

The sniper looked at the Captain, who nodded at him, and then the radio soldier, who shuffled his feet until he could climb back into the Jeep too. The sniper was reluctant to move. He wanted to go and find his friend and bring him back to the camp, no matter how many bits he was in. But he knew that if they lost the light now, their lives would soon follow. They all looked to where the Sergeant was still lying on the ground, clutching his ear and head.

"Get the Sergeant into the passenger seat, and let's get out of here" said the Captain, sliding into the driver's seat and starting up the engine. The sniper rushed to the Sergeant and hauled the man onto his feet, then frogmarched him to the vehicle as quickly as he could. Once they were all aboard the Captain made a smart three-point turn, mud splashing around the big tyres, and drove away at high speed down the slope.

Eric was standing up in the back, intently staring at the treeline. "You might want to put your foot down Captain," he called over his shoulder. He could see bushes and branches moving. The sniper nodded and tapped on the Captain's seat. He too had seen the movement up the slope, and the bodies emerging from the forest on four legs. The Captain checked the rear-view mirror, slammed his foot down on the accelerator, and the Jeep sped off through the long grass.

Once they found the gap in the hedge they had come through earlier and joined a country road, the Captain visibly relaxed a little and let out a nervous sigh. One good thing about the War, there was rarely anyone else on the roads, and speed limits were a thing of the past.

The Captain hated having Eric as part of his unit. It wasn't because he wasn't very good at his job, but he never listened to orders, and the men despised him for not being one of them. Plus he had this annoying confidence about him, as if knowing full well he could talk or fight his way out of any situation, which meant if he got assigned to your unit it meant the higher-ups were probably getting ready to send you somewhere very dangerous.

He'd seen many soldiers and officers try to take Eric down a peg or two, but each time they got the same result, and learned a valuable lesson on not reading a book by its cover. Even though he didn't look all that big and tough, the Captain had seen him take big strong men down as fast as small ones. Occasionally someone might get a few punches past his defences, but he always won in the end. The Captain had heard stories in the officers' club that he had once been very drunk in a pub somewhere, which wasn't uncommon, when the soldiers decided to 'teach him a lesson' or 'make him learn respect for the Army', and all forty-three well-trained men were shown the extreme error of their ways.

After about an hour of driving through twisting country roads, the sun was starting to set, and the sky was awash with all the colours of the rainbow. Although the engine was loud, they could all just about make out the gentle snoring coming from the back of the Jeep. Eric Mason had slid down in his chair and rested his feet over the edge of the vehicle, and was sound asleep. The Sergeant in the passenger seat was gently stroking his bruised ear and mumbling words of revenge under his breath.

They were not far from base camp now. In the distance the Captain could see the tops of city buildings on the other side of their outpost. Each of them was looking forward to eating whatever dinner was on the go, and getting a good night's rest in the first cot they found.

The Captain was dreading getting back to camp however. The other scouts would have been back for a while now, and already given their reports, and he'd have to turn up with fewer men than they had started with. Not to mention that there probably wouldn't be much left for them to eat, and he was starving.

The captain daydreamed about the other scouts, the ones who had actually followed their orders: "Locate and surround the potential Lykor nest. If it does exist you are to observe, but do not engage the Zarda. Once the nest has been suitably mapped, return to base without delay, and do not enter the nest for any reason". The Captain had remembered the orders clearly. The Major had made it crystal clear that if there was a nest, they needed to find out how big it was and how many Lykor they might come up against if they sent in the heavily-armoured Knight squads.

He wished he had simply sent Eric into the nest alone. He knew full well that Eric would have tried to recon inside the nest itself; he might even have tried to go it alone. By all accounts Eric was a fair-minded man, who simply had a bit of a temper on him. But did he do all he could to keep the soldiers he was with safe? They were always put in extreme danger when Eric was around. He had little doubt that if they had been spotted by the Lykor and had had to fight their way out, he would have done all he could to get them out alive. But there was still a small seed of doubt at the back of his mind that Eric might have just left them to fend for themselves.

The Captain drifted off into mindless daydreams. All around him the other soldiers had joined Eric in slumber, and their snores were all harmonising, like a hive of bees.

CHAPTER 16

THE HOTEL

The window shattered into hundreds of tiny razor-sharp pieces, exploded into the night air outside and fell to the pavement far below. If you were able to watch it happen in slow motion, the effect was really quite pretty, the light reflecting off all the little pieces like stars on a clear night. It was a shame no one was able to appreciate it.

The bullet had missed Eric's head by an inch, if that, and if he hadn't moved at the last second it would have gone straight through his eye. Instead, the bullet had passed him by and shattered the window a few feet behind him in the small corridor. There was no time for him to appreciate the twinkling explosion of glass, not that he would have been very interested in it anyway, because he had much more important things to deal with, primarily the man who had just fired at him.

Eric slammed into the corridor wall and raised his own weapon in half a second, took quick and careful aim, and shot the last bullet in his own gun straight down the long corridor and through the heart of his attacker. The man hit the ground with a thump and small cloud of dust, but he was quickly replaced by two others moving at high speed from the connecting hallways and corridors. They skidded to a halt when they saw the man writhing around on the floor. Blood was pumping out of his body, making a very sticky puddle on the cheap and dusty carpet. They stared down at their fallen comrade. He was pointing a blood-soaked finger and gargling something they could not understand. When they looked up, the corridor was empty, and the intruder had vanished into thin air.

Eric was crouched down in the dark. He had taken the door closest to him, which had led to a small bedroom. Yellowish street light from one window, mixed with the silvery light from the full moon through another, was making the room look distorted and unbalanced. All these hotel rooms looked the same, sad faded wallpaper and carpet, a small window with a view of the opposite building and nothing much else. The room was small and could only house a single bed, a tiny writing table and a bedside table with a sad-looking lamp lying on its side. The table may have once had a TV sitting on it, but this had long since been stolen by someone.

The room in general gave off a very depressing air. It had clearly not been used in a long time, and even when it had been it was probably as a last resort. As Eric looked around he could imagine some poor man sitting at the writing table, writing the last letter he would ever write, before tying a rope to the light and hanging himself from the ceiling.

The sounds of the hubbub of city life were filtering in though a gap in the window; just as well the gap was there, or Eric would have probably choked to death on the ancient wallpaper glue, the mould, and the thick layer of dust that was everywhere. Eric could hear the main road outside. Cars were rushing back and forth, the rain hitting buildings and puddles, and off in the distance a police siren pierced through it all. The police car must have been travelling fast. The siren got louder as it got closer and Eric held his breath, but the car travelled past the hotel and off into the distance.

Eric let out a long sigh of relief. You could never tell in a bad neighbourhood like this, most people would probably ignore gunfire, but there was always the offchance that someone might report it. Although he doubted the police would actually enter this building. This was a place where the law would make a detour, just in case it saw something it didn't like.

Eric removed the empty clip from his gun and fished around his pockets for the next, but after much searching he couldn't find one.

"Shitty bollocks!" he exclaimed under his breath. He had already used his spare clip when he got into the building and found far more obstacles than he'd previously imagined. He felt on his belt until he found his hunting knife and silently moved to the doorway. Out in the corridor he could hear the two men talking; it sounded as if they had not seen which room he had gone into. "Finally, a bit of luck," Eric murmured to himself sarcastically.

The owner of one of the voices in the corridor decided that they should check each room one by one, and he was clearly the smarter of the two because he let the other guy enter first. One after the other Eric heard a loud bang as each door was kicked open, and the scuffling of feet as the two men searched each room. The loudest bang indicated that they must have worked their way to the room opposite to this one, so Eric changed his grip on the knife and readied himself. He would only have one chance at this, so it had to go just right.

"He must be in this one" said one of the voices.

The door was kicked open and swung violently into the room, banging against the wall only a few inches from where Eric was standing. A gun entered the room raised at shoulder height, followed quickly by the first man, but he then made the biggest mistake of his life. Once inside the room he immediately pointed his weapon at the furthest corner, turning his back to Eric. Eric grabbed the door handle and lashed out as hard as he could, slamming it into the face of the second man just as he was coming through the doorway. There was a heavy thump as the second man hit the opposite door and fell into the other room.

In one smooth moment Eric reached out and grabbed the hair of the first man, placed the edge of his knife under his chin and slid the blade across the man's throat. The man gasped for air and clutched at the gash in his throat, blood flooding out between his fingers. He dropped his gun. Eric pushed the man away from him, picked up the gun, and spun across the doorway so his back was up against the wall again, but this time on the other side of the doorway.

He stood for a moment watching the struggling man. "Shhh!" Eric hissed sarcastically at him with a finger over his mouth. Then he raised the new gun at head height, aimed at the door, and waited patiently.

"Jimmy!" came a muffled sound from the corridor "Jimmy, did you get him? Are you OK?" His voice was dripping with fear.

"Yeah, I got him" shouted Eric. "Get in here, I'm hurt." The door burst open and the second man was silhouetted in the doorframe, Eric noted the height of the shadow across the carpet, and adjusted the height of his gun.

The second man stepped forward and immediately saw his comrade lying on the floor in a pool of blood. Eric fired the gun and sent a bullet ripping through the man's temple at close range, causing most of his head to explode. He jumped sideways with the force of the shot, and he fell onto his comrade's now motionless body.

Eric took a moment to listen for any more footsteps or voices out in the corridor outside, but he couldn't hear anything, so he took a chance and peered outside, but the corridor was empty.

"Thank fuck for that" he muttered, releasing the new clip, and counting only three bullets left. He dashed over to the two dead bodies and quickly went through their pockets. He found cash, a pack of cigarettes, a deck of cards and a set of keys that jingled in the silent room. The deck of cards went over Eric's shoulder, and he quickly lit one of the cigarettes and pocketed the pack along with the keys. You never knew when a set of keys would come in handy.

After further examination Eric found some fresh ammunition, and prised the gun out of the second man's hand. He fished out his empty weapon and dropped it on the bodies. They couldn't use it now either, but he would rather not carry unnecessary weight. Or get into a pinch and reach for the wrong gun. He'd learnt that the hard way.

Fully loaded, he stood up, taking a big drag of the cigarette, and walked out of the room and down the corridor, trailing a cloud of smoke like a steam engine. Eric had smoked for years, but they were getting harder and harder to find now everyone was being so healthy. Besides, out of all the things that could kill him in this world, smoking had to be one of the most enjoyable.

The hotel was old and had obviously not been cleaned in a while; areas of corridor and rooms had bare walls and cracked plaster showed through where the yellowing wallpaper had peeled off. Some of the wall lamps weren't working very well either; their light was dull and lifeless, and where the bulbs had blown or long ago died, the corridors had ominous and ghostly shadows.

Even the occasional door was hanging off its hinges and, Eric noticed, in several places there were pools of dried blood that had long since soaked into the carpet. There was a lot of blood in this hotel; Eric could smell the metallic scent, even over the musky dampness that was all around him. These corridors had obviously seen a lot of action over the years. He was in the right place.

He came to a T-junction and paused to finish his cigarette. On one wall leading down the right-hand corridor, there were scratch marks scored deep into the plaster. He looked in the other direction, and the corridor leading off to the left didn't seem any different from all the others he had seen. He dropped the cigarette onto the floor and stubbed it out with the heel of his boot. Then he looked down both the corridors again, shrugged, and walked down the corridor with all the scratches. Clearly that was where all the fun was, and Eric was good at fun, although other people might not call it that.

As he walked down the corridor the scratches became deeper, and they seemed to have more and more dried blood in them, and soon there was a tie-dye effect of different blood stains all down the wall and floor. He reached out absent-mindedly and ran his hand along the nearest wall. The scratches were a finger distance apart, but not as wide as his. Whoever had been dragged down here, Eric mused, hadn't liked it much, and equally hadn't had much choice about it. At the end of the corridor was a corner; the lights were out and it was bathed in deep shadow. Eric pressed his back up against the wall and silently slid into the corner, letting the shadow wash over him until he became completely invisible.

Eric stood looking down the new corridor in front of him. There was life down at the far end. Muffled sounds of music and voices could just about be heard, and there was an unpleasant smell of hot sweaty bodies that hadn't showered in a while. At the far end of the corridor was a door. It was nearly shut, allowing light and sound to creep through the small gap.

Eric could hear men laughing and chatting, which gave him the impression that their owners had also been having a few drinks. Each voice was trying to be heard over the music and the other voices in the room. Because each voice was trying to talk over the others, it was tough to work out exactly how many could be on the other side of the door. Eric stood motionless in the shadow, listing to the drunk voices. Maybe four of them?

The volume of noise was a good sign; it meant that Eric would be able to move down the corridor in complete silence, but there were a few shadowy patches he could hide in if the worst should happen. Between him and the door at the end were a few doors along the way, and even though he couldn't hear anything coming from them, there could be anyone or anything behind them. Eric's analytical, tactical and slightly pessimistic, mind raced through a few scenarios.

Annoyingly, the noise from the end room was interfering with his ability to hear sounds from the other rooms, so he decided to take a chance. He took a few steps forward and drew his new gun. Sliding his back against the wall, he made his way down the corridor, his heart beating a little faster in anticipation of the rush of adrenalin.

When he had got halfway down the corridor he saw out of the corner of his eye one of the door handles turning, and quickly moved into one of the shadows, but he knew he wasn't completely hidden. The door swung inward and a man came out zipping up his trousers, before turning and shutting the door. Eric froze and refused to breathe. The man was grinning madly to himself as he turned to walk down the corridor. Luckily for Eric he had not been expecting anyone to be in the shadows, and so he completely failed to see him. Moving as fast as a cat, Eric wrapped a hand over the man's mouth to muffle any sounds, and with the other hand he slammed the butt of his gun into the base of his unsuspecting head.

Usually this would have sent a shock running up a man's neck, causing him to black out. The man's knees buckled slightly and he was obviously dizzy, but still conscious. With lightning speed Eric put away his weapon, and with both hands gripping under the man's arms, rammed him into the nearest wall repeatedly until his head slumped down to his chest. Eric had stopped worrying about causing serious brain damage or concussion to the people he came across on these missions a long time ago, and so long as it wasn't him getting the concussion, he was fine with it. Besides, if Eric came across someone on one of these missions, they probably weren't one of the good guys, and that didn't count, did it?

Eric redoubled his grip on the man – he was heavier than he looked – and carefully elbowed the door open. But when he looked into the room the man had come out of, the sight made him drop the unconscious body back on the floor. In the dark, dingy, and soiled room, there were several beds in rows on either side. Each bed looked like it had been dragged in from other rooms, and it didn't look as if they had had the sheets changed in years. In each bed was a limp, lifeless body.

Eric had to hold a hand over his nose and mouth to save himself from the stench in the air. It was clear that these bodies hadn't been cleaned much either, because the room smelt like rotting flesh and dirty sweat. He'd fought wars in hot countries, down in the trenches and foxholes, side by side with big sweaty men who had no option of getting clean, and it hadn't smelt this bad.

He looked down angrily at the motionless man on the ground and dragged him into the room by his collar, then dropped him. Eric knew there were places like this, but he hadn't expected to find one here in the city. They were usually found outside city limits where police wouldn't accidentally find them. Virtually every bed was occupied. They were mostly girls and woman, but a few men and boys too, and each one was handcuffed to the bed frame by their hands and feet, which would not only stop them from escaping, but restrict movement.

It had probably started off as a symbiotic relationship for many of the girls. They wanted drugs, and the men with the drugs had certain needs the girls could take care of. In these modern times, it was clear to Eric that all of mankind were pretty much split into four main groups: the intelligent, the unintelligent, the useful and the useless. Obviously there were different grades of each group, and other factors would apply, but the bodies in these beds were the dregs of the unintelligent and useless. They wouldn't have had much education, or perhaps they had thought they were too smart to have to join the rat-race and get jobs. But mostly they just didn't have the skills that would have made them useful in any area of modern society. So these drifters mostly wandered from place to place looking for different ways to get through the day, in whatever chemically-induced comas they could find, or died sleeping rough on the streets. They would eventually find men who would invite them into their 'family' and promise safety, of a sort. These men would offer to look after these poor unfortunate souls, give them a bed to sleep in, a roof over their heads, and enough drugs pumped into their system to keep them in a form of numb stasis indefinitely.

In the old days you'd find them out the back of opium dens and gambling pits. But the drug of choice these days was Regretamin, a dangerous mixture of distilled spider venom and a powerful tranquilliser commonly used on wild animals. It gave the user an instant hallucinogenic high, whilst at the same time robbing them of all movement or feeling in their bodies. It was not unlike being paralysed, but the users could still feel everything – they just couldn't move.

Eric felt sorry for these people; they didn't have much hope in their lives. He had once tried closing down one of these operations, only to find the same girls weeks later in a different one. They had nowhere to go, no one to look after them, and couldn't take their lives into their own hands. Maybe there was some spark in them that told them to survive, but not to live.

Eric walked slowly over to the first bed. Its owner looked up at him, and after a moment of her trying to focus on him, blinked a silent message for help. Eric took a small pair of wire cutters out of one of his pockets and cut the handcuff chains that held her in place. Eric then worked his way down the line of beds, cutting all the handcuffs of each occupant, making a large snapping sound each time as the metal succumbed to Eric's strength. He probably shouldn't have made so much noise without first assessing how many attackers might have heard him. But if they came, they came, and Eric would simply deal with them.

Luckily no one seemed to hear him as he moved from bed to bed. The drugs would wear off eventually, he figured, and then the pain of withdrawal would kick in. Hopefully some of these people would be lucid enough to get up and escape, before they lost the luxury of choice. Eric noticed the muscle tone of some of the bodies that must have been there the longest; their legs and arms looked like bones wrapped in thin grey skin, and he doubted if many of them could even walk, let alone run to freedom.

He had nearly finished when he came to a girl who didn't look much more than fourteen or fifteen years old. She wasn't like the others, her skin looked fresher and still pink, and she had some muscle under her skin. Like the others she wasn't wearing much, a short skirt and a bra, but her skirt looked cleaner than the others. She couldn't have been there long – probably traded in by some low life to pay for their own addiction.

Eric reached over to cut her handcuff chains and nearly jumped out of his skin when her hand snapped around his wrist and she dug her nails in. He looked down and saw her staring straight up at him. Her lips were moving, but no voice was coming out. He had to lean down close to her mouth before he could hear what she was saying.

"She left me here" came the whispering voice. "Please help me... I want to go home!" The effort of speaking was clearly very painful.

Eric thought for a moment and then bent down and whispered

"I've cut your chains, when you can get up, go down the hall, and get far away from here". It probably wasn't the most heroic thing he could have said, but he'd never been good at that part. He had a vision of picking this girl up in his arms and carrying her far from this room to safety. But then what, take her home? Eric didn't really have a home himself, it was more like a place to sleep off a few hangovers before he moved on. Should he let her stay with him for a while until she got clean? He had seen people trying to fight their way from the cold embrace of Regretamin withdrawal. It wasn't a pretty sight. Most victims didn't make it through the first few nights, and those nights were filled with screaming, unmeasurable pain. And then what? Send her on her merry way? Where would she go? She might end up right back here, or maybe somewhere else just as bad. Not to mention the fact that people would think he was living with a young teenage girl, even if it was only with the best of intentions.

"Please, I can't move... she just left me here," she whispered. A river of tears was streaming from her eyes and running down both her cheeks.

"I have to go," explained Eric but with not much conviction. "The drugs will wear off soon." In truth he had no idea. "When you can get up, go down the corridor. There's a smashed window. You can get down to the street on the fire escape. If you can get out that way, get far, far away from here."

With that he walked to the foot of the bed to cut her ankle cuffs, but something caught the corner of his eye. Around one of the girl's feet was a grubby pair of knickers, and he remembered the man leaving this room and doing up his trousers. He looked at the bed next to her. It was empty, and there was a massive stain that Eric didn't look at too closely. Eric picked up the man's unconscious body, tossed it into the empty bed, handcuffed him to the frame, and dealt him a punch that broke the man's jaw.

He pulled the underwear back up the girl's legs as delicately as he could to give her a little scrap of modesty, and with his thumb he wiped away the girl's tears.

"Down the corridor and turn left" said Eric clearly. "Down the next corridor, and turn left again. There's a broken window at the end. Go down there and climb out the window, get out of here, and get out of this city. Do you understand?"

The girl blinked and tried to speak, but no sound would come out, and Eric reluctantly dragged himself away from her bedside. He moved quickly through the room, trying not to look back, and went out, closing the door behind him silently. He was very angry now. He hated the fact that he couldn't help her, or any of them in fact, but right now he had bigger things to focus on. If he could, he would come back this way and get all of them out. But first things first.

He glared at the door at the end of the corridor and listened to the voices and music, still at high volume. The stench was still in his nostrils. He stretched his neck to either side and extended his arms a little in anticipation of doing some quite severe physical violence. Then he crept down the corridor.

THE KITCHEN

The small kitchen Eric was thinking of entering was full of noise and movement, and most of the noise was coming from a TV that someone had put on top of a large fridge in the corner. It wasn't a very big TV, but the speakers were doing their best to get the sound to a near-deafening volume. Which of course meant that the group of men were having to talk louder to be heard, although none of them were really watching the screen.

Originally the room had obviously been set up as a communal kitchen and dining room for guests of the hotel. The remnants of old coffee machines, teapots, cups, plates, and even an ironing board were now barely recognisable. Virtually everything was broken or smashed, and every surface was frosted by a thin grey carpet of cigarette ash and dust.

In the middle of the room was a small round metal table, which had once probably been used to serve breakfast or late-night snacks. The table was covered in similar rubbish, with crushed empty beer cans and food wrappers, sticky coffee cup rings, stubbed out cigarette butts and various drug paraphernalia.

Around the table sat three men, all dressed alike and similar to the rest of the guests. They all looked a little strange; if you saw them in a crowd of people you probably wouldn't notice it, but here in this small room some of their features didn't look quite right. Their ears were slightly bigger than normal and slightly pointed. Their eyes were brighter than normal too, and they all looked as if they regularly saw the inside of a gym. All in all they looked like the type of people you wouldn't want to meet in a dark alley.

They were all smoking, drinking and playing cards around the small table. A fourth chair was unoccupied. They had cleared just enough space in the debris on the table to play, but the space was constantly in danger of shrinking as the rubbish tried to take back what rightfully belonged to it. The men carried on their game regardless, occasionally glancing at the empty seat to the wall clock.

"He's been a while" one of the men remarked, laughing. "Two Strokes is normally done by now, he's missing the game."

"Why's he called Two Strokes?" asked the youngest of the trio. He had only been with the group a short while, and all the others were beginning to believe he might be a little simple-minded.

The two other players glanced at each other and burst into laughter. "Because after two strokes he's done," said the first. "He never lasts more than a couple of minutes with a girl."

The trio sat there laughing, while the TV filled the room with the background noise from an advertisement for the latest smartphone, and explained how much happier everyone's lives would be if they had it.

"Maybe we should check on him," asked the first man after a little while. "Do you think any of them would give him any trouble?"

"I doubt it" said the other man. "He's been known to break arms and loosen teeth if any of them give him any issues. But you're right, someone should check on him. Well volunteered mate," he said to the youngest of the group.

"What? Why should I go?" demanded the youngest man. "What if he's still, you know, in the act?"

"It's simple" said the first man, putting a reassuring hand on his comrade's shoulder. "Just open the door and look inside. If he's still pumping, leave. He won't thank you for giving him an audience, so get out of there quick," he laughed.

The youngest of the group stood up and walked slowly to the doorway, "OK, but if I get in trouble I'm blaming you guys for sending me after him, right?"

"Sure, sure" said the third man. He waited for him to reach the door before saying "Oh and kid? Stop being a soft cock, you'll never make anything of yourself in this world by being soft." That got another roar of laughter from the pair. "Man up and get on with it."

The boy put his hand on the door handle, shaking his head. He didn't want to be there, and he certainly didn't like hanging around with these guys. The pay had been all right in the beginning, when all he had had to do was deliver the drugs around the city, to the few safe houses and the occasional customer. But recently they had been sticking him in this dirty, smoky room more and more, and each time he came home covered in a thin layer of smoke and ash, like bad dandruff. At least when he was doing the drop-offs he would meet new, and sometimes interesting, people.

Just as his hand gripped the handle to leave the room, the door was forced open, slamming straight into his face and throwing him backwards. He stumbled back a few steps before falling onto the table, knocking everything into the air. Dust, ash, rubbish, cards, ammo and food exploded in all directions as the cheap metal table buckled under the boy's weight. The two other men reacted slowly, raising their arms to cover their faces from the dust, and saving their beers, with a look of pure shock on their faces.

Eric reached the door at the end of the corridor and crouched down by the door handle, listening intently to the muffled voices. When he heard one of the voices telling someone to go and check on their missing comrade, he straightened up and took two careful steps back.

With his eyes never leaving the door handle, Eric readied himself by pulling both guns from his belt, and as soon as the handle started turning, he launched his body into the air, raising his right leg. His heavy-duty boot landed heel first and slammed into the door just above the door handle, causing it to hit whoever was on the other side of it hard. Eric heard a crashing sound from the other side of the door, and with both weapons raised at arm's length, he marched into the room.

As soon as he was inside, Eric squeezed both triggers, firing at the two men sitting at the table, who were still staring in disbelief at the cloud of ash and dust. The cloud expanded to fill the room, making the place look like the inside of a snow globe, and Eric had to hold one of his sleeves over his mouth to stop himself from choking in it.

The bodies of the two men slumped in unison forward in their chairs, and slowly slid to the ground with two squishy thumps. Eric noticed with amusement that they were both still holding their playing cards, but he could not see who would have won the hand. One of them was even still holding a can of beer. In the centre of the ash cloud Eric could make out two feet sticking in the air where the table had collapsed.

"Please!" came a whimpering voice from behind the table, "I don't know who you are, and I didn't see your face, so if they ask I can't tell them anything."

Eric checked that they were the only two alive in the room,

then took a few steps towards the table and tentatively looked over the edge. "I'm looking for someone important" he stated simply.

"Never heard of him," came a practised, instant reply.

Eric sighed. "He's your boss, you idiot," he said, kicking the table hard with his boot. "Some guy who calls himself the Lizard King. Don't fuck me around, I am not in a good mood."

"Oh, oh him? Never met the guy, honest, I'm a small fish in a big pond, I don't know anything," said the man on the floor quickly. "Please don't kill me, I'm not a bad guy."

Eric looked around the small kitchen. What a dump. He holstered one of his weapons in his belt, then used his free hand to grip the man's ankle and drag him to one side of the wrecked table. The man whined in pain and Eric noticed a streak of blood under him mixing with the dust. He had obviously cut himself on the metal rim of the table.

Eric dropped the ankle he was holding and walked around to the top half. "I'm not in the mood for this sunshine, where's your boss?" he demanded, and kicked the man in the ribs.

The man on the floor clutched his ribs where the boot had landed. "I swear I don't know, I never met anyone in charge, I'm just told to sit here and guard the merchandise in the next room. A few times a day someone comes in to use one of them, I just do the pat down while they pay. I'm just the pat down guy, I swear," he explained. "I never met no one important, they all stay downstairs somewhere, in the basement I think, please don't kill me!"

"All?" Eric asked and kicked him again. "All who? How many are down there?"

"I don't know who they all are, there's like seven or eight of them down there I think, I heard someone saying they saw them go down once," said the young man, holding his side.

"Which is it, seven or eight?" said Eric, moving a few steps to the left and raising a boot ready to stamp on the man's head.

"Seven! It's seven, I think, I'm not sure, I never saw them," he said, cowering under Eric's still raised boot. He was beginning to get dizzy with shock and fear.

"How do I get down to the basement?" asked Eric. The man raised his arm with one finger outstretched and pointed to the door on the other side of the kitchen. Then he fell back, slipping into unconsciousness.

Eric shook his head, stepped carefully over the unconscious man and opened the door a crack. On the other side was darkness, but he could see a narrow landing with a staircase. Eric opened the door fully, seeing his shadow in the middle of the rectangle of light shining through the doorway, and stepped out onto the landing. There didn't seem to be anyone around, so he shut the door behind him, crept over the railing and looked up and down. Was that a door to the roof? He cursed himself for not climbing the fire escape all the way to the top. If he had, he might not have had to kill those men, but at the same time, he would not have been able to cut those handcuff chains.

On the ground floor there were several lights on, and Eric could hear the faint and distant sound of voices drifting up to him. It wasn't the front door, Eric had already checked that out, and there were far too many bodies to go through to get in the building. That was why he had to find that dank alleyway and climb the fire escape to get in. The thugs hanging around the main entrance wouldn't have slowed him down much, but if they had raised the alarm there was no telling how many more would come running. Or however many bosses they had inside, who would definitely have got out of some back door, and then he'd never find them. It was not as if he had any backup to call either; Eric preferred to work alone. It meant he didn't need to look after or babysit anyone, which in this line of work he really didn't have time for.

Despite the dim light on the ground floor, Eric could just about make out the shadows of people moving around, but he couldn't say for certain how many were down there, and it could easily be as heavily guarded as the front entrance. He was going to have to get down to the basement some other way. These old hotels had to have more than one way to get down.

Eric went down two floors, taking each step carefully and trying not to make any sound on the old wooden staircase. All the time he was peering over the banister to see if his movement had been noted. Once he was down to the first floor he came off the staircase. Each floor had a door leading off it, and Eric crept up to this one and listened to what was happening on the other side. He could hear nothing, so he relaxed, gripped the door handle, and swung the door open.

Behind this door was another communal kitchen. It looked exactly the same as the one upstairs, even down to the carpet of ash and rubbish over every surface. Around the table sat another set of very angry and very serious-looking men. The big difference however, was that these four men were neither laughing or joking, nor were they were playing cards or watching TV. Two of the men were reading copies of a magazine entitled 'Women with Guns', and had a stack of similarly titled magazines on the table in front of them. Both front covers had photos of extremely attractive, tanned, blonde, muscular women holding various types of weaponry. The main focus of these magazines, it would seem, was to show off women holding hunting knives and machine guns, in various poses in their bikinis. Eric could honestly say he'd never seen a woman go hunting in a bikini, perhaps due to the lack of pockets. He'd met many female hunters and trackers over the years, and they wore practical attire, like the men. What you need out in the middle of nowhere, or freezing to death in a tent, is a good pair of trousers, top, and jacket.

The other two men were being nice and productive. They had an array of weaponry spread out on the table in front of them, and the pair were cleaning, polishing and reloading them with the skill and precision of surgeons. Eric scanned the weaponry. He recognised most of the pieces, but it was a mystery to him how they all fitted together.

Eric stood for a moment in the doorway, and in unison the men around the table turned their heads and fixed him with different degrees of hatred. Realising there was no turning back now, Eric stepped into the room and let the door swing shut behind him. The two men servicing their weapons slowly reached out and picked up a fully loaded one each. The other two carefully put down their reading material.

"Who are you?" asked one of the magazine readers.

Eric paused for a moment, his mind racing, and then decided just to go for it.

"I'm Eric Mason," he stated. "Who the fuck are you?"

No response – just blank stares.

"How's it going?" he asked. "Working hard are we?"

"What are you doing up here?" said the other magazine reader, standing up. "Where's your man?"

"What man?" asked Eric. He had no idea what else to say or do. He knew he could fight them, but when two out of four people are already holding guns, and they are being aimed at you, the odds are not exactly in your favour.

"You've not been here before, have you," said the man who was standing up. It sounded like a question, but it was more a statement of fact. "Everyone who comes in 'ere gets escorted up after a pat down." He snarled and exchanged a glance with one of the seated men. The three other men slowly pushed back their chairs in unison, a universal sign that a fight is imminent, and stood up too. Not one of them lost eye contact with Eric, and each of them was either Eric's height or bigger.

"Don't need one mate," said Eric by way of explanation for his entire existence. "Probably because I'm well known in all the other houses," he added still in a cheery voice.

"What other houses?" asked the first man "Who do you know?" He glanced around at the other men. This wasn't usual, and these men weren't big thinkers. Anything out of the normal meant trouble to them, and they knew how to handle trouble.

"You know Jimmy?" asked Eric, not missing a beat. Everyone knew a Jimmy.

"No" said the man simply.

Balls, thought Eric. That was the first time that hadn't worked. But he rallied quickly and said, "Oh you must know him as Jim. Look, I don't have time for this, the guys downstairs know who I work for and I came straight up. I need to check the merchandise to make sure no one is messing around, so I can report back to... the warehouse." He was hoping they didn't use some slang term for warehouse he didn't know. "Before I can come all the way back to this dump with the next shipment," he concluded.

It was another long shot, but someone had to keep these guys stocked up, didn't they? Surely a place like this, guarded by this many goons, must have regular deliveries of fresh merchandise. He had met street dealers before. They had a short life expectancy, especially if they had the misfortune of bumping into him, so they might never see the same guy more than a couple of times. It wasn't that Eric was against drugs, far from it, he just didn't like dealers who tried to charge him lots for cheap stuff.

"Nice try" the man said, a grin starting to crest his thin lips. "We got a regular guy that comes here with the stash." He looked around at the other men for confirmation, and they nodded. This guy clearly liked this part, the few minutes before all the violence started.

Unfortunately for these guys, Eric enjoyed it too.

"Him? Youngish guy, yeah? Blonde, about this tall?" Eric said, raising his hand to his eye line and causing his jacket to rise so they could see both his weapons holstered in his belt. "Kind of a soft cock?" he added, which got a few nods of retrospective agreement from the men around the table. "He's dead, I killed him for asking too many stupid questions, fucking snitch," Eric added simply, and dropped his hand back down by his side, with a thumb in his belt about an inch away from his gun.

The four men stood there for a moment in silence. Eric stared the man out and tried to give the impression of someone who really didn't have time for this, which was pretty easy because he didn't. A clock on the wall ticked away the seconds; no one wanted to make the first move.

Eventually the grinning man shrugged. "Yeah I can believe that. Kid probably had it coming then" he said, lowering his weapon. Seeing this the others followed suit, glad they weren't the ones making decisions. This Eric Mason guy looked like trouble.

"How did they find out he was a snitch?" he asked.

"Shit I don't know, pissed off the wrong person probably" said Eric dismissively, walking further into the room. "Jimmy put me in charge of it now, I don't want to be here and I don't have time to chit-chat. Where's the stuff so I can get out of this dump?" He was still using the casual voice of someone getting paid well to do a very small job.

"Yeah that's cool" said the man losing interest quickly. He picked his magazine back up, flicked to the page he was on and gestured to the man next to him. "Get this guy sorted will you?" he asked.

The man next to him sighed and shook his head before standing back up. "Right, this way mate" he grumbled, and gestured to the door behind them.

"Excellent" said Eric, following the man out of the room. "Glad to see you guys got this place covered." He left the room with his escort and shut the door behind them.

THE GLADIATORS

Eric Mason and Major Tolley were standing outside the tent. A sandstorm was working its way up to top gear, and the wind was raging. Tolley grimaced at the wind, and wrapped his jacket around him a little tighter. Eric squinted through his broken sunglasses at Tolley and was just going to make a sarcastic comment when something caught his eye over Tolley's shoulder.

Soldiers were still packing up and running back and forth with supplies, their movement obstructed by the infuriating winds, which were adding more chaos to the already chaotic surroundings. Eric looked around. Almost every tent was empty now, and the soldiers had picked up anything that wasn't nailed down and squirrelled it away somewhere. All around them were the skeleton tent frames where the canvas had either fallen off or been thrown off by some frantic soldier.

"All this work just for a sandstorm?" said Eric.

Tolley slipped his arm around Eric's shoulder. Eric glared at it, but allowed himself to be propelled down the path in the direction all the soldiers were running. The pair walked down the rapidly emptying pathways, Eric trying to keep track of all the movement, but it was like trying to watch the hands of an expert magician. Turning a corner Eric caught sight of something he wasn't expecting and stopped dead in his tracks. He looked from it to Tolley, and instantly didn't like the way Tolley was smiling at him.

Ahead of them the ground fell away to reveal a steep slope made from concrete and stone, which had obviously been worked on for a while. To say it was big would be a gross understatement. The slope was probably fifty metres wide by about two hundred metres long. He craned his neck to see down it, and saw at the bottom the entrance to an underground bunker. It was hard to see inside, despite the bunker having a massive entrance, because it was shut off to the world by a massive metal door that could probably withstand a nuclear bomb.

There were soldiers rushing in and out, and up and down the slope. The ones rushing to get into the bunker had armfuls of supplies, and the ones rushing out had empty hands eager to be filled. Sergeants and Captains were milling around outside the entrance, all wearing big sand-goggles and ticking things off on their clipboards. It took a few moments for Eric to notice, but the Captain's goggles were slightly bigger and slightly better looking than the Sergeant's goggles. Heaven forbid the officers should have to wear the same goggles as the enlisted men and women. Someone, somewhere, must have made that decision, instead of doing something actually important.

"What the hell is this?" demanded Eric, waving his hands wildly at the underground bunker. "You didn't mention this, did you!"

"What, that old thing? the War is taking a turn for the... not so great," Tolley said dismissively. "We built this to train up the perfect army. The best of the best," he added with a grin.

"I see," said Eric. "And all the soldiers are rushing around because?" He pointed them out as if Tolley hadn't noticed.

"We've got to get all the supplies inside" said Tolley. "Because of all the... sand storm, obviously." He was not making eye contact.

Eric looked around. The wind-whipped sand was starting to sting a little. "How long do these sand storms last?" he asked.

"Don't know, this is the first one I've seen," said Tolley in apparent honesty. "Better to be safe than sorry though, come on, let me show you inside." He headed in the direction of the hatch.

When they reached the hatch door a soldier immediately held a hand up to the stream of soldiers to allow Eric through, but he was left with a few soldiers struggling to get past him on their way in or out of the bunker. Eric held his ground for the last one, and the unlucky soldier bounced off him and nearly crashed into a pair of captains who were comparing clipboards. It was probably like hitting a brick wall for the poor man, but after that the soldiers stopped, and gave him ample room.

Inside Eric noticed that Tolley seemed to have the Moses effect. As the officer walked down the corridors, pointing out uninteresting areas of the bunker to Eric, the stream of rushing soldiers parted around him like a river. The stream split about two metres in front of him, and every soldier did his best to stay out of Tolley's way. No one wanted to jostle a Major, no matter how much of a rush they were in. It would have been a nice effect to see, but Eric was following about a metre behind Tolley, and this was the point where Tolley's force-field seemed to wear out, forcing Eric to push his way against the torrent of bodies, like a salmon trying to get up a waterfall.

"Living quarters are down there," came Tolley's voice, just about audible over the background noise of shouts and banging "and down there is the command centre." Eric saw Tolley's sleeve and hand pointing down a stairwell. "Supply and storage down there... are you listening to me Eric?" The question came loud and fast. Tolley had stopped walking, and Eric had to squeeze past two soldiers to get into the safety of his personal bubble. "I said, are you listening Eric?" Tolley repeated, like a teacher addressing a naughty child.

"Yeah, sure" said Eric, not missing a beat "It's a bit crowded in here isn't it?" He was hypnotised by the rushing blur of soldier uniforms.

"For now, yes, we had to pack up and get inside earlier than expected. It'll all calm down later once everything has been put in place," said Tolley dismissively.

"This is all a bit much, Tolley. How long are you expecting the sandstorm to last?" Eric asked.

Ignoring this, Tolley looked around over the sea of heads and found what he was looking for. "Aha" he said, pointing out a direction. "This way." He marched on, Eric hurrying behind.

"How big is this place?" Eric asked, but he was interrupted by Tolley's tour guide impression.

"The training areas are down this way, a lift will take us down. You are on level..." said Tolley, but now it was Eric's turn to interrupt, loudly.

"Who's in charge of all this?" asked Eric.

Tolley paused when they reached the lift. He pushed the call button and said "Please. You don't need to know who is in charge, you just need to know I am in charge of you".

The lift doors opened with the grinding noise of metal on metal, and a few soldiers got out to allow Tolley and Eric to get in. Then the doors slid shut behind them.

Inside the lift Tolley leaned across Eric to push the floor button, and the big lift shuddered into life. Eric looked down the line of buttons. "Are you kidding?" he said. "That says there are thirty-five floors down here."

"Yes" said Tolley beaming with pride, "we've been working on this for a long time, Eric. You'd be surprised at what we have done with some areas."

"You guys must really hate sandstorms" mumbled Eric, half to himself.

"It's not really about the sandstorm Eric" said Tolley, as if letting Eric into a secret. "It's about" – he paused to check the other ranks in the lift – "it's about what caused the sandstorm," he added in a whisper.

The lift shuddered to a halt before Eric could reply, and the lift doors slid noisily open. Tolley took a quick step forward and gestured theatrically for Eric to get out. He opened and shut his mouth a few times, but Tolley gestured again, refusing to make eye contact. So Eric walked out, and Tolley directed them down a new corridor until they came to a hatch door. It looked like something out of a submarine. It was big and heavy, and had a round metal ring door handle riveted to the centre.

"This is where you'll be sleeping," said Tolley, reaching past Eric to open the door.

The metal ring made the same grinding noise of metal on metal as the lift, and went around a few times before the big metal door swung into the room. Inside the hatch was a small, dark, damp-smelling room. It couldn't have been more than eight feet square and contained nothing but a toilet bowl with a small sink next to it, a writing desk that could easily double up as a bedside table, and a bunk. Eric had seen bigger jail cells.

"I don't know about that" said Eric. "You said I was here to do training? Do I not get a bed in the living quarters with all the other officers?"

"You are not an officer Eric. Surely any good trainer would want to be close to his squads anyway," said Tolley sarcastically, and laughed again. In the distance they both heard chants and shouting voices. "Ah, and that must be one of your squads now. Shall we see if they pass your inspection?" suggested Tolley. He didn't wait for a reply but turned and walked off towards the noise.

"I'd suppose I don't have much of a choice at this point" said Eric. After all, how bad could they be? He followed behind Tolley.

The hexagonal training area was large, about half the size of a football pitch, and there were five main areas to it. In each corner of the auditorium were various punching bags and reaction speed testers, and large heavy-looking weights. Each area seemed to have a different set of exercises, depending on which muscle or cardio workout you wanted to do that day.

The reaction tester was a very popular training method in the Army. Not only did you need a high reaction speed, you had to have a lot of physical speed and strength. To complete the test was simple. You stood in front of a large curved metal frame which held sixteen touch pads. The pads would light up in a series of ever-more complicated patterns, and the user had to punch the buttons in turn – some needed hitting harder than others. Hit a button out of sequence, or not hard enough, and you were treated to an electric shock that could knock you to the floor.

But the central area caught Eric's eye immediately. It had a big sparring area cut deep into the metal floor, where two soldiers could practise their hand-to-hand combat skills. The whole training area was surrounded by a platform where people could walk around and view the men and women sparring and training. Eric got a little twinge of anticipation about the sparring area, and his keen eye spotted the blood that had dried but had not been cleaned away yet. These fights obviously didn't end until the victor had finished.

The hexagon was full of soldiers, each with the zombie-like look of men and woman who had only just woken up and weren't quite ready for the day yet. Some men were relaxing by sitting on weight machines, chatting and smoking. Others were over by the reflex tester, where one woman was doing her best to try to reach the squad's highest score, and the rest of the squad were spread out in different degrees of relaxation. All heads turned to see the two newcomers as they entered through the auditorium's big double doors,

It was the Sergeant who noticed that one of them was a Major. "Officer present!" he shouted, and all the soldiers instinctively jumped to form a line across the centre in front of the sparring area. "Come on, come on!" the Sergeant shouted as he hurried each man and woman to stand painfully to attention, glaring at the ones doing their best to hide smoking cigarettes behind their backs. "Aaaaaattention!" bellowed the Sergeant, and every soldier attempted to stand even more to attention than he already was.

"Thank you Sergeant" said Tolley, waving a dismissive hand in the Sergeant's direction. "Yes, very good, carry on."

"Yes sir! Thank you sir! Right, get to work you lot!" shouted the Sergeant. "You, you and you, get on those weights and bag! You, you, and you, work on those chicken legs! Rest of you, get to work!" He pointed at soldiers, and each soldier rushed to a machine and started pumping the various weights and levers to make it look like they always worked out this hard.

The Sergeant shouted encouragement at point blank range into the soldiers' ears as they worked up a sweat. The few that weren't able to make it to a machine in time were forced to do suicide jumps in the centre of the sparring area, the Sergeant's booming voice counting away in time.

"Here you are then" said Tolley, making a sweeping gesture around the auditorium. "This is one of three squads you will be training up for us."

"Can't wait" mumbled Eric, surveying the men and women. He wasn't too impressed with the squad. None of them seemed to be putting much effort into what they were doing. He was half tempted to show them how to do it properly, but hesitated. There was no need to piss off the big muscle people just yet. He eyed the nearest man mountain. They had clearly been working out for most of their lives. They were all very big and looked very strong, but Eric doubted they could take a joke. One of the soldiers lying on a bench looked closer to sleep than working up a sweat. That was until he got a kick from the Sergeant, and was made to do laps around the training yard.

Then Eric noticed the soldiers' uniforms, which certainly weren't the usual army fatigues he had seen worn by other foot soldiers. They looked more rough and ready, designed to give the wearer protection whilst not actually covering much. The men's and women's muscular bodies could quite easily be seen, but that was fairly typical of men and women in excellent physical condition, and Eric had to force himself not to stare at some of the women. Their training outfits weren't made from thick material, like the men's, and just about managed to cover the more eye-catching areas of their bodies.

An alarm bell sounded somewhere down one of the connecting corridors, which led off to other various training areas, Eric had no doubt, and he could hear cheers and shouting coming from the same direction. The noise was quickly followed by the sound of running feet, and soon a second squad of soldiers came thundering down the corridor and into the training room. These two squads clearly didn't get on, because on first sight the squad in unison jumped up and glared at the approaching second squad. The newcomers grouped together and glared back, and Eric got the impression that both sides were about to start a game of rugby, only without the ball.

Both squads stood for a moment eyeing each other up, and the more intelligent or quick-witted soldiers made quips about how bad the other squad was. Each time a putdown was shouted out the rest of their squad would back it up with cheers and encouragement. Eric couldn't help but laugh a little, but he coughed it away when he saw Tolley's expression.

"Enough!" shouted Tolley. He waited for silence before turning around and addressing the soldiers. "Listen up gladiators, this here is your new lanista" he said, putting a hand on Eric's shoulder. "This is Commander Eric Mason. Treat him with respect, and he won't break too many of your bones." It sounded like a joke, but it wasn't.

Now that the squads were all standing still Eric saw that there were twenty-one soldiers in each squad, and every pair of eyes was staring intently at him. It was possibly the most unnerving thing he'd seen in a long time. It took a lot to shake Eric's confidence, but this was doing a good job of it.

Each soldier looked somewhere between twenty and thirty years old, but it was difficult to determine any specifics. Both squads were made up mostly of men, and most of the faces had scars and other war wounds across them; a few even had nasty burn scars. You didn't get many old soldiers these days, especially not in this war. Any soldier who managed to get to the ripe old age of forty was either given a desk job, promoted, or retired to civilian life in one of the built-up megacities. The retired thing didn't happen very often though, and nor did the promotions for that matter, but it was nice to know that if you didn't die at the hands of the Zarda or their Lykor pets, you might be given a nice house to live in, and hopefully all your limbs to enjoy it with.

"Gladiators?" asked Eric out of the corner of his mouth, but Tolley just grinned.

"This… is our new lanista?" demanded one of the soldiers, spitting the words and stepping forward from the first squad, which Eric had mentally named 'Squad A'. The guy who had made the comment was big, not especially tall, but looking him up and down Eric could see all his muscles bulging under what passed for a uniform in these squads.

"Who told you to open your mouth, Jackson!" shouted the

Sergeant. It wasn't a question. The Sergeants in the Army rarely asked questions. The Sergeant had the face of someone who had just had a bucket of worms poured down the front of his trousers, and he was very obviously not making any eye contact with Eric.

The Gladiator called Jackson, who must have been Squad A's squad leader, mumbled an apology to the Sergeant, but he grinned at the rest of his squad when he stepped back in line.

"This little fella?" laughed the squad leader for Squad B loudly. "He don't exactly look like he could handle himself in a fight, how's he supposed to train us?" This comment was backed up by grumbled agreement from both squads.

"Let him train your squad Truck, god knows you lot could use all the help you can get" laughed Jackson.

"I don't know" said one of the women from Squad A, who had been making Eric a little uncomfortable with her staring. "He looks like he can handle himself just fine" she added with a wink and smile, and this was backed up by nods from the other women, Eric noticed. He forced his face to stay completely blank. This was not what he had been expecting, and he was getting the distinct impression that he was going to get stabbed or decapitated in his sleep.

"All you lot, silence!" roared the Sergeant at the top of his voice.

"Major, I thought we was going to get a real trainer" shouted Jackson in exasperation, ignoring the Sergeant completely.

"Silence!" shouted the Sergeant, walking back and forth in front of both squads. "The next soldier who talks without permission goes for a twenty-mile run."

"Eric, I'd like you to meet squad leaders Jackson and Truck" said Tolley jovially, and gestured to the two outspoken men. "These are your squad leaders for Squad 201." He pointed at Squad A. "And Squad 204" he said, pointing at Squad B.

"Squad 202 are in the firing range sir" reported the Sergeant, still staring at both squads. "They won't be done for another couple of hours."

"What happened to squad 203?" asked Eric.

"They're out fighting the War" said Tolley, quickly and in a very loud voice. "No need to let the other squads know about the recent fatalities," he added in a quiet, conspiratorial voice just for Eric. "You're looking at two of the strongest, and most dangerous, squads the Army has to offer. These are the Army's Gladiator squads!" he shouted, raising both hands to cheers from both the squads. "The Gladiator squads were my idea," he said quietly as the shouts and chants continued. "We took the toughest, the meanest and the strongest from all the other squads, and prisons, to form a front line that could destroy the gods themselves!" He roared out the last few words, bringing even more cheers from the squads.

"That's right!" shouted Jackson. "We're the first into danger, and we don't leave until the Zarda are dead and shit under our boots." Jackson turned to let the cheers of his squad wash over him before turning back to address Tolley. "This guy isn't good enough to be Gladiator," said Jackson in an angry tone, but then remembered he was speaking to a Major and quickly added "sir" as a precaution. "He's too scrawny, like the last one we had, he was weak. Give us a lanista with some balls" he called above the noise around him, and grinned at Eric.

"Jackson!" shouted the Sergeant "Twenty-mile run tomorrow morning before training starts!" and glared at the man for disobeying his order.

Tolley laughed and threw his hands in the air for quiet. Then he rocked back on his heels a couple of times. "That's quite all right Sergeant, no need to punish a man when he's right. You men and women have been sent into the darkest, most dangerous places the Army can think of, and each one of you came back stronger." He paused and grinned while the two squads cheered and roared again. After a moment he slowly raised both hands again for silence. "Now, what you need is a leader, a killer of Lykor. Someone who even the demons of hell could not kill. You need a man who could make the heavens rain blood, and turn wind to ice. I have seen what this man is capable of." He placed a hand on Eric's shoulder. "He has what it takes to turn you lot of wild animals into well-trained, efficient, killing machines." The cheers sounded again but not, Eric noticed, from the two squad leaders or the Sergeant.

The two squad leaders exchanged glances and looked Eric up and down suspiciously. Compared to them, Eric probably looked small and weak. The Sergeant was staring at him too, and Eric couldn't help but get the impression that this Sergeant had been expecting to be promoted. He would have to keep an eye on this man. Daggers in the eyes are one thing, but Eric didn't fancy a dagger in his back.

The Gladiator squads were an extremely useful tool for the Army. They were typically made up of men and women who were too volatile and unpredictable for regular units. The Gladiators used to be known as the Canaries, and were held up as a warning to all the regular army soldiers, a horror story told to soldiers who couldn't or wouldn't follow orders, or couldn't keep up in training. "If you monkeys don't shape up" the drill instructors would scream at them, "I'll throw you down the hole and those wild animals will rip you into a real soldier worthy of the uniform". Being sent into one of the canary squads was seen as a worse fate than being locked in a sweatbox out in the middle of a desert, or sent to the front line.

'The hole' was, in its broadest terms, a very remote training facility built on and around one of the country's biggest and highest-security prisons. The original occupants of the prison were deemed unworthy of being integrated into regular army squads, so instead of wasting valuable resources, the Army put them on the front line of the War. If any poor soul found him or herself thrown into one of these facilities, they could not be sure of ever seeing natural sunlight again. Men and women tended to degenerate in the hole; they became more animalistic and savage, fighting over scraps of food and drops of water. Several of them had been reduced to killing each other, just to have something fresh to eat. This came with its own unique social problems, but it wasn't stopped. Each unlucky soul would do all they could not to be killed, until it was their time to prove themselves on the battlefield, and then they would either prove their warrior strength or never be seen again.

The canary soldiers who survived being dropped into the thickest and most dangerous of the Zarda territories needed to be strong, tough and fearless to survive. Over time those who could prove themselves to be great warriors would be given a uniform, which was slightly different from the regular soldier's and was worn with pride, like a badge of honour.

It didn't take long before these animalistic men and women were the strongest units on the battlefield. They were bigger, tougher, stronger, and faster than any of the other 'classically' trained army soldiers, who were much smaller in comparison. Because of the brutal environment they lived in, the rules for the Canaries were slightly relaxed in terms of training, and they were left to their own devices. Soon many of them were using scrap metal, and whatever else they could find, to create a sort of armour that they wore at all times, and over time they began to resemble the Roman gladiators from the ancient days of the Roman Empire, which were generally speaking used as the same kind of resource.

In ancient days, over two thousand years ago, the mighty Roman armies would use gladiator slaves to pad out their front lines, because they were not considered people. These slaves, being bred on battle and harsh training, would strike fear into the hearts of their enemies and cause panic and chaos. Because they were expendable, and not considered fully human, they were not deemed worth of shiny clean armour, like the rest of the Roman soldiers, or decent sharp weapons, so the gladiators had to make do with sheer strength and fearlessness to keep themselves alive. It wasn't until much later that the various cities in Italy realised that their prowess on the battlefield would make a spectacle for citizens to watch, so gladiator fighting arenas were built all across the lands, controlled by Rome. When the name switched from Canaries to Gladiators, the soldiers took full advantage of it by wearing similar body armour to that the real gladiators wore on the sands of the arenas and battlefields. Some chose chainmail shirts, others wore shoulder-and-arm armour and some went in wearing nothing but body paint, but these did not last very long.

On the battlefield the Gladiators were given the choice of a variety of weapons, depending on their skill and mind-set, so hardly any two Gladiators had the same weapon. Some preferred the double-handed axe or sword, some preferred spears and nets, and some went simple and wrapped barbed wire around their fists. The majority carried shields and short swords, because the Army didn't feel they were worth giving guns or rifles to, as many did not survive the missions, and the Army would not get their weapons back. But one weapon every Gladiator could agree on was a two-foot-long razor-sharp machete, and one hung from each of their belts. Many a time on the battlefield this blade saved the life of a Gladiator as a last resort.

Overall the Gladiator squads attracted the type of person you could imagine in high-security prisons or juvenile detention facilities, the sort that like to hang around the workout yard, smoking and lifting weights with their other gang members. They were bad, they were mean, and they had no problem cutting an arm off to steal a ring, or even just to pass the time between battles. Which made them very difficult to control, but of course the Army tacticians and officers still tried to do so. It was like trying to control the wind, or use a sledgehammer to crack a boiled egg. Whenever the Gladiators were used on a mission, it was a roll of the dice whether they would all get wiped out in an all-out blood bath or destroy everything in their path.

Luckily the squads were self-regulating. The weak were squeezed out quickly, and the tough reigned over the weak. New recruits were beaten, broken down, starved out and forced to run through so many tests of strength that the majority died in the first few weeks. But the downside of this was that their ranks were always hungry for new recruits.

It soon became apparent to the Military Intelligence Agency that these units were a valuable asset to have, made up of completely expendable units, where it didn't matter if they survived their missions or not. But after a few short years, the many successes of the Gladiator's missions started to creep through to the regular squads, and even back home to the various highly-fortified Megacities. Children were even seen playing in the streets dressed as the bloodthirsty, monstrous Gladiators. Eventually the units became so popular throughout the Army that the officers were getting transfer requests from the regular soldiers. Men and women seeking blood and glory wanted to join the Gladiator squads. The Army, of course, loved this. More meat for the grinder.

"Ok" said Tolley calmly, "Everyone knows what usually happens to new recruits." This comment got a wave of smirks and muffled sniggering, and in some cases fist bumps and high-fives throughout both squads. Tolley raised a hand for silence. "You boys like to rough up the new recruits, put them through their paces, separate the weak from the strong, and at the end of the first month they take the test of strength" he said. This got more of the same reaction from the squads.

"Test of strength?" asked Eric out of the side of his mouth, but Tolley appeared not to hear him.

Eric looked along the lines of faces. At first glance the

Gladiators' smiles looked innocent enough, but on closer inspection they gave Eric reason to pause. Some of the soldiers now had a spark of fire in their eyes, with smiles so evil that they looked like hyenas or tigers who had just seen dinner walk by. He got the distinct feeling that each one of these Gladiators would take great pleasure in knocking a new lanista down a peg or two if he got the chance.

"So" continued Tolley, "have at it. If any one of you can knock your new lanista to the floor, they will get an extra day's rest and food ration." The room went eerily quiet.

A few of the bigger Gladiators took this cue to step forward, flexing their muscles, and glared at Eric. Eric looked from them to Tolley, who was pretending to be standing alone at this point, and back to the Gladiators. Eric guessed that this had happened before. He wondered what had happened to the last lanista. By the look of some of these men and women, he might well have died of accidentally cutting his own throat whilst shaving, or accidentally falling down some stairs with a knife sticking out of his back.

Tolley took the small staircase up to the viewing platform, leaving Eric standing alone, and casually leaned over the railing. Eric looked wildly from Tolley to the Gladiators that had stepped forward, and back to Tolley again, who gestured to Eric to enter the sparring area.

"Are you taking the piss?" said Eric. "You brought me all the way here for these Neanderthals to kick the shit out of me? Wouldn't a well-placed sniper with a gun do a better job of it?"

"We tried that" laughed Tolley, "but you kept killing them. Why not give them a demonstration of why you are the best man for the job?" He smiled.

The Gladiators all took a few more steps forward, not taking their eyes off Eric. Not one of them was about to pass up an opportunity of getting a day off and extra food. They were even less likely to pass up on an opportunity to go toe-to-toe with an officer without getting in trouble for it, even if this officer had the rank of Priest on his uniform.

Eric whipped off his broken sunglasses and casually threw them over his shoulder. Then he slowly made his way to the sparring area, attracting boos and cheers from the two squads. When he stepped into the sparring hexagon he raised both fists out in front of him, in what he hoped looked like a very inexperienced and relaxed attack stance, and tried to look as small as possible.

Jackson and Truck together were up first. As squad leaders everyone was looking for them to make the first move, and no one did anything without their permission. There was a very good reason why Jackson and Truck were in charge. They had risen authority by beating all those who were stupid enough to challenge them. But challenges didn't happen often, which gave them an undefeated streak very quickly. Despite their large size, they also had excellent reaction speeds.

Slowly Eric took a few steps forward, looking around wildly at all the Gladiators, who had all moved to make a ring around the sparring Hexagon, and jostled and jeered each other. It reminded Tolley of how a pack of angry wolves in the wild might look when surrounding their dinner. The two squad leaders were stretching their arms and flexing their muscles for the crowd, and soaking in the cheers and encouragements. They were going to enjoy this fight with the new guy. It was good to show the others exactly why they were in charge, and it would also stand as a warning to any of the men who were thinking about challenging them in the future.

Eric was hoping that if these two weren't able to beat him, the rest might not want to try. A few might still have a go, and he had better watch out for that, but overall if he knock the two men down as quickly as possible, the others might lose interest. But not too fast of course, that was a good way to find your breakfast sprinkled with broken glass, or something worse.

He had seen this sort of behaviour before, and not always in humans. If they had thought about it for a minute they would have stood a better chance of winning if they all attacked at once, not given him single targets to focus on. Eric seriously doubted he could take on all of these brutes at the same time. He had won with worse odds before of course.

A nervous chill ran down his spine. The two men in front of him stood at least a foot taller than him, enough to give even the best fighter pause.

Eric was in no way an undefeated champion. Over the years he'd been beaten many times, and not just by big brutes like these. Every fight was different, he thought, as if remembering something someone had once taught him. Don't let their size and strength worry you, worry about your own size and strength.

"Come on Eric, we don't have all day" shouted Tolley jovially. Eric turned, dropping his hands down a little, and shook his head at Tolley in disbelief.

As if telepathically linked, Jackson and Truck rushed forward in attack positions, their arms up high to grab and their eyes open wide. Jackson, as fast as lightning, launched through the air to land barely a foot or two away from Eric, who hadn't moved an inch. He'd been keeping eye contact with Tolley, by way of defiance, as the two men charged him. The Gladiator's arms shot out and gripped Eric's shoulders in both hands, and he brought one of his big knees up into Eric's gut, causing him to bend over double.

The blow had knocked a little wind out of Eric, so he decided to take a few theatrical steps backwards. When Eric looked up he saw that Truck had somehow teleported right in front of him, and the bunch of bananas he called a fist was already inches away from Eric's face. The punch landed square on Eric's jaw, making him take a few more steps back. The knee to the gut wasn't too bad, but the punch had really hurt, and Eric recoiled a little, holding both areas. The pain was fairly bearable, but the unexpectedness of the punch had thrown Eric a little, and he was struggling to gather his bearings. It was clear why this guy was called Truck. It felt like he had been punched by a sixteen-wheeler going a hundred miles an hour.

Jackson saw the window of opportunity; Eric didn't have his hands up. He fired a few jabs to Eric's kidneys and ribs, his arms moving like pistons. Each punch landed hard, and even lifted Eric off the ground a little each time. When the punching had stopped Eric fell backwards, but was caught by the ring of Gladiators, who quickly threw him back into the fight.

What the hell is happening here? demanded Eric's internal damage report. *Stop letting them hit you, and do something about them,* shouted his common sense.

Truck's arm was already arching around at head height, and had spun a whole 360 degrees to get the most impact. But Eric saw it coming a mile away, and at the last second he twisted backwards and managed to limbo underneath it. The second he was clear, Eric threw his elbow back to make contact with Jackson's unsuspecting ear. Eric had used his whole body to do it, and if the pain in his elbow was any indicator, it must have hurt the man.

The blow made Jackson howl out in pain and clutch at his head. He had not been expecting the blow, and it had nearly knocked him off his feet. He had seen Truck's spinning attack before on the battlefield and sparring ring, and had seen it once knock down an enemy soldier twice Eric's size. He certainly hadn't expected Eric to have the speed to duck under it, so he had simply been standing there waiting his turn to punch the new guy again. Jackson could now do nothing but stand there dazed and in a lot of pain. His ear was ringing, and when he took his hand away a thin trickle of blood dripped out of it.

When Eric had finished the movement he had spun a few steps to the side so he was standing directly behind Truck, and now he kicked the backs of both of Truck's knees, making him drop very hard to the metal floor. Eric moved with lightning speed to top off the move off by punching Truck square in the back of his head, sending the Gladiator firmly to the ground on his front. The thump of twenty stone of muscle made the sparring area shake slightly, and the onlookers crowed in surprise. None of them had seen either squad leader beaten before, especially not when fighting together as a pair.

'That's it, you bastards' muttered Eric as he readied himself for another attack. 'Don't fight as a team, just fight like idiots.' He knew full well that if one of them held him still and the other one punched him hard a few times, he'd go down, no questions asked.

Eric calmly took a few steps away from Truck and faced Jackson just as the man was charging with both hands raised like a Brazilian wrestler. Eric wanted to punch the man square in the face, and would have done so if he'd had enough time to move. Jackson really was fast on his feet. Eric reduced himself to simply raising his hands to intercept him.

The two men grappled for a moment, neither of them able to break the other's strength. Jackson glared at Eric, and if looks could kill Eric would have been turned to dust on the spot. But despite his extra size, Jackson still had to grit his teeth in the effort of breaking Eric's grip, and eventually the pair pushed each other away to circle a few more times. Jackson tried a few punches that were easily dodged by Eric, who was beginning to pick up speed. The ring of people around the pair were working themselves up into a frenzy, their cheers and shouts getting louder with every punch.

Jackson was getting frustrated now with this little man. Each punch he felt sure would land was easily blocked, and Eric gave him a returning blow that hit its mark perfectly. Eric wasn't trying to hurt the man too much, but he did take pleasure in annoying him, so each punch he landed was no harder than a light slap, but they all struck home. It wasn't the power of the hit that was beating Jackson, it was the number of the many Eric was able to plant over his face, chest, kidneys and ribs. The jeers and chants from the other Gladiators around them did the rest.

Jackson wasn't used to this sort of fighting. Normally the other guy was so terrified he was going to be killed that he made enough mistakes to let through one or two good punches, and the fight was over. He was used to going up against brute strength, like Truck, not speed and lightning jabs. And the man he was facing looked a lot bigger than he had done when he'd first stepped into the sparring area. Now he was even smiling at him.

Eric was faster than he was, and Jackson was starting to get very angry indeed. And some of the crowd were actually cheering on the other guy. He glared at his comrades, who instantly wished they hadn't opened their mouths, and did their best to indicate that they'd been cheering for Jackson all the way.

Eric dodged to avoid yet another punch from Jackson and landed a few neat hits to the big man's kidneys, causing him to hiss in pain. Jackson was furious. He arched his back, rolling his head back, and screamed a war cry at the top of his voice. Then he took a few steps away from Eric, trying to regroup.

Seeing this, Eric relaxed a little. Maybe that was the end of it... but he changed his mind when Jackson drew his machete blade. No Gladiator would dream of leaving his bed without his blade on his hip, and some even slept with them, just in case of an attack during the night. The lights in the ceiling glinted off the blade. The guy must have been up all night polishing that thing. He had to admit that the sight of this blade was a little worrying. Maybe he should have hit him a little harder.

But just because someone had a big and scary weapon, it didn't mean he knew how to use it properly. The volume from the spectators started to reach critical mass, and shouts of "slice him up Jackson!", "kick his ass!" and "stick your blade through his throat!" floated through the hubbub. This didn't fill Eric with much confidence, but he squared up to Jackson anyway, keeping eye contact with him.

The Sergeant, worried that he might get in trouble from the Major, glanced up at him on the viewing platform; he hadn't moved. Tolley had a slightly worried look on his face, but the Sergeant didn't get the impression he was worried for Eric's safety. He shrugged and turned back to the fight, and figured that if the Major was worried he probably would have stopped the fight as soon as Jackson had drawn the blade.

Eric stretched his neck. This wasn't going to be easy, but it might be straightforward. He took a few quick zigzag steps forward, and Jackson waved the blade a few times as a warning. He wasn't sure why this man wasn't calling for an end to the fight. He had half expected his opponent to give up or run away when he saw him draw his blade.

When Eric got close Jackson started swiping the blade through the air as if he was trying to hack away long grass or jungle vines. Eric ducked and dodged the swipes with ease; Jackson was really sweating now, and every time he tried to swing the blade at Eric's head, or stab him through the heart, Eric was able to get out of the way at the last second. A few times, Eric had to pull his arms in tight to avoid them being cut off by the blade's erratic movements, but he was still able to punch at the man in front of him in between attacks. Jackson clearly wasn't expecting this, and jumped each time Eric was able to land a punch on his body. They were the same strength as before, not enough to really hurt Jackson, but enough to annoy him.

Jackson kicked out with a boot, and caught Eric square in the chest, throwing him back a few steps. He had decided that enough was enough. There was just enough space between the two men for Jackson to take a small run up and jump a full three or four feet into the air, raising the blade high above his head.

Time slowed down as the big man floated through the air, and the light reflecting off his blade made him look as if he was holding a flaming sword. Eric stared up at the man and carefully moved, placing his feet in exactly the right places. When Jackson brought the blade down in both hands, in an arc that would have split an oak tree in half, but Eric was already out of the way. It missed him by an inch, and Eric saw his reflection in the blade's polished surface as it went past his face.

When the blade hit the metal floor near Eric's foot, the impact vibrated up the steel and through the hilt, nearly breaking Jackson's wrists. At this moment time rushed back into the world, but Jackson didn't move a muscle. He was staring intently at the pain in his arms, and a hiss of air escaped from his lips making him sound like he was deflating. His brain was trying to comprehend what had just happened to him and push the pain back into the blade, but it wasn't working. A weaker man might have just crumpled into a pile, and lost the use of his hands for a few weeks.

The crowd around the two fighters went silent, and Eric glared up at Tolley, who'd been joined by some onlookers. Tolley was grinning again. A low growl started to rumble from behind Eric, and Eric turned slowly to find Jackson glaring at him and snarling like a Lykor.

Drunk with the hunger for revenge, Jackson charged Eric again, swinging the blade wildly around himself. If Eric had found it easy to avoid his attacks the first time, now the man's attacks were even slower and more apelike. It made him look more like he was waving a flag rather than a blade. Not one of his attempts managed to hit their intended mark, but no surprise there. Eric continued to duck and dodge out of the way of the swinging blade, expecting at any minute that someone would call off the fight. The Gladiator was clearly beaten.

Someone threw something metallic into the hexagon, and the light reflected off it as it spun in the air. The blade landed near

Eric's foot, and the loud clang of metal caused Eric to break his concentration and look down. At that moment Jackson was attempting another wild thrust, and with Eric distracted, he was able to slash a deep cut through Eric's shoulder and arm. Eric pulled away, holding his wound tight, and watched the blood trickle between his fingers.

Seeing that he'd actually drawn blood surprised Jackson as much as it did Eric, but without missing a beat he threw a punch, hitting Eric hard in the chest. The force of the punch pushed Eric off balance, and he slowly fell backwards. On his descent Eric's hindbrain screamed at him, don't hit the floor! If you're knocked down, you lose, and Tolley and this ape win!

Eric managed to swing an arm out behind him, and he felt the cold hard floor beneath him.

He refused to be knocked down. If anyone was getting a day off tomorrow and free food, it was going to be him, he thought, holding himself up off the floor. Seeing this, the crowd burst back into life and started chanting and booing again.

Eric pushed himself back onto his feet, and checked the wound. It didn't seem too bad at second glance, but it was still a deep cut. In the background he heard Jackson boasting to the crowd about his strength and cunning with the blade. He wasn't too annoyed by the man's boasts, they were only to be expected by the sort that craved attention. But what did annoy him was that the ape had not only been lucky enough to cut him, but get a powerful hit in too after that nearly floored him.

The crowd's volume died down a little when they saw the determination in Eric's now very focused eyes, and Jackson slowly turned around. The pair circled a few times, and Eric's foot touched the blade that was still lying on the floor. With a quick flip of his foot, he scooped the blade up into the air in front of him. He reached forward and plucked the blade's hilt out of the air, then gave it a few spins, testing its weight. Jackson's eyes watched bemused as Eric gripped the hilt and moved his body into an aggressive stance, the point aimed between Jackson's eyes. Jackson had never seen an attacking stance like that before, and he was worried.

Now Truck was getting to his feet, and he had the look of an angry bull. He'd only been in the fight a few seconds before he had been knocked to the floor, and this was very unusual for him. In fact, he had built up the reputation of beating new recruits that fell in the first few seconds of a fight, if they were still alive of course.

Truck loomed behind Eric, taking big heavy steps and ignoring the pain coming from both his knees. He had been lying on the cold metal floor, helplessly watching the two fighters. Thankfully no one in the crowd was paying him any attention, but this stung his pride at the same time. No one cared that he'd been floored so early on in the fight, no one cared that their leader was injured, and to a Gladiator, this was the worst kind of pain. His mouth was snarling like a wild animal and his eyes were fixed on his target. He was now going to crush this little man into dust.

Truck stamped and stumbled until he was standing directly behind Eric, and raised both large hands above his head. Eric noticed something was happening behind him, because something about the spectators behind Jackson was giving it away. They were all smiling and pointing, and none of them were looking at him. They were all, including Jackson, looking at something about an inch away on either side of his head, and he doubted it was his ears.

On the floor in front of him, Eric noticed a faint shadow, too big to be his own, which meant someone was either right behind him, or would be soon. And then the shadow moved, fast.

Eric's instincts took over and he spun a few steps to the side, narrowly missing Truck's double-handed blow from above, and watched the big man stumble forward until he crashed into

Jackson. With both his attackers standing in front of him now, Eric moved quickly. He lashed out with hard punches, kicks, and slashes of his blade at the pair. His arms became a blur of speed and precision, and the light glinted off his blade as it swung through the air.

Jackson and Truck quickly became entangled, their arms trying desperately to block and attack at the same time, and they were not doing a good enough job of either. Neither of them had time to think, and they were in each other's ways. Each time they tried to separate, Eric's fist or blade would herd them back together again.

An easy twist of Eric's blade caused Jackson to drop his, and Eric shoulder-barged forward, hitting him hard in the chest and dropping him to the floor instantly. Jackson tried to get back up onto his feet, but Eric was on him. With a short run up, he launched himself through the air, kicking out with both boots, and slammed into Jackson's chest. This threw him backwards and through the crowd of onlookers, so that he hit the wall behind them. The impact made the spectator platform shake a little, and Eric saw Tolley gripping the banister to steady himself. Then he saw Jackson slide to the floor, defeated.

Truck's Gladiator brain told him to keep on fighting no matter what, but his body was pleading with him to stop the fight. He turned to face Eric, who was glaring at him with clenched fists, and despite his better judgement, took a few steps forward. He raised his fists, but without much conviction, and gave Eric a pleading look. He couldn't back down now, not in front of all the other Gladiators.

Eric couldn't have cared less. He jumped forward, ducking a big swing from Truck, and hammered a few punches to Truck's torso. With his arms moving like pistons Eric slammed punch after punch into Truck, each one making the man take a half a step back, until his back was up against the wall. Truck was trapped, pinned up against it, and not able to defend himself any more. Finally he gave up and slid to the floor beside Jackson.

"Get up!" shouted the Sergeant. He was red-faced and angry at this poor display.

Jackson glared at Eric, and then at his squad. "Attack him, you fools!" he ordered, and a few Gladiators took a few timid steps back. "All at once, he can't fight you all!" Jackson added.

Eric spun on his heel and glared at the mass of soldiers, daring them to try. This could be problematic. He didn't fancy his chances against all of them at once. Not after fighting those brutes.

A few Gladiators stepped forward, despite seeing their leaders beaten, reasoning that it was better to try and fail than to risk the wrath of Jackson or Truck later. Eric heard Tolley laughing from somewhere up above. 'I'll fucking show him' he murmured, and raised his fists again.

One by one Eric blocked and dodged the new attackers, as each Gladiator charged at him with arms flailing around like wild animals. With each move Eric made a counter attack, and floored several of them in a matter of seconds. Because of the sheer number of attackers around him, it almost didn't matter what direction Eric chose to punch, and the group gave him a near endless supply of targets.

Within a few minutes, Gladiators were littering the floor. The ones still standing waited until a viable window looked open in the blur of movement that was now Eric's arms and legs, and tried to land a punch or kick. But Eric was moving at full speed, and not one managed to connect a fist or boot. Eric tried not to hurt them too much, but in the heat of the fight, and with the adrenaline rushing around his system, He slowly brought them all to their knees.

When Eric had finally run out of targets, he stood breathing heavily. The sound of hands clapping in slow rhythm made him look around, it was Tolley. More clapping could be heard, and Eric saw by the main entrance that a group of soldiers and officers had stopped to watch the fight. They all had a mixed look of shock and admiration.

"Looks like your Gladiators need a proper trainer after all," Tolley shouted in a loud and happy voice. "Sergeant, make sure the medic has a look at any broken bones, and get the rest back to work. We have a war to win you know" he added, and grinned at Eric.

"Yes sir!" shouted the Sergeant "Right you lot of time wasters, you disgust me! Get up! Get up you scumbags! You lot, get down to the firing range. The rest of you get moving on those machines. If this priest can wipe the floor with you, single-handedly I might add, how do you expect to beat the Zarda?" His face was purple with anger.

The Sergeant marched the squads off to different machines and angrily helped Jackson and Truck to get to their feet again. He was furious that his best trained Gladiators had been soundly beaten by someone who had barely broken a sweat. They had managed to get a few of their own punches in of course, but this didn't matter if you then lost the fight. He was going to make these soldiers suffer for this embarrassment. How was he supposed to get promoted to Lanista if he couldn't prove that he could train these men and women? He could feel the eyes of all the other soldiers by the main entrance staring at him.

Jackson and Truck had a look of thunder about them, and slowly joined the rest of the Gladiators. Not a single word was spoken about the fight, mostly because they all knew Jackson and Truck probably still had some energy left in their tired bodies. The first person to make a comment or joke, or even catch eyes with one of them, would soon seriously regret it.

Eric stared as Tolley slowly came down the metal staircase, still grinning at Eric. A vision of Eric punching the man in the face and leaving flashed in front of Eric's eyes, but he was too tired to run now. Besides, he hadn't really been paying enough attention to how he had got there, so if he ran he would probably be stuck there for days. Although the Gladiators were the supposedly the most dangerous the Army had to offer, not much would slow him down, but he still didn't fancy fighting his way out. What he did fancy was a drink, a big strong one, with the kind of alcohol content you might find in the stuff medics used to clean wounds. Tolley had promised the key to alcohol storage, but Eric could smell a lie a mile away.

"They're good men and women Eric, they just need a little discipline and leadership" Tolley said conversationally. "And you are just the man for the job. Now if you follow these soldiers…" He paused to point out two regular soldiers waiting patiently either side of the auditorium's big double doors.

The soldiers had seen the fight and were a little wary of Eric now, but they reminded themselves they were armed and he wasn't, although this might not make much of a difference by the look of things.

"I could use a drink" mumbled Eric, but this was ignored by Tolley.

The two soldiers stood to attention when the Major and Eric walked over and joined them, "Make sure the Commander here gets to his quarters all right" ordered Tolley, and the two soldiers saluted him. Tolley casually saluted Eric, just to annoy him, and walked off down one of the corridors with a slight spring in his step. Eric gestured theatrically for the two soldiers to carry on, and they moved so that one was standing in front and one behind him.

He was still a prisoner then, thought Eric, and muffled a laugh. These men weren't showing him to his room, they were escorting him top his cell. The trio marched down the corridor away from the training area, turned a corner and marched down a series of short corridors, passing possibly a hundred rushing soldiers, until they reached Eric's sleeping quarters. The soldier in front of Eric turned the big wheel handle and the door swung open with the now-familiar grinding metallic noise. As he stepped gingerly inside, the soldier pulled a thin piece of string hanging from the ceiling by the hatch door, which switched on the bare bulb hanging from the centre of the room.

'At least the prison cells had a little walking around space' he mused, looking around. The light hanging from the ceiling wasn't bright, it was that 'easy light' you got from those long-life bulbs which had been all the rage a few years before the War, but was now pretty much the only option. It was the sort that took ten minutes to warm up and then light up the room, but even then it wasn't exactly bright.

The walls hadn't been painted, but someone had had the fun job of smearing the overly-thick army-grade plaster across the walls, which was intended to give each cell a slightly more homely look, but actually made it look a bit like a cave. On the ceiling, where the heavy plaster had clumped together, small stalagmites hung down a few inches.

"The Army spare no expense, clearly," said Eric sarcastically. "Very cosy, but no mini bar, I notice," he added with a smile, but the smile disappeared when he saw the grim faces of the soldiers. "Yes I think I could be very happy here. Tell me lads, what time is breakfast?"

Just then a grinding metal sound made him spin around. One of the soldiers was slowly shutting the heavy metal door. It slammed shut before Eric could reach it, and he had to shield his ears from the sound rebounding off the walls. "Charming, not big conversationalists then" muttered Eric, lowering his hands. "I don't see a phone, how am I going to call for room service in the morning?" he shouted at the closed door.

Eric sighed, and decided to investigate the bed first. He sat down and bounced up and down a few times, the universal test. Eric hadn't expected much, and indeed it was about as comfortable as a slab of concrete, mainly due to the mattress being only about three inches thick. The blanket was reassuringly made of itchy wool. He would have been very suspicious if the Army had given him something nice to sleep on, or in.

There were no bottles of water that he could see. He stood up and decided to test the taps on the sink; he turned one, and nothing happened. He turned the other, and still no water came out, but a loud banging sound could be heard through the wall. New pipes, probably. He left the tap on for a moment, and the banging got louder and louder until a thin trickle of water fell out of the tap.

Eric cupped his hands under the trickle and tasted the water. It wasn't bad, a slight chemical taste, but it was better than nothing. He cupped his hands again, and waited for what seemed like forever for it to fill. Finally he tapped it with a finger.

The tap exploded. If asked to describe the effect, Eric would have said the pressure was that of an ocean being pushed through one tiny nozzle. It hit the metal basin hard, and the pressure of the water nearly knocked him off his feet. He swore loudly a few times, though this was completely inaudible over the torrent of water, and fought the powerful stream of water using both hands as a shield. Finally managing to reach the basin, he tried to turn the tap, but it simply spun round and round with no effect. Which caused a few more inaudible swear words to be shouted at it.

Getting angrier by the second, Eric slammed the heel of his hand down on the tap as hard as he could a few times, but his hands were hurting badly from the fight with the Gladiators, and this brought a yelp of pain each time. The banging sound from behind the wall seemed to quiet down a little, so he tried turning the tap a few more times, and slowly the pressure began to calm down.

Eric looked around at the drenched room, and down at his dripping wet clothes, "Well isn't that nice, I get my own shower too" he said aloud to himself, and brushed some of the wet off him.

He looked around, but couldn't find anything that resembled a place where someone might have put a change of uniform for him. He tried opening the desk drawers, but they were empty except for religious books. Eric snorted with laughter when he saw them – they were for the four main religions that had survived the War.

There was nothing else for it. He couldn't just stand around in dripping clothes, he was going to have to find some fresh ones, and there had to be a laundry nearby, surely. Plus, if he just happened to find a handy exit on his travels, all the better, preferably via an armoury of some sort too. The urge to get as far away from here as a stolen truck full of petrol could take him was rising again.

Eric then noticed what had been nagging at him, a small thought in the back of his mind which had been waving its hands and jumping up and down trying to get noticed. The door didn't have a handle on the inside. There should have been a big ring handle the same as outside, but instead there was just blank metal. If the room had looked a like a prison cell before, now Eric was sure he was in one.

At eye height there was a small rectangle hatch, which he hadn't noticed from the outside, and again the handle for it must be on the outside. Eric advanced on the small piece of metal, leaving soggy footprints across the floor as he did so, and tried to slide it open with his fingertips. But the hatch wouldn't budge an inch. He clenched his fist and banged a few times on the door, but it was solid, and he wasn't able to make much noise.

He stood with his ear close to the door to hear if there was a reply to his banging, but there was silence on the other side. He couldn't tell if that meant he couldn't hear a reply, or if there wasn't actually anyone on the other side to give one. He tried again, harder this time, but still nothing happened.

"Arseholes!" he shouted, his anger level starting to rise even further. Eric had very little patience for the Army at the best of times, and now they had locked him in a small metal box and expected him to train their meat-head Gladiators. "Fuck this" he muttered, and took a few steps back.

After taking a few deep breaths he turned to his side, and twisted his arms around a few times until he could fall into a self-taught martial art style stance. He brought his right hand back and clenched his fist, and raised his other hand into the air flat in front of him. Concentrating hard on his inner energy, which he could feel bubbling up inside him, he tensed his entire body. His aura started to swell and grow around him, and without moving he seemed to grow larger, and almost a foot or two taller.

He swept his hands around in the air a few more times, and his whole body twisted and spun on one heel. His arms almost became a blur as they twisted and folded around his head and body. Closing his eyes tight, he focused on building up a charge of energy, and quickly felt the reassuring warmth fill his tired arms and legs all the way to his hands and feet.

It wasn't long before the energy could be seen through his skin. It was dull at first, but quickly got brighter and brighter. His veins started to illuminate, as if a fire had been lit deep down inside him, and growing. Small sparks of yellow electric light crackled up and down both of his arms, and he let out a small low hum as he continued to twist and turn. The veins began to pulsate beneath his skin, and the crackling sparks began to spread out until he was sure he had had enough

Then he slammed his fist into the metal door. Where his fist met metal, a small yellow-white light flashed around him. The bang as Eric's fist hit the door vibrated out in all directions and echoed around the small confined cell, and when Eric took his hand away there was a perfect imprint of his fist in the metal surface. Eric couldn't believe it, and he stood in shocked silence and stared. The fist dent was barely an inch deep. The door couldn't be more than a few inches thick, surely. He had fully expected to blow the door completely off its hinges.

In his anger he wrenched off his soaked T-shirt and priest shirt and threw the wet clothes into the corner of the room. He again got into the attacking stance, extending his arms. Sweat from concentration was beginning to show on his forehead, and he stared straight ahead. He was not about to be beaten by a door.

He swept his arms around again and again, twisting and turning and causing the electric sparks to run up and down his arms again, but this time they continued all the way up and over his shoulders and across his chest. He carried on twisting and moving, and the yellowish veins nearly covering his whole torso, glowed brighter with every sweeping move. When he had finished twisting and charging up his energy, his aura becoming thick and powerful, and he really stepped into it this time. Both fists hammered into the door as one, and for good measure he kicked out with one of his boots as well.

Nothing changed, except that the door had a few more dents in its surface now. Eric creamed a few swearwords at it, and without missing a beat, he swung his body and arms around in complicated circles and swirls. This time his energy was nearly at its fullest. His hands and arms were leaving yellow trails of shadowy light behind them, and the whites of his eyes began to glow too. The bulb in the ceiling smashed, the floor beneath him began to shake, and plaster started melting and sliding down the walls. He gritted his teeth, forced everything into his arms, and punched the door one last time.

The world exploded around Eric. White light filled the room, and eerily dark electric snakes burst out from where Eric had hit the door, then spread out, causing the metal to blister and melt. Eric was lost to sight in a flash of blinding white light and energy. And from the corridor outside, light escaped around the very thin crack around the doorframe.

CHAPTER 19

THE CAVE

"Balls!" exclaimed Eric. The echo of his voice travelled off into the inky blackness all around him.

Eric knew exactly where he was. He had been there more times than he wanted to be, but this time seemed to be a little different. He had no idea how he had got there, and he was almost convinced that this had to be a dream, and he was actually tucked up in bed somewhere.

This was no ordinary cave. It was somewhere that could never be found on any map that could ever be drawn. If a traveller found him or herself in this place, it would be the last place they ever saw. Not that that they would be able to see much of anything in this darkness, Eric mused. He turned around a few times, squinting into the black curtain around him.

As if on cue, off in the distance, a pinprick of light appeared, and started to grow, until it sent a beam of light stabbing through the darkness. It took Eric a few minutes to notice it. The darkness in here was trying its best to suffocate the light, but it grew stronger anyway. Soon the pinprick was as big as a tennis ball, and it nearly blinded Eric when he foolishly tried to look into it. As it grew brighter, it illuminated the rough-looking rock floor beneath Eric's feet, and he was given a faint outline of his surroundings. He was standing on one side of an enormous cavern, the walls of which rose up hundreds of metres above him. The cavern was so big, in fact, that he could barely see the other side, despite the stream of light crossing it like a laser beam. The light reflected off some of the smoother rock surfaces, reflecting and refracting hundreds of times and finally reaching the ceiling above. Eric followed the light's path as it bounced around the rocky world he'd now found himself in. As the light reached the ceiling it seemed to jump from one green crystal stalagmite to another, and soon each one was glowing quite brightly. No wonder he couldn't reach the tops of the walls he kept walking into.

He absentmindedly rubbed the wounds on his head. Compared to the darkness all around him, the source of the light looked very warm and inviting. Eric looked around one last time, and shrugged. How bad could it be? Better to investigate the light than keep walking into things in the dark.

The beam of light seemed to have drilled its way through the rock face, and it shone down the length of what could only be described as a tunnel in the wall. Eric couldn't believe what he was seeing. He crouched down, wincing and squinting, as he tried to look into the light, and had to bend double to get into the tunnel.

As he walked towards the source of the light, it seemed to brighten slightly. Eric also noticed that the walls on either side seemed to be getting narrower the closer he got to it, which was a little disconcerting. He realised he could reach out and touch both walls at the same time, and as he got closer still, he had to crabwalk sideways in order to fit. Which wasn't ideal, because it wasn't a natural movement, and he kept banging his head.

When he'd reached the end of the tunnel, Eric was faced with a dead end, and no hope of turning around in such a small space. He couldn't quite make out where the light was coming from. It appeared to emanate from the wall in this long cul-de-sac of rock, but by using the piece of broken glass in his pocket, he was able to reflect the light a little, and see that it was actually coming from the other side, through a tiny gap in the rock face.

Eric couldn't help himself. He raised a finger and covered the hole, and was instantly thrown into complete darkness. He wasn't too sure what else he expected to happen, so he pushed with his finger a little bit, and the loose rock around the hole crumbled away slightly. He started digging. It wasn't all loose rock, and he had to pull quite hard to get some of it away, but bit by bit he made a bigger hole for the light to shine through, and the more he did this, the brighter it got.

Soon Eric had made enough of a hole to look into, which he instantly regretted, as the light was so bright it nearly blinded him. He clenched a fist and started punching at the rock, causing the hole to get bigger and let even more light out, flooding the tunnel he was in.

Eric dropped the shard of glass – it wasn't needed any more. He used both hands to pull away at the rock until he had made a space big enough to crawl through. "This had better be worth it" he muttered, catching his breath. Anything had to be better than stumbling around in the dark. He leant forward, and clambered through to the other side.

On the other side of the hole, Eric was surrounded by warm golden light, and he had to hold a hand up to his eyes to shield them from it. The light seemed to be coming from all around him, but from what he could make out, he was simply in another cave. However this time, instead of the cold darkness that seemed to suffocate everything, the rock around him was glowing.

He looked back, expecting to see the small hole he had just crawled through, but there was nothing there. The hole had vanished, leaving nothing but rock. He stared at it for a moment, and spun around in case he was looking at the wrong place, but there was nothing but golden rock in all directions.

"Well that can't be good," he muttered with a sigh, hoping this was just a dream. He couldn't quite decide what was worse – the cold, suffocating darkness from before or this blinding brightness. It was warmer here though, which had to be better than shivering in the dark.

He looked down, and could now see the state he was in. His clothes were ripped and burnt and the exposed skin was black and charred. It didn't look attractive, and it was easy to see why he had been so cold earlier; there was barely anything left of his clothes to cover his body.

"Right – so?" Eric asked himself, taking in his surroundings. He seemed to be standing at one end of another long cul-de-sac of rock, although this time there didn't seem to be an end in sight. But the light was playing tricks with his eyes; it was thick like a fog, as if he was looking through hundreds of sheets of golden silk. Each time his eyes tried to focus on whatever was in the distance, it seemed to move around so that he couldn't.

"Out of the frying pan, and into a hotter frying pan I guess," he mumbled to himself, and started walking down the tunnel.

After walking for some time, Eric walked into something hard, and swore loudly. He'd reached the end of the tunnel, and found another dead end. He'd tried to keep an eye open for where he was walking, but each time Eric lowered his hand and squinted into the light, the light played tricks on him, so he'd resorted to just keep keeping his head down, and walking in a straight line hoping for the best. He'd been walking for ages, so he wasn't expecting to hit a solid wall.

He rubbed the new wound on his head, and shook the pain away. He tried feeling with his hands along the rough stone in both directions, but couldn't find an obvious direction to go in. It was too much to hope that he had simply come to a corner in the tunnel, and he could continue on this fairly worrying journey, but in a different direction.

There had to be a point to all this, surely, Eric thought. There had to be something at the end of it all, he reasoned, but without much confidence. If he was stuck in here, walking from one side to another of a golden tunnel that didn't go anywhere for all eternity, he would get very angry, very quickly. Annoyingly, there wasn't anyone here to take his anger out on.

And then, as if on cue, a voice said very slowly, "You… are… here."

Eric jumped and looked around. The voice had sounded as if whoever had said it was standing right behind him, but there was no one in there with him, which was a shame because Eric's fists were eager to talk to someone. "Hello?" asked Eric, and then felt a little silly for doing so.

"You are here… again" said the deep voice. "Why are you here again?" It sounded as if the voice was having to travel a very long distance to reach him.

Eric strained to see in all the brightness, and his eyes began to water with the effort. He was alone, he was sure of it, with nothing but glowing rock as far as the eye could see.

"Why… am… I… here?" said Eric, mimicking the voice, and he couldn't help but let out a little laugh. "Where the bloody hell am I?" he demanded in his normal voice, "because I don't know that either." He stood in silence for a few minutes.

"Leave" said the voice at last. The single word hung in the air for a moment before continuing, "…or fight." Menace and violence hung on every syllable.

Eric thought about this for a moment. "I would love to fight, but you seem to have me at a slight disadvantage. So I would like to choose the first option. If you could show me the way out?" He spread his hands, to indicate that there was no door anywhere in sight.

"Leave... or FIGHT," repeated the voice, but louder this time, and angrier. It sounded as if his answer had annoyed the speaker more than anything else.

"Certainly, leave it is then, but I don't see a way out. Could you point me towards the exit? Is there a gift shop? Or at the least, do you think you could manage to lower the brightness slightly? It's a little dazzling in here." Nothing happened for a moment, and Eric got the impression that this wasn't quite the answer the speaker was expecting.

After a minute or so the speaker must have reached a decision, and the light in the tunnel slowly dimmed. Eric was able to lower his hand from his eyes to have a proper look around. He was no longer in the golden tunnel, but in a cave about the size of a football stadium.

OK, thought Eric a little suspiciously, whoever it was could move stuff around, so... so he wasn't under the Mountain then. But this just threw up more questions.

The cave he was in now was still golden, and glowing brightly, just not as bad as it was in the tunnel. Eric stared around, a little in awe of the molten gold stalagmites hanging from the ceiling, but more importantly, he could see no obvious doors or exits. There was nothing of any real interest in this cave. Although there did seem to be something in the far corner, now that Eric could see a little better.

He wondered what the point of the glowing tunnel was; probably a metaphor for something. He shrugged. He had never been too interested in metaphors, and rarely took the time to think about them. Either things were real, or they weren't. He decided to make his way across the cave towards the object he could see in the corner. As he got closer to it, he could make out a little more detail. From a distance it had looked like a small grey cloud or patch of fog, but now it looked as black as midnight. It was so dark in fact that it was like a small piece of the darkness he had been wandering around in before, and it practically sucked in the light from around it.

When he got closer still, the black object turned out to be a person, wearing a big hooded cloak. He, she or it was sitting with its back to Eric in the farthest corner facing the rock, and moving gently in a rhythmic pattern. Eric couldn't quite make out what it was doing. Without a word, he leaned to one side and peered over the cloaked figure's shoulder. It was hunched over something, and seemed to be paying no attention to Eric at all.

This didn't feel right. The hairs were standing up on his arms and on the back of his neck.

The figure seemed to be making a long-drawn-out scraping noise which reminded Eric of metal on metal, or stone. He felt a cold memory run up and down his spine and bury itself deep into his brain. He knew what that sound was. It was the sound of sharpening a sword or blade with a wet stone, and it meant danger.

"You are still here" said the voice, each word escaping from under the cloak like a convict escaping from prison. But the figure didn't stop what it was doing. Eric tried to think of something clever to say, but failed.

"Many have come here before me" said the voice, and the scraping noise stopped. "They did not leave, because they could not leave."

"Well, if it's all the same to you, I'd like to leave," said Eric quickly, and then added a "please" for good measure, because it couldn't hurt to remember his manners. Especially when talking to a figure wrapped in a big black cloak on the far side of a cave that seemed to be glowing. Not a lot was making sense to Eric right now, but if he could get out of this cleanly, he would.

The memory of a silvery sword being sharpened on a whetstone in a golden cave was hanging in the back of his mind. By adding this piece to the "what the hell is going on" puzzle, he was getting some rather worrying results. There weren't many people in this world that would dress in a big hooded black cloak, and Eric refused to let the name of the person he was thinking of appear in his mind, just in case it was true.

The cloaked figure slowly stood up. It was an awkward and jerky movement, and looked as though he was being pulled up by invisible strings like an extremely large puppet. When fully extended, the cloaked figure loomed a good two feet taller than Eric, who rarely came into contact with anyone much bigger than himself. Eric wasn't exactly a giant, but he was a few inches over six feet tall, and most people he met these days were either at his eye line or lower. It was a strange feeling having to arch his neck to look up at where he imagined the face might be inside the hood, which pretty much hid everything inside it. Eric squinted a little. He still couldn't make out who or what was inside, but he could make a pretty good guess.

Out of the corner of his eye Eric could see what had been making the noise. Hanging out of one of the arms of the cloak was a wide silver blade. The figure must have been sharpening it for a while, because the blade looked razor sharp, to the point where he couldn't actually see the edge; instead the blade disappeared into a thin blue glow along the edge.

He had seen that blade before. Out of nowhere a voice whispered in his ear, *"No blade or shield from the finest blacksmith could stand its equal, and no mortal weapon could defend against it."* It was a teacher's voice, but he had had so many teachers that it would be tough to pinpoint exactly which one had said those words to him.

Eric concentrated, and kept eye contact with the place where he had to assume this man's eyes were. The other arm of the cloak rose slowly and a thin white hand appeared and reached up to the hood. The hand was simply a collection of very long bony-looking fingers, with skin stretched thinly over each one. There was no colour to the skin – it was white as a sheet – but in this light it seemed to glow with a silvery haze. The fingers gripped the edge of the hood, and very slowly pulled it back.

Underneath the hood was the head and face of a man, and he looked very old and tired. Like his hand, the skin was stretched tight over the bone of his skull and jaw, and his eyes were two pools of black set deep in their sockets. His lips had lost all their colour, and his skin had a very faded washed-out look. He stared down at Eric. His breathing sounded heavy, and his angry eyes burnt deep into Eric's. With a single smooth motion the man raised the hand holding the sword, and held it in both of his thin skeletal hands, with the tip of the sword neatly placed between Eric's eyes.

Eric had never seen anyone look so intimidating, he stared up at the white man dressed all in black, and desperately thought of something to say or do.

"You remember me" said the man plainly. It wasn't a question. "But… you cannot remember remembering me," he added with a sigh.

"I've met you before?" said Eric, a little unsure. "That seems like something I would definitely remember." He could see his reflection in the sword, and he looked very small indeed.

"We have met several times Eric Mason, in this place. I am Death."

There was no emotion in the sentence. It was deep, as if the writing on a tombstone could speak.

"Really?" said Eric. It was not the strangest thing he had ever heard. Over the years he had seen and spoken to all sorts of men and monsters. Honesty was clearly going to be the best policy in this situation. He remembered the darkness from before, but that was in the cave under the Mountain. He did not remember this golden cave, and where he was or how he had got there was a mystery.

"Why is my memory not right?" he demanded.

Death said nothing. He glared at Eric, but after a minute or so a thin reptilian smile slowly crept onto his white face, which put Eric a little on edge.

"Many times you have come before me, Eric Mason, more times than any mortal should do, I might add" said Death meaningfully, his low voice echoing off the golden walls.

"Have I?" remarked Eric in surprise. He thought for a moment before adding, "where is this place?"

"You already know" said Death, and he was right. As if on cue, a memory long since forgotten slammed into the back of Eric's brain. He remembered everything; walking around in the darkness, trying to climb the walls to find a way out, but only reaching the crystal encrusted ceiling and falling back down. He remembered finding the cave of gold, and the figure dressed in black. But it wasn't just once, it was hundreds of times, if not thousands, he'd been here before.

Eric looked around the golden cave. Images and visions projected themselves into the cave somehow, showing Eric fighting for his life against the man in black. Each image seemed identical, yet somehow they were all different. Sometimes he looked like he was winning, whereas at others he could tell he was close to being beaten by the man in black. His appearance was different in each one. His hair was long and overgrown in some, but cut short in others, obviously depending on the fashion of the time. Eric winced at the clothes he was wearing in some of the visions. He noticed that they all seemed to have a ripped or rough look to them, which was a little worrying. He stared down at the clothes he was wearing now.

Eric sympathised with each of these visions. He knew how little he wanted to die. Death was something that happened to other people, in his view. He knew that he wasn't mortal, or immortal for that matter. He knew he could die, that was obvious when you've been shot at as many times as he had been, or set on fire, or pushed off a cliff, or frozen at the top of a mountain. But he just assumed that he kept on coming back for a reason, and he hadn't wanted to question it too much in case it stopped working. Maybe some god or other wanted to keep him alive, but Eric certainly hadn't expected to have to fight Death for his place in the land of the living.

"Eric Mason," said Death, "you do not allow me to do my duty, my purpose for being. You have sent many souls to meet me, yet yours still eludes me."

"Your duty?" exclaimed Eric. "But don't you kill people?" he added before he could stop himself.

"I take souls" said Death angrily, as if tired of explaining this to mortals. "I do not kill. I take that which is already dead to the other side where they belong."

Eric thought for a moment, watching the hundreds of visions of him around the cave. "So," he said thoughtfully, "you expect me to fight again?" Death nodded slowly. "Right... well, considering I seem to have bested you a lot in the past, wouldn't it just be easier all around to just let me go back?" he tried, and offered a friendly smile.

"No" said Death simply, and his black eyes narrowed on Eric.

CHAPTER 20

THE PRISON CELL

Eric Mason woke up. He hurt, and every part of his body was screaming at him in pain. He tried to open his eyes, and failed. He tried again. In front of them was nothing but darkness, although a faint light somewhere in the distance was creating faint shadows and outlines.

He was lying on his front, of that he was certain, so he tried turning his head to one side, but his neck sent a warning shot up and down his spine which buried itself deep into his brain, ordering him not to try again. He tried blinking, but even his eyelids hurt as they opened and shut over his dry and tired eyes.

"Great, now where am I?" he murmured through the haze of pain, fully hoping for a voice in his head to give him an answer, but failing to get one.

Eric decided to ignore the pain signals his body was giving

him; it would just have to deal with it. He managed to tuck both hands underneath his body, and with trembling arms he pushed himself off the ground and rolled onto his back. He lay on his back for a moment waiting for the pain to subside, but he wasn't sure this was any better than being on his front. But right now, Eric was in too much pain to care. He had woken up on what he was pretty sure was a hard metal floor. Considering he probably wouldn't have chosen to sleep on a metal floor, he had to assume someone had put him here, and knew straight away that that person would regret it. He would make sure of that.

Eric sat up and groaned. A sensor must have picked up his movement because a thick yellow glow started to shine from a long tube which ran along the length of the three in front of him. The light wasn't exactly bright, and it didn't travel very far, but judging by the room's contents, it wasn't really necessary. The room he was in was very small, barely ten feet across, and it had the feel of a prison cell. When was he going to stop waking up like this? It didn't happen all the time, but it happened often enough to be highly frustrating.

He rubbed his face with his hands, and noticed that they were illuminated by a light which was not coming from the strange yellow tubes around the room. If fact, it seemed to be coming from behind him. He twisted slightly and turned his aching neck so that he could see where this other light was coming from, and when he looked around he was greeted by his own reflection.

Behind him was a wall of silvery, shining liquid, like a mirror had melted, and it was framed by the yellow glowing tubes. His reflection looked as bad as he felt, and he sat there staring at himself for a moment. Although there was no breeze, the surface of the liquid rippled gently, warping his reflection like a carnival mirror.

Eric turned back around and strained his eyes to see into the room. There wasn't much in there with him. The main object was a box the size and shape of a coffin which was bolted on to one of the walls. That seemed to be all the furniture he had been given, and he couldn't help thinking that it didn't look much more comfortable than the floor he had been thrown on. Whoever had dragged him there could have at least dumped him on it rather than the floor. His body felt battered and bruised, again.

He braced himself, and let out a long hiss as he carefully got to his feet. His muscles were tired and he swayed slightly, but he was just about able to keep his balance. Taking small steps, he was able to turn around and face his reflection. His knees wanted to buckle under his weight, and he quickly took a few awkward steps backwards to stop himself from falling down, so that he ended up sitting on the hard metal box. He leaned back until he reached the wall, and shivered slightly as he felt the coldness of the metal.

Eric groaned. He was sick and tired of going from one prison cell to another. He wasn't a bad person, not all the time anyway, so why did everyone seem to think he deserved beating up and throwing in a cell? He'd killed people, yes, quite a few in fact, but only people who were trying to kill him. He'd stolen, yes, but nothing that anyone would have missed, and besides, it was usually food or alcohol; it wasn't as if he was a thief who stole people's jewellery. And yes, OK, he'd maybe helped in the fall of a few empires in his time, but he mostly just gave them a little push really.

Eric slumped forward and stared at the multi-coloured bruises and patchwork of cuts and scratches. Under his right eye was a big deep bruise, a gash ran down one cheek, and there was another on the other side which ran down his neck. He felt them with shaking fingers. The one on his neck felt the worst, but the bruise under his eye was in close second place. He continued to stare at his reflection for a while. It didn't look real. He almost expected it to wink, or smile, or something.

Eric had never seen anything like it before, and wanted a

closer look. His legs felt a little stronger after a few minutes' rest, so he got to his feet and walked over to the shimmering wall, keeping a close eye on his reflection in case it did anything different. When he got a few inches away he could hear a low humming sound coming from it, which had to mean it was being powered from somewhere. He looked around the edges, but there were no obvious wires or connectors.

Up close, the wall looked like a big rectangular puddle of mercury. He reached out a trembling hand, but before he could touch it, a static shock jumped up to his finger and ran down his arm.

"Dammit!" Eric exclaimed, and jumped backwards, shaking his hand vigorously. "Fucking... WALL!" he shouted at the top of his voice. He knew it wouldn't go down in the history books as a witty quotation, but it made him feel a little better. He sighed and shook his head "OK wall, let's try that again" he said, taking a step forward and raising his hand again. This time Eric decided to slap his entire palm onto the liquid surface, and white sparks jumped to and from his fingertips. A look of pain streaked across Eric's face, and he instinctively raised his other hand to pull the first one off. But this joined the first one on the wall, and Eric was trapped.

Around the edges of his fingers the liquid started pulsating and rippling outwards. Eric tried pulling his hands away, but silver liquid was starting to creep over his fingers, pinning them down. The thick, silvery liquid extended up his fingers, threatening to engulf his hands, until quickly Eric couldn't see either of them. Each time he tried to pull away, the wall would reach out thin silvery tendrils and he was sucked back down, while the pain shooting up both arms intensified.

Eric arched his back and gritted his teeth, his muscles screaming at him. The metallic liquid stretched up over his hands and flowed sluggishly up his forearms, all the way up to his elbows. The pain was now unbearable. He screamed again through gritted teeth, breathing heavily. He tried to concentrate, but it was hard. At last he found his hidden energy, and let it bubble up inside him a little, just to give him a little more strength. Pretty soon the white glow of the wall where his hands had been started to change to yellow. But the stronger Eric seemed to become, the stronger the wall became. The glowing yellow veins started to appear all up Eric's arms and were now rising up his neck.

With one last effort Eric heaved with all his strength and weight. This time he managed to pull out of the silvery liquid's grip, and his arms began to reappear. But the wall reacted, and Eric was jerked forward. He slammed into it, fully expecting to rip straight through to the other side. But he didn't. The wall held him steady, his entire body pressed up against it.

He stood there for a moment completely helpless, feeling the electricity crackling all along the edge of his body and face, and his skin burning and blistering. He had his eyes shut, trying desperately to push the pain away, but when he opened them, he saw that the wall was charging up. What had once been a silvery glow was now a brilliant white pulsating light. Then suddenly the wall's energy was cut off, and Eric was thrown clear across the small room. He hit the far wall, and then the metal floor below, very hard.

He lay there for a moment in disbelief. What the hell had just happened? Pain was ripping through every part of him. It felt as if each cell in his body was getting fried in hot oil. Lying face down on the metal floor he looked up to see the imprint of his body in the liquid. But the image was quickly fading, because he was now losing consciousness.

He tried to push himself up, and shook his head trying to focus, but he could not stop himself passing out and slumped back down to the floor. His eyes closed and everything went black.

CHAPTER 21

CAMP 53

It was very early morning in the camp outside the run-down city. The sun had only been up a little while, so there were still some frosty shadows around the place. The Army had been there a while now, and had decided to pitch camp in a clearing a mile outside the city limits, a safe distance away from any danger. They had chosen a large grassy area that looked like before the War it had been a park. Many years before it would have been full of happily-playing children. One area was very overgrown, but you could make out the skeletons of a swing and a roundabout. Their metal frames were covered in such a dense forest of frozen weeds and leaves that a passer-by might never notice them. The Army officers had ordered them to be rigged up with explosives and razor wire, so if anything tried coming through the playground, not all of them would make it to the other side.

Just outside the camp, parked near the main road, sat three large army trucks. The trucks were standard army issue, but their owners had taken it upon themselves to build up the bodywork to give them a little more strength, with better tyres for speed and handling. These trucks had been out in Zarda territory so long that they had taken on personalities of their own. One had metal strips welded across gashes and scars that ran along the bodywork, another had spikes riveted where they would catch the Zarda, should they decide to jump on. All three of them had been altered and remastered to give them the greatest powers of defence, and offence, a truck user could want.

The third truck was tricked out with spotlights, spikes, gun hatches and windows, and even a pipe out the back so that the driver could dispense slippery black oil in its trail. These trucks were not intended for simple troop or cargo transport. They were juggernauts which could ride a hurricane and come out the other side without missing a beat.

These trucks were mean, and looked like they had seen way more action than their owner's manual would recommend and survived. They didn't look as if they had been cleaned in a while though, and there were patches of dried blood mixed in with the mud and dirt. Clearly, when under attack by the Zarda, they didn't stick to the roads.

The Army officers had set their tents close together in a line, and the foot soldiers had set theirs in a ring around an ash pile that might have been a small campfire the night before. The officers' tents were off to one side near the medical tent and the command tent. Officers never liked having to walk far to give orders, or to get some aspirin for a hangover they'd got from drinking expired wine and beer the previous night.

At this hour there weren't many soldiers about, and snoring could be heard from the tents. Over the course of about ten minutes, a series of beeps indicated that the soldiers were waking up and turning off their alarm clocks.

Coming from all directions was the sound of distant activity. Squads of soldiers on foot were returning from night-watch duty in the security towers and perimeter patrols. Each squad consisted of six soldiers and a Captain or Sergeant. They trudged silently into camp from out of the frosty gloom and fog and headed straight for the warmth of the mess tent, several of them sighing a with relief to be back home alive.

Inside the mess tent were several large coffee machines, the sort found in the franchise coffee shops people used to love before the War. Each soldier poured himself a large measure of coffee and helped himself to protein bars and food rations before sitting down at one of the trestle tables.

The food and drink were then devoured in silence before they returned to their tents to dig their bunk-mates out of their shared beds. Thanks to a combination of damage through attacks, lack of supplies, overcrowding, and the Army's limited supply trucks and supply routes, virtually every soldier had a bunkmate. The night watch got to sleep in the bunk during the day, and the day squad used it during the night. Sleeping in shifts didn't bother the soldiers too much – they were normally too tired to care where they slept. They were just happy to be getting some sleep after a long shift, and on mornings like this it was good to know that there was someone keeping the bed warm for you when you got back from standing in the cold all night waiting to die of boredom, or Lykor attack.

This camp was one of only two that were left after many fatalities. They were both away from the city, and despite constant pleading from their officers, the Army had no more troops to send out to help them. The area was far too dangerous, and nearly all the supply trucks that were sent had failed to make it. It was becoming clear that the remaining camps would never be able to survive on their own, and the officers from the two camps made the executive decision to combine forces. That meant a quick boost in supplies for the two remaining camps, but they were quickly depleted.

Originally, the first camp's objectives were to enter the abandoned city, clear out any survivors and create a stronghold for the Army to set up a base. This would have been a good relay point for a supply route, with roaming squads, and to build up a base of operations deep in Zarda territory which had been lost a long time ago. But when the first camp failed its objective, the Army decided to push resources into maintaining this area.

The Army's Military Intelligence Agency had expected the odd attack from the Zarda in this area, which is why five camps were felt necessary, but none of them had expected quite so many Lykor nesting sites, or so many survivors in the city. The camps were fully stocked and armed to the teeth, but Military Intelligence hadn't expected the city's survivors to be hostile towards their troops. Based on the scout reports at the time they were expecting the city to be completely empty, and assumed any survivors would gladly welcome them.

The city had been ravaged by the Zarda a long time before the Army had strolled into town. The population, made up from mostly drifters and runaways, had rejected the Army's advances and plans to create a stronghold. On the basis that they had survived just fine before the Army arrived, they felt they would be fine without it too, which didn't sit too well with the type of officer who assumed everyone loved the Army and should consider themselves lucky it had come along when it had.

After early advances into the city's streets, soldiers came back with reports of rocks being thrown at them, shots being fired at them, and even reports of traps set for them. After losing several soldiers the Army and the rebels came to something of an agreement, and the Army restricted itself to the areas around the city limits. This of course didn't stop the officers sending secret squads into the city to map safe areas they could move in to, and to salvage what they could from the dying buildings and homes. Occasionally these squads returned with supplies, but at other times they didn't return at all, and further squads had to be sent to negotiate their release. This usually came at a high price, so each salvage squad was ordered not to be caught, at whatever cost.

The camp's next orders were to patrol the surrounding areas of the city and as much of the Zarda territory as possible, to seek out and map possible Lykor nests and enemy movements. This was done in the hope of earning the rebels' trust and eventually being allowed into the city. Once a nest had been identified, the scouting squads were to return to camp immediately and radio their report to headquarters. HQ would then dispatch fresh troops to reinforce the camp and neutralise the immediate threat. The theory was good, but after several ambushes on the connecting roads, the reinforcements became fewer and the camps were reduced to dealing with the nests themselves. It was fair to say that spirits were not high in any of the five camps, which led to widespread desertions, and the commanding officer's rubbish bins began to fill with transfer requests to other camps and squads. Over the space of a year, the five camps reduced until there was nothing left but to group the camps into two and hope for the best.

One tent did seem to stick out from the others. It was older, and covered in patchwork repairs. All the tents looked pretty old, but this one looked as if it had seen a lot more of the War than the other, and the owner didn't have much prowess with a sewing needle. It stood some distance from the other tents, not quite with the foot soldiers and not quite with the officers. It was close to the mess tent and showers, but if you didn't know it was there, it would be easy to miss.

Eric Mason was sound asleep. The early morning sunshine was filtering through the walls, and an icy morning wind was finding its way in through the gaps in the patches he had painstakingly sewn. But he was wrapped up warm in a cocoon of different coloured blankets. He had nearly died of cold on the first night, so now he wasn't taking any chances.

The morning sounds of night patrols trying to talk in quiet tones and the sounds of alarm clocks drifted through to his slumbering mind, and his snoring abated until he finally woke up. Eric hadn't needed to set an alarm clock in a long time, considering the Surroundsound effect of beeping alarms, the noise of all the coffee machines being used at once and the shouts of the day squads doing their morning callisthenics.

He sat up rubbing his face with his hands, and shivered a little in the cold air. He looked like a man who hadn't had a proper night's sleep in a very long time, and he had dark bags under his eyes. He swung his feet over the side of his bunk and slipped his feet into his boots. Eric had long ago discovered the advantages of sleeping in his clothes. No man should be forced to defend his life in his underwear during a night-time skirmish.

He stood up and slowly walked out of his tent, yawning and scratching. Outside, the camp was starting to fill with soldiers. The day squads were made up of three main patrol squads, and several salvage teams. One squad was in the clearing doing a mixture of jumping jacks, push-ups and other cardio exercises. The soldiers from another squad were either eating breakfast or making their way from the mess tent to the showers. Another squad were checking and maintaining the trucks and other engineering necessities.

Eric yawned loudly and stretched out in every direction. He thought of joining the soldiers for some exercise, but the thought didn't last long. His tent was some distance from the middle of the camp, as neither the soldiers nor the officers wanted him to camp with them, but this suited him just fine. He wasn't an officer and had no intention of becoming one, so he had no right, apparently, to sleep near men and women who were. But this simply meant he could pick where he wanted to pitch his tent, and he had, of course, decided to pick an area close to food and drink, with showers nearby. He looked around at all the moving bodies, and decided to get breakfast in the mess tent.

As he entered, the mess tent fell silent instantly, and all eyes turned to watch him as he helped himself to a large measure of coffee and food rations and sat down alone to have breakfast. No one wanted to be associated with Eric, which meant he usually got a table to himself, and that suited him down to the ground because it meant he could eat in peace. As he started eating his poor excuse for breakfast, the rest of the tent slowly turned back to their conversations, completely ignoring him. Eric didn't notice.

The food was mostly rehydrated meat and eggs, which tasted as unpleasant as it sounds. The coffee was pretty good though, thanks to the franchise coffee shops, and coffee and machines were easy to find. Because of the War, there was very little fresh food in shops and supermarkets, so pretty much all food came from a can or powdered in a packet. But it filled the stomach, and there might have been a few nutrients and minerals in there, somewhere.

Eric could hear the sound of Sergeants outside shouting at men and women to work faster or harder than they already were. Even those eating breakfast got shouted at, as apparently they could not eat, shower and dress fast enough for them. One of the less-experienced Sergeants tried to order Eric to speed up his breakfast and get out on patrol, but Eric simply ignored him, and he went off to shout at someone else.

The trucks outside were loaded up and ready to go with water, fuel, ammo and enough food rations to last a few days in case of emergencies. Eric left the mess tent feeling totally unsatisfied by his breakfast, as usual. He stood watching the soldiers climb aboard the trucks and the dust kicked up by the tyres as each truck headed off in a different direction. He finished the last of the coffee n his mug, pocketed the few foil-wrapped food rations he had taken while no one was looking, and headed for the camp's showers.

The showers were pretty grim at the best of times, having been fashioned out of salvaged sheets of rusting metal and any other scraps the soldiers could find around lying around the city limits. Big tanks of water were suspended in the air by scaffolding, and underneath were several shower heads and pull chains. The idea was simple. An engineer had tapped into the local water supply pipe, so the tanks filled up with fairly clean water, and the dirty soldiers would get clean by pulling on the chain to open the shower heads. The water was always cold, especially on mornings like this, and there wasn't much soap to go around, but nevertheless you didn't want to go too long without a proper clean. Those soldiers who didn't like taking cold showers in the mornings were often shunned by the others, for obvious reasons. And if the other soldiers could smell you, then so could the Zarda's pet Lykor, who could pinpoint your exact position in seconds, and they didn't stay alive much longer after that.

Eric walked into the shower's changing area, pulled his clothes off and hung them up with the others on the rough metal spikes someone had riveted to the thin metal walls. He washed himself in the usual quick-tempo way of everyone trying to wash in cold water.

Hanging around the shower area were a few men whom Eric recognised as scavenger rank soldiers. The barrier that had once divided the men from the women had long since collapsed, and a couple of the women who were showering opposite smiled at him as he took his place under a shower head and pulled the chain, releasing a waterfall of freezing water. The icy water hit Eric hard and ran down his body, making him flinch slightly. He had got used to cold showers, and whenever he heard someone complaining about them, he would remember the days of his youth, when every shower was a cold shower, unless you were lucky enough to have been born into a rich family, unlike Eric.

He rubbed the cheap soap over his body. It was one of the bars that had been salvaged from the city, and it didn't clean much, but it moved the dirt around until the water washed it away.

Eric would not have described himself as good-looking, though perhaps better than average, and he had the sort of body only a high protein diet, coffee and lots of exercise could produce. He knew he was in good shape; with all the running to and from danger, he had to be.

He stood under the torrent of water and listened to the soldiers chatting away, trying not to make eye contact with any of them. But as expected, the conversation soon turned to Eric.

"I hear you lost some more good men yesterday," said one of the male soldiers to Eric over the rush of water. He turned to the others. "How long do you think it'll take for him to kill us all?" He laughed. Eric stood quietly and continued washing, pretending he hadn't heard him.

"Hey, Eric" called one of the other soldiers in a loud voice, "have you ever gone out on patrol without killing someone?" This was followed by loud laughter. Clearly they found each other extremely funny.

"Leave it alone, fellas" said one of the female soldiers, winking at Eric. "I'm sure it's not his fault that they got killed. We are at war you know, deep in enemy territory." Eric couldn't help thinking this was a bit of a back-handed compliment.

"Yeah" agreed another female soldier. "People get killed all the time around here, you boys are just jealous you haven't had any of the more dangerous patrols. I heard they've just found the biggest nest so far," she added excitedly,

"Clearly she hasn't been out on many patrols then," Eric murmured. The newer and less experienced soldiers were always excitable. Fresh from the Academy, eager to do their bit for the War effort, they wanted to kill some enemy, fight some Lykor and come home heroes dripping in medals. The more experienced soldiers knew that every day could be their last, and a big nest simply meant that chances were it wouldn't be medals you would come home dripping in.

"Any patrol with Eric is a dangerous patrol" said the first soldier, ignoring the woman's comments. "The sooner he gets himself killed instead of the rest of us, the sooner this area gets a little safer for all concerned."

"Shut up Dave," snapped the woman. "You're just embarrassing yourself." She gave Eric a sideways glance and a coy half-smile.

Eric flashed her a quick smile and finished washing, then pulled the chain to cut his icy shower. "I've got an idea, if you're up for it I mean?" said Eric calmly. "How about you all come visit the new nest we've found?"

The question hit home. Eric saw all four of the young male soldiers go a little pale. These scavenger soldiers had seen no real action. They liked to talk big, as all young men do, but the thought of actually going out to one of the nest sites sent a chill down their spines. He couldn't blame them though. They were only kids after all – the oldest of the bunch couldn't have been much older than twenty, and the youngest looked in her mid to late teens. There were a few grunts, but none of them came up with a response.

Eric gave a casual salute to the girl who had smiled at him, then turned and walked out of the shower area to collect his clothes, tying a towel around his waist. From behind him he heard the female soldiers laughing at the guys, who he knew were giving the back of Eric's head some really dirty looks.

Eric fished out the food rations he had stolen, dumped his dirty clothes in the hamper by the shower's entrance and selected a clean uniform from a pile of folded clothes. Then he made his way slowly back to his patchwork tent.

A few moments later a soldier appeared running through the camp, dodging and ducking around obstacles and other soldiers before entering Eric's tent at speed. It was then clear to everyone outside that an argument was happening in the tent. Someone was clearly getting pushed into the canvas wall a few times.

After a minute or two the soldier re-emerged from the tent backwards as fast as he had entered it, like a drunk being thrown out into the street. He rolled head over heel on the ground and sprang back onto his feet like a cat, before trying to run back inside the tent. Just then Eric stepped out of his tent, doing the buttons up on his trousers and carrying a vest, and the soldier skidded to a halt.

The onlookers saw Eric shaking his head and trying to go back inside the tent, but the soldier grabbed his arm each time to stop him. Eventually Eric gave up and agreed to follow the soldier, and the pair walked to the command tent at the other side of camp. They both entered, with Eric dramatically holding the tent flap open and ushering the soldier in first. If Eric could have slammed the tent flap shut, he would have.

There was a lot happening inside the command tent; the few officers the camp had were rushing around and falling over themselves to shout orders at each other, or at any foolish soldier who happened to be near the entrance. In the middle of the tent was a large round wooden table, covered in maps detailing the city and the surrounding towns and villages. Eric mused over these while he stood patiently waiting for all the shouting to stop.

Each map had obviously been marked several times, and then the marks had been rubbed out and replaced with others. The different colour markings indicated the different territories in the local area. Red meant enemy bases and strongholds, blue showed Army camps and outposts and green was for the rebels in the city. There were yellow markings too, for civilian-populated towns and villages, but there weren't many of those left.

Eric wasn't worried about the rebels. In his opinion they were poor men and women who had no interest in fighting a war and had been forced to forage in the surrounding ruins for food and tradeable goods. the Army didn't like talking about it, but they had a pretty good trade route with the rebels, mainly because they were able to salvage things the scavenger squads couldn't, or wouldn't, have thought to look for. Eric himself had been in their stronghold a few times, trading things he'd salvaged in buildings, or stolen from the Army, and had made a fairly decent profit on some things, like booze. Most of the rebels had lived all their lives in that city, and knew every street, road, and area worth plundering for goods. They were fast and intelligent, and could pretty much adapt to anything the Army or the Zarda could throw at them. They were builders too, and even the children had become experts in setting quick traps for anyone who was not too vigilant.

The Army, on the other hand, filled its ranks with young men and women straight from the hundreds of military academies across the globe, which in Eric's opinion were dumbing down their intelligence and common sense. In the past, armies had beaten and shouted at their soldiers to turn them into ruthless killing machines that could think for themselves, fight when needed, and didn't care for the luxuries the civilians had, like shampoo or branded clothes. These soldiers were, in Eric's opinion, no more than big children. Eric suspected governments had been adding too much oestrogen to their food and drinking water before the War, because he seemed to see more effeminate boys than actual men, and they were all 'sensitive to each other's feelings' apparently. They needed to be told what to do every step of the way, and Eric had heard that they couldn't fail the Academy's tests because there weren't any. You advanced through an Academy because of age, not exams. So it didn't matter if a soldier wasn't any good at being a soldier, it might hurt their feelings if they were told they were stupid or not very good at their job.

They mused over the maps a little while longer, and the noise was starting to simmer down a little. The blue areas on the map in front of him had been drawn on, rubbed out, and drawn on again so many times it looked like an angry toddler had attacked the paper with crayons in trying to draw a brightly-coloured animal they had only ever heard about. All the maps were a mess of different-coloured smears that made them very difficult to read. Eric was glad it wasn't his job to decipher them.

The noise in the tent was silenced by a crackling of radio noise from the camp's only decent long-range radio equipment. Because of the War, the world had had to shut down several of the usual forms of communications; the Zarda seemed to be able to smell the signals in the air, and the only place you could get internet was in some of the major megacities. Even there, only the very wealthy and influential could afford to enjoy the internet.

Mankind had taken it all for granted; when internet and phone signals first went down, there was uproar across the lands from everyone. But if you asked someone today, they'd probably say they didn't miss the social media and dating websites, or the silly videos of animals playing. It was mostly the younger generation that couldn't cope without internet or mobile phones, as they had never lived in a world without them, which made the older generations laugh. The fashion for uploading everything you were thinking onto social media sites in the desperate hope of being 'found' and getting famous was now a thing of the past. And Eric, for one, was glad. The more social media took over, the less intelligent everyone seemed to be.

The radio static cut through the noise of the tent and everyone stopped to watch the radio technician fiddling with the dials and aerial, trying to change the signal into something audible. After a few moments, and a couple of ear-piercing tones, a voice broke through the static; it was the familiar voice of the headquarters operator. Each outpost, barracks, camp and roaming unit was assigned its very own operator, which was handy in the beginning, because it gave work to all the hundreds of accountants, salesmen and women, customer service advisers and account managers that had been made redundant as soon as the War started.

It was probably a good idea, seeing as these mildly intelligent men and women didn't have much in the way of transferable skills to aid in the War effort. Most people before the War were far more interested in their image, and trying to sell themselves as a brand in a desperate attempt to get famous somehow. After a few weeks of fighting the Zarda their numbers had got fewer, and Eric had assumed, correctly, that the more difficult and arrogant or less than averagely intelligent ones had died at the front line.

All ears were on the radio. The big news everyone was waiting for was information about any Zarda activity heading their way, or when reinforcements would be arriving to help tackle the big nest Eric and the scouting squads had discovered. It was probably the largest nest Eric had seen up close, and he had lost a few good men when they were detected by the Lykor. After Eric's report on the nest, they were all hoping Headquarters would be sending several reinforcing squads, and preferably a tank or two.

Whenever the Army had to send fresh troops to a camp they usually came stocked with fresh supplies and provisions, which, whether they liked it or not, they shared with the camp. Eric had heard of several officers getting into trouble falsely reporting large enemy movements to Headquarters and taking the supplies and rations for themselves. Headquarters took a dim view of officers cheating the system, which was why Eric took every opportunity to do so, seeing as he wasn't a 'proper officer' or a 'proper foot soldier'. Not to mention it was fun.

It amused Eric when he saw the faces drop when the news came through loud and clear on the radio that there were no available troops to reinforce them and no available supplies to be transferred. Because of the reports they were getting from other camps and outposts, their orders were to pack up and bug out of the area immediately.

There was a deafening silence in the tent when the operator had finished her announcement. So much so that she had to ask if they were still there. The radio technician was the first to break the silence. He thanked the voice for her time and switched the radio off.

Eric looked around. He appeared to be standing in a forest of statues, and he resisted the urge to wave a hand in front of them. No one wanted to be the first to speak. Eyes swivelled in their sockets, and the only noise in the tent was the technician putting away the radio equipment.

"We'd um... we'd better start recalling the salvagers and patrol units" said the Major, not making eye contact with anyone.

"What?" exclaimed a voice. Eric looked around and a cold shiver ran down his spin. He had said it himself.

"You have something to add... Commander?" asked the Major. All faces were turned to Eric.

"Oh shitty bollocks" Eric muttered to himself. "Oh well, I figured... if we weren't going to get any fresh troops, we could handle the Lykor nest ourselves?"

He knew this would not get a good response, and he could feel his feet trying to walk him out of the tent. "We... by which I mean you, of course, have the manpower... we could deal with this threat ourselves, couldn't we? I mean you, of course," he added.

This last comment split the crowd in half. Some of the officers who looked a little more accustomed to the War, and had the scars to prove it, were nodding. The other half, who had much softer skin and looked like they hadn't been expecting to do any fighting at all, had shocked looks on their faces. Luckily the Major, who had been the one to address the voice of the operator on the radio, looked like he belonged to the first half, and was staring at the table of maps thoughtfully.

"You're not seriously considering this, are you?" exclaimed one of the female captains, who had a very worried look on her face.

"Those nests are full of beasts."

"I'm not sure," said the Major, looking up. When he saw her rank he snapped, "It is not your decision - *Captain*."

"But you can't seriously be considering... " the Captain continued, like a mother speaking to a small child who has asked to jump off a roof with a towel tied round its neck. She had completely ignored the Major's tone.

"I don't see why not, Captain. We do have fighting men and women in this camp, it's the main reason a lot of them join up as soldiers, to fight the Zarda you see," said the Major to a wave of muffled laughter from the other officers around them.

This Captain was one of those women who had never expected in a million years to find herself in a remote outpost and faced with the prospect of action on the front line. She was determined to make the best of her time in the Army; she'd risen through the ranks, but only so that she could give the orders rather than take them from people she didn't consider her betters, or equals. But right now, she was damn sure she wasn't about to get ripped to shreds by some werewolf out in the muddy countryside. She had made friends with the other like-minded women around the camp, who had made her their unofficial leader, and her few remaining years in the Army were supposed to be simple and easy. No stress, no danger, just an easy downhill slope to citizenship. Then she would move into her well-deserved house, with a husband she hadn't met yet (that was just a minor detail), and live happily ever after.

"What's the matter soldier, are you trying to live forever?" said one of the other Captains.

The woman spun round to face the fool who had dared to disagree with her point of view, and fixed him with a stare that could have stopped a rhinoceros.

"You men are all the same!" she exclaimed in a shrill voice. "You'd rather charge headfirst into a nest of Lykor than do a bit of actual work for once. I take it all you men will be expecting us women to do the packing do you?"

"A bit of actual work?" asked the Captain who had dared to speak, little taken aback by the woman's glare. "We are soldiers, Captain. We're fighting a war. Going into battle and fighting the Zarda *is* our work. It's our job in this territory to clear the surrounding areas, report back to headquarters and then go out and find some more war to fight. When the War is over, maybe you could raise all those little babies you keep chatting about with the other women and all this could just be a bad dream. We all know why women like you join up, and if we keep bugging out and retreating every time we come across a little bit of danger... well, we'd all be living on top of each other behind great big walls. Until the Zarda work out how to get past them too, and then where will you be? Complaining that people like us, here and now, should have done more about stopping the danger."

This little speech got a murmuring of approval from the other officers and some nearly started clapping, but stopped themselves just in time.

"Captain Jarvis has a point," the Major started saying, but he was quickly interrupted by Jarvis herself.

"Oh you would agree with him?" she snapped. "All you men stick together, it's not easy being a woman in this man's army." There were nods from the other women, and groans and eye rolls from male officers, and even a few women. "Well, I for one will not be a part of this," she said, scowling at the women who had not agreed with her straight away, but now it was the Major's turn to interrupt.

"It is not, Captain, a matter of being men or women," said the Major quickly but calmly. "In the Army, as well you all know, we are not considered men and women but human beings, and you will do as you are ordered by your superior officer."

Captain Jarvis looked close to bursting. Her brain told her

many times a day that she was in charge, so it confused her when someone of higher rank put her in her place. Eric did feel sorry for her, she so wanted to be in charge of this situation.

The Major walked meaningfully past the Captain and over to the table in the centre of the tent, where he picked up the map Eric had been looking at earlier. With a theatrical flourish, he walked back to where everyone was standing.

"Not a problem, Captain, no one is ordering you to join this assault if you don't want to. I think we would much prefer soldiers with combat experience," he added, a little more spitefully than he meant to. "Besides, as you point out, there will be a lot of packing to do, if we aren't successful, and if you're not going to fight, there's only one job left that'll need doing." He turned away, concentrating on the map.

This got the desired response. Captain Jarvis stamped her foot hard on the ground, spun around and stormed out of the tent with the other 'mother soldiers' in hot pursuit. Eric strained his neck so he could watch her walk across the camp, and saw her kick what looked like a bucket as hard as she could. If she was a cartoon drawing, she would have had wavy angry lines floating around her.

The officers started to crowd around the map, pushing and shoving as politely as possible and slotting together like a human jigsaw. It was at this moment that Eric felt it would be a good time to leave. There would probably be a lot of questions asked, a lot of orders given, and he didn't feel like having any of them directed at him, despite feeling partially responsible for all this. OK, completely responsible, but if they decided not to attack, and were needing to bug out, he had a few things he would rather keep hidden. There was one bag in particular in his tent that really didn't need finding its way into someone else's hands.

He tried to edge himself out of the way, but the press of bodies kept him locked in, and there was nothing for it but to draw attention to himself, again.

"Well" he said in a loud clear voice to get heard over the mumblings of others, "looks like you don't need me here for this part, so I'll…" He was interrupted before he could finish.

"Ah yes, Commander Mason, we'll need you to detail exactly what we are going up against" said the Major, not taking his eyes off the map. "Do you have any ideas on the size or numbers in this nest? How many of the Lykor did you see?"

Eric tried to think of a number big enough to give them an idea of what they would be up against, but not so high as to scare them off all together. "Er… from what I saw, you may be looking at about thirty, maybe thirty-five?" he suggested.

The intake of breath from everyone around him told Eric that he had gone too high. He wondered what they would have said if he had told them the truth. He was banking on headquarters sending a fresh transfer of soldiers to tackle this nest with them. They had the manpower there sure, but a few extra guns and hands to hold them wouldn't have gone amiss. Especially as there were way more than forty Lykor in that nest, maybe more.

"It might be fewer than that," he said quickly. "Worst case scenario I would say. We could really use a few more soldiers than we have, but it's nothing we can't handle ourselves," he added, looking around at the now unsure faces. "We've faced the rebels in the city before, and there were a lot more of them." Luckily this got a few nods from some of the officers who had been there.

"Yes, but the rebels didn't have razor sharp teeth, or the strength of five men, or move as quickly," said the Major thoughtfully. "If what you say is true, then we really need some reinforcements, I'm not in the business of going back on my word, and I would rather Samantha wasn't proved right about whether we should attack or run." There were nods from a few men who had been on the receiving end of Captain Jarvis's 'I told you so' look.

"What about the other camps in the area, there's still one or two nearby, aren't there?" asked Eric. "Surely they would have been given the same orders as us... I mean you... and there's always safety in numbers. Let's get onto the radio with them, and get them to ship everything they have over here as fast as they can." He figured this would do the trick, but all he got were more unhappy and concerned faces.

There was a pause while the Major thought about this. "Good point, well made. I wonder if any of them are crazy enough to think about taking this nest down with us," he said at last.

"I doubt it" said the Captain who'd spoken out against Samantha earlier. "The few outposts left in this area are manned by skeleton crews, but one or two of the camps might have supplies we could use, if they haven't already been overrun. But I wouldn't put much hope in persuading Camp 215 to help. I went to the Academy with their Captain. He' s not a very bright man and he would follow whatever orders he was, no matter what alternatives there might be."

"Excellent point" said Eric. "I say we get them on the radio and give them a few orders from the Major, and get everyone here to gear up, take out the nest. Then it's medals all around" he added, smiling and waving his hands.

The mention of medals perked up a few ears. After a soldier had served his time and was awarded citizenship, the more medals and commendations he had, the more money and status he could expect as a civilian. An ex-soldier could live out the rest of his life quite comfortably with a bit of money and respect behind him. Even lowly foot soldiers who'd come back missing a few limbs but covered in medals of bravery could expect a relatively expensive house in a decent district in one of the less crowded megacities, along with enough Army Credits for a comfortable retirement.

"Where's the radio engineer?" shouted the Major over his shoulder, and the man appeared at the back of the ring of officers. "Get on the blower to the other camps and outposts within a ten-mile radius and get me their commanding officers. I want to know how many soldiers they have, what supplies they can carry, and how quickly they can be here. OK?"

"Yes sir!" shouted the radio soldier, and disappeared.

"The rest of you" continued the Major, "get me inventory on exactly what we have here. I want lists here in half an hour!"

A few officers rushed away, leaving a gap behind Eric, who took this opportunity to slide out of the circle and walk as casually out of the tent as possible. Outside, he stood in front of the command tent listening to all the shouting and radio static from inside. He fumbled in his pockets and produced a battered-looking pack of cigarettes. Smoking was allowed on campus, but it was frowned upon, seeing as the only way you could have got cigarettes out here was to have either traded for them with the salvage teams or salvaged them yourself. Both of which were chargeable offences.

He lit one and stood there taking a few drags, enjoying the smoke filling his lungs and blowing thick clouds into the air above him. As the shouting from inside the tent got louder he chuckled a little to himself, turned on his heel, and walked slowly towards his tent with smoke billowing out of him like a steam train. He was in a good mood for a change.

Reaching his tent, Eric finished the cigarette, stubbed it out with his boot, and entered. A few seconds went past before he re-emerged carrying a rucksack over his shoulder and brushing dirt off his hands. He looked around to make sure no one was paying him any attention, picked the direction that would get him out of camp the fastest, and walked off in the direction of the city as casually as he could. There was no real rush. It had probably take a while for each camp to radio back with their inventory, and for the officers to persuade the surrounding outposts to join in on this attack.

CHAPTER 22

THE ABANDONED CITY

The city was falling apart. Weeds had grown tall and strong through the cracks in the pavement and roads, and the wind was doing a good job of blowing dust from one area to another and then back again. Several of the buildings had lost their roofs, and glass from windows broken a long time ago littered the ground. The entire place was silent, except for the occasional creaking of buildings in the wind and the sound of Eric's footsteps walking down one of the roads. The sun had melted most of the frost now. There were still a few crunchy patches around, but overall it looked quite attractive, considering it looked as if a hurricane had been through it.

Eric liked walking through the quiet city; it was oddly peaceful. He had seen a fair few deserted towns and cities over the past few years, but none were as nice as this one. The closer to the centre of the city he got, the taller the buildings were. He had been through several of the houses in this area already, and there was never much in them. Most of the homes had been stripped by salvager squads, but he liked just sitting in the rooms. They were mostly filled with broken picture frames and faded photos of smiling faces. He would try to imagine what sort of family might have been living there.

He had learnt a very long time ago not to open any of the fridges or freezers, as after this much time there was nothing but eye-watering smells and mould spores. In some of the cupboards he'd found tinned and dried foods, which he would quickly liberate by putting them in his bag. Even after all this time, some of them were still in date.

The tinned foods were the best finds. They seemed to last forever, but Eric often wondered about the quality of what went into the tin to start with. Before the War you could buy them extremely cheaply, because they lasted so long, and the contents weren't held up to too much scrutiny. They were mostly 'mechanically-recovered meats', which simply meant whatever fell out of the grinding machines after a hose down, which then got drowned in some kind of sauce to disguise the taste, and sold to the poor.

The big money was finding silverware, tools, or alcohol, which could be traded quite easily to anyone Eric came across. Or drunk if it was a particularly good bottle, which happened more often than not. Eric was never one to see good booze wasted on anyone other than himself.

Getting closer to the centre, Eric found himself in the shadows of high-rise buildings and apartments. It felt colder here somehow, and cars and vans littered the streets where they'd been abandoned, gradually going rusty. The occasional decomposed body, more bone than anything else now, told stories of attacks either from the Zarda or the Lykor. Smears of long-dried blood still stained some of the buildings and pavements, and in some areas you could see the spray of desperate bullets etched forever into brickwork and signs. There had not been a reported Lykor attack in the city for a long time now. Eric had heard that a few hunting packs had come by on more than one occasion, but they'd found nothing worth eating, so they moved on. Everyone was a winner – except for the unsuspecting army camp or outpost they happened to find next.

Other cities weren't so lucky. Several places across the land were plagued with constant Lykor attacks, but the residents there had taken precautions, and the Army had made sure they were well defended. It didn't stop the attacks, but it probably helped during the midnight ambushes. The creatures were clearly learning to adapt to the different parts of the world they found themselves in. This city, however, would be a playground for them in comparison, with not a soldier in sight. Eric could walk for hours and not find any sign of life, and from what he could make out, that was how the rebels liked it.

The Lykor didn't seem to worry the rebels much; they were more bothered by the Army constantly trying to move into their city and salvage goods the rebels could use. Eric had explained carefully that if the Army wanted to, they could wipe the rebels off the face of the planet. Or turn up in force, and arrest the lot of them and throw them in jail. Only they probably wouldn't, because it wouldn't be very good publicity for them if word managed to get back to the megacities that the Army were arresting people, rather than fighting the Zarda. Although they would probably describe the Rebels as extremists, or terrorists, or whatever word they could use to make their civilians think it was a good thing they were doing. It had worked fine before the War, so no reason it wouldn't work after. Eric had tried to talk the rebel leader round to the idea of letting the Army into his city too, but he was a very stubborn man.

Eric walked through the maze of alleyways and side roads, taking turns apparently at random with his head down and eyes alert for traps. Just because the Rebels didn't advertise their existence to the world, this didn't mean they liked unwelcome guests. He stepped over the occasional trip wire, and slid carefully past loosely-placed scaffolding that would, if triggered, drop several tons of building onto the heads of unsuspecting Lykor or soldiers.

The traps blended seamlessly into the background, making them difficult to see, and once triggered they would create a very natural-looking disaster, one which any intruder might dismiss as an accident. Eric had accidentally tripped one once. It had hurt, and taken ages to heal. After that he kept a keen eye out for them.

Turning a corner, he heard a sound above him that made him look up. Some tennis balls had come bouncing out of one of the second-storey windows, and they landed less than ten feet in front of him. He'd seen this before, and with lightning speed he pulled a cloth rag out of his pocket and tied it around his face so it covered his mouth and nose. Without missing a beat he ducked down behind a pile of bricks and other construction materials, and waited.

The tennis balls exploded one by one with bangs that echoed off the walls, nearly deafening Eric and sending shards of glass and rusty screws out in all directions. This was followed by clouds of thick dusty smoke that stung the eyes and choked the throat and lungs. The haze of smoke filled the alleyway and engulfed Eric in his hiding space. He looked over the edge of a pile of bricks, and through his streaming eyes he saw four shadowy figures moving fast towards him.

Eric threw down his bag and leapt out of his hiding place like a panther. The smoke was thick, so he couldn't see too well, but he quickly found his first attacker. He'd found what felt like an arm in a jacket, and by gripping it with both hands, Eric was able to throw the first guy into the nearest wall as hard as he physically could. The man he threw must have tripped a wire, because Eric heard the crash and scream as a lot of loosely-built-up masonry fell down in a pile on top of his attacker. He didn't have time to find out the extent of the damage, because he needed to turn his attention to the other shadows that had spread out in the narrow alleyway. The attackers were shouting orders to each other. One of the orders must have been to stay out of his reach, because each time he advanced on a silhouette, it backed into the fog and out of sight.

Eric spun around a few times, trying to find somewhere he could stand where he could see all three remaining attackers at once, but each time he found a spot, they'd move quickly out of sight. His foot kicked something on the floor, and Eric found one of the smoke grenades. In one smooth motion he picked it up and launched it at the nearest silhouette. A yelp came from the direction he had thrown it, which made Eric smile. It was probably quite a shock to catch something and find it was red hot. But it meant that whoever had caught it would possibly stand still for a minute. He ran towards the voice he'd heard, and kicked out hard with a boot, which connected with a something fairly solid. It wasn't a strong kick, but it had a lot of weight behind it, so whoever had been on the receiving end wouldn't be getting up any time soon.

Tears and sweat were starting to pour down Eric's face. The smoke was stinging his eyes, and he could feel them going red. He knew that rubbing them would only make them worse. It wouldn't be long before he wouldn't be able to see anything, and worst of all, his cloth mask was beginning to get damp and heavy. He had to raise a hand to it to keep it from slipping down. He had no intention of breathing in any of this smoke, but this meant he was limited to only having one hand to attack and defend with.

Something hit Eric across the side of his head with a crash, and a tinkling sound on the floor made him assume, correctly, that someone had just smashed a glass bottle over him. Who goes into a fight with a bottle? thought Eric A bat, maybe. A knife, sure. But a glass bottle? His head rang like a bell. He reached down and pulled a long hunting knife out of his belt, and held it ready. If that was how they wanted to play it... He felt the wind of an object as it flew past his ear, and heard the same crash of broken glass by his feet, and then another, and another. His attackers were throwing bottles down from above him, possibly from one of the many windows or roofs.

"Bastards!" shouted Eric to the smoke in general, and a few more bottles hit the ground next to him.

"Is that you, Eric Mason?" came a voice somewhere above Eric in the smoke.

Eric thought quickly and then shouted "Yes! Stop throwing shit and fight like men!" He held the knife by his side, hoping it wouldn't be seen.

There was a pause for a long moment, and then bottles rained down all around him in their dozens, several of them smashing over Eric's head and shoulders and forcing him to the ground. He tried putting out a hand to cushion his fall, but found nothing but broken glass around him, and it was slicing deep cuts into his hand and arm. Each time he tried to get up another hail of bottles rained down on him and forced him back into a half kneel. He tried to run to one side, in the hope of getting to some less dangerous ground, but a bottle that hadn't broken found its way under one of his feet and Eric flew onto his back. Sharp points of glass pierced his clothes, and he felt as if the ground was trying to eat him with hundreds of tiny teeth and claws.

Just then two bottles hit Eric on either side of his head, making him scream out in pain and clutch at his head with both hands. Blood was pouring through his fingers and down his face and neck, mixing with the sweat and making a puddle underneath him. He tried desperately to wipe it out of his eyes, while looking around for the next attack. Without a hand to hold it up the cloth fell from his mouth, and Eric started to hack and cough on the dust and smoke. It filled his lungs with dry pain, and quickly it became difficult to breath. The rain of bottles stopped almost as suddenly as it had started, and the alleyway was silent apart from Eric sliding around in the broken glass.

The smoke started to drift away as the breeze picked up a little, and soon there was very little left in the alleyway around Eric. He heard the sound of glass crunching underfoot, and then gloved hands reached down from all directions and groped at Eric. He tried to see who it was, but his vision was seriously blurred, and all he could make out were rough shapes. The hands swung him up on to his feet, and hauled him forward, with his feet tripping on bottles and shards of razor-sharp glass.

When the smoke finally cleared, Eric looked around to see that he was surrounded by men and women. From what he could see, they were all very heavily dressed, with thick cloth masks tied tightly over their mouths and noses and goggles protecting their eyes from the smoke. Eric was hauled in front of a rough-looking man, evidently the leader, who eyed him up and down critically.

"So this is the great and mighty Eric Mason" said the man, pulling his mask away to reveal a gnarled and scarred face. "I would expect better from someone with your reputation. I've heard you can't be killed."

"Mere rumour, I assure you" mumbled Eric sarcastically. He was getting a little light-headed from blood loss. "I just don't die easily. I came here to trade, not to fight, and I have information your fearless leader will want to hear." He shook off the two men holding him up.

"Really, and why should I care why you are here?" said the man. "I see anything in an army uniform... it dies!" This comment was growled at Eric, and got murmurs of agreement from the others. "What information could you possibly have that would interest us?"

"I said for your boss, not you," said Eric testily. The man swung a punch at his head, which Eric expertly dodged. "I need to speak with him." He smiled as if nothing had happened.

The leader growled loudly, and swung another punch. Again Eric dodged it easily, but then the other men grabbed his arms, and the leader treated Eric to a series of punches to the torso, like a boxer hitting a punchbag, before kicking him in the centre of his chest, which sent him flying. As he tried to stand up, a thick black canvas bag was dropped over his head, and string was wrapped tightly around his wrists.

"Is this really necessary?" asked Eric, his voice muffled by the bag.

The leader spun around, grinning at his audience, and held a single finger up to his lips for quiet. He then raised his other hand for all to see, and made a fist. His grin made him look like a jungle cat about to pounce, and Eric could feel the tension around him growing. He strained to hear every sound around him through the hood.

The man carefully positioned himself in front of Eric and pulled his fist back. Eric heard a soft tinkle of glass moving under the man's foot, and the slight intake of breath from the other men. He caught the soft sound of the man's jacket creasing as he moved into action. Eric ducked. The gloved fist missed Eric by less than an inch, and the unexpected miss pulled the man off balance so that he fell forward into Eric. Eric allowed the man to lean back before kicking out. The blow caught the man in the gut and sent him to the ground, crunching across broken glass.

There was muffled laughter from the rebels around them, who enjoyed a good show, and there wasn't much street theatre in this war-torn, broken-down city. At one time or another each of the rebels had been the victims of this man's wrath, so it was good to see him get knocked down a peg or two, especially by a guy with a bag over his head.

The man growled as he stood up, and when he got back on to his feet, he removed a hammer from his belt. He hit the bag as hard as he could, and laughed as Eric slumped to the floor unconscious.

"Nice chatting to you, Eric" he scoffed. "Get him up, we'll take him to see the governor." He spun on his heel and marched down the alleyway with a big grin on his face.

CHAPTER 23

THE CITY REBELS

In the centre of some tall residential buildings was a large open courtyard. Long ago, before the War, it had been used as a market place and a kids' play area, but things had changed over the past few years. The area had endured the Army trying to take over the city, as well as the Zarda and their beasts rooting through areas looking for food. At one side or the small courtyard was a heavily built-up barricaded entrance area made from scaffolding and thin metal wire. A lot of thought and many man-hours had been spent meticulously designing and building this area to withstand an attack.

The alleyways leading to this courtyard were narrow, so a large attacking force wouldn't be able to get down them without setting off traps and tripwires. Even if an attacking force could get through the alleyways, there wasn't the space to mass an attack on the main gates to the rebels' lair. Not to mention that this main entrance had several pairs of eyes fixed on it, and from every possible angle too. If the Army did decide to overrun this place with soldiers, they would be fired upon from all angles until the sewers ran red.

Eric had seen the gate a few times, but mostly from a safe distance, and he'd seen the rebels in the surrounding buildings with sniper rifles bought from the Army quartermasters on the sly, or travelling merchants who were either ex-army quartermasters, or stolen from army supply trucks.

The gate was a very impressive sight, although Eric knew full well that the rebel base was nowhere near. The gate was just for show. It gave the scouting squads something to report back on, a big impenetrable gate that they had no chance of getting through. It had worked too, except that Eric had a more curious nature than the Army, and had investigated further. He had followed some of the rebels one night, and had lasted nearly three hours in their base before being detected and having to escape. Because of this the rebels felt a mixture of respect and hatred for Eric, and because he had taken down groups of soldiers with relative ease, and the rebels had failed to hit him with their bullets, they believed him to be some kind of superhuman.

The rebels entered the courtyard to the Surroundsound from the windows overlooking them of guns being loaded and cocked. Eric was positioned in the very centre of the courtyard, with his captors surrounding him on all sides, and the group leader prowling through them like a lion in tall grass. He was very proud of his catch.

From inside the hood Eric could feel hundreds of pairs of eyes upon him, and then a call was shouted out from behind. He didn't quite catch what the person said, but he could hazard a guess by what happened next. He was struck behind the knees, forcing him to drop to the ground, and then the hood was pulled off sharply, leaving him blinking in direct sunlight. A shadow moved in front of the sun, allowing Eric the gift of sight again, and Eric looked up. Standing in front of him was Titus Duff, the leader of the rebels and the self-proclaimed Overseer of the City.

Duff had assumed the position of Overseer by careful strategy. He had bribed all the right people, blackmailed others, and killed anyone that stood in his way, as any good politician would. He wasn't necessarily a bad man – he could be good-natured and kind – but he was a man of singular vision, and that vision was him on top. He was a man who knew what he wanted, and had the intelligence and cunning to get it, no matter who or what got in his way. On the outside he appeared a smart businessman, making deals with new traders, offering help at a price. But behind closed doors, and under the expensive suits he wore, was a world of burns, scars and more pain and suffering than any human being should be able to endure. He had killed his fair share of men and women on his journey to the top of the pile, but some of them had fought back.

Eric had watched him from a distance on many of his late-night observations of the city. He saw through the plump face and businessman attire and knew Duff was a devious, callous man who would cut your throat before you could say anything against him, and he would do it with a smile. One night Eric had seen him torture a boy with knives and hammers, shouting questions he had no answers to, and then casually sit down to dinner with friends and tell jokes over the appetisers.

"It's only fucking Eric Mason" exclaimed Duff with an evil grin on his face, and Eric tried not to breathe his cigar breath. "I knew they'd send someone, but I hadn't thought you were stupid enough to come back into my city, not after the last time. You'll be here for the scavengers we found this morning then?"

Eric looked around at the rebels, who were all glaring at him. "What scavengers?" he asked.

This brought a mighty belly-laugh from Duff, as if he'd never heard such a stupid question in all his life. "I must say you soldier boys act quickly don't you? We only found them a couple hours ago. Naughty little kids, shouldn't be playing where they could get hurt. He turned and signalled something to the rebels above the big gate.

"What soldiers?" repeated Eric, but Mr Duff didn't seem to hear him.

"What were you stealing from my city, soldier boy? Maybe I should hoist you up with them," he grinned, but the laugh was quickly replaced by an evil glare.

"I'll give you fucking soldier boy," grumbled Eric to himself under his breath, and looked up to see what Duff was gesturing at. Most of the windows in these buildings were missing glass, and in one of the buildings on the far side, shapes were moving in the shadowy interior. As the shapes moved closer to the window, and stepped into the light of day, they turned out to be soldiers, two women, and one man, in ripped and blood-soaked uniforms. They were gagged and bound. The two women looked as if they'd been badly beaten; even from this distance Eric could see the bruising. The man had a look of extreme pain on his face, suggesting broken bones or dislocated joints. Eric recognised all three. They had been among the soldiers he had seen earlier that day in the showers back in camp.

Behind the trio were three much larger figures, each holding his prisoner up on his feet. The man was the one who had been jeering at Eric. He winced and started to cry a little; he really wanted to be rescued, but not by Eric. Not by a man who, if all the stories were true, would just leave him to die if things got out of hand. He was obviously praying that Eric was not really the kind of guy they'd all been joking about that morning.

Duff looked back at Eric and smiled, showing his slightly yellowing teeth. He looked like a crocodile who had learnt to talk.

"Here to save the day Eric?" he asked cruelly.

"Who are they?" asked Eric innocently, not taking his eyes off them.

"These naughty kids were scavenging in our territory. You know the rules, Commander Mason," said Duff, and his reptilian smile grew a little wider. "Anything in a soldier's uniform comes near our territory, we kill without question," he explained, as if Eric didn't know.

The prisoners' escorts bent them over the window ledges so that they were hanging precariously over the big drop below them. Eric's eyes calculated their path to the ground. Normally a drop from a second-floor window would only result in a few bruises or broken bones, but beneath them lay wooden boards into which someone had hammered six-inch nails, and the spaces between the nails were filled with broken glass. The fall might not kill them, but for the few minutes they stayed alive, they would wish it had.

"Never seen them before" said Eric quietly. "They aren't from the Army camp outside the city. They must have stolen those uniforms."

"Oh really?" said Mr Duff theatrically. "You won't mind if they drop to their deaths then, impersonating your army and all?" He spoke in a cheerful, sing-song voice.

"It's not my army" growled Eric. "But I still wouldn't want to see them die."

"Ah, but I hear any scavengers caught impersonating your army get thrown in the clink, then taken out and shot" said Duff.

"It's not my army" repeated Eric. He was tired of telling people he wasn't actually with the Army, but no one seemed to believe him. It must be the uniform they made him wear. "But it is well known that raiders or slavers impersonating army soldiers are thrown in military prisons to rot, so if you could just hand them over, unharmed – or rather, no more than they have been already – I will make sure they go in front of the relevant authorities."

"Oh yeah?" said Duff, clearly enjoying the situation, "and what's in it for us?"

"I came here to trade, Mr Duff. I have a bag of goodies somewhere, and information you may find useful" said Eric.

"Bag?" asked Duff, "What bag?" A rebel stepped forward holding Eric's backpack and handed it to Duff, who opened it and peered inside theatrically. "I don't know what bag you have Eric" he said, looking around Eric's feet, "I can't see one. I have a bag, see?" Eric heard sniggering. "In my bag I have… let's see, oh lots of goodies that I probably would have traded quite highly for maybe even one or two of our prisoners' lives. But this isn't your bag, it's mine. So I don't have to give you anything." He handed the bag to a stern-looking man.

"Really?" said Eric sarcastically. "Don't be that guy Duff, you're not that much of an arsehole. That lot took me a long time to find… you're not going to give me anything for it?"

"Not likely, my friend. I guess I could let you live? For now, of course. Long enough for you to give me the information you spoke about, hmmm?" Eric saw the spark of curiosity in his eyes.

"Let them go, keep the bag, and I'll let you in on a secret" said Eric in a matter-of-fact tone. "If they die, I tell you nothing – and then you all die." This comment left the rebels muttering among themselves, and Mr Duff looked around at his audience disapprovingly.

"Really? That is an interesting deal" he said, putting on a thinking pose. "I tell you what I'll let you do. You can tell me everything about this little secret of yours, and if I don't think it's worth anything I'll kill you, and that man up there, and feed the women to my boys. They'll make them wish I had let them die instead."

Eric jumped to his feet, making those around him take a quick step back in unison, and pulled his hands apart. His bindings snapped. He had been quietly cutting at them with a small piece of glass he had picked up. He took a menacing step towards Duff, who took a half-step back, and held out a hand.

"Fine, it's a deal then" said Eric, grinning.

Duff stared at Eric's hand as if it had been a loaded gun and looked Eric up and down questioningly, paused, and then tentatively reached out and shook it vigorously.

"Excellent!" said Duff, grinning like a madman. "Let's go talk in private, shall we?" He turned and waved a hand at the figures standing behind the prisoners. Black bags were pulled over the soldiers' heads and they were dragged back into the shadows kicking and squirming. Duff led Eric to the side of the courtyard, followed by a few of the armed rebels, and a previously-hidden door in a wall opened for them. They entered, and the door slammed shut behind them. The other rebels took the opportunity to relax and dispersed in different directions through hidden doors, and down alleyways. Within seconds the entire courtyard and surrounding buildings were empty.

CHAPTER 24

THE BURNED CELL

It was early morning in the bunker, and most of the soldiers had risen early to get an hour and a half's callisthenics and exercise in before breakfast. For the Gladiators, getting up involved their Sergeant quietly walking into the centre of their sleeping quarters and sounding two air horns before shouting at everyone to get dressed and get out of the door. Some mornings the eardrumbursting sound of the horns wouldn't stop until every soldier was up and standing to attention in a line by their bunks. Once everyone was up and ready to start the day, they were given their exercise and training orders. That could be anything from weights and sparring in the hexagon to running around one of the base's many obstacle courses.

The breakfasts were never much to look forward to. Each Gladiator was given a bowl of slightly warm runny oatmeal to eat and a high-protein shake to wash it down with. Their basic diet pretty much revolved around high carb and high protein meals to give them energy and strength, and it worked. The Gladiators exercised harder, trained harder, and built up much bigger muscles than the regular army soldiers.

On this morning Jackson and Truck were sitting together within a large group when the Sergeant entered their food hall, looking very angry.

"Gladiators!" said the Sergeant.

"Morning Sergeant," came the casual response from the table of Gladiators.

"I notice our new lanista has not joined us for breakfast," said the sergeant, looking around.

"No Sergeant," said Jackson.

"He wasn't around for the morning exercises either Sergeant" said Truck loyally, looking around the food hall. "Maybe he ain't woken up yet?"

"Yes, you may be right about that" said the Sergeant thoughtfully. He produced two of the wooden training rods and dropped them on the table. "Maybe he could do with a wake-up call. Go and wake him up, and show him what happens to new recruits who skip the morning exercises."

The Sergeant and the two squad leaders smiled knowingly. There had been a long tradition of beating the new recruits into submission, and often these beatings came with a lesson to be learnt, even if it was only not to give Gladiators a reason to beat you with sticks. The Sergeant walked away to help himself to a big bowl of oatmeal while Truck and Jackson got to their feet and left the food hall carrying the wooden rods.

The two men walked down the corridors in a playful mood, swinging the training rods back and forth and laughing and joking about old times when they used to be woken up like that, and saying the new recruits had never had it so good.

They turned the corner to Eric's cell and stopped dead in their tracks. All around the doorway and across the floor outside the cell there were soot and burn marks. The thick metal around the cell had been bent until it looked close to falling off. The door was still there, and the lock was still in place, but every other part of the cell looked like it had been hit by a nuclear bomb. The paint had melted and burned away, leaving swollen and blistered raw metal underneath.

Jackson edged a little closer, feeling the heat of the metal radiating off the door, and peered inside. When he saw what was on the other side his eyes widened even further.

"We need to get this door open," he ordered.

It took about half an hour and five men, three of which Truck had grabbed at random from a squad who were absentmindedly walking past on their way from breakfast, to prise the door off its hinges and pull the bolt out of the lock. The door was heavy, and even with two Gladiators taking most of the weight, they could only move it a little. But at least now they could see into the room.

Inside the cell was pretty dark. The light bulb had blown and the paintwork on the walls had been burnt to bare metal. The walls were covered in a thick wallpaper of soot. Jackson and Truck poked their heads in and looked at the carnage. All around the inside of the doorway were tentacle-shaped scorch marks, still glowing red hot against the black soot. The bunk was barely recognisable. The thin mattress was nothing more than a molten mess that had dripped into thick puddles on the floor around the burnt metal frame.

In the centre of the room, lying face down on the floor, was Eric Mason. Most of his hair was standing on end. His exposed skin looked badly burnt, and wisps of smoke were curling out from between his fingers. Strangely though, the blast seemed to have come from the very spot Eric was lying on. The metal was rippled like water when a stone is dropped into it. It was clear that whatever had happened in there had happened to Eric first.

"Did he try to use explosives to get through the door?" said one of the regular soldiers.

The question hung in the air, and everyone turned to look at the door propped up opposite the room. In its centre was a concave patch the size of a dinner plate. It looked as if it had the imprint of a clenched fist in the centre, but that couldn't be right.

"He would have been mad to try using explosives in a room this small" said Truck. "This base was designed to withstand a nuclear war." He walked over and touched the dent in the door, but then he pulled his fingers away sharply. "It's still hot" he exclaimed, waving his hand in the air.

All eyes turned to look at Eric. He didn't appear to be breathing, and no one wanted to see what they might find if they turned him over. They could already smell the burnt flesh and hair, and dreaded the gut-wrenching view of his face and body.

"We'd better tell someone about this" said Jackson. He looked around for volunteers, but no one moved.

"Funny" said Truck mournfully, "he didn't seem like an enemy spy. Maybe he was a terrorist or something. You know, one of those idiots who try to stop the War by chaining themselves to tanks and stuff."

"He fought like a demon in the sparring area" muttered Jackson to Truck, and turned to the regular soldiers. "You lot, just go. Tell no one you saw this, this is Gladiator business."

The regular soldiers disappeared instantly. These men didn't need to be told twice. In theory the Gladiators were of lower rank than regular soldiers, but it was hard to argue with a man or woman who was over six feet tall and had more muscle in one of their arms than the soldiers had in their entire bodies. The soldiers raced off down the corridor, their boots hammering on the metal flooring, and fought to get past each other.

"Even if he was an enemy spy" continued Truck, "he'd be mad

to think he could get away with blowing up the bunker from in there."

"Yeah" agreed Jackson, looking closely at the tentacle shaped scorch marks. "It must have been a hell of an explosion. Look at these lines, they don't look like any fire damage I've ever seen."

"That's true" said Truck as he looked around the room. "They almost look like lightning strikes." As he leaned over Eric's prostrate form, he lost his balance and fell on top of him. Eric writhed and moaned in pain, making Truck jump with shock. The men looked at the groaning figure on the floor.

Eric Mason hurt. His whole body was screaming in pain, and to make matters worse a very heavy weight had just fallen on him. He opened his eyes and blinked a few times to force them into focus, and painfully stretched out his arms. He rolled over slowly, and looked up to see the startled faces of Truck and Jackson.

"What the fuck?" exclaimed Eric. "Where am I this time?" He looked around at the bombsite that had once been his room. "Oh right," he said, memory gradually returning. "I'm in the bunker, right?"

He looked at the burns on his arms and could see them visibly fading. He scrambled to his feet, grabbing Jackson's arm to steady himself. The two Gladiators stared in shocked silence as Eric patted his pockets, produced a slightly singed packet of cigarettes and lit one. "What the hell did you fellas make that door out of?" he asked. By the looks on their faces he probably shouldn't be expecting an answer. "Sorry about the room, but if I'd known you had built this place out of some bloody ridiculously strong metal" – he banged a fist against the door frame, making a gonging sound – "what's this from, some kind of meteorite? I haven't seen metal like this before. Any food going?"

"Er... yeah, breakfast is being eaten in the food hall," said Jackson.

"Yeah" agreed Truck. "Sergeant wanted us to er... come get

you… you missed…" his voice trailed off as he remembered the training rods they had dropped outside the room when they had tried to pull the door open earlier.

"You missed the morning exercises, too" said Jackson.

"I did? That's a shame" said Eric in a jovial tone. "Breakfast though, yes? My favourite meal of the day. Bacon? Eggs? Sausages? Maybe some toast and hash browns?" But he could see the two men weren't really listening. He took a step forward, and they flinched slightly. "You boys had better show me where it is then, I'm new here after all. Take me to your breakfast," he said in a happy voice.

"Your skin" Truck managed, still gaping at Eric. "I mean, look at this place. It looks like a bomb went off. Are you a spy? What the hell happened in here? Your burns, how come they…?"

"Oh, right, that… well, I have excellent health," said Eric quickly, "and I eat all my vegetables of course. Come on, which way to breakfast?"

The Gladiators stepped backwards as Eric advanced on slightly unsteady legs, and nearly tripped over the lip of the doorway trying to get out of his way.

"This way lanista, we'll take you straight there," said Jackson. He patted Truck on the shoulder and gave him a look that said they'd better let the Sergeant decide on this.

The three men stepped out into the corridor and Eric paused for a second to kick the door with his foot as he went past. "Bloody strong stuff you guys have made this place out of," he said thoughtfully. "What are these sticks for?" Truck quickly swooped down and picked up the training rods.

"Nothing" said Truck, quickly handing them to Jackson.

"They're for training" explained Jackson, holding the rods out of sight behind his back.

"Fair enough, shall we go then?" said Eric, gesturing towards the corridor.

The two men walked down the corridor, Eric following. He had to struggle at times to keep up. His legs were still a little weak, and Jackson and Truck were walking a little faster than necessary. Eric's entire body hurt, but he did not want to show this in front of the two Gladiators. Not to mention he was starving hungry, and the thought of getting a big meal in his stomach was taking priority.

The lunch hall was full of noise by the time they arrived. The different squads were all sitting around laughing and joking and telling stories of their bravery against the Zarda. The Sergeant was walking down the lines of tables, nodding and smiling at the Gladiators who had proved themselves to him, and pausing only to shout at a new recruit.

The new recruits could easily be distinguished from the established Gladiators. They were the only ones still wearing regular army uniforms for a start, and they were smaller than the other Gladiators, who exercised and lifted weights when they weren't out on a mission, eating, or sleeping. They were also the ones who had to 'earn respect', and traditionally this meant they had to pick up after the true Gladiators. They were for all intents and purposes, slaves and dogsbodies. They would continue to be considered as such until they proved themselves, which usually meant either going on a dangerous mission and not dying or by completing some of the hundreds of dangerous tests dreamt up by the Sergeant and lanista. These tests could be hand-to-hand combat in the pit against one of the Gladiators or racing against each other over vast distances, dangerous assault courses, or anything else the Sergeant could possible dream up. On the whole it was easier to try to survive a difficult and dangerous mission than attempt some of the ridiculous tests.

Jackson and Truck entered the food hall and stood sheepishly by the entrance, not wanting to meet anyone's eye. The Sergeant had been keeping an eye open for their return, and spotted them across the hall. He quickly got out of his seat with a big grin on his face. He wished he could have been there to knock the new lanista down a peg or two, but he was happier that he would have an alibi for the bruises Jackson and Truck would have surely rained down on him.

His smile vanished when he saw that there was no blood on the training rods. Maybe they hadn't hit him hard enough. His face fell even further when Eric pushed past them both. Eric peered into the vats of oatmeal. From what the Sergeant could see, he didn't have a scratch or a bruise on him Surely he hadn't beaten Jackson and Truck again? The Sergeant made a mental note to punish them severely.

The Sergeant charged towards Eric, promptly crashing into one of the new recruits, who was trying to balance a stack of dirty breakfast bowls. The bowls and cutlery went flying in all directions, and slops of oatmeal spattered some of the Gladiators. A spoon bounced off the head of one of the female Gladiators, making her spin around in her seat and growl at the unfortunate recruit. The room fell silent. Every one of them knew Frankie had a very short fuse, and even the biggest of Gladiators would think twice before messing with her.

Frankie leaned down, picked up the offending spoon and held it up for the recruit. But just as the man reached for it, she brought her hand back and hit him as hard as she could with it. The blow sent the recruit crashing into the rest of the oatmeal-spattered men. The recruit disappeared into a crowd of very unhappy men and women, who proceeded to take out all of life's frustrations on him. It was accepted that being mean to the new recruits wasn't mean, it was training. Perhaps the recruit had got off lightly – she had been seen to break bones just because someone used her water bottle in the training yard without asking permission.

Meanwhile Eric was at the food counter, arguing with the recruit on serving duty.

"I want bacon, eggs and toast," Eric was saying to the petrified recruit, who had seen how Eric had fought Jackson and Truck the night before and was paralysed with fear. "Come on soldier boy, there has to be something better than this slop" Eric demanded, pointing at the vat of oatmeal, but all the recruit could do was shake his head nervously.

"Good morning lanista," said the Sergeant in the smooth voice he usually only reserved for officers, with just a little sarcasm. "Can I help at all?" He looked from Eric to the recruit and back to Eric.

"This kid doesn't have any breakfast for me" said Eric glaring at the recruit. "This is a food hall isn't it? Where's the food?"

"We are Gladiators, lanista" said the Sergeant, waving away the recruit, who ran back to the kitchens relieved.

"I'm not a bloody Gladiator!" laughed Eric. "And I want some breakfast." He picked up the ladle of oatmeal and let it pour back into the bowl. "This is not breakfast."

"We require a high carb and high protein diet," the Sergeant explained. "This is a good hearty breakfast."

"Not as hearty as bacon, sausages and eggs" said Eric, dropping the ladle and splashing oatmeal over the sides of the vat. "Where can I get a real breakfast around here?"

"The regular soldiers have their breakfast in their food halls," said the Sergeant. "We Gladiators don't mix with them."

"Sergeant?" came the voice of Jackson behind them. The Sergeant turned to him. With his captor distracted, Eric took the opportunity to walk away. His stomach was in charge now, and it was determined to have a proper breakfast. He quickly walked across the hall and headed for the doors.

As he reached the doorway a horn sounded, silencing everyone in the food hall. The Gladiators paused in their task of pouring oatmeal over every part of the helpless recruit. The horn sounded again, but this time it was long and drawn out, and turned into a pulsing and more frequent alarm sound.

"Right, you lot!" bellowed the Sergeant over the noise. "It's probably just a drill, but let's get suited up and in to battle stations, go, go, go!"

In each corner of the food hall's ceiling, circular disks slid aside and large red spinning lights dropped down and began flashing in time with the horn. The entire base was on red alert. Eric could feel the tension start to rise with every pulse of the alarm, like a giant heartbeat. All the Gladiators jumped to their feet in unison, and both squads turned and ran towards the doors, where Eric was standing with his hands over his ears. He'd been standing right next to one of the horns when they'd gone off, and it had bounced around the inside of his skull like a pinball. When he took his hands down and looked up, he saw a tsunami of bodies all running towards him, like a terrifying rugby team. He threw himself to one side to let them all pass, and they ran down the corridor and split at the T-junction to get to their squad's designated armouries. The Sergeant reached Eric and pulled his shoulder down so Eric's ear was in front of his mouth.

"It's probably just a drill," the Sergeant shouted.

"What?" shouted Eric, and theatrically put a cupped hand to his ear and leaned in.

"It's probably, just, a drill, lanista!" repeated the Sergeant.

"WHAT?" Eric yelled.

"We have to go, suit up!" The Sergeant pointed down the corridor.

"Ok!" shouted Eric nodding and smiling, "you go on ahead. I'll be right behind you."

With that the two men jogged out of the food hall and down the corridor. When they reached the T-junction the sergeant took the right turn and sprinted towards the armoury, and Eric watched him go. He looked left and saw a concrete staircase. On the wall were signs telling the reader what was on each level, upstairs and down. The sign that caught Eric's eye had been edited; the word 'regular' had been added to the words 'food hall' and it was only a couple of levels above. It took all of ten seconds for Eric to look back and see the sergeant turn a corner, then make his decision and run up the stairs.

On the staircase Eric launched himself upwards, taking the steps in twos. The thought of bacon fuelled his speed. He had managed to get halfway up the next flight of stairs when the entire base began to shake as if it was inside a tumble dryer. Eric was sent flying head over heels down the concrete steps, until he hit the landing between floors, hard.

The shakes didn't last very long, and Eric was able to get to his feet on the second attempt. After they had stopped Eric could hear, between alarm horns, the sounds of things crashing onto the ground and people shouting. All around him the fluorescent light tubes from the fixtures above him were falling and crashing onto the stairs, sending dust and broken glass in all directions.

"What the hell is happening now?" he asked the world in general, and the world replied with another stomach-churning shake. He darted up the staircase, dodging the broken glass, took a quick glance at the wall signs and ran off down the corridor. He had to slalom past running soldiers, clearly frantic about getting to anywhere other than where they were now.

Halfway down the corridor he skidded to a halt. His nose had sensed the unmistakable smell of cooked meat. He turned and followed his nose through a doorway, finding himself in one of the regular soldiers' food halls. He did not stop until he had reached the serving counter at the far side.

He checked around to make sure no one was watching, but apart from the occasional soldier running past the entrance he was completely alone. Someone had foolishly left this counter completely defenceless, and he scanned the counter's contents with hungry eyes.

Laid out in front of him, in all sorts of hot plate contraptions, was everything a hungry man could ever wish to find; bacon, eggs, sausages, toast, beans, and a number of other hot and cold foods. Eric didn't hesitate to scoop it all onto a very large plate. It took both hands to lift the plate off the counter, probably because it was actually meant as a serving platter. Eric spun around and headed for the nearest table.

At the table he arranged the condiments and prepared his meal like a conductor about to lead an orchestra. With a fork in each hand, he began to shovel the food into his mouth, pausing only to chew briefly and then swallow. After a few minutes he had polished off a third of his giant plate.

But something was annoying him. he could feel eyes watching him.

He looked up and saw the Sergeant and Major Tolley standing in the doorway. The Sergeant's face was a picture of disgust, but Major Tolley had a look of admiration, even envy. Eric smiled happily at the pair and turned back to his breakfast.

"That looks good" shouted Tolley over the noise of the alarms. He walked over to Eric's table. "I hope the sirens and alarms aren't bothering you too much."

"Disgusting behaviour" snarled the Sergeant, who was close behind. "Is this really the sort of person to train…"

"Sounds like you worked up quite an appetite last night Eric" said Tolley, interrupting the Sergeant. "If I hadn't seen your bedroom I probably wouldn't have believed what the good Sergeant here had told me."

"Yeah, destruction of army property, endangering all our lives with a fucking bomb" the Sergeant began saying, but was waved into silence by Tolley.

"Sergeant, I don't think all this is a drill," shouted Tolley. "Please attend to your squads and get them ready for battle, and have them all lined up ready for inspection by your new lanista."

He sat down opposite Eric. The Sergeant looked from the back of Tolley's head to Eric Mason, and then back to Tolley's head in disbelief. He had expected fireworks, but years of training had taught him not to speak out of turn to officers, and to follow orders no matter what his opinion. He sighed, spun on his heel, and marched out of the food hall. Eric's turbine-operated forks slowed slightly. Tolley was giving him a strange and fascinated look.

"What?" asked Eric. He was beginning to get a little disturbed by Tolley's look, and the sirens were starting to give him a headache.

"I don't know if you've noticed" shouted Tolley over the noise, "but there seems to be a certain amount of commotion going on."

"Nah, just a drill" grunted Eric dismissively. He turned his attention back to his plate, scooping up the rest of his food. "Nothing to worry about, yeah?"

"I'm not so sure about that, Eric" said Tolley.

CHAPTER 25

NIGHT IN THE CAMP

It was a very cold night. All the stars were out in the cloudless sky, and the full moon was shining its silvery light down on the desert landscape below. The flash and bang of explosions could be seen and heard for miles around, bright against the darkness of the sand dunes. The explosions lit up an area of desert to show the skeletal remains of an army camp the size of a city, the wind blowing at the few scraps of canvas that remained.

The Zarda had found the Army's underground super-base, and they were coming down on it with the full force of their military might. Balls of electricity spiralled angrily through the air, spitting sparks and static out before crashing down in an eye-watering display. It was like firework night, but with more screaming.

The sands around the Army's base shook as if a suppressed earthquake was ripping through the area. In a giant ring around the camp small sticks extended into the air, and red lights began flashing along a wide perimeter around the base. The explosions became fewer, and the sound of sirens could be heard piercing the air in between the bangs. They were old sirens, used during the Second World War to alert the citizens of London to an attack by Nazi Germany. They wailed like cows in pain.

There was no movement for a little while, apart from sand and debris falling from the sky. Everything seemed to be peaceful, until the ground started to shudder and shake again. In certain areas around the base, big metal boxes seemed to emerge from nowhere, raising some of the red lights higher into the air. If anyone was foolish enough to be standing near one of the boxes, they would notice that inside there were ramps leading down into the underground parts of the base. Emerging from each entrance was the ferocious, eardrum-bursting roar of hundreds of engines starting up. Within a few seconds the air was full of jet fighters, each taking its turn to shoot up the ramp to take off. The jets whizzed through the air like angry wasps, gathering together in their tightly-drilled battle formations. They were going to tackle the Zarda head on with as many waves of attack as possible.

Once they were in formation, full power was applied. Now the attack would be taken to the Zarda.

"What do you mean, this is not a drill?" demanded Eric. He was being dragged down a corridor, hopping up and down as he tried to put a fresh set of clothes on.

"We're under attack by the Zarda!" shouted Tolley as they walked past a siren. His fist was clamped onto Eric's arm and he was dragging him at high speed down the corridor towards a bank of elevators. "Get in and shut up, Commander, you will do as you are ordered." He pushed Eric into the small service lift past some regular soldiers. "You lads can take the stairs" he shouted, and they men all fled towards the nearest staircase.

Tolley joined Eric in the service elevator and pinned him up against the back wall. In the mirror behind Eric, Tolley could see the shocked faces of the regular soldiers and officers. Tolley knew that word would have got around by now about the explosion and the fight with the Gladiators last night, and he was not about to look weak in front of the lower ranks. He had brought Eric in at great cost, and in the eyes of everyone he was fully responsible for him.

The big metal doors of the elevator slid shut behind them, and both men felt the floor judder a little before the elevator took them through the levels. The whole box shook, but it shook a little more when Tolley was thrown clear across it, and hit the doors hard. Tolley sagged to the floor, clutching at the areas of his body which had hit the metal doors.

"Need I remind you, Tolley, that yes I am a Commander, and I do not take orders from you," said Eric.

"I'm sorry about that, but it doesn't do to lose face in front of the men" said Tolley. He flinched as Eric took a step forward.

"I know" growled Eric, "that's why you're only slightly bruised and not picking your teeth up off the ground. Come on, stand up. I just wanted to make a point. Don't try doing that again because it won't work a second time."

Tolley tentatively took the outstretched hand and pulled himself up off the floor "Yes, well, I'm sorry, but appearances are important here. Can't let them see fear, can't let them see you not in control, and so on... especially an officer like me. That's why I needed to get you here, Eric. That's why I did everything I physically could to get you here. The Army needs you, Eric".

Tolley's pleading tone did nothing to quell the anger that was rising in Eric. "You drugged me, dragged me out here to the middle of a fucking desert against my will, had some big bastards try to kill me, and then locked me in a small metal box with... what the hell did you make this base out of by the way?" exploded Eric counting the offences on his fingers.

"You've always helped the Army in the past" said Tolley. "I hear it was you who first warned us about the Lykor invasion. You helped on several early missions, and that was well before the War broke out across the world."

Only a handful of officers had access to the hidden case files with Eric's name in them. Most of the pages and reports were censored with a thick black pen, and some of the files had suspicious brownish-red stains. A few even looked older than Tolley himself, and had singed edges as if at some point they'd been rescued from a big fire. Tolley had read them with wide-eyed fascination. It had been like reading a great fantasy or science-fiction novel. It had taken him months to get access to the files; it seemed there was less red tape involved in building a nuclear bomb than there was in accessing the restricted files in Military Intelligence Agency archives. But as he was trying to bring Eric in, he had begged, bribed and brown-nosed every higher-ranking officer until he got what he wanted. The most curious thing about the files was that he wasn't at all sure how far back the files on Eric went. Some of them had clearly been typed on a typewriter, but some of the old ones were shakily hand-written, as if the author had been scared to write down what they had seen or done.

"The only reason I have had to help your army was that if I needed help with something, or needed supplies, I would have to help you first" he explained. "That meant dealing with your Lykor nests, playing the diplomat with rebels who didn't want or need your army's help, retrieving stolen weaponry or food from the more difficult civilian terrorists, and all the while being looked down on by any idiot monkey in an officer's uniform." He was shouting now. "Fuck your army Tolley, they have given me nothing but grief and misery for a very, very long time. I've been around for a while, longer than you know, and this is the first time I have ever sympathised or joined up with the Zarda, just to bring your Mickey Mouse army down a peg or two!" He was red in the face.

Tolley stared at Eric, stunned. Everyone knew he had a temper, but not everyone got the chance to experience it from a range of two feet.

"You help us and we help you" said Tolley as casually as he could. He had seen how the Army had treated trading favours with Eric, and he agreed that the Army's favours by far outweighed the small favours Eric was asking for. "You can't expect the Army to drop everything to give you handouts" he added, but without much conviction. If Tolley wasn't careful Eric might get violent, and in a box this size he was unlikely to come out on top.

"A bed to sleep in and some food," Eric said, counting on his fingers again.

"That aside, Eric, I need your help – not the Army, me. The Zarda are attacking this base, and every able body is needed to fight. You are here now, whether you like it or not, and you're not likely to just walk out of here with their army waiting for you outside. And wouldn't it be easier for you to fight them with some good soldiers behind you?"

"The Zarda only ever attack in small numbers, they don't have an army," snapped Eric. "You're worried about one of their little attacking squads - against this big underground base?" The lift ground to a shaky halt at their destination.

"No, we're not worried about one of the Zarda's little attack forces" said Tolley, hurriedly straightening his uniform before the doors opened. "We're worried about an army that's a hundred times larger than anything we, or you, have ever seen."

The doors slid open and Tolley and Eric stepped out of the elevator and into an auditorium that could probably have comfortably held six jumbo jets wing to wing. It was full of soldiers, all standing to attention. An ocean of bodies stretched out in front of them, and Eric had to admit he was impressed.

"Behold" said Tolley sweeping an arm theatrically. "The Novum Orbis."

Both men walked past the rows of soldiers, Major Tolley leading the way. Eric looked down the rows. Every soldier had that half-determined, half-terrified look in his eyes, the look Eric had seen so many times before a battle.

"How many soldiers do you have living here?" Eric asked, trying to hide his admiration. "There must be bloody thousands."

"Thousands? Probably not, but close," said Tolley jovially. "This is just one third of our total number of foot soldiers. By now our aerial attacking units should be well in flight and shooting anything that moves out of the sky, and we have a few armoured vehicles and juggernauts ready to go at a minute's notice." He spoke like a waiter announcing that evening's specials.

"You mentioned in the elevator that we're facing an army a hundred times bigger..." said Eric, but he was interrupted by the Sergeant, who appeared carrying a set of body armour.

"For you, lanista" growled the Sergeant, handing over the body armour to Eric.

"Er..." said Eric, staring at the armour. He was about to say something along the lines of 'I don't need any armour' when a hand from the sergeant propelled him further down the lines of soldiers, all the way to the front. "Right this way, sir" said the Sergeant, pushing Eric into line with the Gladiator squads were standing. None of them looked too worried about the imminent fight.

Eric looked back, but Tolley had vanished. Typical, thought Eric, always disappearing when there was some real fighting to do. The Sergeant gave the command for the Gladiators to stand to attention. With a scraping of heavy boots on the fresh concrete floor, the Gladiators all stood to attention in one fluid movement.

Ahead of Eric the big metal hangar doors opened slowly, letting in a blast of cold night air, which blew in carrying the sand and dust of the desert with it. The full force of the wind and sand slammed into the Gladiator ranks, but they did little more than shut their eyes. Eric, however, who had been staring at the armour in his hands, was nearly knocked to the floor by it. He swore loudly as sand and dust got into his eyes, but luckily didn't notice the Gladiators closest to him sniggering.

A crackling sound indicated that the large speakers fixed along the walls were turning on, and someone not accustomed to using a microphone was getting ready to speak. The unseen speaker blew and tapped on the microphone, which sent loud banging sounds echoing around the hangar.

"Soldiers of Novum Orbis!" came a loud booming voice from the speakers. "The time for training is over. We are under attack by the Zarda, and the brave men and women defending our skies are in need of your help. The Zarda are looking to wipe us off the planet, our planet, and we are not going to let them. We will not be wiped clean from the history books. Instead, we are going to write them in the blood of our enemies!"

"In the what?" Eric said, laughing, but no one else seemed to get the joke. The speaker continued to spout the usual rubbish men say to people who are about to fight, and probably die, when they are not doing any of the fighting or dying themselves. A loud clanging noise indicated that the hangar doors had opened fully, and Eric craned his neck to look outside. As if on cue, a set of jet fighters whizzed past the opening, their bright lights contrasting against a sea of sparkling diamond stars.

The sounds of explosions and gunfire could be heard far off in the distance, and the occasional bang or crash of something big sounded a little too close to home for Eric's liking. The cacophony of explosions was only slightly louder than the screams of the burning engines that preceded them. Some Gladiators jumped in surprise at how close they sounded. Then came a deafening roar; something big was heading towards them. In a brilliant shower of sparks and twisted metal, a fighter jet crash-landed into the hangar doorway in front of them. As the flames licked at the air above the Gladiators' heads, Eric felt a blast of heat, and a chill ran down his spine. War never changes, he thought, but the explosions do get bigger. He laughed to himself.

Eric pulled on the Kevlar vest and the helmet, then stretched in all directions to limber his body up. The battlefield was no place to get cramp. He could feel the eyes of all the Gladiators on him, but he didn't care. He'd rather be nimble and ready to fight than get caught short on a battlefield.

Despite the deafening drum and bass sounds of war, Eric could hear sniggering from the Gladiators behind him. He ignored them and continued to stretch, but there was something about this vest he was wearing; it was too tight, and allowed him little movement. He compared it with the one the nearest Gladiator was wearing. It seemed to be several sizes too small for him. He thrust the helmet into the neighbouring Gladiator's chest and ripped off the body armour. He held it up in the air to inspect it, and threw it to the floor before reclaiming his helmet again. That was too small as well. He tossed it to one side. He probably wouldn't need it anyway. It wouldn't help much if one of the fighter-jets landed on him.

He looked down the lines of Gladiators and saw the Sergeant grinning at him. The grin quickly disappeared when Eric gave him the universal middle finger salute, and carried on stretching a little more.

"Gladiators... ready!" bellowed the Sergeant at the top of his voice. Eric stopped stretching. He patted his pockets until he found the singed pack of cigarettes, and lit one. He blew a big cloud of smoke into the air in front of them, and leaned back in the line.

"I don't have a weapon" he whispered to the Gladiator next to him.

"That's a shame" came the reply. The Gladiator didn't even look at him.

"What do you expect me to do, run around and shout encouragement?" asked Eric, turning to the nearest group of

Gladiators. "Come on, come on, let's see a little teamwork here" he snapped impatiently.

After a moment of hesitation, two of the men held out sidearms and three others offered him spare blades. Eric took the two pistols and the blade that looked in the best condition. He hefted them to test their weight, rammed the blade into his belt and checked the clips in each gun. Once satisfied he put the guns away, nodded a thank you to the volunteers and spun back around.

"Gladiators, you will go on my signal!" the Sergeant ordered, ignoring the commotion coming from Eric's direction. "Once the immediate threat is dealt with, the regular units will then follow us out. This is not a drill. Our orders are to destroy the Zarda at all costs, take no prisoners, and leave no one standing." He turned on his heel. "Gladiators... ready! Forward!" With that he marched towards the open door, followed by the ranks of Gladiators, all marching in casual unison.

As the lines of soldiers neared the hangar doors, Eric marched slightly faster than the rest, and in a few quick steps he was out in front, so he was the first to exit the bunker next to the Sergeant.

"Good luck mate" said Eric in a jovial tone. "I'll see you for a well-deserved kicking later, if you survive of course." The Sergeant said nothing. Eric felt a little sorry for him. He had gone a sickly shade of white.

CHAPTER 26

ATTACK ON THE ARMY BASE

The aerial battle was in full swing now. The jet fighters dodged in and out of each other's way at breakneck speeds, their silver bodywork reflecting the moon's silvery-white glow. The Zarda were in full force, their great black flying machines almost camouflaged against the night sky, making a very difficult and fast-moving target.

From a distance it looked as if the Zarda were so far winning the fight. The sands beneath the attacking skies were littered with twisted, burning wrecks and the air was full of balls of electric light which could rip straight through their bodywork. Despite the pilots' extensive experience of combat situations, and although they were flying the most technologically advanced aircraft with the latest in aerial ammunition, they were gravely outmatched. This had never happened before. The Zarda had previously been content to fight in small groups around the globe, covertly sneaking past barricades, bombing from above and ambushing men, women, and soldiers on the roads between towns and cities. The largest force the Army had had to deal with so far had been no more than a few hundred Goblins, a few heavily armed Zarda-soldiers and Lykor and their powerful flying machines. But here and now, on the biggest battlefield to date, tens of thousands of soldiers had massed, thousands of pairs of hands held weapons and thousands of green-scaled fingers grasped triggers. From a distance the Zarda's black battledress made the desert look as if it been flooded with black oil. Waves of movement rippled throughout the ranks, and great drums thumped rhythmically above the snarling and growling of the warriors. Dotted among the mass of black bodies were the Zarda's mighty artillery guns, each moving slowly through the crowd towards the front.

A call came over the radio to all pilots. Their new orders were to take the fight to the Zarda's long-range artillery and draw their deadly flying machines away from the barracks and infantry soldiers. The command was acknowledged by each squadron leader, and the jets manoeuvred into one large attack formation, heading straight for the Zarda.

At various points around the bunker, the big hangar doors slid noisily open. A fighter jet, damaged, broken, and leaving a long trail of smoke behind it, escaped the fight, the pilot struggling to keep the jet in the air. Her controls were failing and alarms were screaming at her, but she had no way of manoeuvring the jet out of its current trajectory. At the last second she pulled the cord and her chair ejected out of the top, the parachute flying free. She hung there for a moment, staring wide-eyed as the jet continued on its trajectory and hit one of the big metal entrances.

There was a pause before two men emerged from the base and marched through the debris. They were quickly followed by several more men and women, all marching in rows from the different hangars like snakes leaving a nest. At the head of one of the snakes were Eric Mason and the Sergeant. They walked with their heads up high, and each snake slowly moved into position between the bunker and the Zarda's front line.

The Zarda's aerial fighting machines and enormous artillery cannons were hammering the Army jet fighters hard, and soon there were would be few left in the sky for them to aim at. The voices of dying pilots could be heard screaming over their radios. The Gladiators stood motionless. Not a single shout or call could be heard. Compared with the Zarda's front line, the Army looked like a brick wall.

The order came at last to silence everything; the aerial attack had failed, and it was time to retreat to safety. The pilots were each ordered to different air bases in the surrounding areas, so as to split up the survivors, in the hope that the Zarda would not be able to mow them down before they reached safety. Each pilot did as ordered but the Zarda were quick to react, and groups of enemy fighters split off to follow the retreating fighter jets. One by one the fighters were shot down in fiery explosions of black smoke. Only a handful were lucky enough to escape, some being chased over miles of desert landscape.

Up on the sand dune, the Zarda's heavy artillery was moving. Each unit consisted of a large base with complicated tubes and wires interlocking and cocooning the main firing element. The primary damage mechanism of these big artillery weapons was the thermal plasma they fired; it typically caused serious burns, and resulted in the immediate death of any living creature it touched, while it melted or evaporate anything in a wide area around the impact site. But it was highly unstable, and could explode in the air before it reached its intended target.

Over the years the Army scientists had done their best to study the strange and highly advanced weapons the Zarda were using to wipe them off the planet. The balls of plasma were fused and charged, and could hit small targets from great distances.

From a distance, it looked as if the Army base had a ring of glass around it where the plasma had fallen short and melted the sand. In the moonlight it shone silver. Each artillery cannon sat on a multi-wheeled carriage which was tightly fitted into long metal tracks for better grip on the moving sand. They were all moving slowly apart to allow the Zarda's transporter trucks to pass between them and reach the battlefield.

The Zarda had a number of different transport trucks at their disposal. The ones Eric had come into contact with were used for short distance, and mostly ferried soldiers deep into an attack. But the flying machines Eric had seen could travel across country in a matter of minutes and were used for moving larger numbers of troops or prisoners. These were much faster moving, as the only way to chase an Zarda flying transport ship was to be in another one. They were fragile though, with most of their space taken up with the weight of their unwilling cargo. They had been fitted with engines the likes of which had baffled aero engineers for years.

The transporters rolled past the heavy artillery on their big tyres and slowly descended the sand dunes towards the Army base. They lined up, well spaced out, a few hundred metres in front of the ranks of Gladiators, who did not look very impressed.

It was all quiet around Eric. Every pair of eyes was watching the transporters' doors. This wasn't unusual behaviour, but it was usually a gamble as to what was going to come out of them. Sometimes the Zarda loaded them with hungry Lykor, so you did not want to be standing anywhere near when they opened. Other times there'd be explosives, or they would be packed full of foot soldiers with weapons. In the Gladiators' eyes, nothing was more important than finding out.

Eric felt a little chill run up his spine and into his skull. He hated this part, the waiting, the anticipation and the nerves. He'd not seen this many transporters in one place before, and he had a very worried feeling that this was not going to be as easy as he'd thought. Eric liked fighting and got a lot of practice at it, which meant he was very good at it. The problem he had right now was that this all seemed different somehow, more serious than the other fights he'd found himself mixed up in. The Zarda meant business this time, and they weren't messing about by the look of things. Eric counted twenty transporters in close proximity, and if he looked down the line of them, he could probably count about the same on either side. He wasn't completely sure he was going to get out of this alive.

Lights started to flicker on the transporters. Very soon the locks would blow and whatever was inside would get out. No matter what came out of them, they needed to be ready.

"Ready weapons!" shouted the Sergeant, and everyone did so.

The lights flickered a little more, and then faster and faster until mini explosions released the heavy metal doors, and they swung open. In a flash enemy soldiers burst out of the transporters and rushed towards the Gladiators in a massed frenzy of movement.

"FIRE!" came the order, and every finger squeezed the trigger.

The Zarda foot soldiers were terrifying. Each of them was wearing the all too familiar midnight-black body armour, which covered them from head to boot with no gaps at all. Their long tails that hung down to the backs of their knees. The tail was pure muscle, which not only gave the soldier excellent balance but could be swung like a wrecking ball. The material they wore was like the wetsuits people used to wear for diving, but much stronger and more resilient to attack. They were not bulletproof, but it took a few shots on target to penetrate them and kill the wearer.

In one hand they carried large Spartan-style defensive shields, which glinted golden in the light of the full moon, and in the other they had pulse guns capable of firing liquid electricity with devastating accuracy. The air was instantly filled with the sound of gunfire and the crack of bullets. Each Gladiator was picking his target carefully so as not to waste ammunition, but their targets were very fast moving. The Zarda began to dodge and zigzag their way towards the Army, their shields up high.

"Forward!" came the order over the din of weapon fire, and the lines of Gladiators marched a few steps forward in unison. "Again!" came the order moments later, and the lines advanced further. Eric was astounded, for the Zarda were showing no fear at all, despite being opposed by an entire army of Gladiators. Ordinarily the Zarda stuck to the shadows, and rarely came out into the open like this.

A light caught his eye and he looked over to where the Zarda's heavy artillery had moved to. Their long cannons were pointing straight at the Gladiators, and they looked very much as if they were about to start firing again. Eric looked from them to the Sergeant, who didn't seem to have noticed but instead was firing his machine gun in all directions like an amateur. A flash of light came from each of the cannons, and large balls of plasma were fired into the air, heading straight for them.

"Hey!" Eric shouted, but the Sergeant couldn't hear him over the noise of gunfire. Eric ran the short distance to him and grabbed his arm.

"What the fuck do you think you're doing?" demanded the Sergeant, his face full of anger and surprise.

"We've got to move!" shouted Eric, and pointed at the sky.

The Sergeant looked up and all the colour drained from his face "Disperse!" he screamed "Incoming!" He pushed everyone out of his way as he tried to run.

Panic spread through the ranks of men and women, and Eric cursed the Sergeant for not calmly ordering them all to retreat to a safe distance. The Zarda had stopped advancing, and were now standing their ground and sheltering behind their shields, safely out of blast radius. Eric raised one of the pistols to take out a few attacking enemy soldiers who had got a little too close for comfort, but a pair of Gladiators ran straight into him, knocking them both down. As he fell the world around him was lit up by the explosions of plasma hitting the ground, and he saw some of the Gladiators burst into flames and then simply disintegrate. He felt the heat of the plasma on his face, and the weight as the two dead Gladiators landed on top of him. He had to struggle to move under their sheer.

It took a minute or so, but eventually Eric wriggled free and stood up. All around him was chaos and death. Zarda soldiers in front of him were shooting at the panicking Gladiators, and the air was full of burning electricity. He looked down at the charred remains of the two who had been on top of him. If they hadn't knocked Eric to the floor and landed on top of him, he'd be a smouldering mess himself.

But he didn't have long to ponder the situation, because the Zarda were advancing again, attacking any soldier they could get close enough to. Eric searched the ground for his pistols, but they were nowhere to be seen. From his belt he pulled out the blade he'd been given, and then he set to work adding his own brand of chaos to the pandemonium around him, twisting this way and that, dodging friend and foe alike. He was very good at this part, and there were many targets to choose from. His blade began itself slicing through every body part it could reach and plunging deep into chests and stomachs.

In a blur of movement a Gladiator fell into his arms. He was covered from head to toe with blood, and tried desperately to gurgle out a message, but Eric didn't stand a chance of understanding him. What he did understand was that this man was not going to need the gun he'd just dropped again. Eric dropped the corpse and picked up the gun in one smooth movement, and carried on down his path of destruction.

Eric soon became a main target for the Zarda. Gladiators were falling like flies around him, but he was able to make use of their dropped weapons and continue his descent into the heart of the attacking ranks. Then, out of the corner of his eye, he noticed that the Army were now sending their regular soldiers out to fight. He sprang to his feet, and with his head down he charged as fast as he could. He knew that if the Zarda artillery saw the soldiers they would destroy them before they had left the bunker.

Eric charged through the crowd like a rugby player going for the winning try, but then he saw something which made him skid to a stop. Alongside the foot soldiers the Army had released their big fighters, the large armour plated tanks and Jeeps, quickly followed by the juggernaut-knights in their robotic heavy armour. On top of each Jeep was a large machine gun. The tanks were an impressive sight, their great gun barrels unleashing shells the size of footballs, which took out large numbers of the enemy in one hit.

Eric watched wide-eyed as one of them fired with deafening precision into the throng of fighting bodies. The shot hit a group of Zarda soldiers, but there were Gladiators in there too. Eric sprinted as fast as he could, his mind whirring, trying to think up several different plans at once. The Army might train their soldiers to fight, but they forgot to add common sense into the mix, it would seem. In the old days an army could move and adapt to what their enemy were doing on the battlefield, but now it seemed they needed an order to tell them not to kill their own people.

He slowed to a stop in front of one of the giant armoured tanks, unfazed by the bullets and shells flying only a few feet above his head. On the ground in front of him he noticed a shadow creeping away. Then he saw the next volley from the Zarda's heavy artillery coming his way. He was too late; the Zarda had already seen and targeted the armoured vehicles. Eric tried waving his hands and shouting to get the attention of the drivers and gunners, but they could not hear him from up there.

Balls of plasma came crashing down only a few yards away from Eric, hitting the vehicles in the centre and turning them instantly into fiery explosions. The entire area was showered in molten metal, and the blast set off a chain reaction of explosions throughout the ranks of vehicles.

"Oh shitty bollocks!" Eric shouted. He turned on his heel and ran as fast as he could, but the force of another explosion lifted him off his feet and sent him flying through the air. He landed bumpily on the ground and rolled several times across glass and sand before he stopped moving.

He lay there for a few seconds trying to shake off the pain that was radiating throughout his body. His skin was burnt and blistered and some of his ribs felt cracked, but luckily his arms and legs didn't feel too damaged by the fall. He got to his feet and quickly realised he was in the middle of a crowd of Zarda soldiers. He looked around wildly, but before they could react to his presence he was already off at a sprint. 'Shit, shit, shit, shit!' were the only words running through Eric's mind as he pushed through a forest of bodies. This was the worst situation imaginable. Even he couldn't fight an entire army single-handed.

After about a hundred yards he found more space, but that just meant he was an easier target. the Zarda raised their weapons and fired their plasma bolts at his retreating back, narrowly missing. Up ahead a few dead soldiers littered the ground in his path, and he leaped high to clear them. But the leap had made him a clear target, and he felt the terrible force of the bolts striking him.

Eric landed on the ground and screamed out in agony. He could feel his uniform melting and burning, and the skin underneath was doing the same. He clawed at his battledress to get the molten material off him. Now he was in real trouble. He felt his belt for a weapon, but he had nothing left. He was unarmed, and about to face an entire regiment.

Some distance away Jackson and Truck were in their element. This was the sort of fighting they had been trained for. They filled everything that moved with bullets, and when their bullets ran out, they sliced and hacked with their razor-sharp machetes. They were both still feeling the pains and aches from the fight with Eric the day before, and were beginning to wish they hadn't trained so hard that morning. But this didn't stop them from separating arms and heads from their enemy's bodies. They didn't need to move too fast, for the Zarda were charging all around them, and the light from the explosions lit them clearly.

After plunging his machete deep into the chest of another enemy soldier, Jackson saw Eric through the haze of fighting. The new lanista was surrounded, but this was of no concern to Jackson. "Good riddance, lanista!" he shouted, but Eric couldn't hear him.

Jackson retrieved his blade from the body by his feet, and looked up to see if Eric was dead yet and how many pieces he had been cut into. He was puzzled to see that Eric was still in one piece and still on his feet. There seemed to be light coming from his eyes, and his hands were glowing oddly, as if they were on fire.

He watched Eric's fist demolish one of the Zarda soldiers. The fist and the arm it was attached to seemed to be covered in what looked like glowing veins. But he couldn't stop to puzzle over that, not in the middle of a battle. He shook the thought from his head and carried on hacking and slashing.

The Zarda soldiers came at Eric in pairs and threes, knocking him every which way with their shields and slashing at him with long golden blades. No sooner had Eric put one soldier on the ground than he was replaced by another. The commotion pulled enemy soldiers from all around the surrounding area, and soon a thick ring of black-clad figures with golden shields were waiting their turn to fight him.

Half way through an attack Eric's foot kicked something sharp on the floor, and he pulled a long shard of glass out of the sand. One of the plasma bolts must have melted the sand into this very long and sharp piece of glass; it was even still warm to the touch. Finally he'd found a weapon. He swung his glass sword like a baseball bat and managed to connect with a few new attackers, but one soldier managed to block it with his shield, and the glass club shattered in his hands. Eric was left holding a small piece out in front of him. The Zarda soldier swung his blade at Eric's neck, but he was able to dodge just in time, and felt the wind as the blade passed by his skin.

The Zarda soldiers were beginning to get angry that Eric was able to avoid their attacks, and began closing in on him. Eric blocked a swinging attack from one soldier's shield, nearly breaking his arm, and shoulder barged another in the chest in the same movement. The soldier threw his arms up and Eric took the opportunity to stab him in the chest with the fragment of glass he had left. The Zarda soldier fell backwards, dead before he hit the ground, and Eric looked around wildly. One more down, but still a hundred or so to go. The soldiers closed in again, and he eyed up the bigger fighters, deciding that he probably didn't stand much of a chance. Beyond the ring of bodies, he could see Army soldiers either dying or fleeing.

"Fine, fuck this!" shouted Eric to no one in particular. "I give up. I surrender." He raised his hands above his head and dropped to his knees in the soft sand.

"Human scum!" growled the nearest soldier in a deep reptilian voice. It sounded like someone having a lot of trouble speaking a language it didn't like using. "We take no prisoners, and we don't accept surrender."

"Who said I was human?" asked Eric. He raising himself up on his knees slightly, so he was crouched on his toes. The Zarda soldier paused in swinging its blade to finish Eric off. Eric had confused him slightly, and he had failed to notice that Eric was now in a sprinting start position.

"If you're not human" said the soldier, "then what are you?"

Eric noticed the extra symbols carved on the creature's shield which indicated that it was one of their officers. This was probably why it could speak human. It also looked smarter than most of the foot soldiers.

Under Eric's clothes, yellow light was beginning to illuminate the veins in his arms, legs and neck. "I'm Eric Mason" said Eric in almost a whisper, and unleashed the energy he'd been building up. He shot off like an Olympic runner and sprinted at full speed into a wall of enemy shields, knocking their owners straight into the air. With his head down and arms flexed Eric was able to ram his way through the mass of soldiers like a wild bull. It took a couple of minutes, but Eric finally freed himself from their army, and he was running full power towards the safety of the Army base.

Behind him he heard the order to fire, and immediately balls of plasma began shooting past him. He zigged and zagged as best he could, but he knew it would only be a matter of time before he was hit. Finally he was hit three times in the back, sending him tumbling across the sand. Pain streaked through his body until he felt as if he was being ripped to shreds from the inside. His vision blurred and dimmed until he could no longer see anything around him. He collapsed, and his heart stopped beating.

Eric was dead.

CHAPTER 27

DEATH'S CAVE

The memories slammed into Eric one by one. He was reliving every blade-thrust, every drowning, every bullet, and every other time his life force had been drained from his body over the years. He remembered the heat of the fires, the pain of metal blades ripping through skin and muscle. Most of all he remembered standing here in this golden shimmering cave, and challenging Death for his life, over and over again.

"You now see" said Death plainly, "and now you are here once again" His eyes were boring deep holes into Eric.

Eric's hand brushed against something hanging from a belt around his waist. He looked down to see the ghostly outline of a sword at his side. It shimmered in the light of the cave, but it looked about as solid as a whisper. The hilt sat on the top of a long scabbard that hung down to his knee, and it felt as familiar as one of his own arms.

In a quick, fluid movement he reached down, pulled the glowing silver-white blade out of the scabbard and held it up in front of him. The sword was practically as long as his arm; he waved it in the air, watching the hypnotic trail of light it left. He hefted the weight, and it felt good. It had taken a very long time to craft this sword, and it was something he used only when he needed the purest power. Clearly it knew something he didn't, because he didn't remember calling for it.

A movement on the other side of the blade made him snap out of his trance. Death had taken a step back and was brandishing his own blade in front of him, his thin, skeletal hands gripping the hilt tightly. Death's sword looked big and heavy compared to the one Eric was holding, but something about the way he was holding it told Eric that it was as light as a feather.

Each time Death swung his blade, Eric could see a faint shadowy shine around it. The sword of Death was sharp, but the trail of light it left was different from Eric's; where his sword left a silvery light, Death's was blacker than midnight.

Again Eric's mind was hit by memories of how he had fought Death in the past, and how he had won his right to be taken back to the world of the living to carry on his journey. He winced at the memory of being cut by that sword. Many foolish men had challenged Death to final combat, and Eric wondered how many had managed to win. Death had done this a thousand times by the sounds of things, so he couldn't have been the only one.

Death swung his mighty blade around his head, the shadowy edge shining, and brought it round in a long arch at head height. Time slowed down and Eric took a very long and heavy step forward, raising his own blade. His hands gripped the handle tight, making his knuckles go white, and the two blades collided.

The clash of the two mystical blades caused an explosion of light and energy, and the energy engulfed them both. When time finally flowed back into their world, a shower of bright sparks flew out in all directions, shimmering through the air around them. The pair stood locked together like statues, Eric's muscles bulging and straining against the mighty force of Death. He gritted his teeth to hold Death's blade away from him.

Death grinned and bared his teeth, which for a man who was mostly skeleton was not hard. Death had the strength of time, a force so strong it could crush stars and level mountains. He pushed forward, inching Eric's blade back towards him, and brought his own blade closer and closer. But Eric wasn't about to lose so quickly, and he pushed back with all he could.

When it was clear that neither were going to win this exchange, the pair pushed away from each other and stepped back. The veins in Eric's arms and face slowly began to glow, and he felt his body start to regenerate from the plasma wounds. He held his sword in both hands, allowing the yellow energy to swarm up into the metal, which began to glow as golden as the sun.

"You dare use that power here?" demanded Death, sounding genuinely surprised. "Very well." He raised one of his white skeletal hands and traced out a series of mystic symbols in the air around him, all the while keeping perfect eye contact with Eric. The symbols left strange shapes in the air like smoke rings, distorting, warping and dancing menacingly around him. They were pointed and evil looking. Eric had never seen them before, and could not decipher their meaning.

"I have beaten you before, more than once" said Eric, watching Death's hand intently.

"Yes" came the plain and simple answer from Death.

"Then why do we continue fighting over and over again?" Eric asked. The symbols were beginning to worry him, although the golden energy had now completely filled his body and his sword.

Death looked surprised. "You wish to stop fighting? Have you finally decided to come with me to where you belong?" he asked.

"Where I belong?" exclaimed Eric. "I belong in the world of the living. What I meant was, why continue to fight when I continue to beat you?" He knew this wasn't the cleverest thing to say, but he was feeling a little cocky right now. Besides, if the most he had to lose was his life, what was the worst this man could do to him? He had already died.

"Because one day you will not win" said Death simply, and pointed the symbols at Eric.

The smoky symbols flew through the air like daggers, heading straight for Eric. The glow from his sword pulsed, and with a few quick swings he cut the symbols in half. Each one burst with a pop, like a tiny firework.

"I see all the years of being part of the living world haves not dulled your power, like so many others" said Death, obviously perplexed to see that the ancient curses had not ripped Eric to shreds. "The power you have installed in your favourite blade is still as strong as the day it was crafted. I had hoped that it would have weakened over time."

Death's sword disappeared from his hand. The metal seemed to dissolve into dust in a split second and then vanish as if it had never existed. Death gave Eric an evil grin. He slowly raised both arms up and began twisting and swaying, creating bigger and angrier-looking symbols than before. They seemed to hang in the air around Death like loyal guard dogs protecting their master. They were thick and heavy, and seemed to glare and growl at Eric.

When Death had finished carving the symbols out of the air, he held out a hand and his sword reappeared as if it had never gone away. Death stood encircle by his new curses, which twisted and changed colour around him but never left his side. Eric could not read these symbols either, nor was every likely to. These curses were older than words, older even than sound or sight; even older than death himself.

Eric didn't miss a beat. He twisted and swung his sword

around, carving out a few symbols of his own which he reserved for special occasions. Compared to the intricate symbols around Death, they looked as if a toddler had been let loose with some crayons, but they would suffice for what Eric needed.

The pair charged towards each other, swords swinging back and symbols circling. Death's mystical smoking symbols instantly came alive, and shone white and blue with dark, sinister centre. They crackled as Eric ran through them. It felt as if he was running through a mass of electrical wires, giving him a sharp static shock each time one of them connected with him. His own symbols helped a little, but they were no match for Death's.

With their swords leaving long trails of light, the pair clashed blades, trying to find gaps in the other's defences, and began to circle one another. Eric made an attack, but Death avoided it easily and then took full advantage, delivering a blow with his bony fist to Eric's chest. It was as unstoppable as a wrecking ball, the bony white fingers stronger than the toughest steel, and sent Eric flying.

The rocky floor of the cave raked Eric as he rolled across it, but on his final tumble he jumped back up onto his feet like a cat. A flash of memory came to him. This had happened more than once before, and from memory Death had always followed up this attack with an aerial assault and driven his blade deeply into him to end the fight.

He glanced upwards and saw Death already halfway to him, his long black robe waving, his sword above his head ready to strike.

Not this time, he thought. He had just enough time to react. He raised his sword above his head, holding hilt and blade in both hands like a shield. Death brought his sword down hard, his face creasing slightly as he grimaced with the effort. The sword struck Eric's and forced him back down to his knees, the point of Death's blade inches away from his face. Eric tried to push back so he could get back onto his feet, but it was like trying to lift a house, and Eric was pushed down further.

Refusing to be defeated, Death raised his sword slightly, and hammered at Eric as if he was trying to crush rocks with a sledge hammer. Sparks from the two blades started flying around Eric's head, but he held strong against the attacks.

Then Death kicked out and caught Eric in the chest with the flat of his bony foot. The power of the blow was enough to lift Eric up and across the cave again. Again Eric rolled across the floor and jumped back up. Death had already leapt into the air for another attack, but Eric was ready for this and was already swinging. The pair clashed swords again, neither managing to get the advantage. The pair were showered in sparks and flashes each time their blades touched, and the sound of metal hitting metal echoed through the cave.

Sweat began to drip down Eric's forehead with the effort of trying to keep up with Death's attacks. It wasn't that the blade was heavy or that Eric was getting tired, but it had been a very long time since he'd needed to fight someone of this calibre. Death was of course not tired. He never slept, he never ate, and he never admitted defeat to a mere mortal. Yet even he would begrudgingly admit that he had doubts about winning this fight. Death knew that Eric was not an immortal; he just refused to die, which only angered him more. Each time Death thought he was going to make the final blow, Eric somehow managed to dodge or defend against it.

"Call it a draw?" asked Eric, out of breath as the two pressed against each other's blade again.

"A *draw*?" asked Death, puzzled, as if it was a word he had never heard before. "There is no draw! You, Eric, will die and be taken across the void!" he barked angrily, but Eric could see that the remark had broken his concentration for a moment.

"Maybe one day" said Eric, "but not today. If I have to, I can do this for the rest of my life."

"That can easily be arranged!" screamed Death.

Eric brought his sword round in a wide arc across Death's chest, slicing through the thick black robes and deep into his paper-thin skin. The impact of the blade made Death scream out in pain and frustration. Out of the wound in Death's chest wisps of green smoke started to spill out, forming into wide-eyed ghostly demons which clawed at the sides of the wound, desperately trying to pull themselves free from their cage. But Death held them down with a hand, and when he moved his hand away the wound had vanished. He glared at Eric with eyes glowing black with anger, and began to slash at Eric, who evaded every stroke.

Eric grinned. He was winning. Death had lost his cool, and Eric was as calm as a mountain. He read each attack perfectly, so much so that he didn't even need to use his blade to defend some of them. He ducked and dodged each swipe and thrust, making Death ever angrier and more careless.

Finally, when enough was enough, Eric swung his blade like a big hitter in a baseball game and knocked Death's sword clear out of his hand, sending it clattering across the rocky floor. The blade skidded to a stop and dissolved into dust.

Eric carried on in his attack. Now his blows were striking home. Gashes were appearing on Death's back and stomach. He was losing his balance and couldn't move out of Eric's way fast enough. The misty demons clawed again within each wound, and squealed with triumph as Eric plunged his blade deep into Death's heart. Death opened his bony jaws wide in silent pain; no words or sound could describe the feeling of being beaten by a mere mortal.

The pair stood motionless for a moment, Death glaring at the glowing blade sticking out of his body. With all his strength Eric heaved on the hilt of his sword and pulled the long blade clear, allowing him to fall forward onto his knees. There was no blood on the blade as Eric withdrew it.

Eric knew he could never kill Death; the paradox alone would give even the most enlightened mountain dwelling monk a headache. He stood up straight and slowly put the silvery-white blade back into its scabbard on his belt. Without its owner's touch, the blade began to fade.

"What do you want?" asked Death, his booming voice now quiet and full of defeat. "You win your prize of life, and what else?"

Eric thought about this for a moment. "What else is there?" he asked, slightly confused.

His opponent stared up at him. "Few mortals have ever managed to win their life back from me, and none as many times as yourself," he said. "But eventually they all fall to my sword, as will you one day. I am constant, you are not. It is traditional that I may bestow on you another prize. Riches, enlightenment, some have asked for the strength of ten men." Death's voice was trailing off to a whisper.

Eric stood for a moment trying to think. "All I want is for you to send me back to the world, as healthy as I have ever been," said Eric carefully. "I still have things to do, and I'm not ready for my time to end just yet."

"You may not want to go back" said Death in a hushed whisper. "Would you like to know your future? Would you like to know what you are going back to?"

This confused Eric. Knowing his future was an interesting idea, but wouldn't that take the fun out of experiencing life first hand? Besides, did he really believe in fate? He was the master of his own destiny, wasn't he? So any future he could be told right now might never happen, not if he didn't want it to.

"I didn't remember being here, that darkness and cold was as if for the first time" said Eric thoughtfully. "And I didn't remember winning the fight last time, or the times before, or being sent back to the land of the living. If you told me my future now, how would I know you were telling the truth, or that I would remember it anyway? Any future you could tell me now will be worthless if I don't remember it tomorrow."

Death grinned. He had asked Eric that question many times, and each time Eric had given a similar answer. It puzzled Death that Eric was the only one to refuse a mystical gift. Perhaps he was the only one who wanted nothing but to be alive. Death rarely saw the same person twice, but Eric was different. He was beginning to feel a certain respect for him. He kept coming back time and time again, each time refusing to let the inevitable take its course.

This time was different though. This time Death actually wanted to tell Eric what his future held.

"I am not responsible for you not holding the memories of this place in your mind" he lied. "Are you quite sure you would not accept a fortune telling?"

"If I won't remember what you tell me, what would be the point?" said Eric. "Send me back, the future can wait until I get there. Then I will be the one to decide what the future holds." Once it was done there wouldn't be any turning back, so what did it matter? Knowing the future is only helpful to those who are scared that they are not in control of their own destiny.

Death very slowly stood up and placed a freezing cold skeletal hand on Eric's shoulder. It was like being gripped by a row of icicles. "I've followed you a long time Eric, and I will continue to do so as you continue your journey" he said. "I will give you a rare piece of advice. There will be much pain and destruction in your future, and there will come a time when you will have to kneel in front of a white-haired old woman. At that moment you must find strength, or else we will meet again."

With that, Eric's world went blank.

CHAPTER 28

BEHIND ZARDA LINES

Eric Mason woke up. He hurt. Every part of his body was screaming at him in pain. He opened his eyes and squinted up at an early morning sunrise; it was really quite pretty. There wasn't a single cloud in the sky above him, and he could just about make out a few faint stars.

A memory flashed across his mind. When he was younger he used to stay awake all night, just lying on his back looking up at the stars, until the sunrise came and he went home for breakfast.

Breakfast - he remembered breakfast. There had been a lot of it recently, big plates of cooked meats and breads. But when was that? His stomach felt nearly empty again. There was pain too, more pain than he felt he deserved. There had been a fight, of that he was certain. He had been running, he had been worried, he had been tired, and then he had been hurt.

He was lying on something soft and bumpy, which shifted slightly when Eric tried to sit up. He fell back down straight away; he was clearly in no condition to move just yet. His muscles ached, his skin felt itchy and his stomach was ice cold and burning hot all at the same time. He looked down at his body. He wasn't wearing much. His black commander's uniform had been ripped and melted, and his skin looked burnt and painful. He felt around to assess the damage, but even his fingers were stiff and painful.

He was surrounded by a smell. It was like taking a deep breath from a bag of dead poultry. The air around him stank of sweat and blood, with a hint of burnt flesh and smoke. If Eric hadn't had an empty stomach the smell would have emptied it pretty quick. It was thick too, like sitting in a fog. No matter which way he turned the floor would move and another waft of smell would rise up.

Eric lay still for a moment, trying to concentrate. It took a few breaths of foul-tasting air, but soon he was able to focus his inner thoughts on his pain, and feel his skin starting to heal itself. In the old days it used to take months for his wounds to heal properly, but after years of practice he was able to get even the most deadly of wounds healed in a few days. He'd had a very good teacher.

From all around him noise started filtering through the haze; he could hear sounds of running feet, the occasional scream of pain, an explosion. It was clear that wherever he was, it was not the best place to have woken up in.

He always felt disorientated when he woke up like this. Flickering memories of a golden cave were fading fast, and he could vaguely remember speaking to someone, but for the life of him he couldn't remember who. A voice came through the mists, a whisper from somewhere deep inside his mind: "you need to peel a white-haired wagon" it seemed to say. Eric dug around in his memory. Surely that didn't sound right, but he couldn't find the memory. He mentally logged this for later study, and attempted to sit up again to have a look around. He managed it on the third attempt, which wasn't too bad considering how bad he felt.

What was important right now was working out where he was. He vaguely remembered a battle and fighting, which wasn't much of a surprise as he always found himself fighting someone. But he should really find out why he had been fighting and who, and if he needed to do any more of it.

Eric's vision was slightly blurred, but he forced his eyes to focus on his surroundings, and instantly wished he hadn't. He was lying on a pile of dead Army soldiers.

Excellent. That would account for the smell. He checked his surroundings and a shiver of fear ripped up and down his spine. He was back on the battlefield. The fighting was over, and he was deep behind the Zarda front line. In all directions black-clad Zarda soldiers were running around. Some were dragging dead or injured Army soldiers towards large piles of dead men and women, some were torturing and beating survivors, and the officers were shouting orders at each other in their reptilian language.

It didn't look as if anyone was paying attention to him. A group of officer-type soldiers were marching through the ranks, easily spotted because of their golden spiked helmets and engraved branded shields. They were the ones shouting most of the orders. The senior officers were in the centre; they were clearly in charge of everything that was going on. They wore golden crowns rather than helmets, and their shields were covered in so many engravings and symbols that it almost seemed a shame to use them in combat.

Two Zarda soldiers were walking towards the pile Eric was sitting on, each one dragging a corpse by its ankles. When they reached the pile the bodies were unceremoniously dumped at the edge. One of them looked up and saw Eric sitting there, and gestured to the other soldier. The other soldier sighed, and they both started clambering up across the bodies to where he was sitting.

"Oh bugger" mumbled Eric. He got to his feet, a little

unsteadily, and had managed to stop swaying by the time they reached him. The closest soldier drew a golden blade in one long smooth motion and reached out a black-gloved hand to grab at him, but this was awkward as it isn't easy standing on a pile of dead bodies. Each time they moved, so did the pile.

Eric swung out a fist, and was almost as surprised as the soldier when it hit home. The soldier went tumbling down the side of the pile and hit the ground hard. Not wanting to lose momentum, Eric threw out his other fist and hit the other soldier, who followed his counterpart to the ground. The commotion sent a ripple of interest radiating out over the surrounding ranks, and every faceless gaze looked up to where Eric was standing, high above them like a statue. The light from the new day sun was behind him, and he was the picture of a hero.

Eric shook a bit of feeling back into his shaky legs and half jumped and half skidded to the ground. Once down he quickly fished around the bodies of the soldiers he'd hit, but they weren't carrying weapons. "Bugger" muttered Eric. The golden sword was a little too far out of reach. Zarda soldiers were heading his way, and to Eric's annoyance, they were all holding their plasma guns in one hand and their shields in the other.

When they reached him Eric lashed out, managing to connect with some of them, but the Zarda's shields did a good job of blocking most of his punches. The Zarda clearly weren't expecting someone looking this close to death to keep fighting; they crowded around him to watch.

One by one the soldiers attacked again, and one by one Eric dodged them like a matador, sending the attackers head first in to the wall of bodies behind him. These foot soldiers were not very talented fighters, their punches easily blocked, their kicks easily dodged, and Eric could move a hell of a lot faster than any of them, even though he felt as though his legs and arms might fall off any minute.

The commotion attracted the attention of the nearest group of officers, who stopped in their tracks and turned to watch this pitiful man trying to fight for his life. They were half impressed that he was managing to fend off so many of their soldier's attacks in quick succession. But this not go down too well with them. The largest pushed though the throng and knocked Eric back so hard with his shield that he flew several feet across the ground and landed back on the pile of dead soldiers.

Stunned, Eric looked up at the officer. He was far bigger than any of the others. The only way to deal with him was to get him away from the others, so he could focus on him alone. He stumbled forward, playing the part of a dazed and confused man, and allowed the officer to hit him again.

The officer removed its golden helmet and tossed it to the nearest soldier to carry. Eric could tell by their body language that the soldiers were enjoying themselves at this display. Just then his hand brushed against something hard and sharp – one of the Gladiator machetes. He gripped the blade and stood up, keeping it behind his back. The officer advanced again, but in an instant Eric whipped the blade round and rammed it deep into his chest. When he pulled it out, dark green blood sprayed out in all directions. A gentle kick from Eric, and the officer fell to the ground dead.

Eric looked around furiously for the next attacker, but no one moved. A higher-ranking officer stepped forward and barked an order at Eric in their language, but the voice was muffled by the black covering they all wore. Eric didn't understand what it had said, but guessed it was along the lines of "kneel you dog, and prepare to die", because that's what they all said in these situations. He didn't know it, but that was exactly what he had said.

The officer creature, clearly angered by Eric's defiance, slowly raised its hands to its spiked golden crown and lifted it off its head. Then the officer reached behind its head and pulled at a short length of string that was keeping the black hood attached. It pulled the hood away to reveal green and red scales. The soldier-reptile shook its head and each of the scales stretched out a little. The reptile had a long fat snout and small dark eyes, and when the mouth creased into a grin, it showed a line of small razor-sharp white teeth.

Eric didn't hesitate. He leapt forward brandishing the machete, but his attack was easily blocked by one of the officer's arms, and a punch to Eric's chest sent him staggering back again. Eric straightened up and glared at the reptile. Judging by the amount of red on the scales, this one was very senior.

Eric had worked out a long time ago that the reptile warriors achieved seniority by the number of humans they killed in battle. The scales came in all different shapes and colours, and Eric had noticed in the past that the red-scaled reptiles were the biggest and strongest. The bluer-scaled reptiles were more cunning, and prided themselves on tinkering with war-machines and technology. Most of the foot soldiers had light green plain scales all over their bodies.

The General stepped menacingly closer to Eric. The soldier carrying its crown held it up for the officer to take, and it slowly replaced the spiked helmet onto its head. It barked an order in its reptilian language, but this was wasted on Eric.

"I know what you're thinking" Eric said quickly, lowering the machete slightly, "but I'm not with the Army, I'm just passing through this battle. So if one of you could just show me the way out, I won't kill any more of your soldiers."

The officer hissed at him. Eric lowered the blade a little more, in the hope that this reptile would wrongly assume Eric was done fighting. When Eric clearly wasn't going to do what the reptilian was ordering him to, it made a gesture to one of the other officers, which took a few steps forward carrying a weapon – a seven-foot-long thin black staff with large black spikes on either end. As soon as the reptile gripped it, sparks ran up and down the spikes. The reptile spun the staff a few times before pointing it end at Eric's head, which then glowed with electric energy.

"Ah" said Eric, "now there's no need for any of that. I'm sorry about your soldier here" – he indicated the dead officer by his feet – "but they attacked me. Self-defence yeah?" He really didn't like the look of that staff thing.

The electricity started to charge up, and the glow got brighter. The reptile fired a bolt of electricity from the staff and it hit Eric in the chest; it felt like being hit by an entire lightning storm. The blade fell from his hand, and Eric began convulsing in pain and shock. All around his torso white and purple glowing lines appeared, and tightened around him until he was completely confined. The weapon wasn't designed to kill, it was designed to disable a prisoner, and it was very effective at it.

Eric's body hit the ground hard, but the pain from this didn't even register over the level of pain from the electric shackles the thing had wrapped around him. The pain was unbearable. Eric screamed at the top of his voice, and strained to break free from these bindings. The whites of his eyes started to glow and pulsate yellow, shining veins began to cover his body, but still he couldn't break free. The stronger Eric pushed against them, the tighter they became.

Slowly Eric began to lose consciousness. The last thing he saw before blacking out completely was the reptilian officer standing over him, laughing. Two of the other Zarda walked over, lifted Eric up into the air and carried his unconscious body away.

Standing by were ranks of flying transporter ships, which one by one were being loaded with prisoners and flown off. The Zarda rarely took prisoners, but when they did they didn't hang around. Eric was carried onto the nearest one, and the hangar door closed behind him with a loud clang. The bright light of the engines shone in the early morning light as the ship lifted off the ground and set off in the same direction as the others.

CHAPTER 29

THE ABANDONED CITY

"There's a *what*?" exclaimed Titus Duff.

"A nest" said Eric patiently. "Bigger than I've ever seen in this area, and it's just a few miles outside the city. Find me a map and I'll show you where, if you don't believe me."

The pair were sitting at a small kitchen table in a dark room. The only light was filtering through a thin set of brown curtains across a small window. Eric looked around the room while he waited for the rebel's thought processes to catch up with the new information. Sometimes this took a few minutes with Duff.

The building they were in had clearly been a block of cheap flats before the War, and the designer and decorator had brown very much in mind when they put in the curtains, wallpaper, carpets, and even the kitchen cupboards. Even most of the furniture was brown, or beige. Eric had heard that these had been known as 'earth colours', but they had only really been fashionable in the 1970s, and then again several decades later, thanks to hip people looking for a 'rustic' or 'natural' look.

In each corner of the living room was a rebel soldier. They all looked alike to Eric. Their only distinguishing feature was their clothes, yet they were all wearing the same desert drifter style. The look would have been right at home out in a windy desert where you needed the tinted goggles and the bandana over the mouth, or a large scarf that can be turned into a head dress. But here in the broken-down city it was clear they just wanted to look cool. Eric hated cool.

"So what are you army boys going to do about this 'biggest beast nest you've ever seen' then?" the rebel leader asked thoughtfully.

"I would like to point out" said Eric with only a hint of a sigh "once again, that I am not actually with the Army, I just happen to be travelling through."

"That's funny, because you look very much like a soldier boy in that uniform" said the leader.

"Yes, yes" said Eric in the tone of voice of someone who had explained this far too many times, "it's a commander's uniform. I'm not part of the Army, but I am under their protection, so long as I actively work for them."

"Protection? From what?" asked the rebel leader. "From what I've seen and heard, they can't even protect themselves. Besides, I hear you of all people don't need protecting. Anyway, those three outside were easy enough to capture, and I want top dollar for their lives."

The pair sat there in silence for a moment, each staring the other one down. The rebel leader was used to negotiating with regular army officers, who usually just gave him whatever he wanted if he threatened them or their soldier's lives. The rebel leader's biggest weakness was his arrogance. H surrounded himself with big, tough looking men with guns, and had no idea that if Eric decided it was time for him to leave, he could do it without batting an eye.

"Look" said Eric at last, "I don't mind telling you that this nest is worrying the Army, and they are happy to simply pick up and go. If they do, and you're left here all alone, the nest will quickly expand when the Lykor and their pups get hungry, and then this city will look very enticing. They like to tunnel, and with a nest this big, they might have already reached the city limits. They could be sitting right under your feet, and if they decide to come up... Well, you'll all look very tasty." He grinned.

"So?" said the rebel leader looking around at his entourage. "We don't need you soldier boys here, do we lads?" This got a murmur of agreement from each corner. "The beasts don't scare us" he said in a slightly louder voice, but Eric noticed his guards were absent-mindedly looking down at their feet, just in case the floor fell away and they were snatched up by a whole nest of hungry beasts.

"OK, that is as maybe" said Eric, "but if I leave here and tell those officers you are holding three lives hostages..." he let the last words hang in the air for a moment. "Then before they leave you with the nest they'll come in here and stick a grenade up your arse" he added with a smile.

This got the response Eric was looking for. Each man took a few steps forward and aimed his weapon at Eric's head, and the rebel leader had to quickly raise both hands to calm them down.

"So far you and they have lived quite peacefully" continued Eric as if nothing had happened, "but what do you think the Army will do if the outpost sends word to their HQ? They won't send simple soldiers you can throw rocks and smoke grenades at, they'll send tanks and those armoured Knights, and then what are you going to do?" He looked around at the rebel guards as if for the first time. "Think you could take out a heavily-armoured Knight Soldier with that?" he asked the nearest one, nodding at the machine gun he had aimed at Eric's head.

"We'll fight them!" said Duff. "We have guns, and we have walls, big walls. Your army doesn't scare us! And anyway, Eric Mason, what makes you think we'll just let you walk out of here and back to your little army camp?" He thumped the table with his fist to punctuate his sentences.

"You may not live to regret trying to stop me" said Eric. "You're a businessman, Mr Duff. Be reasonable. All I want is to make a good deal that benefits us both. Just think about it. You give me those three kids out there, and I take them back to the Army outpost. Then the Army will pack up and go, leave you to it, and you won't need your guns or walls, because you're not scared of those big bad wolves either, are you?"

He stood up and offered his hand for Duff to shake. Instantly the rebels surrounded Eric, two hunting knives were thrust up against his throat and weapons were cocked and aimed at his head again. Eric didn't dare move in case one of those hunting knives was actually sharp. He looked around without moving and saw every eye was on him – except Duff's. Duff wasn't looking at anyone. He was still staring at the empty chair Eric had been sitting in moments before, deep in thought.

"I can't just simply let you walk out of my city with them soldiers Eric," said Duff thoughtfully.

"What could you possibly want more than to just be left alone? How much is peace worth to you?" said Eric quickly. At the word 'peace' he noticed a slight shift in the rebels around him. He could see Duff thinking about it – or maybe he just needed the toilet, it was hard to tell with someone who thought so slowly.

"Hmmm, you might be right, but your biggest problem is that I'm a businessman, as you rightfully said, respected throughout the city I am, and if I didn't get a better deal out of this little meeting than what I already have done, what kind of businessman would I be?" he asked, straightening out his jacket and brushing some invisible dust off his shoulder.

"How good will business be when the Army leave and the Lykor are at your door?" asked Eric. The question hung in the air like a bad smell, and despite the warmth of the sunlight coming in through the window the room felt very cold all of a sudden. "You won't get much passing trade if all the other cities and towns in this area find out you've got a beast problem on your doorstep" continued Eric unabashed. "Look," he said in his best conspiratorial tone, "give me the soldiers and I'll take them back, you keep what I had in the bag as a... goodwill gesture or whatever, and I'll speak to the Army boys and get you something good." He held his hand out again for Duff to shake.

"We want guns, food, and clothes" said the rebel leader, grinning and counting on his fingers quickly "and I'll give you one soldier. Take it or leave it. You return with what I want, and we won't kill the soldiers, can't say fairer than that, eh?"

"It's a deal," said Eric quickly, and offered his hand again. The rebel leader stood up and spat on his hand before shaking Eric's. "Excellent" said Eric, staring at his spit-covered hand. "I'll be off then?" He indicated the knives around his throat.

Duff gave a humourless laugh and gestured for the rebels around Eric to relax. Begrudgingly they lowered their weapons, and Duff gestured for Eric to leave the room. Eric took a couple steps forward, and was pushed along by one of the rebels standing behind him. Luckily he didn't lose his footing, and when he looked back he saw two rebels grinning at him. He glared at the two men, their eyes hidden behind dark sunglasses and their faces shrouded in big desert-trawler wraps. He was just about to say something when Duff said "Now, now, boys, let's not let violence get in the way of a good business deal," and the rebels slowly walked away from Eric.

The effect was probably supposed to intimidate Eric, but Eric didn't do intimidation. He watched as the men took up their positions in the corners of the room. One rebel stood by the door. Eric walked to the door as casually as he could muster, and pulled it open so fast the rebel standing next to it didn't have enough time to get out of the way, and was knocked flying into the wall. Eric left the room without a second glance and walked across the courtyard towards the windows where the prisoners had been standing.

Outside Eric heard the rebel he had knocked to the ground shouting and arguing with Duff, and then the click of a weapon being uncocked. Duff appeared by Eric's side. "Jimmy?" shouted the rebel leader to the line of windows where the scavenger soldiers were being held, "Bring down one of them prisoners." He did a quick step to catch up with Eric's fast pace.

A few minutes passed and then a very big man, dressed like an English football hooligan on holiday somewhere hot, appeared at a door dragging someone in army uniform. They had put one of the thick black hoods over the prisoner's head. Eric could see it was one of the scavenger women soldiers, but he couldn't tell which. She was thrown forward hard and skidded across the ground in front of him. Eric could hear muffled sounds of whimpering and crying coming from under the hood, and the noise ran straight down his spine. He clenched his fist, resisting the urge to hit the thug standing over her. He was laughing coarsely and had a strange glint in his eye. Instead Eric carefully bent down, picked the woman up, and walked her away.

"Don't take too long, Eric" called Duff. "We wouldn't want anything bad to happen to the other two while you're away."

Eric escorted the woman slowly down the alleyway, and turned a few corners before stopping. Then he removed the hood from her head and the rope from her wrists.

"Where are the others?" she demanded, looking around wildly.

"I could only get you" said Eric, throwing the hood and rope to one side.

"Why me?" she demanded suspiciously.

"I'm afraid I didn't get to choose who I brought back first. I didn't even know I was getting you until the hood came off" Eric said, inspecting her injuries.

"We have to go back and get them" she wailed, and turned to run back down the alleyway, but Eric caught her arm and stopped her. "You have to save them!" she screamed, and managed to wriggle out of Eric's grip.

"I don't think so" said Eric, grabbing her arm to stop her again. "Don't worry, I'm coming back for them later. Let's get you back to camp first and get your wounds looked at."

"I'm fine!" she wailed trying to shrug him off, and growled a little when she realised she couldn't get out of Eric's vice like grip a second time.

"Calm down girl" said Eric. "I'll be back for the other two, I promise, but for now we need to get you back to camp so you can have those wounds looked at." The scavenger soldier continued to fight against Eric's grip, but after a about half an hour she reluctantly agreed to walk alongside him without a fuss. Eric refused to lessen his grip on her arm, in case she ran back to the city and got herself killed.

"My name's Hayley, by the way" she said conversationally after a few more minutes of walking in silence.

"What?" said Eric. Her words had derailed his train of thought.

"My name, not that you've ever asked," said Hayley a little testily. "They said they knew someone would come for us." They had left the city limits, and the camp was in sight in the far distance. "They all sounded surprised and worried when it turned out to be you. They all got armed really quickly..." but here Eric gestured for her to be quiet. "We weren't the only ones in there..." she tried to continue, but Eric waved her into silence again.

"Don't worry, we'll get your wounds looked at, and then I will be back to deal with... how many people?" asked Eric, stopping dead in his tracks.

"I don't know, they had that fucking hood over my head most of the time when they were..." her voice trailed off, there was something about the way she had said this that made Eric pause.

"While they er..." he started saying, but stopped when he couldn't think of the right word for what he could only imagine an ogre might do to a young girl like her.

The pair carried on in silence, neither of them wanting to broach the subject of what had happened back in the city. The scavenger girl kept her head down and stared at the road, and Eric kept an eye out for any rebels that might have been keeping any eye on them.

CHAPTER 30

ARMY CAMP

The three scavengers finished off their shower and rushed to get dry and clothed before their Sergeant noticed they were late. Once fully dressed and ready to go, they rushed to meet up with the other scavenger teams to receive that day's orders. The others were already waiting patiently in the middle of the courtyard.

"Come on you three" shouted Sergeant Davies, "get in line immediately!" He glared as the three latecomers joined the line of soldiers in front of him. "Right, now that we are all here, here are your orders and city co-ordinates for this week. Same as last week, but for a few of you there are a couple of new areas to explore." He began handing out pieces of paper with their week's orders. The scavenger soldiers stared at the orders they had been given and sighed. It was pretty much the same thing week after week, nothing new ever happened for them. The regular soldiers got to go out on patrol and see the local countryside or towns, something a bit different, but they had to trawl through the same areas of the city, looking through the same piles of rubbish and bringing back half-full bags of junk. All the good stuff was deeper into the city limits, in the blocks of apartments, offices, shops, and so on.

"Can't we delve a little deeper Sergeant?" asked Hayley, looking at their team's co-ordinates. "We've been doing these two areas for the past month, there's nothing there."

"You do as you are ordered, soldier" came the automatic response from Sergeant. His tone was that of someone who had had this argument a lot over the past few months, and now had an automatic response ready.

"But Sergeant..." said another soldier.

"No," said Sergeant Davies. "You will search and report back on your given areas, that is all private, it is not your job to question my orders, it is not my job to question the orders I get from the officers. You do as you are told, and so do I. So if these are the areas the Captain and Major want us to search in, then these will be the areas we search, got it? Good," He turned on his heel. "Recon units ready!" he shouted. "Get your things together, and get out there... oh, and good luck." He marched off in the direction of the Command Tent. There seemed to be a lot of commotion in there this morning.

"This is bullshit!" exclaimed one of the scavenger soldiers when he was sure the Sergeant was out of earshot. "What areas have you guys got?" He snatched papers from the soldiers around him. "Ha! Same as last week, same as last week, ah something new... but we did this area two months ago" he said, looking through a set of orders.

"It's not fair" agreed Hayley. "I'm fed up of stripping copper wire from stuff just to make it look like I found a lot. These areas are dry. We need to move closer into the city." She looked around at the others, hoping for agreement from the others, but suddenly the floor was the most interesting thing anyone had ever seen. All eyes turned down, no one was willing to make eye-contact with anyone else, especially not Hayley. "Oh come on!" said Hayley looking around. She was the sort of girl who stamps her foot to punctuate her sentences and to show she is serious. "I bet we could find loads more good stuff if we move into the city," she went on. "We don't have to tell them where we found the stuff, do we?"

"I don't know Hayley," said one of the male scavengers. "If we start coming back with lots of stuff they'll know we didn't just stumble across it in the same place we've all looked a hundred times." This got murmurs of agreement from the other teams.

"Fine, don't take a chance, search through the same old crap you always do, we'll go into the city" said Hayley and looked for back up in her team, who were still busy staring at the floor. "Won't we, team?" she added meaningfully.

"Sure Hayley, whatever you want" said the other two in Hayley's team. They didn't want to go through the same areas either, but at the same time they didn't want to get caught breaking orders.

"That's settled then" stated Hayley. She stamped her foot again. "Let's get moving then."

The scavenger teams all inwardly sighed at Hayley. They would never say anything out loud, but Hayley was the sort of person that got bullied at the academy because she'd rather study than go to a party, but would still wind up in the same job as those that had gone to the party. They all rushed off to get their packs and supplies and dispersed out of the camp in different directions towards the city.

CHAPTER 31

RETURN TO CAMP

Back in the camp there was plenty of movement. Soldiers were running this way and that, some emptying tents, some loading supplies onto trucks and some even dismantling the showers. Officers stood around doing what officers do best, shouting at the soldiers to move faster, carry more, and generally do the work that the officers could have done if they weren't so damn busy shouting at other people to do it.

Eric and Hayley turned a corner of one of the rundown buildings on the very edge of the city's residential district and walked towards the ants' nest of an army camp. Eric's eyes picked out each soldier and calculated the chances of his tent already being taken down like the rest. But as they got closer he could see that his was the only tent that hadn't been taken down, and it didn't look like it was going to happen any time soon. It had a very lonely and neglected look to it.

"What's going on?" Hayley asked.

"I'm not sure, but it looks like they're bugging out" said Eric, eyeing his tent suspiciously. It didn't seem to have been touched, but he couldn't see the inside from there.

"We're moving camp?" she gasped, "but what about the others?"

"Leave that with me" said Eric. "You go see if they still have any medical supplies, and get those wounds checked out." He pointed across the camp to the medic tent.

"What are you going to do?"

"I'm going to find out what's happening. We're supposed to be gearing up to tackle the nest, not running scared" said Eric over his shoulder as he walked away in the direction of the command tent.

"Really?" exclaimed Hayley. "We're going to be taking on that nest you found?"

"No, we are going to tackle it, not you, go get yourself looked at by the medic" said Eric. He shooed her away from him and carried on walking. The pair parted ways and headed in different directions. Both of them had to dodge the other soldiers who were rushing around doing impressions of headless chickens.

The command tent had been stripped of nearly all its contents. A couple of officers were standing over the central table studying the few maps of the surrounding areas that hadn't been rolled up and packed away somewhere. One of them glanced up when Eric entered the tent, but quickly returned his attention to the map at hand.

The Major entered the tent behind Eric and bumped into him.

"Commander Mason!" exclaimed the Major. "What are you doing here? I figured you'd heard we were ordered to bug out, and had already gone on your way."

"Without my stuff or my tent? What's going on, Major?" asked

Eric. "Why is everyone running around?"

The major pushed past Eric and walked over to where the other officers were standing around the central table. "We have had new reports about the Zarda and this particular beast nest, Commander" said the Major over his shoulder. "The nest is too big for us to take on ourselves or with the help of the other outpost, but that's not the worst of it. There have been reports of enemy soldiers in the area heading this way." He was not taking his eyes off the map in the Captain's hands.

"That can't be" said Eric, joining the officers around the central table. "The Zarda are no threat in this area. There are only a few camps I've seen, and they're dotted around the place." He pointed at various areas on the map.

"That's what we used to believe" said one of the Captains, not looking up, "but new intel says they have started massing together, pooling multiple units to form bloody regiments."

"Oh right, that's not good" said Eric.

"It's very troubling that along with this big nest you found, well... it's time for us to make like a tree, and get the fuck out of here" the Major added with a little chuckle.

"But you can't just up and leave" said Eric. "Is the Army afraid of a few Zarda and a couple of big dogs?" He knew this wouldn't work, but it was worth a try. Pride was a wonderful thing in an officer – it made them easy to goad into a fight.

"From what we hear, Eric, there's a lot more than a few Zarda, and after hearing the reports from the scouts that didn't die in your investigation into that nest" – the words hung in the air for a moment – "the nest could be filled with several hundred beasts, all much bigger than average I hear."

"The Army will send in the Knight troops to deal with the nest" said another Captain, "and by all accounts your services are no longer required, Commander" he added snidely; he had never liked Eric.

"You can't just leave" snapped Eric. He opened his mouth to say more, but was interrupted by the Major.

"Oh really?" asked the Major. "you're giving the orders now are you?" He smiled coldly.

"No, of course not, but we have a situation that will require your attention before you go anywhere."

"And what might that be?" asked one of the officers around the table.

"Well…" said Eric hesitantly, "I was in the city earlier…"

"You were what?" the Captain exclaimed. "Soldiers are not permitted in the city. Even the scavenger units are not allowed into the inner limits!"

Eric could see he was the type of officer who obeys orders to the letter, and his world view would be distorted if he ever found out that anyone might be insolent or stupid enough not to do the same.

"I'm not a soldier, remember Captain?" he said, imitating the Captain's snide voice. Childish, Eric knew, but he did it anyway.

"What are you getting at, Commander?" asked the Major, holding a hand up to control the Captain, who looked as if he was about to explode.

"When I was in the city I saw some of your scavenger units being taken hostage by the rebels" said Eric quickly, keeping eye contact with the red-faced officer. "I went in to try to get them out…"

"Can't anyone follow orders?" the Captain interrupted, throwing up his hands to the gods. "They will be severely reprimanded when I get my hands on them!" he added, glaring at Eric.

"I think they have been through enough already" said Eric in his most calming voice. He wanted to see this officer explode. He turned to the Major. "They were badly beaten when I found them, and who knows what other kinds of hell they were put through."

The Major nodded. He had been in this war a long time, and had served in a few others, and knew full well the horrors some of the female prisoners had gone through. "I was able to negotiate for the life of one of them, a woman, who is I believe is getting her wounds looked at – assuming you still have a medic tent," Eric continued. "But the rebels still have two more prisoners. Major, there needs to be something done right away, or else I'll have to go back and let Mr Duff know where to send the bodies." He slammed his hand on the table for good measure. He instantly wished he hadn't, but it had made the Captain jump, so it was probably worth it.

"Well" said the Major thoughtfully, "good news that you were able to get one of them back here safe I guess. But bad news that they still have hostages."

"Good news?" shouted the Captain "We do not negotiate with the rebels. If they have taken some of our men, we should march in there and take them back!"

"What a good idea" said Eric sarcastically, "march in there with lots of soldiers and guns."

"Exactly" said the Captain in agreement, and then paused at the shock of what he had just heard. "What?" he demanded.

"You get your soldiers armed up and rush straight in there, and you'll have more rations to go around in the new camp you're headed to. You'll either lose good men and women as hostages for the city, or they'll simply be killed. Either way you won't have to feed them, although you'd have fewer people to help move camp."

The three men stood for a moment in silence. The Major looked around and saw all the soldiers staring at them, waiting for him to make a decision. "What do you suggest, Eric?" asked the Major.

"*What do you suggest, Eric?*" repeated the Captain mockingly under his breath.

"Delay bugging out for now, that order can wait surely. We're probably not in any immediate danger or HQ would have said something sooner, right?" said Eric.

"The order can *wait*?" exclaimed the Captain.

"Assign me a small taskforce…" said Eric, but he was interrupted by the Captain, who had heard enough from this non-officer.

"Assign you a bloody taskforce?" the Captain exclaimed at the top of his voice. "Major, you can't seriously be considering this madman's plan. We have orders…" But he was silenced by the Major, who held up an authoritative hand.

"I think" said the Major carefully, "that maybe you need to go out and get some fresh air, Captain, clear your head a little. What would you have us do? Leave our own in the city as hostages? Go take a walk, Captain, and don't come back until you have a proper head on those shoulders."

The Captain looked from the Major to Eric and then back at the Major, and then around the tent for back up from the other officers. But everyone else suddenly had much more important things to occupy their minds, like staring at their boots, or studying the maps, or writing stuff down on some paper, but all trying desperately not to catch the Captain's eye. The officer stamped his foot in disgust. Then, realising he wasn't going to win this argument, yet, he marched out of the tent and across the camp.

"I can get them back," said Eric after the officer had gone. "I just need a few light-footed experienced soldiers, and I can go in there and get them out. I don't think we have much of a window of opportunity here, and the time is ticking, sir." He looked at his wrist watch. He thought the 'sir' part was a good addition. It never hurt to let an officer think he was better than you, especially a Major.

"You're not going to take a whole squad and get them all killed trying to save two hostages are you?" asked another Captain, a man whom Eric recognised from the nest scouting party a few days before. "My advice, Major, is don't let them take any grenades." He gave a snort of laughter.

"Are you volunteering to go with the Commander then?" asked the Major over his shoulder.

"I'm volunteering to go in and help save the hostages, sir, if that's what you mean," said the Captain, stepping forward and saluting the Major.

"Excellent" said the Major happily. "I like a soldier who isn't afraid to do some fighting for a change." He stared Eric in the eye. "You are not to let any of them die, Eric. I heard what you did at that nest. I don't blame you, I don't know what I would have done in that situation myself, but just see it doesn't happen this time, all right?"

"You have my word" said Eric. The Major's stare was unnerving him a little. "I know where they will be keeping the hostages, and I reckon with a select few we could easily get in and out without being seen or heard." He turned aside. "So long as they don't do anything stupid, like get caught, or get themselves shot" he muttered.

"I can't stop the camp from bugging out. Orders are orders Commander, it might raise suspicion within the ranks." He turned to the volunteer. "Captain, assemble a team of soldiers and get them ready to move out as soon as possible." The Captain saluted again and left the tent.

"That's fine by me" said Eric, turning to leave too, "but we'll need to do this under cover of night, so I recommend we meet just before sundown."

"What are you going to do until then?" asked the Major as Eric walked towards the tent entrance.

"I'm going to check on the patient, and make sure none of your soldiers try to pack up my things. I don't plan to be moving on to the next camp with you, I'm sure you can do without me hanging around getting your brave men and women killed."

With that Eric turned on his heel, left the tent and walked

through the camp in the direction of the medic tent. He rarely needed to use the medic tent, so it took him a few attempts to find it. He had kept up the pretence that he was just a normal guy for the first few weeks by rushing to the medic each time he was hurt, but this got a little tiresome, and he hadn't realised how many wounds he collected on each mission to a Lykor nest. After the third time the Medic asked "How are you still alive with all those wounds and lack of blood?" So Eric had given up going, and healed himself in his tent when no one was looking.

CHAPTER 32

THE HOTEL

The door to the small kitchen slammed shut behind Eric and the hotel thug and they started down the corridor. Eric noticed each door was locked with a thick bar across it and a padlock. Whatever was in those rooms, someone didn't want it to be found.

The guard stopped suddenly, took a set of keys out of his pocket unlocked the nearest door and threw it open. Inside, all was darkness. He gestured to the interior, grunted, turned and walked back down the corridor towards the kitchen.

"Thank you kindly" called Eric. "Can I request a wakeup call in a few hours?"

"Do what you need to" growled the guard, without looking back. "Just don't make a mess."

"Ok" Eric called after him, "I'll tell Johnny you were all very helpful." There were a lot of keys on that keyring, Eric reflected.

Surely they wouldn't bother giving him a key to all the doors, would they? Surely they'd just assign a troll like him the important room keys. But if that was the case, they must have a few rooms on each floor. How many floors were there? He vowed to come back and investigate once the mission was complete – he didn't have time for all that now.

He stuck his head through the bedroom door and looked around. Inside were several boxes on either side of the small room. A couple of the boxes were open and Eric could plainly see that on one side someone had stacked vials and bags of the Regretamin drug, while on the other side were containers full of money. The notes looked old and very well-used, and there were many of them, all neatly put in bundles ready to be laundered.

Eric walked into the room and inspected the boxes of Regretamin. Laid out in front of him were enough tubes of liquid and bags of white crystal powder to sink a ship, or destroy an entire city. The window at the end of the room was locked tight, and there were metal bars running across it, so there'd be no way of getting the drugs or the cash out that way. Not that he wanted to of course. He pocketed a few bags of the white crystal powder and some of the money – mustn't be too greedy. Then he turned on his heel and marched out of the room and into the corridor outside. He shut the door behind him as quietly as possible, checked the kitchen door at the end of the corridor was still shut, and relaxed a little.

Eric quietly tiptoed to the kitchen door and put his ear to the keyhole. He could hear men talking in muffled voices and a radio in the background. From what he could make out the men were bitching about the boss sending someone new to check their operation without sending word first. One of the men said something about giving Eric an hour with the 'merchandise' before he went in to check on him. Presumably he was planning to use a baseball bat, or a sock with a rock in it. Eric only had a little while before the alarm would be sounded.

From his back pocket Eric fished out a crumpled piece of paper. On it was a very crude drawing of a floor plan of the hotel. There was only one floor shown, so he had to hope the building was laid out the same way on each level. He continued down the corridor, and took a few turnings, occasionally referring to his map. In the furthest room at the end of all the corridors Eric found what he was looking for, and replaced the small map back into his pocket.

The room looked like every other room in the building. He could imagine middle-aged, recently-divorced men sitting on the beds in the cramped little rooms, shedding silent tears and wondering how life had gone so wrong. The whole place stank of desperation and damp. The carpets were mouldy and the wallpaper was hanging off in places.

Eric moved quickly to the furthest corner of the room and inspected the carpet. After a couple of pulls it came away from the floor, revealing rotting wooden floorboards underneath. From an inside jacket pocket Eric fished out a small hooked metal tool, which he used to pry up the floorboards to find concrete and water pipes underneath. Once all the boards had been moved he crouched down on all fours and pressed his ear against the concrete, but he could hear nothing. How much noise could a group of armed men make whilst not doing anything? He shrugged.

Eric took a deep breath, raised his foot high, and brought his heel down hard on the concrete, which cracked slightly under his boot. He tried again and again. The concrete cracked and crumbled a little more, but he could not make a hole in it.

He took a couple of steps back and held both hands out at shoulder height. He shut his eyes and slowly folded his arms so he had one hand on top of the other in front of him, and when he pulled them apart his palms glowed with a warm yellow light that illuminated the room around him. He drew himself up to his full height, and stuck both arms out to his sides in the pose of

Leonardo's Vitruvian Man. The light from his hands left thin streaks of light in the air as they moved. He jumped into the air, bringing both fists down as hard as he could on the concrete floor like an Olympic diver. The floor buckled under him, and Eric disappeared in a cloud of smoke and creaking stone.

The hotel was seen, before the War, as a place where a man could get a cheap bed for the night, no questions asked. Many men used the hotel as a place to entertain moderately attractive women who usually charged by the hour, at a rate negotiated beforehand. Its other redeeming feature was that it was well known for being a place where a man could get a cheap drink, cheap company, and even cheaper food, and it was never quiet.

It was the hotel's large kitchen that Eric found himself crashing into though the ceiling. In a hail of rock and dust the ceiling exploded and Eric hit the floor shoulder first. The noise of the explosion radiated down the halls and corridors of the hotel, echoing across the restaurant and bar, and armed men and women throughout the building heard it.

"Shit!" grunted Eric. He jumped to his feet, looking around wildly for a hiding place, and ran across the kitchen. He threw himself inside one of the big metal cupboards and shut the door behind him just as the big kitchen double-doors were thrown open.

Inside the metal box Eric had to curl up into a tight ball. The golden light from his hands illuminated his face and chest and sent flickering shadows around the cupboard's walls like light from a candle being blown around. He cupped both his hands over his nose and mouth, limiting the amount of light shining out. Then he took a deep breath and blew into his hands, hard. The light in his hands flickered like an old light bulb. Sparks flew out between his fingers, but the light soon sputtered out. Wrapped in darkness, he tried to edge himself into a more comfortable position, which wasn't easy, and press an ear up against the cold metal cupboard door.

Three men came rushing into the kitchens with weapons cocked and raised. They spread out around the room and inspected the hole in the ceiling and the pile of rubble underneath it. Off to one side, they failed to notice the yellow glow around the edges of the cupboard door. If they had been looking, they would have seen the light darken, and then flicker out. As it was they were too interested in checking the hole Eric had come through.

"What the fuck happened here?" asked one of the men, aiming his assault rifle up into the hole in the ceiling.

"Must have just caved in" said another man. "This fucking place is falling apart."

Just then two more men burst into the kitchen with their weapons raised. They only just stopped themselves firing at their comrades.

"What the hell is going on in here?" demanded one of the newcomers suspiciously. He lowered his weapon slightly, but not all the way in case of trouble.

"Ceiling fell in by the looks of it, Rambo" said the first man dismissively. The man called Rambo was carrying three large hunting knives, a sawn-off double-barrelled shotgun, two pistols, several belts of ammo with knuckle duster type rings hooked from them and a small machine gun that was strapped half way up his leg. He made the other men in the gang cringe with embarrassment. He was a one-man army who couldn't move very fast and clanked when he ran. By the time he could decide which weapon to use in a shoot-out, he would have been shot dead himself.

The men lowered their weapons. "What a dump" said one of the guards as they turned to leave the kitchen.

"What did you do?" demanded Rambo suspiciously. He had never like these guys because of their constant teasing, and he was sure he could outshoot any of them.

"We didn't do anything, mate" said one of the first three.

"Come on lads, let's get out of here."

"No one leaves until I have done a full sweep of the quadrant" exclaimed Rambo, raising his weapon again. He rushed around the kitchen, opening cupboards at random, checking through doors, checking the pantry, and then inspected the hole in the ceiling. It was more theatrical than thorough. Luckily for Eric, he completely missed the cupboard. The other men waited. It was easier to let Rambo do what he wanted than get in his way.

Rambo finally gave the all-clear and dismissed the men back to whatever they had been doing before he had turned up to take charge.

The last man was just about to leave the kitchen when something on the floor caught his eye. The man let the two double-doors bang shut and walked over to where the dust from the ceiling had settled on the floor. He crouched down and examined what had caught his eye. He could just about make out a footprint in the dust.

Meanwhile inside the metal cupboard, Eric heard the door to the kitchen bang shut and sat listening for a moment, because only a fool would rush out of their hiding place straight away. After a short pause, he gently opened the cupboard door a crack. In front of him the man who had stayed behind was kneeling down with his back to the cupboard, inspecting something on the floor; Eric's footprints.

Eric fished around frantically, but without moving and giving himself away he could not reach any of his weapons. All his hands could find was the metal hook he had used to pry up the floor boards upstairs. It would have to do. He took a deep breath and burst out of the cupboard, throwing himself across the kitchen floor like a pouncing tiger, and landed on top of the man. He took a big swing in mid-air, stabbed the hooked tool deep into the man's throat and pulled hard. The man tried to scream, but Eric's other hand clamped down hard over his mouth, muffling the sound. Eric pulled the man backwards across the floor by his head. The man thrashed about, desperately trying to connect a hand or fist with his attacker, but Eric was able to dodge each blow. He reached to his belt and found the hunting knife, then brought it across the man's throat. The life slowly slipped away from the man's body until he let out one long last breath, as if his lungs were deflating. Blood spurted out from the gash in the man's neck and ran down his chest and body, and a puddle began to form on the tiled floor.

Eric stood up quickly and wiped the blade on the man's sleeve. Then he gripped the man's shoulders and dragged him to a large walk-in freezer. It took a little effort, but Eric managed to get the door open on the third attempt and dumped the body inside before kicking the door shut behind him. The freezer stank. The thing must have died a long time ago, and no one had thought to fix it. There was no ice left, and the small room had that distinctive defrosted smell to it. The body probably wouldn't make it smell any worse, and it would be a nice surprise for the next person who opened the door.

Eric walked quickly to the kitchen door, narrowly managing to avoid slipping on the puddle of blood, and looked through the small window that looked out into the restaurant. A group of men were walking through the restaurant laughing and joking together, and when they reached the far end they split up and went through different doors. Eric did not like the look of the biggest man.

Before the doors in the restaurant closed, he was able to get a glimpse of hallways and corridors, none of which interested him much. The men looked the same as the ones upstairs, but there was something different about them. Their ears looked slightly pointed, their eyes slightly brighter, and judging by how many had managed to get into the kitchen that fast, the hotel must be full of them. Eric wasn't prejudices; he didn't see the point in discriminating against skin colour or species, but these guys were always a pain on missions. Their hearing was far too good, their reactions were far too fast, they were usually a lot stronger than normal men and they could move silently, which annoyed Eric and slowed him down.

He fished out the scrap of paper again and studied it. The other door into the kitchen seemed like the best way to get into the cellar. He hadn't been expecting to have to go into the cellar, but if that guy's information was correct about some big bosses down there, then down into the cellar he must go.

He looked around and saw in the far corner a small door. He stuffed the paper back into his pocket and strolled over to it. After a few seconds of putting his ear up against the wood, he decided that there was no one on the other side and pulled it open. On the other side of the door was a narrow staircase leading down. The light from the kitchen illuminated only the top few steps. Eric had excellent eyesight, but even he was finding himself squinting into the darkness. The steps disappeared into the darkness below.

With a quick glance back into the kitchen, Eric began to descend the steps. The boards squeaked under his feet, so he decided to get it over with and took them two at a time. The shadows embraced him as he moved out of the light's reach, and when the door shut behind him, he vanished into darkness.

CHAPTER 33

THE TRANSPORTER SHIP

Eric Mason woke up. His entire body hurt, and every inch of his skin was screaming out in pain. It felt like someone had moved from the top of his head down to the tips of his toes while hitting him very hard with a very small, but very accurate, hammer and chisel.

He was lying face down on an extremely cold, hard surface; he managed to move both aching arms underneath his body, and with trembling hands he pushed himself off the ground and rolled himself onto his back. The warm yellow light coming from the tube that ran around the room hadn't got any lighter whilst he had been unconscious, and his internal body clock told him that that had been quite a while.

He raised his hands up to look at them and forced his blurry eyes to focus. His fingers and hands were badly burnt, but they had already started to heal, and he could see fresh pink skin around the burnt areas.

At the fourth attempt he managed to sit fully upright without wincing or falling back down, and looked around the cell. The big shimmering liquid silver door was still glowing at one end of the room, mocking him, but in two areas there seemed to be slight impressions. Eric squinted at the liquid's surface. The impressions looked like hand prints, but they were fading, and soon he couldn't see them at all. Eric sat there for a moment and asked all parts of his body to send damage reports. Some were more disturbing than others.

He slowly got up and walked over to the only thing in the cell that could be described as a bed. It was a narrow metal slab that had been welded to the wall and floor, and he was able to sit down on it without too much pain. He held his hands out in front of his body. They were shaking wildly and he had to clench and unclench them a few times to make them a little steadier.

He took a closer look at his fingers. On the surface of the burnt skin there seemed to be a silvery sheen, as if he had put both hands down on a table that had recently been painted. He sat there for a moment letting the dull light from the room reflect off the silvery haze on his fingers. It would appear that he was staying put in this cell, whether he liked it or not. He could probably charge the liquid door and try to force himself through it, and it would probably work too, but Eric doubted if many people tried that approach with burning fingertips, and he didn't fancy getting the burns all over his body.

The sound of laughter snapped Eric out of his trance, and he looked up and around the room. It came again, and Eric jumped to his feet.

"Hello?" said Eric to the empty room, and immediately felt stupid for doing so. The laughter got louder as Eric moved across the room to the silvery liquid wall, and Eric stood for a moment, making sure not to get too close to the rippling surface. "Hello?" he tried again.

"You dumb bastard!" came a voice from the other side of the silver wall. It was a male voice, gruff and dry, and it appeared to be laughing at something hilarious.

"Hello?" asked Eric "Who are you, where am I this time?"

"We're on a transport ship to hell, my friend" said the voice after a moment's thought.

"Been there," said Eric dismissively under his breath. "Who are you?" he asked the wall in a much louder voice.

"Does it matter?" came the instant response.

Eric thought about this for a moment and shrugged. "I guess not" he said, and walked to the nearest wall and leant up against it. "How long have we been in here?" His body was still aching like crazy.

"Who can say, my friend? I am not wearing a watch. I saw you try to open your door." The laughter began again. "It was very funny the way you flew across the little room."

"Yeah, yeah, very funny," mumbled Eric. "It hurt like shit by the way, thanks for asking." More laughing.

"I bet it did, I bet it really did" said the voice. "My name is Jack, but everyone either calls me Jackal or Jax" it added by way of introduction.

Eric sneered at this. "Jax it is then," he mumbled.

"What was that?" the voice asked. It sounded as if it was coming from far away.

"I said, how you can see me in here?" called Eric without missing a beat.

"The door is made from their strange technology. The more violent or dangerous the prisoner, the more difficult it is to see through it. Mine is crystal clear because I came quietly, eventually" said the voice proudly. "I killed several of them, of course, but when I was finally captured I came in quietly. You must have put up a lot of resistance my friend, I can only just see through yours."

"Fair enough" said Eric, now wishing he had played dead instead of getting up on that pile of bodies. "So, how are we going to get out of here then?"

"You got hit on the head before you tried to touch the electric door?" the voice asked.

"A few times, yeah" replied Eric. "Why do you ask?"

"Only a guy who's not thinking straight would try to put his hand through one of their electric-liquid doors. They're obviously not meant to be touched, or at least it was obvious to me. I would have to assume that the shock of the door must have blown a fuse in your brain, my friend, if you think you are getting out of that cell before they want you out of it."

"Why is that?" asked Eric.

"Because you'd have to be mad if you think we are ever going to escape this. You, my friend, are on a direct route to hell, and so am I. There is no escape, and when we get there, we will be tortured and killed."

"Is that so" said Eric thoughtfully. "I think they may have trouble with me, I don't tend to die easily." He tried changing his position on the wall he was leaning against.

"That's the spirit" said the voice of Jax in a happy tone. "Keep that in mind for when we get out the other side, and they start cutting you."

"Great, will do" Eric said "I'd better have a sleep so I'm well rested for all the excitement." He pushed himself off the wall and walked to the big metal slab on the far wall.

Eric lay down on the metal bed. He could still hear dry laughter coming from his new friend Jack, and he could feel his body trying to heal itself. He shut his eyes and instantly slipped into a deep and yawning slumber. Eric could quite literally sleep anywhere, if he was tired enough.

CHAPTER 34

THE ARMY CAMP

The sun had started its final descent across the sky, and was nearly at the horizon. It now illuminated the sky in every shade of red and yellow, framed by the dark blue of the approaching night sky. The Army camp had been pretty much all packed up now, leaving heaps of rubbish in several areas and bits deemed unnecessary to be transported. The trucks were all loaded up, and several were bulging at the sides. Soldiers were rushing this way and that, trying to fit in the smaller items they had been told to pack. Only one tent remained where the camp had been, an island in the open space, and if you listened carefully you could hear faint snores from inside it.

A small squad of soldiers, led by a Captain, was marching across the derelict campus towards Eric's tent. They came to a noisy halt a few metres away and waited. When the snoring continued, the Captain walked to the entrance and coughed politely. Or rather, as politely as someone could when trying to wake up someone who had a reputation for being violent when woken. When this had no effect either, the Captain gingerly opened the tent's entrance and peered inside. His eyes widened a little, and he threw open the tent flap.

"Commander Eric Mason!" the Captain bellowed in a loud clear tone. The snoring stopped. The Captain hesitated for a moment, and when there was no sign of movement, he entered the tent.

Inside were several army bags, obviously full of clothes, cooking equipment and objects the Captain didn't dare look too closely at. He had heard the stories of what happened to officers when they tried to confiscate any of Eric's belongings, or were caught going through his bags. But more worryingly, laid out on the small standard army-issue chest of drawers were a number of different weapons, including three pistols, an automatic machine gun, an assault rifle, a pump action shot gun and a range of knives and other implements obviously designed to inflict a great deal of pain. The Captain did his impression of someone who had completely failed to see anything of interest, and turned his attention to the half-asleep Eric lying on his cot. He had stopped snoring, but he was definitely asleep.

"Commander" said the Captain in the quiet tones of someone who does not really want to wake someone up, but has no choice. "We would appreciate it if you would be so kind as to join the squad" he said sarcastically. There was no response. He waited a moment, then picked up Eric's heavy boots and dropped them onto his feet from shoulder height.

The impact of the boots made Eric jump up instantly, both fists clenched. The Captain stepped cautiously back out of reach, but instead of disembowelling him Eric looked around and rubbed his eyes with a hand. Then he tried to focus on the Captain.

"Piss off" he said simply when his eyes focused on the uniform. "I thought we weren't meeting until sundown." He lay back and got himself comfortable again.

"The sun will be down shortly, Commander," the Captain went on. "We've been waiting at the command tent for over an hour. We need to get going if we don't want to have to find our way through the city in the dark." He turned and marched out of the tent.

Eric, his eyes still shut, stuck two fingers up at the place where the Captain had last been standing and very slowly sat up with a groan. He was beginning to regret drinking that bottle of whisky earlier, but the sleep had marginally helped. "I can see in the bloody dark" he muttered to himself, and slowly turned and swung his feet over the edge of the cot. The boots banged as they hit the floor. He groaned again, and then put them on.

"We're losing sunlight out here, Commander" came the voice of the Captain from outside. Eric raised two fingers in the Captain's direction and then pulled on his Army issue black shirt and jacket.

He picked up his weapons one by one and checked them, then stowed them in various holsters and other hiding places around his body. When he had run out of places to hide them, he stuffed the remaining few into his bags. "Coming boss" Eric called over his shoulder, "running all the way". He picked up the last whisky bottle and drained it. Then he looked for a certain area where the ground had been disturbed and used one hand to brush away enough dirt to revealed a rough-looking metal road sign. He pulled it aside to reveal the deep hole where he had stashed several more empty bottles. The one in his hand was placed carefully down with the others. He stood up and adjusted his clothes to look a little more respectable, then pushed his way out of the tent and into the dim light of the dusk and twilight evening air.

Out in the empty campsite he looked around, rubbing his face. As soon as the Captain saw him he shouted "Attention!" and the squad stamped their feet and stood alert. The noise made Eric jump. He sighed and waved for the squad to go away, then turned to go back inside the tent, fully prepared to go back to bed. The Captain grabbed his shoulder. "Your squad is ready for inspection, Commander Mason" he said loudly, and gestured at the squad behind him.

Eric shuddered. "Just Eric will be fine, Captain. So these are the brave men and women who will be going into the mouth of hell, are they?" he said. He did his best to look like he knew what he was doing. He didn't really care what the squad was like, because he didn't intend them to be anywhere near him when he dealt with Mr Duff.

He inspected the squad the Captain had picked for the mission. They didn't look like much. The Captain might have gone to the food tent and simply grabbed the first six soldiers he saw. Eric didn't know it, but that this was almost exactly what the Captain had done. He had asked for volunteers, but only two people had put their hands up, and when they found out it was a mission with Eric Mason they had quickly melted away, so the Captain had tapped the closest five soldiers on the shoulder and ordered them, much to their dismay, to eat up, get suited up, and meet at the command tent as soon as possible.

That would have been the end of it, but as the Captain marched the unlucky five men out of the food tent, he heard a shout from behind him. Hayley, the female scavenger soldier, now somewhat recovered and sporting some new bandages over her cuts and bruises, was rushing over to him. She demanded to be allowed to join the squad, and even though the Captain had explained that the mission was with Eric, she was determined to join in and help. Scavenger soldiers were notorious for not having much skill in combat, which is why they were scavengers and not real soldiers, but she had insisted, so he had reluctantly agreed. He had never seen or heard of anyone before who gunned for a place on one of Commander Eric Mason's missions.

The Captain wasn't too impressed with the selection, but his orders from the Major were to get Eric into something he couldn't get himself out of, leave him there and get the hostages back to camp, where a Jeep would be waiting for them, all fuelled up and ready to go. The squad didn't need to be tip-top, they just had to be there to help get Eric into the city and get the hostages out safely. Although he wasn't entirely sure what situation he would be able to get Eric into that he couldn't get out of.

"They don't look like much" said Eric. "Why are they carrying so much?" he was staring at the packs on the soldiers' backs.

"Standard army issue pack, Eric" said the Captain. He watched the big transport trucks on the other side of camp start up their engines. "They need them to carry their stuff around." As the trucks moved off they revealed a single Jeep standing on its own.

Eric turned his attention back to the squad. "Right boys and girls" he said, pulling the pack from the nearest soldier's back. "You will not need any of this crap. You will need two hands, a gun, and your wits about you. This is going to be a stealth mission, and carrying a big heavy bag that clangs is not my definition of stealth."

The squad looked to the Captain for confirmation. He begrudgingly nodded, and they all shrugged off their packs.

"You, what's your name?" the Captain asked the nearest soldier.

"Private Tolley, sir" he replied, jumping to attention and saluting.

"Well Private Tolley, take the packs over to that Jeep and get them loaded on the back" said the Captain, gesturing towards the loan Jeep that had been left behind for their quick getaway after the mission was finished.

Tolley saluted again and rushed to pick up all the packs, then bustled them over to the Jeep and rushed back.

"Ok Eric, lead on," said the Captain.

"Right you are then" said Eric, giving a very casual salute and turning on his heel. "Follow me, ladies and gentlemen. Do not dawdle, do not make any unnecessary noise, and if I tell you to get down, I expect you to hug the ground like it's your long-lost mother."

The soldiers looked from one to another and glanced to the Captain, who sighed and nodded at them. Then they marched off to follow Eric towards the abandoned city.

CHAPTER 35

PRISONER TRANSPORT SHIP

Eric Mason woke up instantly. He was flying through the air; whatever this prisoner transport ship had hit, it had hit it hard. He landed forcefully on the metal floor and rolled into the silvery liquid door, which instantly electrocuted him and sent him flying back across the floor until he found himself banging heavily against the metal bed slab.

"What the fuck..." Eric rocked on the ground trying to clutch at all the areas that hurt, but he didn't have enough hands. He was cut short by sounds of yelling and screaming coming from all around him. He glared at the silvery wall. He would find who had invented it and do something horrible to them, like lock them in a small box made from the electric liquid and watch them fry.

The dull light from the tubes around the cell started to fade out, and soon Eric was lying on the floor in almost pitch darkness.

The only light was the cold, silvery light from the door. Eric shook his head, trying to dislodge the ball of pain in the centre of his brain caused by the electric shock and the impact with the metal bed. He glanced at the small puddle of blood he had left on the edge of the bed, which was slowly dripping to the floor. He got to his feet a little unsteadily. The screams and shouts were getting louder as more voices joined in, and the effect was nearly deafening.

The glow from the silvery wall seemed to brighten a little. Eric walked over to it trying to make out singular voices in the orchestra of shouts and screams, but none of them were making sense. They were mostly cries for help or howls of pain, and shouts filled with the sour tint of fear. There were a lot of very scared people in here. Their fear was intoxicating to Eric, and he almost felt a little lightheaded because of it. It had been a very, very long time since he had felt this much fear and pain in one place.

The silvery liquid shone extremely bright for a few seconds, causing Eric to squint and take a step back, and when he opened his eyes again he saw that the silvery liquid was dissolving into thin air. After a second or two there the silvery liquid had completely vanished, leaving only a hollow cell doorway, but the doorway wasn't empty. Standing in the narrow corridor between the lines of cells, was the largest Zarda Eric had ever seen. Standing at least seven and a half feet tall, the reptilian monster had to duck as it placed a large foot inside Eric's cell.

This warrior was not wearing the usual thick metal plate armour that most of the Zarda soldiers wore, or the black suit of the foot soldiers. It wore a big leather apron, covered in blood and bits of what could have been skin or bone, and a pair of tough-looking trousers. It was hardly dressed for style and looked more like a butcher than a fighter. Its scales were a very dark green, but each one had a dark red tip, which usually meant a fighter, and a reptile of great strength. Eric wondered what it used its strength for.

The reptilian mountain lumbered forward and reached out a

big three-fingered hand to grab at Eric, who, without missing a beat, stood up straight, clenched his fist, and slammed it into the creature's chest as hard as he could. The resulting shock ran up Eric's arm and buried deep in his shoulder. It felt like his arm was going to fall off.

"Bet that hurt you as much as it hurt me" said Eric.

The giant reptile grinned a little more and clenched its own fist, Eric backed away slightly, thinking that this was definitely not how things were meant to play out. He had fully expected the door to open at some point, and had decided that whoever was stupid enough to be on the other side was going to be very, very sorry. It didn't matter that Eric hadn't been expecting such a big target, but it did matter that his punch didn't seem to have had the slightest effect on this guy. That punch was supposed to have knocked him to the ground so that Eric could simply step over the body, decide which way was out and fight his way out of this transport ship, probably assisted by a few other prisoners as a sort of revolution thing no doubt. They could throw off the shackles of their current oppressor together, and be home in time for dinner and medals.

The scales around the reptile's neck started to glow red and the skin around its mouth curled up into a snarl, revealing a mouthful of razor-sharp teeth. The reptile began making a long-drawn-out noise which sounded like a growl, but as the reptile got closer Eric realised that it was in fact a laugh. All he had done was awaken the big green bastard's sense of humour.

He tried shaking some life back into his arm. As the lumbering giant got closer again, Eric raised both fists and moved his feet into his favourite fighting stance.

"I would just do as he says," came the voice of Jax behind the reptile.

"He hasn't said anything yet" Eric called back, not breaking eye contact with the reptilian butcher.

Jax laughed. "Well I hope you know what you're doing" he said.

The giant swung a fist at head height. It moved in a big slow arc and Eric easily ducked it, but when the second fist followed it was a rising uppercut, which Eric had read all wrong, so he ducked into the punch. The big fist struck the centre of Eric's face, nearly flattening his nose and sending him flying back so that he rebounded off the wall above the metal bed.

He managed to regain his feet and rushed forward, sending four quick jabs into the giant's chest. This had no effect at all, and the giant's grin got wider. Eric tried again and again, like a boxer training against a punch bag, but not one punch seemed to cause him more than a little discomfort. He spun round to give his next punch a little more strength, and now a faint yellow haze surrounded his fist, but the giant simply reached out, caught the fist in mid-air and held him to the spot.

All the blood drained from Eric's face. He knew he was beaten. The giant used Eric's hand to propel him around the room and slammed him into one of the metal walls. Eric fought to retrieve his hand, but the giant reptile held on tight. The grin widened further, and now he began to use Eric like a hammer, smashing him repeatedly into the walls on either side of the cell. Eric looked like a rag-doll in the hands of an excitable child. Finally Eric hit the wall with such force that he felt a bone in his arm break and his shoulder pop out of its socket. His body went limp, and he shrank to the metal floor.

The giant turned slowly, gave a deep rumbling laugh and walked towards the door, dragging Eric behind him. Eric winced at the pain ripping through his arm and shoulder and flailed around, trying to stand up. It felt like someone had filled his shoulder with broken glass.

Eric looked past the giant and saw Jax for the first time. He was standing in the cell opposite Eric's, behind another reptilian giant. They had both taken a moment to watch the display, fully enjoying themselves. As Eric was dragged past them and down the narrow corridor, he looked back and saw Jax being pushed out his own cell and forced to follow.

"OK, OK, no need to push" Jax growled over his shoulder, revealing slightly pointed white teeth.

Eric and Jax were taken to the large hangar door at the back of the ship, passing maybe thirty more cells. Eric looked up and saw that although the ship did not appear to be very big, they had managed to put in three levels of prison cells. For a species which was known for not taking prisoners, they certainly seemed prepared for them. Several of the cells contained nothing but motionless bodies. No doubt that was what happened when you tried to force your way through a liquid-electric silvery wall door thingy.

Eric had to squint to look outside. The sun was high up in the sky, and shining blindingly bright rays down upon them. The wind picked up and blew hot air at them, baked by the sun and the transporter ships' red hot engines. Spread out in front of the transport ships was a sea of moving people. Some were Zarda, but most were human, and the reptilian brutes were ushering their prisoners into what looked like a giant hole in the rocky ground. Stretching out to the horizon was brownish-red sand as far as the eye could see, and in all directions, stretching out to the horizon, was barren wasteland, relieved by the occasional patch of grass and some anorexic-looking trees. It was painfully clear that there wasn't much water around, which meant any would-be escape artist probably wouldn't get very far.

Eric and Jax were among the last to be pulled out of their cells and ushered down the transporter ship's gangway, followed by a line of sheepish-looking soldiers who looked at Eric through red and tear-filled eyes. When they were out in the fresh air Eric looked around some more and saw the lines of transporters on either side of their own, each with a steady trickle of civilians or soldiers being marched in the same direction. From above they must have looked like lines of ants, all marching in lines towards a big nest.

The wind picked up again, and carried the sound of shouting from the mass of bodies in front of them to where Eric and Jax were standing. They could make out screams of pain and suffering coming from the hole in the ground too, and Eric remembered Jax's comment about being taken to hell. Eric had been to hell himself once and he hadn't much cared for it, it was far too hot, and dangerous too. But if hell came to earth, this was probably what it would look like.

Just then a fight broke out in the sea of prisoners; it seemed that some of the soldiers had decided now was a good time to try and fight their way out of this situation. A circle opened up in the crowd, and Eric could see several soldiers clustered together with their backs to one another, doing their best to fight off the smaller and much faster Goblin soldiers. The Goblins, despite their size, were even nastier than the big reptile brutes. They were fast, cruel and extremely intelligent.

In the surrounding crowd Eric could see ripples of movement as the larger reptile brutes homed in on the soldier's location, like bouncers in a busy night club, only with less care for the people who were trampled on or pushed out of the way. The scrapping soldiers all screamed in fear as the large reptile men closed in on them. Some tried to defend themselves, but they were all quickly subdued. Most of the big reptiles carried long clubs the size of Eric's arm, and these were used to deal with difficult prisoners, in a bone-breaking kind of way. The smell of fear was worse than the stink inside the transporter ship, and the unmistakable metallic smell of blood quickly filtered up through the haze.

"See what I mean?" said Jax. "Welcome to hell."

Just then the pair were pushed forward to join the queues of prisoners.

"How do I not know about this place?" asked Eric, and winced in pain as the giant reptile let go of his broken arm. "Ouch! Yeah thanks for that... lesson learnt. What's in the hole?"

"Death and torture, my friend" said Jax. "Can't you smell it?"

"I don't have your feline nose" said Eric dismissively.

"So you know what I am?" asked Jax, a little taken aback.

"I have eyes and ears, and yours are slightly pointed, same as your teeth, and the way you speak... and smell" he added with a little laugh.

"Oh is that all?" asked Jax. "You are a clever man Mr Eric Mason, a very clever man. But I fear it won't do you any good here."

"This guy could find something to laugh about in a morgue" murmured Eric to himself. He laughed a little at how quickly Jax backed away from the big brute.

A light punch to the backs of both their heads silenced the pair, so they continued to walk forward like naughty schoolboys to join the nearest line of prisoners. Eric noticed some of the men and women around him were civilians. They were probably the only survivors of an attack. There were even children there, being marched in line, tears streaming down their faces, and calling desperately for their parents. When Eric saw one of the reptiles grin at a little girl just to scare her even more, it was all Eric could do not to try and rip its head off. The girl couldn't have been more than six years old. Her clothes with sodden with tears and she was still holding on tight to her teddy bear.

The queues of men, women, and children were lined by Goblins barely more than five feet tall. All were carrying whips and chains, and they were dressed in leather overalls. Eric stretched his hand down by his side, extending his arm a little, and beneath his skin he felt the click as the broken bones snapped together and started to heal. He shook some feeling back into his hand and looked around to see if anyone had noticed.

One of the Goblins raised his whip high in the air and aimed it in the direction of Eric's left ear. Luckily for Eric his instincts took over, and he moved away so that the crack of the whip sounded a few inches away from his head. The Goblin hissed and drew the whip back. Eric was very angry, and it was all he could do not to snap and go berserk. But if he did that, innocent human lives would be lost. He took a deep breath to help himself calm down a little. He was going to find out what was in this hole and destroy it, along with every reptile or Goblin that got in his way.

CHAPTER 36

THE ZARDA PRISON BASE

The underground network of corridors and tunnels under the hotel was made from cold, rough brickwork, and someone a long time ago had deemed it unnecessary to put many lights down there. On the wall of each corridor was a small, roughly attached light fitting which spat out a very small patch of light. On many of the walls the light bulbs had blown years before, and entire corridors were bathed in shadowy darkness. Most of the corridors were empty, but a few still held remnants of old furniture, decorating equipment, and even the odd plate of mouldy food left behind by some hotel worker trying to sneak a quick break when no one was looking.

Some of the walls had graffiti on them, but the further you went into the labyrinth, the fewer marks could be seen. Even the toughest street hoodlum would not delve too far in, for you never knew what monsters dwelled below the city. There were even some rotting sleeping bags dotted about the place, as the basements in this district had doubled up as shelters during the last war.

Eric Mason rounded a corner and walked down yet another dark corridor. The light from one of the wall lamps behind him gave him a strange shadowy appearance. His features were distorted by the light, and the shadow he cast on the nearest wall was almost demonic. When he came to a T-junction he stopped, looked both ways, and then back the way he had come. He was lost.

"Shit" he exclaimed under his breath, and frantically rummaged in his pockets. Pulling out the scrap of screwed-up paper, he attempted to read the faint lines drawn on the paper, but after a few attempts he gave up with a sigh and looked down the corridors again. Down one of them he could see another lamp not far off, and he marched up to it and held the paper to the light. After turning the roughly-drawn map round and round a few times, Eric eventually gave up trying to read it, and screwed it up into a ball, dropped it and angrily kicked it down the corridor. Eric wasn't a patient man. No matter how hard he tried, he just couldn't seem to stop the world from getting in his way and pissing him off.

From his pocket Eric absentmindedly pulled out the pack of squashed cigarettes and lit one. Then he remembered that he had brought something else, and took out his small brass compass. In the dim light Eric looked at it closely, and then tapped it on the wall a few times. The needle was spinning round in all directions. Eric grunted in dissatisfaction and tapped it against the wall a few more times before inspecting it again; it was still spinning. He sighed. This was a nightmare. He wanted to just give up and go find some back alley bar somewhere, but he had accepted the mission, so he might as well stay until the job was done, and collect what meagre pay he might get.

He picked a corridor at random and started walking. He was just about to put away the compass when he noticed something odd; the needle had slowed down. He stopped dead and examined it. It was definitely spinning slower than before. He took a few steps backwards, and then a few more, and then a few more. The compass needle was spinning a little faster again each time he retraced his steps. Surely this had to be a good sign.

So he had a direction, of sorts. Now he needed to find out what kind of force was affecting the needle. He rubbed his cigarette on the brickwork and flicked the mangled filter away. He raised the compass to shoulder height, and with his eyes not leaving the spinning needle, he continued his mission.

CHAPTER 37

A Night in London

It was a snowy night in the city of London, and an icy wind was blowing. Eric Mason had visited practically every city on the planet over the years, but he had never liked a city more than this one. Built up over many centuries without any overall plan, it was a warren of streets, and anyone asking for directions had better bring pen and paper to write them down on. The people, the smells, the food, the pollution, the stray cats and dogs and the overall feel of the place somehow made visitors feel welcome and told them to bugger off and mind their own business at the same time. The people were gruff and unhappy most of the time, unless they were trying to sell you something, in which case you were their best friend. Until they had your money of course, and then they would return to their usual miserable selves.

The city was baking hot in the summer and freezing cold in

the winter, and the government had only in the past hundred years stopped people throwing their muck and sewage in the river. The River Thames was the main reason people had settled there in the first place, but now it was simply home to a few boats, thousands of abandoned trolleys and tons of rubbish, along with the odd skeleton of someone who had done something they shouldn't to someone else.

On the roads and pavements puddles of half-frozen slush lay in wait for any poor unsuspecting soul who was trying to rush from one place to another, and sent them skidding to a painful stop. It was nights like this that forced people off the streets and into their homes, or one of the many pubs and bars, for warmth. Here they would be greeted by their friends or co-workers and by a good strong drink to take the edge off the cold.

In one part of the city was a small dimly-lit bar, themed, as a lot of bars were in this area, in an 'American junk' style. On the walls hung photos of supposedly famous people, miscellaneous musical instruments and whimsical street signs. It looked like someone a long time ago had decided he wanted the bar to be fun, but hadn't realised people would mainly go there to get drunk and forget about work. The original owner probably had visions of family gatherings, with fat little children eating piles of American-themed food, their parents laughing manically whilst sipping from one of the bar's famous cocktails. He or she probably imagined waiters and bar-staff dressed in whimsically bright uniforms with permanent smiles across their faces, and thought their customers would tell all their friends that they were lucky enough to get a table there, because it was always so busy and popular.

Nowadays the bar was manned by a single barman, who didn't care if you enjoyed your drink or had a good time. The bar was rarely very busy, which was how the barman liked it, but on this particular night there was quite a gathering of people sitting at tables or on bar stools. He didn't like it when it got busy like this, as it meant he had to actually move around, clear dirty glasses and serve customers, rather than sit there with a cigarette and watch the small TV in the corner of the bar. The barman's name was Joe. He wasn't old, maybe in his mid-forties, but he had got used to being his own boss in a forgotten bar where he didn't have to work too hard. Plus he had the occasional perk of chatting with women who ordinarily wouldn't have given him a second glance. It must be the uniform, he reasoned, or maybe he got better looking the more they drank.

Tonight's customers were all escaping from the freezing wind and trying to forget the fact that they had to work the next day. There was no inter-table mingling or chatting, in fact there wasn't much chatter from anyone in the bar, unless they were ordering another drink. But then the bar would go back to quiet, and the only other sound was the TV.

Then the door swung open and in an icy gust of wind, two women entered the bar. Their cheeks were rosy from the cold and they stamped the ice and slush off their shoes before taking off big thick overcoats to reveal smart office attire underneath. Nodding and smiling at one or two of the customers, they quickly walked to a pair of empty bar stools and greeted the barman, who grinned when he recognised them.

"Hi Joe" said one of the women. "So cold out there!"

"Hi Joanne" said Joe. "how are you Katie?" He reached under the counter for two tall glasses. "Been working hard today? A few drinks will warm you both up, no worries." He poured two steaming hot and highly alcoholic drinks into the tall glasses. The women picked them up and drank, smiling like Cheshire cats, and started to discuss their day at work, and the possibility of calling in sick the next day.

At the end of the bar a man raised his hand to attract Joe's attention, and begrudgingly the barman turned his attention from Joanna and Katie and walked slowly towards him, picking up a whisky glass along the way.

Eric Mason pulled a slim roll of money out of his jacket pocket and counted off a couple of notes while Joe poured three very large measures of whisky into the three glasses on the counter. Eric was looking unusually smart, in suit trousers and a white shirt. His tie hung loose around his neck, and he was still wearing a slightly damp and expensive-looking overcoat. Joe mumbled a price and Eric handed over the money. Immediately Joe went back to his favourite female customers.

Eric watched the barman attempting to flirt with the women. Once they had their drinks, they began gossiping about people at work. He picked up the first glass of whisky and sloshed the contents around, watching the brown and red colours swirl in the dim light. Then he poured the contents down his throat and replaced the glass neatly on the counter.

A crunch from the front door signalled that newcomers had arrived. Eric glanced over and saw three large, mean-looking men enter the bar and demand drinks from the barman. Eric took an instant dislike to them, and he could detect similar hostility from the rest of the customers in the bar, and especially Joe the barman. All three were similarly dressed in jeans, T-shirts and heavy leather jackets. They looked like the sort that are constantly ready for a scrap or a brawl, and Eric imagined they were members of some sort of gang, although he couldn't think of any gangs in this city that had such a dress code.

The biggest man, the one who appeared to be the leader, had slightly elongated and pointed teeth. All of them had bitten their fingernails down to the nub, and the big man had a number of scars on the backs of his hands and wrists. They took their drinks from the bar and sat down at a table at the darkest end of the bar, saying very little. Eric shrugged and turned his attention to his whisky. If these guys were going to start trouble, it would seem he had a little time to finish his drinks first.

CHAPTER 38

ABANDONED CITY

The sun had gone down over the broken-down city, and it was beginning to look like a clear and pleasant night. It was quiet on the outskirts of the city limits, and with very few clouds in the sky, the moon made strange and interesting shadows across the roads and in the patches of dry dead weeds and grass. In this silvery light the buildings with broken windows looked like strange and angry monsters, mouths open bearing razor sharp teeth, ready to devour any unsuspecting passer-by.

The wind broke the silence by carrying the sounds of soft footsteps; there were several pairs of feet, all walking in the same direction. As the footsteps got closer, voices could be heard too. Two men were talking in the flat tones of people who were being forced to spend long hours with other people they didn't much care for. It was hard to make out the words, but it seemed they were discussing the stories they had heard the old men tell about the days before the War. A third voice could be heard occasionally butting in, trying to add to the conversation, in the tone of a younger brother trying to keep up with the bigger boys, because mostly it just agreed with whatever the last voice had said.

The wind changed direction and blew a solitary cloud in front of the moon, which threw down a dark shadow that glided across the buildings and roads like a shark looking for its next meal. When the wind had blown it past, the moon's rays shone down on an uninviting-looking house. Up in the top window a face could just about be made out in the shadows. Eric Mason was listening for an indication of where the distant voices and footsteps were heading. The wind was playing merry hell with the sound and made it very difficult to pinpoint this.

"How many are there?" came the voice of the Captain from somewhere in the dark room.

"Four I think, maybe five" said Eric and went back to listening.

The squad were all crouched down in what had once been a child's bedroom. Crudely-crayoned pictures and family photos lined the walls, and there was a broken cot in the corner. Hayley had picked up a stuffed bear and was staring at it. Perhaps remembering her own childhood, or maybe the child she wanted in her future, Eric wondered. He caught her eye for a split second, and a meek smile flickered across her face. Eric felt sorry for her. She was clearly deep in thought, and not just about the bear in her hands. She had that look Eric had seen a hundred or more times before, usually on soldiers. It was the look of someone doing something they thought they ought to do, but really didn't want to.

The rest of the squad were all holding their weapons ready and staring intently at Eric and the Captain, who were crouched down by the broken bedroom window.

"Which way are they going?" hissed the Captain, his voice testy and full of frustration. As a Captain, he knew he should have been giving the orders. It had been Eric's directions that led them here, Eric's decision to hide in this house, and it was Eric who had heard the rebels walking down the street and ordered them all to be quiet. Every Captain knows that he should play to his squad's strengths – the soldier with the best eyes is put on lookout, the fastest soldier is sent as a messenger or scout, and the best shot's job will be to pick off any enemy soldiers coming at them. Annoyingly, all of these were Eric, and he had taken it upon himself to do everything without needing to be told to by the Captain.

"I'm not sure yet" said Eric, and risked another look outside the window. In the distant gloom he could see moving shapes. "They're nearly at the crossroads" he reported. "We need to wait to see which direction they go before we move on from here."

"Which way do you think they'll go?" asked the Captain.

Luckily the Captain couldn't see Eric's expression. He sighed with impatience and risked sticking his head out of the window again. "They're just standing on the crossroads, not sure," he said. Then he jumped up. "North, they're heading north, let's go!" he hissed, and rushed quickly out of the room.

The squad stood up as one and stepped in the direction of the bedroom door, but then they remembered at the last minute who was meant to be giving the orders, and all turned to the Captain.

"Yes, yes, yes" said the Captain, reluctantly standing up, "follow him then!" He shooed the squad out of the room. The men bumbled salutes and in unison the squad rushed out of the room and down the stairs. Eric was waiting impatiently for them at the back door of the house. He put his finger to his lips when they were all finally down the stairs, and carefully opened the back door. He motioned the squad to follow him and to keep down low, then led them out of the back and down the side of the house.

When he reached the front of the house, he opened the gate. The hinges whined and squeaked and Eric grimaced. The squad crouched in the alleyway waiting to hear if the rebels had had heard the noise. After a moment Eric decided that they hadn't, so he swung the gate open quickly and the squad moved forward.

Out in the streets the rebels stood in a small circle on the crossroads. A lighter was being passed from hand to hand, and each man was lighting a cigarette. They were in good spirits, despite the bitter wind, and they were all joshing each other about the stories they had heard from before the War. For many of the younger generation, the War was all they really knew, many of them being too young when it first broke out across the globe, and hadn't really understood it at the time. Most of the older men and women had been around before the War, and regularly regaled the younger ones with strange and hard-to-believe stories of what life was like before the War.

"No, I'm telling you they did!" said one of the rebels in the tone of someone who had been arguing his point for some time without success. "They called it parker, or something" he added as one of the other rebels pushed him playfully.

"Yeah right" said the rebel that had pushed him. "People running around and jumping off stuff for fun? I don't believe it, where's the fun in jumping off stuff?"

"It's true, that's what my dad told me" said the first rebel.

"Oh yeah right" said the second rebel, "your dad says a lot of things." He ran over to the rusted shell of a burnt-out car. "See?" he shouted, climbing on top and jumping off, "that's not fun, where's the fun in that?" The other rebels laughed.

"No" said the first rebel, walking over to the car shell. "I think you're supposed to do it off higher places, and faster and... you know, with more style, or something."

"Oh yeah?" called a third rebel sarcastically. "Show us how it's done then" he added, laughing.

The first rebel was clearly the sort of person not to let something go if he thought he was in the right. He carefully placed his rifle on the ground and stretched a little. With a quick look back at the other rebels, to make sure they were watching, he ran towards the car. When he was close he sprang into the air with his legs high up, planted both feet on the side of the bonnet and flipped his legs over his head. He landed on both feet about a metre away and stood up straight. His heart was thumping like crazy, and his face was a picture of shock and pride. He heard the clapping and cheers of his rebel friends behind him and turned to grin at them, even doing a little dance of excitement.

"There you go!" he exclaimed. "Told you I could do it!"

At that moment a strange whistling sound made the rebels stop clapping and look around. Something was flying through the air towards them. A grappling hook struck the triumphant jumper, and a wire attached to it whirled around his neck. He was instantly pulled off his feet, over the car and into the shadows. The rebels stood watching in stunned silence.

There was another whistling sound, and this time a large knife flashed in the moonlight before burying itself deep into a rebel's head. It took a moment for the victim to register what had happened to him. He blinked and stared up at the long blade sticking out of his forehead, then his eyes glazed over and he dropped like a fallen tree. His body hit the road with a loud squelch.

The rebels were now beside themselves with fear, and spun around trying to look out in all directions at once, but they could not see their attacker. They all fumbled in their pockets for their torches, which they pointed in all directions. The weak beams of light were swallowed by the shadowy darkness all around them. But on the other side of the car's shell, there was movement in the shadows; something large was headed their way. Eric Mason.

Eric exploded out of the darkness, launched himself over the top of the car and flung himself high in the air at an impossible speed. The remaining rebels raised their weapons and fired desperately at him, but not one bullet managed to find the target. Eric felt the wind as the bullets flew past his head and body as he crash-landed on the group, pulling two of them to the ground and crushing their skulls on the road with an eye-watering crunch. Their cigarettes dropped out of their mouths, and sizzled out on the wet ground.

Eric was up in an instant. Reaching out with the speed of a snake, he gripped the last remaining rebel's rifle, narrowly managing to avoid being shot at point blank range. The rebel struggled to pull his rifle away, but Eric's iron grip held it steady, and eventually he had to accept the inevitable, and let the weapon go. The rebel dropped to his knees and threw his hands straight up in the air, and within seconds the pair were surrounded by the rest of the squad. One soldier moved smoothly behind the rebel, producing a plastic tie, and quickly bound his hands behind his back.

The rebel looked around at his dead comrades, staring wide-eyed at the pools of blood around the two broken skulls, which looked as black as ink under the pale moonlight.

"You Army bastards!" shouted the rebel as his wrists were tied behind his back. He glared at Eric, who was casually wiping blood off his jacket.

"He's just a fucking kid, I thought these rebels were supposed to be tough" replied the soldier who had bound the rebel's hands.

"Now then Tolley" said the Captain, "no need to exchange insults with this youngster." He looked the rebel up and down. He was clearly a teenager, possibly twenty at the most.

"Sorry sir, what do we do with this kid?" asked Tolley saluting the captain smartly, and smacking the back of the rebel's head as he raised his hand.

"You'll just have to kill me" the rebel growled. "I won't tell you where our base is located. That's what all you Soldier boys do is, isn't it? You come along and kill the innocent, torture the rest...

well not me, I don't break under torture!" he added. He nearly shouted the last part.

"Oh really?" asked Eric devilishly. "Seen a lot of torture have you kid?" He pulled the hunting knife out of the dead man with a nasty squelch and turned menacingly on the young rebel.

"Whoa Eric" warned the Captain, and held a hand up.

"We are a free city! And we will keep it free!" shouted the rebel. His eyes swivelled around as he peered into the darkness around them, desperately looking for signs of backup.

"Shut up" said the Captain, and punched the rebel in the side of the head. He slumped to the ground and looked as if he was about to burst into tears. "Damn fool will have every other patrol down on us in minutes" said the Captain, catching Eric's eye.

"Their patrols are usually about an hour or so apart" said Eric. "That means when we leave this guy here, he'll probably get picked up fairly soon."

"We're just going to leave him here?" exclaimed Tolley.

"Yes" replied Eric, turning to walk away.

"But you killed..." began Tolley. His voice dropped when he saw that the Captain was deep in thought. "Captain?"

"I agree with Commander Mason. However, I think he and I need to have a little talk about his approach to dealing with teenage rebels," said the Captain.

"The next patrol will pick him up in an hour or so" said Eric. "I saw a threat and neutralised it. I didn't stop to check their birth certificates. And we do not execute prisoners, especially those that surrender."

Eric didn't like the fact that he had just killed a couple of kids, but they had been in the wrong place at the wrong time, and carrying guns. There was a big difference between killing someone and killing someone holding a gun which he would happily use on you if he saw you first. They wanted guns, they wanted to be big and tough, they wanted to shoot people. They should realise that those people might shoot back.

"You can't just leave me here!" exclaimed the rebel, tears rolling down his cheeks and looking on the edge of panic. "No, you have to take me prisoner or something, you can't just..." He stopped talking when Tolley kicked him in the leg.

"We don't have to do anything, little boy. You'll stay here and explain to rest of your scumbag rebel friends why a child like you shouldn't have been given a gun in the first place. Take my advice kid, leave the fighting to the grown-ups." Tolley turned to follow Eric.

The Captain ordered a soldier to collect up the rebel's guns. Then he walked away.

The squad looked from one another and quickly followed in behind Eric, and together they marched off into the night, heading towards the city. The buildings were larger here, with fewer houses and parks, suggesting that they were getting close to the centre. Occasionally Eric would hold his hand up to signal to the squad to stop moving, and then point to the ground signalling them to get low. Eric found this most amusing, and did it as often as he dared just for a laugh. He found it funny watching these soldiers crouching down desperately trying not to make a sound and stay deathly still. The Captain really didn't like taking orders from Eric, so whenever he was about to say something Eric would raise a hand quickly for silence and pretend to be looking or listening out for something important.

The squad made good time, rushing from shadow to shadow, occasionally having to take a detour around yet another rebel patrol. There were quite a few, which allowed Eric to play with the squad quite often, but eventually they reached the inner limits of the city. The buildings were now stabbing up at the night sky, while the roads were full of rubbish and long-abandoned cars. They would need great stealth if they hoped to get into the centre of the city, where Mr Duff would undoubtedly be hiding.

CHAPTER 39

IN THE BAR

The bar was in full swing. Joe the barman didn't reckon they would get any more customers in that evening and he was now watching the minute hand on the bar's only clock, willing it to move faster so he could kick them all out and go home.

Nearly every table was filled, and Joe was having to rush around to collect glasses, wipe tables, serve drinks and even refill the bowls of peanuts on the bar, which even he didn't dare to eat. He doubted that any of his male customers washed their hands after using the toilet; he had seen them happily scoop up small fistfuls of peanuts, leaving the rest slightly damper than they should have been. He was actually working up a little sweat tonight, which was very unusual. Thankfully no one asked him for anything complicated to drink, apart from Katie and Joanne, but he didn't mind doing it for them.

The guy at the buy was a little unnerving, but easy enough to serve. He sat patiently until the barman had done what he needed to do, and drank all his whiskies in threes. He didn't take his coat off like the rest of the customers, and he didn't look like he was waiting for anyone in particular. In fact, Joe got the impression that the guy was ready to rush out of the door at any minute. Perhaps it was in case the missus saw him. He poured Eric three more big glasses of whisky. This guy could certainly hold his booze.

Behind Eric the noise was getting louder with every drink, and the three leather-jacketed men were in the centre of it all. Joe didn't like them. They were chatting, joking, even dancing with Katie and Joanne. Joe wanted to step in, play the knight in shining armour and rescue the ladies, but to his annoyance they actually seemed to be enjoying the attention, and he would feel stupid if he interrupted without just cause.

Thankfully a few customers now got up and left, and Joe did what all barmen do when they want to make it clear they want to go home; he wordlessly collected all the dirty glasses, wiped and upended the chairs and called for last orders.

There were a few murmurs from people wanting one last drink and a bigger groan from the guys chatting to Kate and Joanne. But Joe didn't care. It had taken him ages to clear up this mess, although normally he just didn't bother at all.

CHAPTER 40

THE RUINED CITY

The Squad came across one or two patrols on their journey to the centre of the ruined city, but they were easily avoided or neutralised. The ones hiding in the buildings were the toughest to spot, so Eric had decided to change tack, and the squad were now moving much faster by using the rooftops. Luckily most of the buildings rubbed up against each other, or were only a short distance apart, so if the squad couldn't jump the gap then the grappling wires would swing them through windows that had long ago been smashed. The route had been mapped out by Eric a long time ago; it was one of six routes they could have used to get to the centre of the city undetected. Even now, Eric had to silence a few rebels along the way. The squad were not really trained for this sort of stealth, and regularly one would trip or fall onto something noisy. If Eric hadn't been in the right place at the right time,

Private Tolley would have fallen to his death after attempting a jump that was slightly too big for him in an effort to keep up with Eric's fast pace. Eric had looked back just at the right time to see Tolley in mid-jump, halfway between buildings, and calculated quickly that he wouldn't make it. He had just managed to catch Tolley before he slammed into the brickwork.

Eric signalled everyone to follow him and went crashing through a skylight window. When the squad joined him, they found him surrounded by nine dead rebels and one who was badly hurt. The squad was surprised to find him casually lighting a cigarette.

"Time to regroup and take a head count" said Eric, wiping his knife on his trousers and putting it away before wandering over to a table in the corner of the room. The soldiers were busy staring at all the bodies. "Are we missing anyone?" asked Eric.

"Tommy, sir" said Tolley, when they all looked around. "He tried jumping a gap. I warned him not to, but he must have mistimed it or something. He landed hard in one of those big metal container things. I don't think he survived."

"Are you quite sure?" asked the Captain, and Tolley nodded solemnly.

"Bugger" said Eric to the air in general, and the squad turned to face him. "Tommy was fast" he said by way of explanation "We need fast people for what we need to do next."

"And what exactly is that?" the Captain asked accusingly. He was out of breath from all the running, and he hadn't liked heights since he was a kid, so being forced to traverse so many had put him in a very bad mood.

"Well, once we get the hostages out of their cages we're going to need to get the hell out of here quick" said Eric. He walked over to the nearest window.

"They keep them in cages?" asked one of the female soldiers. "That's barbaric!"

"We were kept in a damp basement" said Hayley meekly.

"That's as maybe, but that is why we are going to get them out" said the Captain. He turned to Eric. "Where are the cages? By my calculations we're miles away from the main fortified gates."

Eric was standing with his back to the big window now, and jerked a thumb over his shoulder. The Captain joined him and looked out at what Eric was pointing at. In the distance, nearly a mile away, was a clearing in the buildings, and it was lit up with the angry orange and red light that only big open fires can create. Hanging in the air, high off the ground, was what looked like a giant birdcage. The Captain peered at the cage. Inside it was just about possible to see two people-shaped shadows inside it.

"How're we going to get in there and get them down?" asked the Captain.

"Well," said Eric thoughtfully, "I've been thinking about that. We'll have to go in two groups if we want this to work." He looked around at the squad. "I'll take you, and you" he said, pointing to Hayley and another soldier, Private Riley.

Hayley and Riley looked imploringly at their Captain, who looked back at the cages thoughtfully. Finally he said, "Agreed, what's the plan?" The other two volunteers groaned, but they were ignored.

Eric fished in one of his pockets and produced a folded sheet of paper. Then he walked back over to the table and signalled to them all to follow. The paper looked as if it had been well used. Eric laid it on the table and smoothed it out as best he could, revealing several notes and drawings. It looked as if he had used it to meticulously map out the city, the buildings, patrol routes, supply areas, and weapon stores.

"You've certainly done your homework" said the Captain, leaning over the map. "What's this?" He pointed to what looked like a patch of dried blood.

"I spent a long time mapping this city out" said Eric. "One time I got caught – not for long mind, but I couldn't find any more paper to redo the map."

Eric proceeded to point out the places on the map where the squad were, where the cages were, and where he needed the larger squad to be if they were going to pull this mission off.

"If you and your squad can be here" Eric said, pointing to places on the map, "I think the rest of us would have be able to create a distraction to draw their attention away while you lot go in and get them out."

"What kind of diversion are we talking about?" asked the Captain, still staring at the bloodstain.

"We'll figure something out when we get there, shouldn't be too difficult" said Eric dismissively. "You guys just need to be ready to get the hostages out of there."

"And how do we do that?" asked Tolley, who had walked over to the window to see the cages.

"You'll just have to use your imagination" said Eric, folding the map up and holding it out for the Captain. "Take this and be in the right place. We don't have radios, so when you see the diversion, you'll need to act quick. We'll meet up back here in this building after and wait out the initial search, then get back to camp."

The Captain put the map away. He felt the Major would be interested in seeing it, and it shouldn't be too difficult to leave Eric stuck somewhere. If this diversion worked, they could have the whole rebel force bearing down on them, and the rest of them would be in the clear. Although, he reflected, it wouldn't be easy to get those two soldiers out without him.

Eric and his team walked over to the fire escape exit. "Good luck" said Eric jovially. There were mumbled replies, and then Eric opened the fire exit and shooed Hayley and Private Riley out. He turned to see the other team rush away down the stairs, and gave the Captain a nod. Then the room was empty.

CHAPTER 41

BACK ALLEY

Behind any good bar is a back alley which allows drunks to be ejected quickly and efficiently without dragging them through the front door. It also provides an out of the way place for the bar workers of the world to sneak out for a quick smoke break. The alleyway behind Joe's bar was mostly there to just store old kegs and rubbish for the collectors to pick up, along with the usual chair and ashtray of course. What was unusual about this alleyway was that five customers were now using it to exit the building voluntarily.

"Come on let's go," said the big man. "The other bar is just down here." He was doing up the buttons on his leather jacket.

"I still don't see why we couldn't just leave through the front door" said Katie, who was ever practical, and had been warned by her mother not to walk down dark city alleyways, especially not with strange men who'd had a few drinks.

"Nah, we wouldn't want to walk all the way around in the slush to get there" said the man. "This is much quicker." He was urging everyone to hurry up and follow him. He was clearly the alpha male of the group, and used to telling everyone what to do.

All five of them started walking away from the exit they had just taken, Katie quickly linking arms with Joanne, and the men arranged themselves with one guy in front, one walking behind, and the alpha male alongside them. The five of them wandered down the network of alleyways, occasionally getting a glimpse of main roads and people, but they continued on, all the while being directed by the alpha guy, who seemed to know where he was taking them without needing to look around.

"You ladies are real lookers" the alpha male was saying to Katie and Joanne. "I am very surprised you don't have boyfriends or husbands, someone to treat you right and buy you nice things." He spoke in a lecherous tone which made Katie shudder.

"Yeah, thanks," said Katie. "I think we should just go home," she added in a whisper to Joanne, who nodded in agreement.

"When we go round the next corner I say we run for it," whispered Joanne.

However, when they reached the end of the alley, Katie and Joanne realised that the three men had them surrounded. And now they saw that they appeared to be heading towards a dead end.

"Here we are ladies, a beautiful spot," said the big man. It did not occur to Katie and Joanne to kick him in the crotch and run like hell. They continued, hoping against all odds that there was another bar entrance in this alleyway, and that the anxiety they were both feeling was unfounded. Then they realised that the men's footsteps had stopped. They slowly turned around. The men were standing together, and they were all smiling hungrily.

A door opened in the alleyway with a metallic squeal and a bang as it hit the wall. So there was another bar here. Katie was about to laugh and walk towards it when a shadowy figure stepped through the doorway. He was dressed the same as the other three, although the leather jacket looked a little older and so did the wearer. The look he gave the women was definitely not friendly. The man nodded silently to the alpha male, who nodded back, and then walked to the end of the alleyway and stood with the other two men to bar any possibility of escape.

Katie was beginning to curse her own stupidity for drinking so much alcohol, and wondered if it had just been just alcohol in the glasses. She resisted the urge to stick her fingers down her throat just in case. If these men were about to do what she thought they were about to do, she'd rather the alcohol kept her numb. The cold fresh air had sent the alcohol straight to her head, and on her arm she could feel Joanne swaying slightly. Katie squinted at the three men. Their eyes were so bright that they looked like they were almost illuminated from behind, and their teeth seemed strangely pointed. Both women were now practically paralysed by the cold and fear.

The big man walked forward, slowly taking off his jacket and tossing it to one side. Underneath he was wearing a plain T-shirt with the sleeves rolled up a little to show his biceps, which were large. Neither of them fancied their chances of getting away from this monster. He was now looking the pair up and down with a ravenous and lustful look.

Katie felt sick. She wanted to scream for help, but the noise was stuck in her throat.

"Now ladies," he said in a smooth tone, "we can do this the hard, and usually violent way. Or you could just enjoy it." But his voice trailed off. Something was wrong. He spun back around. Where there should have been three men standing to catch the women if they managed to run past him, now there were only two.

"Where the hell did he go?" he hissed angrily under his breath. "Find him!"

The two men looked around and started to walk down the alleyway to look for their missing comrade. They had only got a few steps when they both got a bit of a shock.

Few people know that the lit end of a cigarette is exactly the same size as the average person's ear-hole. The first man suddenly became one of those people. Eric Mason reached out of the shadow he had stepped into a moment before they had walked down the alleyway, and neatly put the lit end of the cigarette he was smoking into the man's ear. Eric's other hand came flying over the man's shoulder and planted a punch neatly across the second man's jaw. The punch was so perfect that it spun the man around, and sent him slamming into the far wall, to the sound of screaming from the one with the burnt ear.

Eric pulled the cigarette out of the screaming man's ear and dropped it down the back of his jacket and T-shirt. The man's screams got louder. The man turned to face Eric and snarled, showing the pointed white teeth. Normally a flash of those teeth would give even the toughest opponent second thoughts, but this guy just stepped forward, raising his fists.

The pair exchanged a few blows, Eric managing to defend and deflect the majority of them, and the fight ended pretty quickly when Eric managed to slam the palm of his hand over the man's burnt ear. The force of the punch blasted a bubble of air through the man's eardrum, making him scream out in pain again, but much louder this time. To silence him Eric punched his throat, and while the man was still coughing, spluttering and fighting for breath Eric sent him flying across the alleyway. He tripped over the moaning body of his comrade and hit his head hard on the brick wall behind him.

The second man looked down at his unconscious comrade, and snarled in anger. His jaw was hurting like crazy, and he was determined to rip the head off whoever had punched him. He spun around to face his attacker, to find himself alone in the alleyway.

He narrowed his eyes and peered into the nearby shadows – or rather, all the shadows except for the one Eric was standing in, holding a brick he had picked up. The brick came hurtling out of the shadow and hit the second man between the eyes, knocking him flying. He was unconscious before he hit the ground.

Eric checked there was no one else coming, and decided that was all for now.

The alpha male heard the first scream, but thought nothing of it. His boys must have found someone stupid enough to be lurking somewhere off in the distance and sorted him out. But the second scream had familiar tones to it, and it sent a slight shiver down his spine. He dragged his attention away from the two women and saw a solitary figure standing in the mouth of the alleyway. He didn't seem too intimidating; he was wearing a shirt and tie under a smart coat, and didn't look much like a fighter, more as if he was on his way home from an office job.

And yet... he might not look like a fighter, but you'd have to handle yourself pretty well to take on three of his best men. He hadn't just become leader of the pack because of his sense of humour or his dress sense. It was a tough world. If you caught someone stealing, they were dead. If you caught someone sleeping with your woman, they were dead. If someone challenged you for authority, they were dead. It was survival of the fittest, fastest and strongest in their world, and this alpha male was all three.

He stalked towards the figure, straightening up to his full height and puffing out his chest in the attempt to look even bigger and meaner than he already did. He smiled when the figure started to back away slightly.

"You ladies might want to run away now" Eric suggested, not taking his eyes off the alpha male.

"You two stay where you are!" shouted the big man over his shoulder "I'll be dealing with you as soon as I've sorted this rat out."

Katie and Joanne didn't need telling twice. They glanced at each other and ran as fast as their high heels could carry them. The alpha male heard the footsteps and pounced on the two women. They managed to struggle out of his grip, but the man held onto their handbags, one in each hand.

"Leave the bags!" Eric shouted, and both women instantly let go. The alpha male fell to the ground, still holding onto the handles of the bags, the mysteries of each handbag spilling onto the floor around him. He got to his feet and threw the bags down with a growl of anger.

"You!" he said accusingly through gritted teeth, "You are going to pay for that, they were a sure thing." He walked towards Eric with long, menacing strides, teeth bared. In the shadows of the alleyway he looked like a panther about to devour its prey.

With lightning speed Eric reached a hand inside his jacket, drew his knife and hurled it at the alpha male with all his strength. The knife struck the man square in the middle of the face, the blade slotting in neatly between the man's upper and lower teeth, and the hilt almost disappeared inside his gaping mouth. The alpha male stood still for a second, rolling his eyes and clutching uselessly at his throat. Then he tottered to the ground with a dying gurgle.

Eric reached down to pick up the girls' handbags, and after a little rummaging he found a driving licence in one of them. On it was Joanne's address. He stuffed the bags inside his jacket in case some passer-by got the wrong impression, and walked back to the main road to hail a cab and arrange for the bags to be reunited with their rightful owners.

CHAPTER 42

LYKOR TERRITORY

Out in the countryside the sky was blue and the sun was shining its warm glow down on the fields and rivers. Birds were singing, and the only thing spoiling the picture-perfect country scene was a long main road that carved its way across the landscape between cities, towns, and villages. It stretched a fair distance; before the War it had probably been full of commuters at all hours of the day and night, but now that the War had been going for several years, the road ran deep into Zarda territory. The only thing moving out here was the occasional pack of Lykor looking for slow-moving animals or people. The grass was now wild and unkempt, and after years of abuse from the pollution that came from thousands of motor vehicles, the trees and bushes had started taking on a spikey and gothic look.

The only other thing spoiling the view was a small area not

too far from the main motorway, a little clearing framed by forest on either side. The Army convoy was in pieces. Metal and debris littered the roadside and the surrounding grassy areas, and there was the stink of death and drying blood in the air.

The entire convoy had been attacked, that much was very clear; the convoy looked as though it had been chewed up by a hurricane and spat back out. One of the trucks looked as though it had nearly managed to get away. It had scored deep grooves into the muddy ground on the side of the road, running pretty straight for a fair distance before swerving wildly, until eventually the truck had ended up crashing into a big tree.

A few of the other trucks were lying on their sides, the doors and canvas coverings looking as though either something had exploded out from inside, or had been ripped apart by some very large, and very strong, claws and teeth. Although the action was long over, there was still a fair amount of black smoke in the air. Thin columns of it spiralled up, allowing the wind to catch them and playfully blow them this way and that.

But the worst sight of all was the bodies. In all directions, bodies and bits of bodies surrounded the wreck, the stale blood soaking into the dry thirsty soil. All the ravens from miles around must have smelt it, because there were hundreds in the air and on the ground, desperately eating their fill and fighting each other for more. Death had been very busy here this day, collecting up the souls of the recently departed and ferrying them to the next world.

Nearby was a sloping field stretching out into overgrown grassy countryside. Rough and ragged-looking trees littered the fields, looking like slow but determined zombies. On the far side of this was another road, cracked and worn. Before the War it had probably been used regularly by commuters to get to the main highway, but now it had grown old from neglect.

If you looked carefully, possibly through binoculars, you would be able to see the distant shapes of two figures moving along the road. They were difficult to make out from this distance, partly because they were so far away, but also because one of the shapes was attempting to carry the other, which was having trouble walking. But both figures had a very determined look to their progress, and after a little while they turned off the road and began to walk through the tall fields of grass. They were clearly heading towards the wreckage of the convoy, having seen the smoke rising into the air.

Up close it was apparent that both figures were men, and they were both wearing army uniforms. The man dragging his leg and having to be held up as he limped was a private. There was blood and dirt all over his uniform, and each step left a few drops of blood behind him. The other man was an officer. The brass bars on his jacket and shirt which indicated that he was a Captain could still just about be seen through the dirt. The men were leaving a deep groove through the overgrown grass.

"How much further sir?" asked the injured soldier. "My leg could fall off at any minute." He tried to laugh, but it quickly turned into a cough.

"Not much further, soldier" said the Captain in a tired but reassuring voice. "If we can get up over this slope, there must be a camp of some sorts just on the other side." He felt exhausted, but didn't want to show it in front of the private.

"I'm beginning to wish we hadn't lost that map he gave us" said the injured soldier. "I hope this camp is friendly." They had all heard about the men and women who had been forced out of their homes by the Zarda to wander from place to place ransacking every building they found. They were not the friendliest, especially towards the Army, because it was often because of the Army that they were homeless.

"I don't think we have the luxury of a choice" said the Captain. "I think we could both use a bit of medical attention." He was looking at a deep wound that could be seen on his shoulder through a rip in his clothes. Blood had been oozing out of it for some time and trickling down his chest and back, although he had packed it with some cloth. It had not helped much, and now he was starting to feel light-headed.

"A soft place to lie down would be my favourite" said the injured soldier, and they both smiled at the thought of resting for a while.

The pair continued in silence, looking as if they were the only entrants in a three-legged race, or more likely a marathon. When they reached the slope they started crawling up it on their hands and knees towards the columns of smoke that could be seen just over the ridge. They managed to crawl over the ridge, fully expecting to be picked up and carried off to the nearest medic tent as soon as they were spotted, but to their surprise, nothing happened.

The Captain looked up from where he was lying, and had to blink a few times to make sure the upside-down image he was seeing was not some grotesque hallucination. He could see unspeakable carnage sprawled out in front of him. He looked up to where the black smoke was hanging in the air, and a chill ran down his spine.

He slowly rolled over to his front so he could see properly, and took in the horrific view in front of them. A bang to one side made him jump as something fell off one of the trucks and hit the ground, and then he spotted a hand which was moving slightly. It was difficult to describe the hand, which looked like something out of a cheap zombie-horror movie. It was bleeding and scorched black from dirt or oil burns, and it seemed to be trying to find something to grab hold of.

"Stay here" the Captain ordered weakly. The soldier waved the Captain away and nodded silently with his eyes shut.

The Captain got to his feet and stumbled towards the truck. Hesitantly he looked inside it and saw an injured soldier. He reached out to take the hand and helped pull the soldier up and out of the wrecked truck.

It was a woman. Her long blonde hair might have been neatly tied back before the attack, but now long strands hung from her head, matted together with sweat and dirt. He laid her on the ground as carefully as he could and she stared up at the Captain with big blue frightened eyes. She was shivering, and the Captain wondered whether he could make a blanket out of the truck's canvas.

"Are you OK?" asked the Captain, although he knew it was a stupid question. "What happened here?"

"Water" came the only sound from her dry throat.

The Captain looked around. "I'm not sure" he said and rummaged in the debris around the truck. Eventually he found a bag full of plastic bottles and canteens, and after drawing a few blanks, he found one that had water inside. He rushed it over to the soldier and handed it to her, she took it gratefully and coughed when she drank with shaking hands. As she drank the Captain saw her rank and could see she was one of the engineers, 'probably just there to drive the truck, not get into any actual fights' he thought.

"What happened here?" asked the Captain again. looking around at the site. It looked as if the convoy had been attacked by an entire army of Lykor, not just some wild hunting pack.

The engineer coughed for a while and said in a dry voice, "We were... attacked on the road".

"Yes, I can see that" said the Captain patiently. "Who by? The Zarda?"

"We were bugging out" she said. "We had to move from Outpost 53, outside the city, to the new site. There was a new nest... but we were attacked." Her voice trailed off and she shut her eyes and lay back.

"We're from Outpost 53," said the Captain, shaking her arm

to wake her up. "We were meant to meet you at the new site. Wake up woman, please! Who attacked you?"

But the woman didn't open her eyes or move. He put his fingers to her throat and tried to find a pulse; it was faint and getting fainter by the second. He quickly moved onto his knees and opened her shirt, but a river of blood washed out from underneath, and the Captain nearly threw up. He inspected the wound. It looked as if her stomach had been ripped open. There was nothing he could do. He had had some medical training at the Academy, but even the best surgeon wouldn't have helped. He carefully replaced her shirt and checked for the pulse again but couldn't find it. She had gone.

"Captain, what's happening?" came the voice of the injured soldier on the ground behind him. The Captain scrabbled for the bottle of water and rushed back to find him sitting up and staring at the debris in wide-eyed disbelief. He handed a bottle to the man, who grabbed it and half drank, half showered in the water. Then he shook like a dog and wiped the wet blood and dirt off his face. The Captain did the same, and soon both soldiers were relatively clean faced. They could now be identified as the Captain who had gone into the abandoned city with Eric Mason to rescue the scavenger soldiers, and Private Tom Berate, one of the scavenger soldiers being held hostage by Mr Duff.

The Captain turned his attention to Tom's leg. There was a big rip down his trouser leg and with a bit of effort by the Captain, he was able to pull the trousers open. The force of this made Tom scream out in pain, as the blood had dried and hardened, gluing the fabric to his leg hair. With the leg and wound now exposed, both men could see that Tom had a long gash running down the outside of his leg. The wound was oozing blood, and Tom's trouser leg must have soaked up a couple of pints. The Captain turned away in horror at the sight of the exposed wound and took a few deep breaths to stop himself from being sick. The mingled stench of blood and smoke was nearly too much for him to handle.

"That's going to need stitches" said the Captain, standing up. "We'll need to pack it until then. I'll go see if I can find any medical supplies." He stood up and swayed slightly before walking back over to the truck. He very carefully stepped over the body of the dead engineer, who looked like she was just sleeping there on the ground, and found a length of the charred rope that would normally have held the canvas cover in place. It took a couple of minutes for him to unthread the cord from the canvas covering so that he could use a piece of bent metal to cut it away.

He returned to the injured Private and tried to ignore his screams as he tied the rope around the man's leg, trying not to breathe or look directly at the wound. He had seen this a few times in desperate situations; you had to close the wound, and hope it would stay closed until you got it stitched up. Trouble was, the slightest movement and the wound would open again, so you had to tie it tight.

"Well done soldier, we'll get you fixed up in no time" he said, patting the man on the shoulder. "Don't move, I'm going to find the medic truck, it has to be around here somewhere." With that he walked back off into the debris.

The wounded Private sat trying to catch his breath. All the colour in his face had drained away, and he looked like a ghost. He stared at his leg. The pain was almost unbearable, but somehow it seemed better now that the Captain had bound the leg up tight. He refused to think about how dirty the rope probably was.

The Private was starting to lose consciousness. He could feel himself getting light-headed, and his vision was starting to go. He looked back and saw the Captain disappear into one of the supply trucks, but he could not see the insignia on the canvas. Water, that was what he needed; he didn't want to pass out, not out here in serious Lykor territory, especially if the birds and flies mistook him for one of the corpses.

He leant over and winced as he rummaged through the empty bottles the Captain had dropped next to him, but before he could find one with any water in, he felt himself blacking out. His body went limp, and he slumped to the ground.

CHAPTER 43

ANCIENT DAYS

Back in the very early days of Earth, when the world was still fresh and new, peace reigned on the planet. The reptilian dinosaurs, the hairy mammals and the giant swimming fishes were all living in peace and harmony with each other. Well, that's not strictly true. The bigger, angrier, meat-eating animals would chase and eat the smaller ones, and so the circle of life went round and round.

The sun rose and set each day, and the animals soon forgot all about the war of the creatures made from oily cold darkness, and the beings filled with the sun's warm glow. Over the years there was no sign of either. Until one day, after many, many, generations of dinosaurs walking across land, swimming in the deep oceans and lakes and gliding on the winds, something new began to happen. Again.

A rumble shook throughout the different continents across the planet, the shockwaves radiating out in all directions and shaking the bedrock up to the surface. Trees began to tremble and lose their grip on the land, volcanos erupted and spat molten rock into the air, cliffs cracked and shed large chunks that fell down on whatever was passing, and the dinosaurs fled in all directions, not knowing where to find safety. From deep below the tallest mountain, a light began to shine up and burst out of the cave entrance, and it shone into the sky like a beacon. Even though it was still daytime, the light could be seen for miles around and shone out into the cold darkness of space.

For miles around every animal and dinosaur turned to look at the strange new light. The ones who moved in herds around the bottom of the mountain were used to having light above them, but none of them had seen light from under the ground. Dinosaurs from all around migrated towards the base of the mountain, eager to find the cause of the disruption of their Eden.

The sound coming from the mouth of the cave started getting louder and louder. If the dinosaurs had been able to describe it, they would have said it was a buzzing sound, but a loud one, the type of sound you might get from the beating of billions of tiny flying wings, like the world's largest beehive. This description would turn out to be very accurate, as what emerged from the cave entrance to the mountain were all things black and evil looking – black flies, black crows and other predatory birds, and all manner of flying spiders and other creatures that plague the darkest corners of nightmares. The swarm exploded out the mountain as if fired from an enormous cannon and spread out across the sky, and what didn't fly would crawl down the mountainside.

From a distance the mass of black creatures looked like a horrific oil spill, seeping out into the beautiful garden that the dinosaurs had previous been enjoying in abundance. Where the creatures spread out, webs of stringy white fibres were left hanging from the trees and twisted through the long grass where the spiders made their new homes. Ravens and crows took over the nests of more timid birds, eating their eggs and killing the parents, and called their terrifying cries to make their claim on their new territories. All the black creatures and insects started taking over the lands surrounding the mountain, and any of the sun-loving dinosaurs that tried to put up a fight were overpowered instantly. The creatures destroyed the dinosaurs like a shoal of piranhas demolishing a hunk of meat in a mad frenzy of blood and death.

The light from the mountain entrance started to get brighter and stronger, and the beam of light shone even further into the blackness of space; whatever the source of the light was, it was getting closer to the surface. The black creatures were moving fast now, and it looked as if they were fighting to get further away from the mountain. If you could look closely at each one you would see a very real fear in their eyes. Whatever was about to come out of the mountain was no friend of the Darkness.

With a flash of light the cave entrance exploded like a volcano, and fragments of light flew out in all directions like ash from a bonfire. They floated up into the air and were caught by the wind, travelling across the lands and seas, for the beings of light were back, and they had won their battle deep inside the Earth. The haze of twinkling little lights drifted down to the ground and brought life to the dying and damaged ground the dark creatures had destroyed.

The particles fell like golden shiny snow. Saplings began to grow, grass came back to life and stood to attention, feeling the winds rushing through it, and the world around the Mountain became its usual emerald green again. Any dark creatures with the misfortune of not getting away fast enough were instantly turned into a fine black dust that dissolved into thin air. The light consumed the dark creatures, growing stronger and brighter each time, and regenerated the lands they had devastated, forcing away the black monsters, which climbed over each other to escape the light's warm embrace.

More light was shooting out of the cave entrance now, and the balls of light were getting larger, and flying out to try to cover more ground around the planet. Finally five very large golden objects emerged from the cave. The dinosaurs stared at them in disbelief. They looked strange compared to the other balls of light they had just seen, as they had arms and legs. They all crawled and climbed very slowly out of the mouth of the mountain. They looked tired and injured, and the centuries-old fight with the creatures of darkness deep underground had left them weak and frail. They left glowing yellow marks on the rocks as they went. When they reached the open-air cave they all did something none of the animals would ever have expected – they slowly and painfully stood up on their hind legs.

They stood there for a moment, swaying slightly in the breeze, looking out at the land they had only seen briefly hundreds of years before. Silently they looked from one another through small pinpoints of light. Their faces started moulding and changing, and defined facial features began to appear.

From a distance they looked identical. From their shoulders, and all down their bodies, muscles could be seen to form on their arms and legs, and fingers stretched out of newly-formed hands. The five of them looked at each other as if inspecting each other. Three of the beings of light were male, while the other two had taken on a female appearance. Each being flexed its new muscles and stretched its new arms and legs, twisting this way and that. Finally, apparently satisfied with their new forms, they looked up at the bright sun in the big deep blue sky above them. It shone down its warmth and light upon them, and they were happy.

CHAPTER 44

BENEATH LONDON

Deep below the city of London, Eric Mason felt very tired. He was leaning up against one of the cold cellar walls staring at the small brass compass in his hand, and he was beginning to get very frustrated again – not that that took much these days.

The dim light was starting to bug him and giving him a bit of a headache. He closed his fist around the compass and shook it violently. That was starting to annoy him as well, because the needle was still spinning uncontrollably. In some areas of the cellar the needle slowed down, but it never seemed to stop long enough to show him his destination. He must have walked for miles up and down these long corridors, and if he wasn't sure he had been going round in circles, he would have believed it if someone had told him he was now outside the city limits. His stomach was starting to grumble as well. It had been a while since he had eaten a good meal, and even longer since he had had a good drink.

He slowly raised the compass, the thin metal chain dangling in the air like a tail, and held it out in front of him, shutting one eye. He grimaced as though the compass might jump out and bite him. He slowly opened his fist and stared at the needle, which was still spinning. As if in a trance he stared at it, willing it to stop moving, but it defied him. He let the compass drop from his hand. It hit the ground with a soft metallic clink, and in a burst of frustrated anger he kicked the rebellious compass down the corridor.

This cellar was starting to get to him. He had once lived in the endless rat's nest of tunnels and sewers of the London Underground system for well over a year, and this was easily worse. The walls felt as if they were bending and closing in on him all the time.

A single bead of sweat ran down his forehead and down the side of his face. He flicked it away angrily, spun around on his heel to face the offending brickwork, and punched the wall. The force of the punch caused the brickwork to shatter and explode into dust, which floated in the air before gently settling on the floor by his feet. Unseen by Eric, the dust moved slightly before it landed, as if being dragged away by invisible fingers.

He spun back around and planted his back against the broken wall, banging his head against the hard surface, which only angered him more. He let out a groan and looked down at the cut that was starting to bleed on his fist. As he watched, a small amount of blood came to the surface and ran down his hand Immediately the skin started to heal and the wound quickly closed, and soon it looked as if nothing had happened. He absent-mindedly wiped the blood on his trouser leg, dug his hand into his pocket, fished out the battered cigarette packet and peered inside. There was a single cigarette left in the packet. Eric ripped it out and screwed up the pack, and without looking launched it at the opposite wall. He found his lighter and lit the cigarette, taking a big deep pull.

He was just about to put the lighter away when he noticed that the flame was blowing to one side. There was no wind down here, not that he could feel anyway, and when he gently breathed out a big cloud of smoke it drifted off down the corridor. He took another drag of the cigarette, but without inhaling it fully this time, and let the smoke rise through the air, making him look like an angry dragon. This too started to dance and roll in the air and drift down the corridor. He held the cigarette out in front of him and inspected the thin column of smoke coming from the tip.

Holding the cigarette out in front of him like a burning torch, Eric walked down the corridor very carefully, stopping occasionally to take a drag from the cigarette to keep it lit. He looked like an old drunk with a back problem. He walked a few metres, stopped to inspect the smoke, and then continued down the corridor. Then he stopped, spun on his heel and walked back down the way he had just come. Now the smoke trail was playing silly buggers with him. He stopped and took a final drag from the cigarette. By now it was near the filter, and he dropped it onto the floor.

He was just about to stub it into oblivion with the heel of his boot when he noticed something strange. He carefully lowered his foot and crouched down to get a closer look. The smoke was faint now, but it could just be seen curling into a small crack in the wall's brickwork.

Eric stood up and looked quizzically at the wall in front of him. The brickwork looked the same as all the other walls he'd seen down here. He crouched back down and inspected the crack in the wall. Now when he held a hand over it he could just about feel the air being sucked into it. Perhaps there was a room or something on the other side – although he thought he had been on that side already.

With a fingernail he scratched at the mortar around the crack. It was dry and loose, and came away quite easily. Soon he was able to trace a rough vertical line in the wall. He stood up straight and thought for a moment, looking at the line he had drawn. On the ground in front of the rectangle he had made there were faint scuff marks in the dust. It was a door.

A glint of light made him look sideways, and he saw the compass lying on the ground where it had landed, the dim light reflecting off its curved surface. "I suppose I can't lose you now, can I?" he said to the compass, and quickly retrieved it and put it back in his pocket.

He glared at the brickwork, and thin yellow glowing veins starting to appear on his hands. He clenched his fists tight, and the veins grew a little brighter. He grunted in annoyance at not having seen the door the first time he had passed this wall – he must have walked past it a dozen times. He stood sideways to the wall and raised a fist; now the glowing light had enveloped his entire arm. Then he struck the wall with the force of a wrecking ball. Brickwork and dust flew in every direction, and when it had settled there was a large hole in the wall in front of him.

It took him a few seconds to pull the bricks away and peer inside. It was dark and cold, but it was clear that there was a stone staircase leading down away from him. He craned his neck to see down the steps, which could not have been used in years by the looks of things, as thick dust had fallen on them and the air smelt stale and old. He could not see how far down they went, but this wasn't about to stop him.

He entered through the doorway and walked down, each step echoing in the narrow stairwell. The steps felt hard, like solid rock, and they definitely were not the same as the previous stairs he had taken to get into the cellars. They must have been carved out of the very bedrock under the city, and must have been built long before the hotel or any other buildings, possibly even before the city had been built.

Eric continued down the stairs and was quickly enveloped by the darkness. He ran a hand along the narrow walls, which also felt like they had been carved straight out of the bedrock. They were smooth to the touch, as if they had been chiselled out over many years and smoothed down. Eric was not an expert in construction but even he knew that this staircase must have taken a heck of a long time to get done.

Occasionally his hand would brush over a small square window in the walls, and after a little investigation of one of them he decided that whoever had built and used these stairs must have put candles in them to light the way. The wicks had long ago corroded, but sticky wax could still be felt around the base of each one.

When he unexpectedly came to the bottom of the staircase, he nearly lost his footing. With both hands he felt the sides of the corridor. It was getting narrower, and soon he had to turn and shuffle crabwise down it. The ceiling made him duck a little too. He knew people were shorter years ago, but this was getting stupid, he thought as he banged his head on the ceiling again. This was not what he had been told about this hotel by his informant. The moment Eric got out of here he would find the guy and stick his head through the first window he saw – or drag him down here and leaving him here to rot.

After he had been crab-walking for about twenty minutes the corridor suddenly opened out into what felt like a very large space. Eric waved his arms around wildly, looking for another wall. "Oh, shitty bollocks!" he said to the curtain of darkness all around him.

The sound of his voice echoed out in all directions. He was apparently sitting on the floor of a massive underground cavern. He felt slightly foolish sitting there listening to his echo. He also had a strange feeling of déjà vu, as if he had been in a dark open space like this before. It felt like the darkness stretched on forever, and it was oddly familiar. Instinctively he looked up, but wasn't sure what he was expecting to see. The air above him was just as dark as everywhere else.

Suddenly he heard a long-drawn-out screech from somewhere in the distance. It was like nothing Eric had ever heard before, like a creature sounding a battle cry or raising an alarm, and it sounded very angry.

Then he sensed movement around him. There were things in here with him, large things, possibly dog-sized, maybe bigger, and they were scurrying around in a circle where he sat. He reached out tentatively and something brushed past him. He rummaged in his jacket and pulled out the gun he still had tucked away; in his other hand he held aloft his cigarette lighter. He lit the flame and held it out to one side so as not to destroy his night vision, then held the gun out in another direction. He couldn't quite make out what was running around him. Every time he caught sight of something it darted back into the shadows. Whatever they were, it sounded as if there were a lot of them.

Eric sprang to his feet and spun around with the gun and the lighter held out. By its light he caught sight of one of the creatures; it was now standing still and watching him carefully. It was bigger than a dog, and looked like the offspring of a horse and a lizard. Eric supposed that as the other creatures hadn't attacked him yet, they must be waiting for a signal from this one. Eric moved a little closer and the light illuminated the lizard thing a little more clearly. It was turning its head to one side, and Eric decided to fire off a shot to see what would happen.

The bullet bounced off the rock behind the creature's head. It did not seem to notice, but the other creatures scurried off in all directions away from him. Eric stood for a moment. He and the lizard were locked in a staring contest, but Eric could sense that they were not alone. In the darkness he could make out faint outlines of other reptilian creatures, each one the same size as the brute in front of him. They all seemed to be watching him and waiting to see what he would do next. As Eric spun around he quickly realised he was surrounded by a ring of the animals.

Eric's finger hovered over the trigger of his gun. Just as was reflecting that he would rather have had a machine gun, they attacked. The reptilian monsters launched themselves forward and Eric was quickly covered by heavy, scaly bodies. The light from his cigarette lighter blinked out, and the cave was in total darkness.

Eric tried to scream out in pain, but his voice was muffled by the sheer weight of bodies on top of him. He gritted his teeth and tried to fight back, but there were just too many of them. He pulled the trigger a few times, but heard the bullets ricochet off rock. He had hoped the noise would scare them away again, but it only seemed to make things worse.

CHAPTER 45

ZARDA PRISON BASE

Far out in the desert the sun was sinking from the sky, and finally the heat of the day was starting to get a little more bearable. This had no impact whatsoever on Eric Mason, who was deep underground along with Jax and lines of people who were being ushered into a maze of small passageways and tunnels. The tunnels appeared to have been dug out of the rock by hand, and many of them looked moments away from caving in.

On the walls were fixed lamps connected by wires, but many of the bulbs had broken so the light was very dim and far apart. Occasionally Eric and Jax would pass one of the large reptilian guards who were watching over the lines of men and women as they walked past. Anyone stupid enough to make eye contact with them quickly regretted it. There wasn't much room down here, and even if Eric had had the energy to fight his way out right now, he would have found it difficult to push past all the people down here.

There was a rhythmic thumping sound around them, the sound of mining with hammers and pickaxes, interrupted by the occasional crash of falling rock.

"Jax?" said Eric in a whisper over his shoulder.

"Yes Eric?" Jax's voice had a tinge of fear and apprehension in it rather than its usual jovial tone.

"What the hell is going on, what is this place?"

"This is hell without the fires. Haven't you heard the stories about these places?"

"Funnily enough, a big hole in the ground where the Zarda funnel in human prisoners has never come up" said Eric with bitter sarcasm. "Is it a prison or something? I thought the Zarda didn't take prisoners."

"It's not quite a prison" said Jax. "It's a lot worse, but tough to describe."

"Ah, that explains everything very clearly, thank you" muttered Eric as they turned yet another corner. The tunnels were getting narrower and tighter the further they went down, and the taller men were now banging their heads on low-hanging rocks. They moved in silence for a while before entering a large underground cavern. Huge stalactites hung down from above, and Eric could see alongside them that people were hanging from the ceiling by chains. Well, not all of them were people any more. Clearly some had been up there a long time. Their skin was grey from lack of blood, and in some cases they were missing vital body parts, like arms, legs or heads.

Eric could see that several of them had started to rot, which was obviously where the stench was coming from. The nearest body was that of a woman who had been strung up by her wrists, and the lower half of her torso looked ready to drop off. He stared at her as they walked forward. Her eyes were glazed over in death. Just for a moment it looked like she was focusing on Eric, but it was clearly an illusion.

The line of people were ushered into a group in the middle of the cave, where they were surrounded by guards, evil-looking reptiles and grinning goblins. Eric slowly moved until he could stand somewhere with a decent view. Just then there came a mad screech which made most of the group jump and look wildly around the cave. Eric had heard a screech like that before, and it hadn't ended well. Some of the group were now shaking in fear, and a puddle was forming on the ground under the man nearest to him.

"One of the soldiers I met told me about this" whispered Jax conspiratorially. "They let loose some of these reptiles, vicious buggers I heard, and they attack all the weaker ones in the group and turn them into food for the rest. If you happen to survive you're taken off for torture and brain washing. Look up there."

Eric followed Jax's gaze to the ceiling of the cave and saw that in between the stalagmites and the hanging people were maybe twenty or thirty small lizard creatures. They looked hungry, and they were moving single-mindedly in the direction of the group. On top of a large rock in the centre of the cavern, a much larger lizard was sitting. It was glaring down at them, turning its head this way and that, as if it was trying to see and hear them at the same time. It sat bolt upright when the lizards got close, and let out another blood-curdling scream that seemed to fill the entire cavern.

Some of the people clamped their hands over their ears, while others dropped to the ground clutching at their heads as if to try to stop them exploding. One woman was so gripped by fear that she screamed, turned, and ran as fast as she could. Eric reached out a hand to stop her, but she brushed past him. He watched helplessly through gritted teeth as the woman run straight into one of the oversized reptilian butcher-guards. The guard looked down at the sheepish woman and growled. The brute's big scaly hand wrapped around the woman's throat and he sent her flying across the cave. The noise of her skull breaking when she hit the ground would stay with everyone who heard it for the rest of their lives – not that this seemed likely to be very long.

Eric was the first to turn away, as he was more worried about the army of smaller lizards climbing towards them from the ceiling. They were gathering around the reptile sitting on the rock, and if Eric was any judge, they looked as if they were all trying to decide who to eat first.

"Bugger this" muttered Eric, "I'm not going to be food for these bastards." He cracked his neck, took a deep breath, and waded through the group of prisoners. All heads in the group turned to watch him. Jax was following fast too.

"Kill or be killed" stated Jax in a matter-of-fact voice, Eric nodded. The pair stepped forward together, raised their hands and took attack positions. Eric had one hand out in front of him, with the other in a tight fist at his waist, whereas Jax held both hands out in front of him like a tiger, and crouched ready to spring into action. Eric noticed that Jax's fingernails looked a little longer all of a sudden; they now looked more like claws than fingers. None of the soldiers had stepped forward, he noticed.

The reptiles on the rock stared at them in puzzlement. Normally their food cowered on the floor beneath them. There were growls of annoyance, and then in unison they all jumped up and charged towards the pair.

Eric moved quickly. He was beyond angry now, and not just for the child he had seen being beaten, not just for the woman that big brute had just killed, not just for being in the battle that he hadn't wanted to be in which had led to him being here. Not just for the poor souls who had been ripped to shreds by these dog-lizards either. He was angry because he knew that if he didn't save these people, no one would.

One of the reptiles was flying through the air on invisible wings, with its claws out stretched ready to rip its prey's head off, when Eric caught it in mid-air. The reptile screamed its anger and thrashed around, but Eric spun around full circle and threw the creature at the attacking horde. Suddenly the pair were surrounded by green, scaly bodies.

Eric and Jax threw fists out in all directions. It almost didn't matter where they punched because there were so many targets. But then one of the things dodged past Jax's claws and sank its teeth deep into his arm. Jax howled in pain, threw the reptile to the ground and stomped on its head until it stopped twitching. But then he was set upon by more of them.

Eric meanwhile was covered by reptiles clawing and biting at every inch of skin they could find. It seemed that each time he was able to throw one off, two more took its place. Then they heard a loud scream, and turned to see that some of the reptiles were heading for the group of prisoners. He dashed towards them as fast as he could. A few men in torn army uniforms had stepped forward to defend the group, but they had little defence these fast-moving killing machines.

Eric was getting really frustrated now. The reptiles were all over him, and no matter how hard he hit or kicked them, they still seemed to be able to jump straight back up and return to the attack. Everything hurt, and blood was everywhere. Eric didn't have time to heal any wounds. He had managed to damage a lot of the creatures, but there were just too many. The yellow light started to glow around his hands and run up his arms. He really didn't like using his special powers in front of people, but enough was enough. The glow started to radiate around him like an aura, the yellow light got brighter as it spread across his body, and it shone out from behind his eyeballs giving his face mini-headlights. He crouched down low, as if charging it all up inside himself, and the ball of moving green bodies got smaller as he did so.

Jax heard an explosion from behind him and was nearly thrown to the floor when the shock-wave hit him like an invisible tsunami. He was in the middle of wrestling with two of the smaller lizards to keep them away from the terrified prisoners, and he felt the whole cave shake and shudder around him. Everything stopped moving. It was as if time had slowed right down and everyone in the cavern had turned to stone, as rocks and stalagmites crashed to the ground all around the cavern.

With a final effort Jax threw the reptiles to one side and picked up a rock to finish them off. Then he glanced at the group of prisoners, who were staring open-mouthed at something behind him. When he turned around, he couldn't believe his eyes. Eric was standing with his back to them. Around his feet a golden ring of light was scorched into the solid rock around him. A semi-circle of rock had been cut from the big rock in the centre of the cavern, as if something had taken a bite out of it. The ring around Eric was pulsating and beginning to fade, like red-hot metal taken from a forge. Eric looked as if he had been injected with radioactive material. The yellow glowing veins covered his entire body, and light was shining out from behind his eyes.

Eric stumbled forward, and Jax quickly leapt to catch him before he hit the ground.

"Who *are* you?" asked Jax, bemused. He struggled to hold Eric's surprisingly heavy body up on its feet. Eric was hot, as if he had just pulled himself out of boiling water.

"Are they all dead?" whispered Eric in a dry and tired voice.

"Yes, I would say you got them all" panted Jax, surveying the lake of reptilian blood that stretched out in all directions.

"Good" mumbled Eric. "Let's get the fuck out of here." H was trying to stand up on his own, but his legs were too weak to hold him.

"Well…" said Jax, "you got all the little ones, but I think the bigger ones might have something to say about us trying to walk out of here."

"What?" Eric exclaimed. He started to rub his eyes and blink. His vision was blurred, but he could just about make out some shapes. They were big shapes, and they were headed straight for them. "Any fighters in the group?" Eric called towards the prisoners.

"Yes," came the call from several voices, but they didn't sound too enthusiastic.

"OK." He tried to blink his eyes into focusing. "The rest of you get to one side." He watched as the blurred figures did as they were told. What concerned Eric was the much bigger mass now standing in front of him, which had to be the big reptilian brutes. Eric felt the strength coming back to his feet a little, and found his balance on the second attempt. He shook his head violently and the vision came back a little more. Now he could make out seven or eight of the biggest of the reptilian brutes, and they were all staring angrily at him. He almost wished his vision was still blurred.

Eric looked from one side to the other. Jax was standing next to him with a worried look on his face. Backing them up were ten soldiers, most of them looking very much the worse for wear with broken limbs and bleeding wounds. One of them was missing an eye, and half his face was a burnt mess of blistering skin. They looked determined enough, but they did not look capable of tackling these monsters.

Eric stepped forward and addressed the brutes like an annoyed teacher. "As you can see, you big ugly scaly bastards are clearly outnumbered. So I suggest you all just bugger off, OK?" The lizards did not move. "Fine" he said. He straightened up to his full height and moved into his favourite fighting-someone-twice-your-size stance.

Then they all heard a new sound from one side of the cavern. It was coming from one of the tunnels, and it sounded like the howls of very angry Lykor. The soldiers started to shake in fear. There was a rhythmic grumbling sound as well, like the thundering of heavy feet. A primal fear gripped each person in the cavern, something that made them instinctively want to escape as fast as possible.

Then a light appeared at the end of the tunnel. It grew brighter as it got closer, and soon Eric could see the shadows of horse-sized Lykor coming straight for them, and they sounded very hungry. They had muscular, fur-covered bodies with claws and fangs, and they were all fighting each other to get down the narrow tunnel. The howls and growls got louder as they approached, and the shadows being thrown up the walls were getting bigger.

Eric turned to face the group of soldiers. "Get over there!" he ordered, and pointed to the tunnel mouth. "What comes out of that tunnel is not going to be pretty, but you either fight and die, or you just die."

The soldiers jumped instinctively at the sound of the order and ran to the opening. Some of them found rocks on the floor and got ready with them on either side of the opening.

"Civilians!" shouted Eric, not taking his eyes off the big brutes. "Are you just going to stand there and let your brothers and husbands die?" The prisoners rushed to stand with the soldiers, several of them following their example and picking up rocks to arm themselves with.

"I don't like dogs much" said Jax as he sauntered over to where Eric was standing. He turned to the snarling brute standing in front of Eric. "I'd rather fight you, big boy." Eric wasn't really listening; he was looking at his arms. He could still see the glowing veins under his skin. He clenched his fists a few times and the veins glowed a little brighter.

"You going to do another of those explosions?" asked Jax, carefully taking a step away from Eric "Because if you do a little warning first would be nice."

Eric grinned and held his hands up in front of his face like a boxer. Jax could see the veins of light stretching up into the air, extending away from Eric's hands through his fingertips. They were stretching up, twisting and clinging together in the air, glittering like liquid gold, and through the tendrils Jax could see Eric grinning.

"Not quite" said Eric. He flicked one hand and sent the glowing liquid tendrils shooting out to one side. Suddenly they had turned into a solid-looking metal blade. It was glowing slightly as if hot, and there was a yellowish haze around it. Jax couldn't believe what he was seeing. It would be a long time before he told anyone however – they would think he was crazy.

He was about to say something when Eric did the same to his other hand, and again the tendrils collected together, and Eric was holding another sword, a little shorter than the other, more like a long dagger. Eric flicked it into the air and Jax caught it in mid-flight. It was as light as a feather, but it felt stronger than anything Jax had ever held before. He inspected the blade. It was one long solid piece running from the tip to the bottom of the handle. Jax waved it in the air a few times. It left a yellowish-white trail in the air in front of his eyes.

He looked at Eric, confused, but Eric was staring at the brutes in front of them, and he somehow looked bigger and stronger than he had a minute ago.

Jax swished the blade in the air a few times, then turned his attention to the brutes. "Are you quite sure about this?" said Jax out of the corner of his mouth to Eric.

Eric grunted. He stepped forward, and in a flash both men launched their attack. The monsters raised their big clubs and blades high in the air and swung inexpertly at them.

The pair rushed in and dodged quickly between their slowly-swinging weapons and fists. One of the brutes tried to stamp on Jax, but he was able to jump out the way at the last second, and treated the brute to a swipe of his new blade. It sliced through the brute's leg and torso like a hot knife through butter. There was barely any resistance, and after a strange pause the brute keeled over clutching at its wounds and a gush of dark green blood poured out onto the floor.

"Oh, I like this" said Jax. Eric looked up and grinned. The pair continued to work together to take down the creatures one at a time.

Then a noise made them look up. The beasts were very close now, and when they turned a final corner to see the soldiers and civilians, they started to speed up. A mass of fur and teeth came thundering towards the prisoners. The beasts leapt like fish, teeth ready to rip throats, claws ready to slash and bellies waiting to be filled with fresh meat.

The soldier who was bravely standing at the front of the entrance gulped and tried to control his breathing. The swarm of beasts leapt from the tunnel into the cavern, and at the last second the soldier shut his eyes, waiting to be ripped apart.

CHAPTER 46

UNDER THE CITY

It was dark inside the cave deep below the city, and Eric Mason was being dragged by what felt like hundreds of pairs of little hands and teeth across what felt like the roughest, sharpest, stoniest floor ever. It was like being dragged across burning hot gravel. All around him he heard screaming and screeching. By the sound and feel of it he was being dragged down a small tunnel taking him even deeper underground.

Amongst all the scaly reptilian bodies, Eric struggled to free himself by kicking and punching his way out, but no matter what he did he couldn't break free from their grip; there were just too many of them.

The yellow light began to creep around his eyes, and up and down his hands, and the scaly hands let go of him. He fell from what felt like a great height, and landed heavily on a very, very hard surface. The glow under his skin flickered out instantly, but around his pupils the yellow glow shimmered into life and Eric was able to see in the darkness.

His body hurt, not just from the fall and being dragged across what felt like endless broken glass, but because the reptiles had been digging their teeth and claws into him and he could feel the blood starting to soak through his clothes. His gun had landed nearby. He rolled over, snatched it off the ground and raised it above him in case there was another attack from the reptiles. He lay on his back aiming directly above him for a moment, but nothing happened, they seem to have dumped him there and left him to it.

He rolled painfully onto his front and got to his feet to have a look around. He was in another cavern, but it was smaller this time, no bigger than a football stadium. This time he barely needed his night-vision to see in the dark, because in several areas around the cavern the rock had a strange green glowing liquid bubbling out of it.

As there didn't seem to be another attack coming straight away, curiosity got the better of him, and he got up and walked over to the nearest glowing wall.

The strange glowing goo appeared to be sweating out of the pores in the rock and dribbling down to the ground, where it had pooled into a thick, glowing puddle. Eric instinctively reached out to touch it, but then thought better of it What if it was acid, or worse?

He turned his attention to the cavern and began to explore it, trying to take it all in. Vast pillars and columns were holding the ceiling up, and stairs led off into what looked like man-made corridors and pathways. The entire place looked and felt ancient, as if it had been there for thousands of years patiently waiting below the city for someone to find it. Eric knew all about ancient caves and tombs, and the traps and monsters you usually found in them.

In the centre of the cave was an enormous rock that must have been more than twenty feet in diameter. Eric walked over to it and looked up. He could see a big hole in the ceiling above it where the rock must have fallen from. Around the base of the rock the ground was clear, other than the dust of years that had settled there. That meant it must have fallen a long time ago and someone had cleaned up the debris it must have left. That meant someone cared about other people seeing it. Perhaps it had fallen when this place had been in regular use, but judging by the amount of dust and lack of footprints, it had been a very long time ago.

He walked around the rock and stopped in surprise. Carved deep into the fallen rock, someone had meticulously cut steps leading up to a big carved throne at the top. So this was a throne room. Who could have built it, and when? It had been a long time ago, for sure.

He had never heard talk about anything being hidden under the city like this, so whoever had built this place was very good at keeping secrets. He had heard all the tales about hidden treasure and secret rooms under the city, but they were mostly just stories. Eric had found this out for himself by spending a year once travelling the city's underground systems.

He stared at the carvings on the throne and steps. They were barely visible in the smooth surface, and he couldn't for the life of him read what they said. They were probably something dull and boring about a war or whatever that had happened thousands of years ago. Eric didn't have much of a head for languages, so to him these carvings were just collection of lines and circles, although they looked somewhat mathematical in nature.

A noise behind him made him and spin around, behind him were three figures, seven feet tall, and they were laughing at him. Eric was often attacked on sight, but rarely laughed at. This laughter was not human, however, but a kind of reptilian hiss. There was no humour to it, only contempt.

The three reptiles looked almost like monks, in long, dark red robes that went down to their scaled feet and big dark red hoods that hid most of their faces for long jaws and noses. Just above their snouts Eric could see small black dots which were presumably their eyes. The glow from the goo in the walls was giving them a strange and unnatural look. Each figure had a gold metal chain hanging around his neck, carrying a stone that shone with a faint greenish glow, like the walls. On the end of their arms, poking out from the wide sleeves of their robes, Eric could see long, thin scaly fingers with sharp-looking claws.

"Good evening gentlemen" Eric said cheerfully. "I'm from London's Health and Safety Department, and this cavern you have here under the city really doesn't look too safe to me. I'm afraid we're going to have some of the guys in construction come down here, maybe put up some safety structures. Maybe they'll just fill the whole damn place with concrete." He smiled and swung an arm around the cave like an interior designer. "And as for the strange goo coming out of the walls, I personally have no idea what it is, but I'm sure it would go against every health and safety rule in the book to have it pooling into puddles where any man, woman, or child could slip and hurt themselves."

The reptilian monks had stopped laughing now and were glaring at this intruder angrily.

"Yes, I think we will get the boys in and fill this place with concrete, up to the brim would be my favourite, you wouldn't want a law suit on your hands now would you?" Eric went on. "Do you have your insurance documents, your health and safety certificate? Hmmm? No I didn't think so." Eric was feeling for his gun.

"Silence, Eric Mason!" came a hiss voice from somewhere behind the three monks. Eric paused, and the three monks shuffled to one side to reveal a very old-looking reptile. The trio started bowing and grovelling in a strange language, and were promptly silenced by the aged figure. It stepped forward to reveal that it was dressed similarly to the other three, but its robes were much older and dustier, and the orb around its neck shone more brightly. It was clearly the leader of the group.

"Sorry, who is Eric Mason?" Eric asked, trying to sound confused. The ancient reptile was staring at him hard, and Eric could feel its gaze going through his eyes and into the centre of his brain. "Never heard of him, we have a Billy Mason over in marketing if that helps?" he added as an afterthought. The way this strange dinosaur was staring at him was unnerving.

"You" said the ancient reptile in a wheezy voice, "are Eric Mason. Yes... we know exactly... who you are!" it said angrily. Its voice was broken up by shortness of breath. "We have watched... you... for many, many years now."

"Oh really?" said Eric, slowly inching his hand towards his gun again. "If I had known you were watching me I wouldn't have sung in so many karaoke bars. Or gone to so many brothels." As he spoke he pulled the gun free with lightning speed and aimed it at the old reptile's head.

The whip came from out of nowhere. It was made from fine metal chain links ending in a mass of spiked wire, and it moved much faster than Eric. The spiked metal snapped the gun out of Eric's hand before he could pull the trigger.

Eric stared at his empty hand, not believing what had just happened. The whip had scored deep cuts. Now he heard the laughing again. All four of them were sniggering at him, and one of the monks was reeling in the metal whip. Eric took a menacing step forward, raising both hands, with the intention of ripping the monk in half, or maybe strangling him with his own whip. But when he got close the older monk simply raised a scaly hand holding the glowing orb, and a thin beam of light shone from the orb and hit Eric in the chest, sending him flying backwards to land in a heap on the stone steps to the throne.

There was a sharp throbbing pain in Eric's head, and more

pain in his ribs from the impact with the stone steps. He climbed unsteadily to his feet. The creatures looked surprised that he was able to stand up, let alone walk, after a blow like that.

"You are... as strong... as they say," said the dinosaur monk. "For a human, of course" he added with a sneer.

"Who said I was human?" asked Eric, fighting the urge to be sick on the floor. "Now, who are you, and what is this place?"

"We, are the Darkness, Eric Mason. We are the nightmares that dwell in the minds of the living all across this filthy, disgusting planet," said the old reptile in the practised tones of a teacher. "We are fear, we are panic, we are the terror in the shadows, and we are the rightful owners of this world."

Eric thought for a moment and then looked around at the cavern they were standing in, at the throne behind him, and back to the monks. "Doesn't look like there are many of you left any more" he said at last, and fought the urge to laugh.

"Oh, there are quite a few of us left," said the aged dinosaur. He hissed something to the nearest monk, who nodded and produced a small silver bell. The monk shuffled behind the old reptile, held the bell high in the air and rang it. The bell's tinkle echoed in the cavern, bouncing off the walls and fading into the distance.

Eric stood frozen for a moment, his eyes darting from side to side to try to see all of the cavern at the same time, fully expecting the swarm of lizards that had brought him there to arrive, but nothing happened. He opened his mouth to say something sarcastic, but shut it when he heard the sound of drums. They were quiet at first as if coming from a distance, but getting louder. From behind the reptiles light started spilling into the cavern from corridors and pathways leading off in all directions. The reptilian monks began to snigger at Eric again, and soon he could see shadows, as of bodies marching.

Eric felt a chill run down his spine, and stepped back. Just then a figure armed with a big scaly shield and a long, jagged blade and covered from head to foot in thick metal-plate armour came down the stairs behind the four reptilian monks. Eric looked him up and down. Every inch of this warrior screamed death and destruction. He had seen armour like this once before on the monsters of the old days, hideous creatures with twice the strength of a man, and twice the anger. But this wasn't like those beings; it had the pointed ears, teeth and nose of a goblin. The big helmet covered most of its face, but the green skin and yellowing teeth were visible, and they weren't a pretty sight.

Behind him soldiers spilled out of the corridors and into the cavern. Eric looked around wildly at the snarling soldiers who were now forming ranks in the cavern, all of them staring at him with hungry eyes. Eric might just be outnumbered. As if to settle the matter, another horde of the creatures arrived and fell in line.

"We are going to take back this world!" screeched the old reptile, who was now standing at the head of hundreds of goblin soldiers. "The humans above this temple will feel the wrath of our power, and soon your world will tremble beneath our feet!"

Eric started backing away. Out of the corner of his eye he could see his gun on the ground, although even if he could get to it, he didn't nearly have enough bullets. This was going to need some very special tactics.

CHAPTER 47

THE WAR BEGINS

So the New Global War started that early morning, deep in the centre of the city of London. The ground shook, the roads and buildings gave way and fell into deep craters that opened under the city. Masses of people on their commute to work, still half asleep, were overtaken by the calamity. Many of them simply stopped to take photos on their mobile phones, post them on the internet and send them to their friends before trying to carry on with their journey into work. Few of them made it. Throughout the city was heard the sound of twisting metal and concrete and the screams of people falling to their deaths as the ground beneath them dropped away. When the dust had settled a little, people tried to climb into the craters and fallen buildings to look for survivors, but none of them were seen again. Women screamed for their husbands and lost children and men called for their wives and girlfriends as mass panic swept the city.

Survivors later said they had heard a drumming noise coming from the craters before the creatures emerged, but most people put this down to their imagination. Out of the craters, the Zarda emerged in their thousands. Swarms of lizard soldiers with sharp teeth and claws and deadly weapons came climbing out from deep underground. They came screeching and shouting out of the crater and dispersed in all directions. The people fled in panic from the lizards and the armoured goblins, trampling over each other in an effort to get away. But no one was able to escape quickly enough. Armed task forces were called in and tried shooting at the reptilian horde, but their bullets could not penetrate the metal armour. Those civilians who tried to take on the invaders were ripped to shreds in seconds.

The city was taken within hours. For days the fires burnt high into the sky, while all around the city innocent men, women and children were slaughtered. For miles around, people outside the city could hear the screams and see the light of the flames.

The lizard soldiers weren't the worst thing to come out of the craters. There were nine-foot-tall ogres and trolls and dog-sized spiked lizards which screeched as they pulled out people's eyes and ears and ate them. But the worst creatures to come out of the main central crater came on four legs, very big and very fast. with incredible speed. Mankind throughout history had never seen such beasts as the giant wolves that emerged. They were fast and cunning, and were able to sniff out even the best of hiding spaces.

In a city this size, there were plenty of hiding places. People hid under stairs, in cupboards and even in the boots of their cars. But the enormous wolf beasts could smell their fear from a great distance. The fear only intensified when people saw the jagged blade being wielded in the reptilian hand, or the gentle patter of four paws, as one by one the Zarda carved a new page into the planet's history books.

CHAPTER 48

Novum Orbis

That was when the Great War started. It was a war that would turn Planet Earth on its head. This was where mankind met its greatest enemy, one which was far stronger than anything they had encountered before. The War knocked an entire species off the top of the food chain, and forced them to put aside their petty differences and band together to fight this new evil. All across the planet, capital cities fell simultaneously to the great swarms of killing machines. From under their feet came the vicious hordes of darkness, and no one was safe from their slaughter. The world would never be the same again.

END OF BOOK 1